DARKEST SIN

Sheridan Anne
DARKEST SIN

Copyright © 2024 Sheridan Anne
All rights reserved
First Published in 2024

Cover Design: Artscandare
Editing: Fox Proof Editing
Formatting: Sheridan Anne

CONTENT WARNING

Darkest Sin is a Dark Mafia Standalone Romance.

This piece was originally published in 2023 as a short 25k word novella in the Billionaires and Babes Anthology. It has been reworked to a full length, 107k word novel.

Your mental health is important to me so please carefully consider these triggers in determining if this book is right for you.

Darkest Sin is not suitable for persons under eighteen years of age.

DARKEST SIN CONTAINS

Abduction

BDSM themes

Bloodshed/Massacre

Bondage

Castration

Drugging

Exhibitionism

Explicit sexual content

Graphic murder

Graphic rape

Graphic violence

Hired hitmen

Human trafficking

Kink exploration

Organized crime

Possessive MMC

Revenge

Sexual assault

Suicide

Ahhh, beautiful girl. I've been waiting for you.

You're so fucking gorgeous when you smile like that. I can't wait to smudge that pretty lipstick.

I know you're waiting to start this adventure and fall in love with my wicked ways. You've been so patient for me, but your wait is over, Sweet Angel. Now be a good little girl and settle in for a wild ride.

Get a glass of wine, restock your batteries, and put those skilled fingers to use and swipe to the next page.

Mmmmm . . . I liked that.
I knew you were going to please me.

CHAPTER 1

Chiara

The harsh, bright lights shine down against my clammy skin as I suck in a shaky breath, wishing I could wake from this nightmare. Men wearing expensive business suits fill the dark room, their chilling stares sailing over my lingerie-clad body like a piece of meat. They're nothing but sick hunters searching for their next victim.

Tears of humiliation linger on my cheeks as fear and rage pound through my veins like a lethal cocktail, threatening to take me out. And for the first time in my life, I wish it would. The sweet agony of death is my only salvation now.

I don't belong here.

One minute I was walking home from the bar where I work, and the next . . .

I cut off the memory before it gets too far. Replaying that moment only sends me into a whirlpool of vicious thoughts. It's a tragic cycle I can't break free from.

My hands shake violently as I grip the bars of my cage, trying not to make eye contact with the men lingering around me. Their putrid stares scan over my body, assessing everything from the size of my tits and the shape of my curves to the color of my skin and every little imperfection. It's unsettling and undignified. It's like they're looking over the prize for some fucked-up business deal . . . but I guess that's exactly what I've been reduced to.

A prized piece at an auction, the highest bidder takes all.

I'm struggling with what to do and how to act. I don't know what they're looking for, and one wrong move could be disastrous. Do I follow the disgusting commands spat at me by the man who snatched me off the street, or should I put up a fight and die with dignity? But more importantly, when a man inevitably drags me home, what should I do when he throws me down, pries my legs open, and tries to take what isn't his?

Bile rises in my throat, and I force myself to swallow it down.

The idea that this has become my life in just a matter of days is unbelievable. This isn't real. It's just some fucked-up nightmare I can't escape.

A thick, black harness decorates my body, starting at my throat like a choker. It travels over my shoulder and to my tits, making geometric shapes across my skin. Bands strap around my ribs then down to my waist, connecting to my thighs like suspenders. I wear a matching thong with my long golden hair pulled back into a tight pony to complete the look. If it weren't for the messed-up situation I was in, I might even consider buying something like this for myself. But wearing it in front of all these strangers makes me feel like a used whore.

The first night as their captive, they threw me into a cold, dark cell, and eventually, the distant cries of other prisoners lulled me into an uneasy sleep. I startled awake hours later to a bucket of ice-cold water thrown over my head, and as I screamed for help, a group of men stripped me from my work uniform. Their hands were all over me, scrubbing me clean and cataloging my every scar, tattoo, and piercing.

The fear of the unknown gripped me. What was happening to me? What did they want with me? Where the fuck was I going to end up? I've never been one to be home-sick when away, but I've never wanted the safety of my home more.

I told myself that was as bad as it was going to get. That I'd be locked up in a dirty cell for some asshole's sick pleasure, that listening to the other girls weeping was what my life would be from there on out.

I shouldn't have been so naive.

Standing here in this cage as a pawn in their sick game, I realize this is only the beginning. There are at least four or five other girls I can see, each of them locked in identical cages around the room and dressed just like me—hooker heels and dark makeup—under the watchful eye of the asshole in charge.

I don't know his name, only that he has the most sinister stare I've ever seen. He watches us like a hawk, his sharp gaze missing nothing.

The very second I get the chance, I fully intend on slitting the bastard's throat. I've never been one to wish death on anyone. I was raised to be a good girl with high standards and excellent morals, but right now, I'm ready to throw it all away. My soul be damned.

The room is like some kind of underground warehouse decked out with a bar and dirty couches. Men linger in every available space, their gazes sailing over the caged women with interest. Their designer suits and expensive Rolexes warn me that these are the type of men who are not used to the word no. Some are older, probably looking for a girl to suck their dicks because their wives won't anymore. In contrast, others are younger, mid-thirties with sickening stares. The new generation of business rapists who purchase women like it's an elite sport and boast over a glass of whiskey just how hard he hit it.

Is this what my life is going to be? A bought whore for a sinister man?

Trying to look past the men, I focus on the room. There are four exits, two of which I've been down already, and they only take you deeper into the connected tunnels—somewhere I don't plan on ever going again. The two remaining exits are across the room, almost the furthest point from me.

One is guarded and used as the main entrance. A set of steep stairs leads up to the metal door where a big burly man stands watch over the events below like a security guard. Every now and then, he turns to the door, checks off a name, and allows another asshole into the lair below.

The final exit is behind the bar with an identical set of stairs leading up to the door. It's not guarded, but with the heavy padlocks and chains, it's clear no one will be escaping through there tonight.

Glancing at the other girls, I see them looking around, just as I am, with nothing but defeat in their eyes. We all know the likelihood of getting out of here is non-existent. And I hate to say it, but if I got free somehow, I'd take off at a million miles an hour, never looking back. It's every woman for themselves.

A filthy old man steps up to my cage, his sickening gaze trailing up and down my body as his eyes fill with hunger, a nearly empty glass of whiskey resting in his hand. He must be well into his seventies, old enough to be sporting wrinkly balls and a leaky cock. He carries himself with an air of importance, and I bet he's the CEO of some bullshit Fortune 500 company, raking in billions of dollars. He's probably got countless sexual assault charges against him from all the secretaries he's abused, though I'm sure each case is mysteriously resolved before seeing a courtroom. His wife probably got fed up with the embarrassment of it all and told him to go purchase himself a whore. I wonder if this is what the old bitch had in mind.

"What's your name, girl?" he rumbles, his deep tone making my skin crawl.

I fix him with a dead stare and indicate the nameplate on the top corner of my cage. "What? Don't you read?" I question.

The old man's gaze shifts up to the nameplate, probably not used to having a young woman speak to him in such a tone. "Misty?" he says with a scoff. "You and I both know that's not your real name. Who are you?"

A grin pulls at my lips, and I let him see exactly what kind of woman he'll be dealing with if he doesn't fuck off and leave me alone. Gripping the bars, I lean in close, watching the way his eyes fill with hesitation. "I'm your worst fucking nightmare."

Without warning, something flashes in his eyes, and his hand shoots through the bars and grips my throat. "You want to put up a fight, little girl? I'll give you something to fight about."

My heart races, fear filling my veins as my airway narrows, but there's no way in hell I'm about to let this asshole get the best of me. My arm snaps out, my fingers knotting into his thinning hair, and with every last bit of strength I possess, I yank him hard toward me, his nose crushing against the metal bars of the cage.

He roars out in pain, and as blood gushes from his nose, he releases me to clutch his face. "You bitch," he spits, gaining the attention of the men around him. Some of them who'd disregarded me before now watch me with keen interest.

The old man reaches for me again, but I spring back out of the way, my back slamming against the bars of my cage. He goes to say something when the big burly security guard from the door shoves him back, stepping in front of the cage and blocking my view. "You know the rules," he grumbles, in a thick accent I can't place. "Touch the girls before purchase, and you'll lose your right to bid."

"She broke my fucking nose," he argues. "What am I supposed to say to my wife?"

"Tell her you're a handsy fuck who got his ass beat by some bitch," he says, shoving him back. "You want to touch, you pay up first."

"I want her punished," he insists, making my back stiffen.

"Not my fucking problem," he growls. "Purchase her first, then do whatever the fuck you want to her. Until then, keep your hands off."

With that, the security guard gives him another shove, pushing him deeper into the crowd, leaving me to the slew of men who probably have some fucked-up rape fetish. These are the kind of guys who get off on beating women. I know their type from years of working at the bar. Holding down a woman and taking what they want makes them feel big. These are the type of men who play sick games when they think no one is looking, but I'd rather die than be one of their toys.

Another man approaches, maybe mid-fifties, and while he doesn't look as wicked as the last, there's definitely something poisonous in his eyes. "You know how to fuck, girl?" he questions, his gaze narrowing as he glances at my body.

I scoff. There's no way in hell I'm entertaining this line of questioning. "Why don't you go home and fuck your wife?"

His gaze narrows as he lifts his chin, making some kind of assumption about me. "Virgin then?"

Ah, this man has particular tastes. Why am I not surprised to find men with virgin kinks in here? He's definitely looking in the wrong place if that's what he thinks he'll be getting from me. I like cock. Big ones, small ones, angry, and pierced. But the ones with that slight curve, goddamn, they're my favorite. I wouldn't call myself a slut exactly, but I'm not known for being shy when it comes to asking for what I need. Though, there's no way in hell the men in this room will ever know that.

Glancing away, I let him make up his own mind about me, and

when he scoffs in distaste, I find myself looking back. "You're just a common whore, aren't you?" he says, almost sounding disappointed. "What about your ass? Ever had someone claim that?"

Realizing he won't stop until he knows just how many cherries I've popped, I step right into the bars, letting my tits squish up against the cold metal. "You're right. I'm nothing but a common whore, the perfect little slut. I've had more cocks buried in my ass than you could imagine," I tell him. "I'm not the sweet little innocent bitch you're looking for."

He watches me for a moment longer, and when he finally steps away, I feel a weight dropping off my shoulders. As he walks away in disappointment, I realize my mistake. I should have played the part of a little angel. He would have purchased me, taken me home, and fucked me until I bled, but then it would have been over. He would have been done with me. I would have been thrown aside and he'd be out searching for the next innocent girl. Instead, one of the other sick men will own me and use me until there's nothing left to give.

While it would have been the worst moment of my life, it might have been my only chance at freedom.

Glancing around the room, my gaze sweeps past the bar to find the asshole with the broken nose, his lethal stare locked onto mine, and I know without a doubt he's not going to let this go. He'll be bidding on me tonight, and he won't stop until he wins.

Swallowing hard, I try not to let my hands shake, but it's like asking myself for the impossible. My heart races erratically, pounding in my ears and drowning out the sounds of the underground warehouse.

I need this to be over. I need to get out of here.

Gripping the bars again, I try not to cry. I've been doing what I can to fend these assholes off, but in doing that, I'm only forcing their attention on the other girls in the room. The nasty tone and bite in my words aren't real, and it will only be so long until one of these assholes sees right through my facade to the scared little girl hidden within.

Time seems to slow, and I feel as though I've been standing here for hours. With everyone confident about where they want to place their bids, most of the men in the room have resigned to talking shit between themselves while sipping on their drinks, leaving us girls in peace. However, that doesn't change the fact that I've felt their sickening stares on my body all night long.

My feet ache in these heels, and I'm on the brink of passing out when a loud static squeal of a microphone tears through the warehouse. My blood turns cold as an auctioneer takes his place on a pedestal overlooking the crowd. "Gentlemen, if I could kindly have your attention. Tonight's event is about to commence."

CHAPTER 2

Chiara

As if on cue, the bidders begin shuffling toward the auctioneer, abandoning their conversations as the men they were just talking to suddenly become their greatest competition. As I watch them move around the warehouse, I realize this isn't just a case of highest bidder takes all. It's a pissing contest, proving to the elite men around them who has the deepest pockets.

Once everyone is where they need to be, the auctioneer gets on with it. "Standard auction rules apply," he says into his microphone. "Raise your hand to make a bid. We're moving up in hundreds with a starting bid of five hundred thousand. No half bids permitted. Once the auction has finished, all winners will be required to make payment within the hour before they will be permitted to collect their prize. We will accept cash or a wire transfer, considering immediate clearance in our account. If you do not possess the funds or cannot arrange payment within the hour, then you are not permitted to bid. Do not waste our time. Otherwise, your name will be blacklisted, and you will not be invited to attend another event."

He glances around the room, making sure his instructions are received clearly before waving a hand toward the first girl, her nameplate reading Stacey. "Alright, I know you are all eager to get this started. So, without further ado, let's start the bidding. For our first girl of the night, Stacey, do I hear five hundred thousand?"

"Right here," someone says, raising their hand. My gaze snaps across the room to find the asshole with the virgin kink eagerly watching the auctioneer. He clearly found what he was looking for.

"Six hundred," another man responds, prompting the auctioneer to do his thing, his voice like nails on a chalkboard as he seeks new bidders.

Another hand flies up. "Eight."

"Nine."

My stomach starts to crawl.

"A million," the virgin kink asshole fires back.

Fucking hell. I can't watch.

Spinning around, I grip the bars of my cage, struggling to breathe as I try to block out the auction behind me. Tears well in my eyes as it all becomes too real. I'm being trafficked—sold to a high-end purchaser to do with as they please.

I brace my head against the bars, feeling a panic attack coming on as I will myself to take slow, deep breaths. The thought of these monsters relishing in my tears makes me sick. I need to be stronger than this. I can't allow them to break me.

The first girl goes for just under two million dollars, and as the word "sold" comes from the auctioneer, I hear the girl let out a pained sob. Knowing there's not a damn thing I can do to help her, I don't even bother turning around to find her purchaser or to get a look at her face. All it's going to do is leave me with nightmares.

A tear falls to my cheek as the auctioneer moves on to girl number two, Brittany, and my hands shake violently against the bars, knowing I'm next. The bidding starts, and as I go to wipe my tears away, I feel someone's stare on my face.

It's intense, and I lift my teary gaze to the back of the room, and right there, deep in the darkest corner and away from the bidding, I find a man covered in shadows. He's tall with dark features, Mediterranean maybe. It's hard to tell from so far away. All I know is that there's something dangerous about him, something that warns me to run in the opposite direction.

Those dark, piercing eyes seem to penetrate right through me, capturing my stare and holding it hostage. He's too far away to hold a conversation, but even with this distance, the silence between us is deafening.

My heart races, and he refuses to look away, the intensity growing by the second. He doesn't try to look at my body, doesn't try to gauge what kind of fight I'll put up in bed. He simply stares back at me with those lethal black eyes.

The name Misty rings through the warehouse, and my eyes widen with fear. Breaking my stare away from the scary stranger in the shadows, I whip around, my gaze locked and loaded on the auctioneer.

Men stare at me from all over the room, and my legs quiver as I try to stay still.

"Do I hear five hundred thousand?"

The old fucker with the broken nose grins manically as he raises his hand. "Five hundred thousand. Right here."

Fuck.

Bile rises in my throat, and if it weren't for my sheer will to get out of here, I would have let it come out.

"Six hundred," is heard from across the room, and my eyes whip back and forth, trying to keep track of who's bidding what.

"Seven."

"I'll take the bitch for eight," broken-nose guy rumbles, his dark gaze shifting back to mine once again. A fucked-up smirk crosses his bloodied face, silently telling me that he'll take this right to the end just so he can be the one to have the pleasure of ending me.

My stomach sinks with each new bid, and I watch with wide eyes, taking in the slew of twisted men who fix their sick gazes upon my body. I wonder just how much fucking me into submission is worth to them.

"Nine hundred."

"A million," Broken Nose throws back, the confidence in his tone making me want to tear his testicles out through his throat and strangle him with them.

"A million, one."

"A million, two."

Each new bid tastes like poison on my tongue, and I watch broken-nose guy closely as hesitation begins creeping into his stare. He's almost at his limit, and that's proved only a moment later when he raises his hand again. "A million, two fifty."

The auctioneer shakes his head. "No half bids, Sir. Can you give me a million, three?"

"A million, two fifty," Broken Nose argues.

"You know the rules of my auction. I'll accept a million, three. Otherwise, bow out and make room for the real bidders."

Broken Nose clenches his jaw and glances back at me. Just to rub salt in the wound, I raise my hand to the base of my throat, drawing my thumb across it and signaling just how quickly I'll end him if he were to win. He narrows his gaze, then raises his hand. "A million, three."

The auctioneer nods. "Welcome back to the party," he says before looking around at the crowd. "Do I hear a million, four?"

"Right here," a new bidder says, raising his hand and making Broken Nose's eyes widen in outrage, his face turning red with rage.

The numbers continue rising, and I turn in my cage, gripping the bars and resting my head against it, no longer caring who wins. It's all the same. Whether I go to Broken Nose or some other asshole, they're all going to treat me the same. I'll be a prize. Something to destroy. Property to be used.

A shadow falls beside my cage, and I lift my head from the bars to find the intense, strange man I'd seen earlier staring right back at me.

His gaze narrows on mine, and I'm struck by just how dark his eyes really are. It's like staring into two deep pits of hell that beckon me in. There's no doubt in my mind, this man is the devil.

His gaze falls away, and I let out a shaky breath, my hands still trembling against the bars. It's as though his stare alone is enough to hold me captive. This man is worse than I could have thought. Seeing him up close like this rattles me to the bone.

He takes just a single step past my cage, and I watch as the men around him hesitantly shuffle away, their sharp gazes quickly morphing into unease. The man raises his head and looks straight at the auctioneer. "This one is mine," he says in a deep, thick, Romanian accent.

The auctioneer fumbles, his eyes widening as everyone whips around to take in this strange, terrifying man. I watch as the auctioneer glances toward the piece of shit running this show, visibly shaken by the newcomer's presence. The man who snatched me off the street and put this whole thing together glances down toward my cage, looking over me before turning his sharp stare on this Romanian nightmare.

"We can negotiate in private," he says. I realize that every last person in this fucked-up underground warehouse knows exactly who this man is. And the fact that he's shown an interest in me is some kind of big deal—I just wish I knew why.

"No," the terrifying man says, that thick accent waking something lost deep within me. "I said she is mine. I will take her now."

My back slams against the bars, and I realize I've been backing up to put distance between me and my new owner. While nothing has been formally agreed, I know without a doubt this man will get what he wants.

"O . . . okay," the piece of shit trafficker says, watching as the Romanian narrows his eyes, the sight making my knees shake. "Yours. She's yours."

"That's what I thought," he mutters before glancing back at my cage, this time letting his gaze travel over my body. He starts at my head, taking in every inch of me. The soft curl in my blonde hair, the subtle arch of my back, my tits and waist, right down to the way my ankles hold me up in these ridiculous black heels.

Approval flashes in his eyes, making my stomach clench, and I hesitantly take a step forward into the center of my cage, my eyes locked firmly on his. Just like earlier, I can't look away. I suck in a breath, every second of this connection growing more intense, more wicked, and more terrifying.

As if on cue, the large security guard who'd stepped in with Broken Nose appears at the door of my cage, and I tear my gaze away from my new Romanian captor. The security guard, who'd so casually disregarded my life, now looks at me with such pity that it almost tears me to shreds. "May God have mercy on your soul," he murmurs, meeting my stare as he slips the key into the lock and opens the door, his gaze filled with darkness.

Fear pounds through my veins. Only an hour ago, this man was more than happy to allow some asshole to purchase me, to spend their time abusing and destroying me without a fucking care in the world. He didn't care if I lived or died. But now that this Romanian has claimed me as his own, it somehow warrants him to fear for my soul?

Fuck.

The cage door swings open, and I find myself glancing back at the auctioneer to see the same pitying look in his eyes. Hell, Broken Nose doesn't even try to put up a fight.

The Romanian dude captures my stare, and the way his eyes burn into mine sends a chill over my skin. "Come to me," he says in that thick accent, his words penetrating deep into my chest like an agonizing command, summoning my unbreakable obedience.

I swallow hard as the warehouse settles into a chilling silence, every eye in the room watching as I shakily step from my cage, the sound of my heels clicking against the blood-spattered concrete.

I take one step and then another, each daunting move bringing me closer to my undeniable end.

What does this man want with me? Who the hell is he to be able to walk into a room filled with men like this and command authority in such a brutal, unsettling way?

My heart races and my palms sweat, but his ghostly stare draws me in until I'm standing right before him, my whole body shaking with unease. "Understand me now," he says, his voice so low yet somehow heard throughout the warehouse. "You are mine. You belong to me. There is nowhere you can run or hide. No escape. No freedom. No reprieve. If you follow my rules, you will find life with me quite satisfactory, comfortable even. If you do not, if you refuse me, you will spend every waking hour wishing for death. Is that clear?"

Swallowing hard, I will myself not to crumble and nod my head, knowing without a doubt he means every word he says. The terror has a chokehold on me, and I try to get the words out past the fear weighing me down. "Yes, I understand."

Those dark eyes blaze, refusing to break away. "What is your name?"

"Chiara," I tell him, his height and brute size overwhelming me. "Chiara Matthews."

"This will be the last time you hear the name Chiara Matthews. She no longer exists," he says, stripping me of my identity with nothing more than a thick Romanian accent. "Forget your old life, scrub it from your memory. Your friends, your family, schooling, or work. Your world revolves around me now. You cater to only me. My every will and desire will be your only priority."

Fuck.

I nod, the weight on my shoulders making me feel smaller than ever before. I can't help but wonder if this asshole has a Daddy kink, but I think it might be more than that. He's not looking for some whore to call him Daddy and act like a brat. This man wants complete submission, and I don't mean the *Fifty Shades* type of submission. I'm talking about the real messed-up shit.

This man wants complete ownership. He wants to strip me of my identity to the point where my world no longer exists. My name will be wiped from public record, my life wiped from existence. Those who once knew me will be made to question if I was ever really there. My friends, my work, my life . . . all of it gone, just like that.

He watches me a few seconds longer, daring me to challenge his word, but while I might have the tendency to run my mouth and fly off the handle, I'm not fucking stupid. I know when to argue and when to back down.

Approving of my silence, he gives a curt nod. "Follow me."

Without another word, the tall stranger turns on his heel and stalks toward the exit, every eye in the room watching him with fearful caution. He doesn't bother to look back at me. He simply expects that I will follow every last demand given, and that's exactly what I do. Sticking to his side, I'm spurred on by the idea of finally stepping outside of this wicked warehouse.

We take the stairs, and as we reach the top to find the burly security guard, I can't help but meet his stare. It's still so full of pity that I'm forced to look away. The guard opens the door, and I expect my captor to walk straight through it. But when he stops and waves me through, allowing me to pass in front, I'm taken aback. Trusting my situation enough to know nothing is about to happen in the next few seconds, I hesitantly step past him and over the threshold.

His hand drops to my lower back, guiding me through the door as any gentleman would, and my back stiffens at his touch, a shiver sailing over my skin. Trying to ignore it, I step out into the cold winter night, the chilling breeze settling right into my bones.

Quickly glancing around, I take in my surroundings and find us in what looks to be an abandoned industrial estate. Each broken streetlight and run-down building looks as sorry as I feel.

My gaze settles on a black SUV with darkly tinted windows parked right by the door as if waiting for me. I stride toward it, my gaze shifting from left to right, waiting and watching for any chance I have to make my escape.

"You do not want to discover what lies in wait for you if you try to run from me," he warns, moving in beside me to reach for the door handle of the SUV.

Swallowing over the lump in my throat, I shoot a timid glance at him as he holds the door. "I wasn't going to."

His gaze narrows slightly, and it's clear as day he doesn't believe me, but instead of calling me out, he nods toward the open door. "Get in."

I flick my gaze between the door and him, knowing the second I get into his SUV, it's all over for me. "Who are you?" I ask, waiting only a second before blurting my next question. "Where are you taking me?"

"There will be time for questions when I get you back to my manor," he explains. "Until then, you will remain silent." Then with another pointed stare, he indicates for me to get in his SUV, but this time his sharp gaze warns me of my fate if I do not obey immediately.

Not wanting to put my life on the line any more than I already have tonight, I silently slide into the back of the SUV and watch with unease as this mysterious man gets in beside me. He closes the door, and the tension rises in the car.

A tear sails down my cheek, splashing onto my collarbone, and with that, the driver hits the gas. I take a moment to grieve the life I once knew because, from here on out, I'm as good as dead.

CHAPTER 3

Killian

The heaviness of this sweet girl's despair fills the air like an impenetrable tension as she sits in the car beside me. Her hands curl into tight fists on her bare thighs to mask how they shake. She's fucking terrified, but she can't hide it from me. I know fear when I see it. I can sniff it out in any room. I'm drawn to it like a moth to a flame, and once I have it in the palm of my hand, I corrupt it.

I've never met a person I couldn't break, and as for this innocent woman who just became mine? Well, fuck. Breaking her might be the best fun I'll ever have.

I live and breathe off the fear I invoke. It's like an illicit drug I've become addicted to, and the moment my gaze connected with hers across the warehouse, that potent fear within her spoke right to my soul. I knew I had to have her. I was going to make her mine, and when I set out to do something, I never fail. It's not in my blood.

I'm not known for being a man who negotiates for the things I want. I take. Whether it's by contract or force, and she is no exception to that.

It's after two in the morning, and we still have a three-hour drive ahead of us. I turn to look at my new prize, letting my gaze sail over her face. There's no denying how beautiful she is, even through the dirt and grime stained across her slim face and the blood matted in her long golden curls. There's no telling how long she was held captive in that cage, but looking at her like this, it's clear Ezekiel and his men didn't exactly go to great lengths to take care of the women they traffic. But truth be told, the kind of men who were bidding on these women aren't the type who care if a woman appears clean or not. They care about the assets of her body, how tight her cunt is, or just how loud they can make her scream in agony as they fuck her until she bleeds—a fate this mysterious beauty only narrowly escaped.

It's not as though I'm any better. I plan to fuck her. All day and night if I could, but I'm a busy man, so luck is on her side. She will cater to me. My every need and desire will be her responsibility, but I'm not a fucking pig like the men back in that warehouse, and I will give just as eagerly as I receive.

I don't know what possessed me to claim her. I don't particularly care for having a pet, and judging by the fire in her eyes, she doesn't strike me as the type to submit willingly. But she will. I'll leave her no choice.

She's going to be work, and probably a huge pain in my ass, and despite knowing this the moment I laid eyes on her, I still claimed her. I'm painfully aware of the fact that I require an heir to inherit my legacy in the event my life shall be taken from this world, though it's still undecided whether she will be the one to bear my child.

All I know is that the moment our eyes collided across that filthy warehouse, I could sense her pure desperation. She was silently screaming for me to save her, and as those other bastards bid for what already belonged to me, I couldn't stomach the idea of watching her being gifted to another man. Don't get me wrong, had she been claimed by someone else, I would have still found her and slaughtered the pig who dared treat her as his own. However, letting it get that far only meant I was lining the pockets of Ezekiel and his asshole employees, and taking that payday away from them was a prize I simply couldn't pass up.

Ezekiel and his men are the scum of the earth, and the second I no longer require them to run my drugs, they'll be slaughtered like the animals they are. My cousin, Sergiu, insists that we keep them around, but turning a blind eye to their shit has been challenging. Considering everything they've got their toes dipped in, it's clear they're capable of keeping a tight lid on their business, but every time I walk in there and see it for myself, my skin crawls. If they weren't such an integral part of my operation, I would have dealt with them long ago.

Most of the time, I'm able to turn a blind eye to the women Ezekiel traffics, but something about this woman caught my attention. I usually leave Sergiu to deal with business here, but Ezekiel needed a reminder about just how disposable he really is.

The question is, what the hell am I supposed to do with her now that she belongs to me?

Do I lock her in my cells to use as I see fit, or do I allow her freedom within my home?

My gaze drops down her body. The dried blood on her thigh and the fresh scratches and bruises decorating her skin are a clear indication of the mistreatment she received while in Ezekiel's clutches. The very sight of her has me wanting to teach her how to ensure this bullshit never happens again. Though, I suppose there's no need for that anymore. Not now that she belongs to me. Whether she likes it or not, my home is not a place she will ever escape. She will live under my roof from now until her dying breath, whether that be in peace or as a prisoner.

As my gaze trails back up to her face, I find her stare already on mine. There are a million questions in her lifeless green eyes, probably wondering what happens from here. "When was the last time you drank water?" I ask. She needs to maintain her energy if she is going to keep up with the demanding lifestyle that's about to be thrust upon her.

She visibly swallows. "I, umm . . . can't be sure," she says in a quiet tone. Though something tells me the moment she finds her comfort within my home, that quiet tone will morph into a fierce demand, and that's exactly what's required of a woman in my world.

I nod, and as if on cue, my driver silently hands me a bottle of water. I quickly uncap it before passing it to her. She slowly takes it from me, but there's a strong hesitation in her eyes, wondering if she should trust me, but she sips on the water anyway. Her body is far too deprived to resist.

She keeps that penetrating gaze on me, clearly not trusting me, but I don't expect her to. I'm not her savior, and I'm sure as fuck not her hero. As long as she's clear in that understanding, we'll be good.

Realizing just how long this trip home is going to be if she's incapable of relaxing, I dig into the pocket of my suit jacket and curl my hand around a small bottle of pills. Pulling it out, I open the cap, and with every passing second, I feel her gaze like laser beams trying to penetrate right through me.

Tipping a single pill into the palm of my hand, I hold it out to her, my brow arched with expectation. Only she doesn't submit to my will, she simply stares at my hand with trepidation. She shakes her head. "What is that?"

"Take it. It will help you relax."

"I don't need to relax."

"Take the damn pill. I will not ask you again."

She clenches her jaw, anger flashing within those fearful eyes. "Do you think I'm stupid?" she questions, somehow seeming offended. "I take that pill, and in a few hours, I'll wake up to find you and your driver tag-team raping me. No thanks, I'll pass."

I take a deep breath, willing myself to calm down. It's one thing to have her fear me because of who I am, but it's another to have her fear me out of distrust or foolishness. Shit like that is how men get killed. "I do not believe you are stupid," I tell her, spitting the words with venom. "But let me get one thing straight. If I want to fuck you, *which I will*, I won't need to knock you out first. I will take it just as surely as those men back in that warehouse would have. However, you are in luck because, unlike those assholes, unconscious women are not my thing. What kind of man do you take me for?"

"As far as I'm concerned, you're the kind of man who purchases women who've been kidnapped and trafficked, and honestly, I think that tells me everything I need to know about the kind of man you are," she mutters, disdain clear in her tone.

Ahh. So she's just as feisty as she appears. I like that. I wonder if she'll be quite so forward with that mouth of hers when I'm fucking it.

"You are right to question me. I am not a nice man, so believe me when I say this. If you don't take this pill in the next two seconds, I will physically force it down your throat. Take your pick. Do you care to discover what it means to be on my bad side, or will you play it smart and do everything within your power to remain in my good graces?"

Her eyes flare with fire as she reaches out and finally takes the pill from my palm, and as she places it on the end of her tongue and closes her mouth, she refuses to break eye contact. I can practically hear her screaming thoughts as they're aimed at me like venom-laced arrows, but her intimidation tactics won't work here. I appreciate her attempt though. It's rare when somebody has the balls to argue with me, and honestly, it's refreshing. Stupid, but certainly refreshing.

She lifts the bottled water to her lips, and I watch with a keen stare as she swallows the pill. It's strong and will take effect in a matter of seconds, and as the pill begins to dissolve in the pit of her stomach, her brows furrow, no doubt already feeling the drowsiness.

She holds my gaze, confusion flashing in those green eyes. "What's happening?" she asks, her body steadily growing heavier. "What . . . What is this? What did you give me?"

"Rest your pretty head, Sweet Angel," I murmur. "It's a long drive."

And just like that, she's out cold.

Her head lolls to the side against the headrest. As I reach over her, my arm skims across her blazing skin, and the unexpected contact unleashes a rapid current of excitement that courses through me. My brows furrow, pausing just a moment to look over her face before swiftly ignoring it. I work my hand down beside the chair and find the lever before gently pulling it and reclining her chair. The second she appears comfortable, I remove my suit jacket and drape it over her lingerie-clad body to keep her warm.

As I settle back into my seat and prepare for the long drive ahead, I can't help but watch her. There's an innocence there, a softness in her face that suggests perhaps before she was stolen by Ezekiel's men, she might have had an easy life. Perhaps been a college student just going about her day, or maybe she was newly graduated and trying to figure out where she belongs in this cruel world—something she will never have the chance to discover, not if I have a say in it.

We've been on the road for almost an hour when the sound of an incoming call fills the silence of the cab, and I let out a heavy sigh. It's already been a long day. The last thing I want to deal with is business, but when you're in my position, the luxury of having a choice isn't something I come across often.

Realizing my phone is still in my suit jacket, I lean toward my new prize and fish it out of the pocket before checking that she's still out cold. She likely will be for another hour or so.

Turning my attention to the phone, I glance down to see my cousin's name across the screen. Sergiu is my second-in-command, and he's the closest thing I have to a brother. However, given the chance, he would rip my beating heart right out of my chest and take it all for himself. It's just who we are, who our grandfather raised us to be, and because of that, I'm the most dangerous man walking this earth.

Friends close. Enemies closer.

My name is Killian DeLorenzo, and I am the head of the DeLorenzo Mafia, a position I have more than earned. I am ruthless. Unforgiving. And because of this, our reputation has flourished with fear. Our competitors don't stand a chance as long as I stand at the head of my family. And Sergiu? While he might be foolish enough to challenge me, he knows I'm his best chance of survival.

"What do you want, Sergiu?" I growl, frustrated that this rare moment of peace has been disturbed. "Do you have any idea what time it is?"

"Sorry, Killian. I thought it was best you heard this from me."

"What?"

"There's been a raid on our warehouse downtown. The place is a mess."

Fuck. I mentally go over everything we have stored in that warehouse, and while it's a pain in the ass, it's not a complete loss. I have four warehouses spread across the state, and the one downtown that we use for distribution is our smallest. After a large shipment went out last week, anyone who dared raid my warehouse would have come up empty-handed.

"FBI?" I ask, wondering just how much trouble is about to come knocking on my door.

"No," Sergiu says, his accent thickening with his rage. "This was no police raid. It was . . . messy."

I nod, quickly going over my current list of enemies, competitors, or anybody else who'd be so fucking reckless as to steal from me. The only issue is that list is longer than the fucking Nile. "What did surveillance pick up?" I ask, my hand curling into a fist on my thigh.

"Nothing identifying yet. I have a team on it," he explains. "Maybe ten or so men in black hoodies and balaclavas. They came prepared for a full house. Automatic weapons and trucks. They were clearly expecting to find product."

"They take off with much?"

"Nothing that's going to push back our schedule," he says, knowing the exact answer I was looking for. "Perhaps 100k worth of E and a few of the weapons for the DeAngelis shipment next month."

I let out a breath. Those DeAngelis brothers aren't to be messed with, and I was honored when Roman wanted to work with me, but I'll be damned if his shipment is anything less than perfect. I don't often get in business with other mafia families, but like I said—friends close, enemies closer.

"Alright. We can work with that. Let me know once you've got something concrete," I tell him. "I want to know exactly who these bastards are, and when we do, I want their fucking heads. Nobody steals from me."

"Yes, boss."

"How many casualties?"

"Twenty-three," he says, his tone dipping with heaviness. "Most of the workers were able to run or hide, but these assholes were brutal."

"I want a list of names and contact numbers for their next of kin," I tell him. "We'll cover funeral expenses, but Sergiu, when I tell them we're going to find the bastards who did this and make them pay, you better fucking come through."

"Of course, Killian."

"Cops are going to swarm the warehouse soon enough," I remind him, though I'm sure he's already on it. "I want a team down there to clear out anything left behind, and make it fast. The last thing we need is to hand the FBI more ammunition against us."

"Already on it," he says. "How'd things go with Ezekiel? That asshole still in line?"

"For now," I admit, pressing my lips into a tight line as my gaze shifts to the sleeping beauty beside me. "I want him watched. He's getting too cocky with his side businesses. It was too loud. He's been inviting all sorts to his auctions, and I don't like it. Too many witnesses looking around."

"Speaking of Ezekiel's auctions and having too many people," Sergiu says. "I've heard whispers from tonight."

"What kind of whispers?"

"That you made a rare appearance and claimed some whore for

yourself."

My jaw clenches, not approving of the casual way he called her a whore. None of the girls in Ezekiel's cages should be classified as whores. They didn't ask for this, and if they had their way, I'm sure they would have chosen to be anywhere but there.

Sensing I don't plan to respond, Sergiu goes on. "I think it's great. Once you're through with her, I'll happily take her off your hands. You know how I like them young."

"Why don't you fuck your wife instead and keep your nose out of my business?"

Sergiu laughs. "Just messing around with you, boss. But should I assume this new girl is going to be a permanent fixture?"

"Haven't decided," I admit. "Until then, I want every detail you can find on Chiara Matthews. Birth certificate, school records, employment. I want to know the last time she ordered takeout, and once you have it all, scrub her from existence. I don't want a single trace of her leading back to me."

"Right away."

"I want it on my desk first thing in the morning."

And with that, I end the call and put my phone down, wondering just how much trouble my new little prize is going to be.

CHAPTER 4

Chiara

Feeling the subtle sensation of movement, I peel my heavy eyelids open and come back to reality. I'm still in the backseat of a car, and my new Romanian captor is right where I left him. I feel as though I've either been hit by a brick or knocked out for a whole lifetime. My body is heavy, and my limbs can barely move.

He knocked me out.

I don't know what was in that pill he gave me, but it did a shitload more than just help me relax. On the plus side, my filthy lingerie is still intact with the addition of his suit jacket to keep me warm. Though, I don't know how to feel about that. It's a sweet gesture, but something tells me this man is anything but sweet.

When we first got in the car, we headed right out of the city and deep into the mountains. Despite the late hour, I could see cars passing every few seconds, especially when we were still within the city limits, but now, glancing out the dark-tinted window, there's not another car in sight.

"Good timing. We're almost home," that thick Romanian accent says from beside me.

Home. Right, because that's what his place is about to become for me. Though the jury is still out on what kind of living conditions I'll be provided. I'm assuming cuffs and a murky dungeon are probably his style.

I sit up, realizing my seat has been reclined, though how that happened is beyond me. After adjusting the seat to its proper upright position, I pull his suit jacket off me and hesitantly place it down between us. "How long was I out?"

"A few hours."

Shit.

The roads are windy and uneven, and my stomach begins to grow uneasy when the driver approaches a huge property hidden deep within the mountains. Every inch of the land is perfectly manicured and well presented, purposefully built for isolation and privacy—the perfect place to hide something you wouldn't want found.

We pull into a wide driveway and stop at a black, iron gate as the driver enters a code. I'm completely taken aback by the sight of armed guards standing on either side of the gate. My hands shake, and I try to convince myself that this was expected, but honestly, I hadn't given it a damn thought.

What kind of powerful man requires armed guards? What the hell have I just been brought into?

Trying to breathe through the uneasy feeling growing in the pit of my stomach, I do what I can to look past the guards and peer through the windshield at what awaits me. The big gate starts to peel back, and I find myself lost for words.

The expansive driveway is lit on both sides, and the stunning bushland leading deep into the property creates an eerie treetop canopy overhead. I know without a doubt that daylight has nothing on this place. If my Romanian purchaser built this property, he did it with his nightlife in mind. The driveway is architecturally designed with stunning natural stones that take my breath away. The soft lighting on either side of the driveway only makes the scene that much better.

We drive through the winding entrance, and I'm struck with the sight of a stunning stone mansion with a modern take on the traditional Georgian style. It incorporates soft grays and natural sandstone and is the perfect estate to suit this Romanian mystery beside me. There's a grand entrance with tall pillars, and a stunning balcony rests on top— probably accessible from the master bedroom. This place has got to be at least three or four stories high and wider than a football field.

Lights are on inside, and the way the soft glow sails through the darkness is breathtaking, leaving me desperate to explore the rest of the property. I can only imagine the type of secrets this home has to discover. Just the thought of the type of pool this home could have gets me stupidly excited—natural stone waterfalls, a hidden cave, and of course, a faux beach and spa. Although, it's not like I'm here for a vacation. I doubt I'll be enjoying the place one bit. This man put me on a train with a one-way ticket to hell, no refunds or exchanges. I doubt I'll ever step foot outside the dungeon he probably has waiting for me.

As we get closer to the home, the thick forest begins to thin out until it's nothing but manicured grass with tidy bushes lining the driveway. It opens up wider into a big circular bay, and as the driver begins to pull around it, a wave of anxious nerves pulses through my veins.

I sink lower into my seat and spare a glance at the stranger beside me.

He sits casually with one foot propped up on his knee and his elbow resting against the groove in the door as if he hasn't got a care in the world. He glances out the window overlooking his expansive property, but he knows I'm watching him. I have a feeling this is a man who misses nothing. However, if he doesn't care that he holds my attention, then I'll take in every last detail until he demands I stop.

He's so tall that even in this huge SUV, his head is nearly skimming the roof while his knees are almost touching the driver's seat before him. On the other hand, my knees are nowhere near touching the seat in front of me. I'm barely five foot three.

The SUV pulls to a stop, and my hands shake violently in my lap. The engine idles as the driver puts the car into park and pushes his door wide, making his way around. My Romanian captor exits the car first, and just as I'm left wondering what the hell I'm supposed to do, the driver appears at my door, pulling it open before waving me out. "Miss," he says with a curt nod, barely sparing me a glance.

I swallow hard, my stomach flipping with unease as I slide out of the SUV and trail around to face the impressive home. Mr. DoAsISayOrSufferTheConsequences is already halfway up the stairs, and I hurry after him, not sure what it would mean to keep him waiting, though I doubt I want to find out.

It seems so much colder here than back at the abandoned industrial estate, and I try to ignore the way my body shakes. It could be the temperature, or it could be out of pure fear of the unknown. It's all too clear that my life changed the second I laid eyes on this man in the darkest corner of the underground warehouse, but stepping inside his home makes it real. I don't know what to expect or what he intends for me. All I know is that one foot out of line is going to see me occupying a shallow grave.

By the time he reaches the top step, the door opens from within, and he strides right through it without bothering to glance back at me. I scurry after him, finding his home alive with staff, despite the late hour.

A doorman stands just inside the foyer, silently welcoming me and ignoring the state of my undress like it's a regular occurrence. He simply closes the door behind me and takes a step out of the way, silently blending into the background but staying close to be available to his boss.

My stride slows as my gaze sails around the large foyer, trying to take in as much as I can before he catches me lagging behind. But when he moves to the adjoining living area and hands his suit jacket to an older lady who I can only assume is his housekeeper, I make sure to be right there at his beck and call.

He turns toward me in a black dress shirt, his top two buttons undone, showing off just a sliver of tanned skin and the top of what I can tell are very defined pecs. He slowly rolls up his sleeves to his elbows as he watches me, and while he looks casual and relaxed, I doubt he's anything but.

"This is my home. *Your home*," he tells me in that thick accent. I keep myself a few feet away and watch nervously as his housekeeper scurries out of the room. "This is where you will stay. You will live freely here. You may roam the halls and explore as you please, so long as you continue to behave as required."

My brows furrow as I stare up at him, hating just how uneasy I feel in front of this man. I don't think I've ever been intimidated by a man in my life, and yet here I am, barely able to meet his eyes in fear of him pulling me in with that wicked intensity. "I get to roam freely?" I question, confusion rattling my bones. "I was under the impression that I was a prisoner here."

"I do not like the term *prisoner*," he tells me. "That is reserved for those who have wronged me and require punishment. You have done no such thing. You are not my *prisoner*. However, you are my *property*. I own you, your body, your mind, everything that you are belongs to me. You will be in my company, and I intend for our time together to be pleasant. So yes, I will allow you to live freely in my home. Generosity does not come easily to me. I am not a kind man by nature, and if I feel my generosity has been disrespected in any way, then it shall be stripped without question. And trust me when I tell you that you will not like the conditions you find yourself in."

I swallow hard and nod, nerves blooming through me once again. I don't doubt him for one second.

Unable to hold his stare a second longer, I drop my gaze to the open living space, glancing around in wonder. Though it's not quite as enjoyable as it could be with my present company. "Might I ask what will be required of me?" I question as his movement across the room draws my attention.

He approaches a small table, and I watch as he fills a glass of whiskey and lifts it to his lips. He turns back to me, and his gaze darkens as he takes me in, reminding me that I have absolutely no idea how he intends to use me. "I have but one requirement," he says, that accent so damn smooth. "That you cater to my every will and desire. When I eat, you eat. When I call for you, you come. And when I eat your pussy, you scream like you will never feel pleasure again."

Holy fuck.

My breath catches in my throat, and I watch as that lethal stare drags over my body, every last hair standing on end. He strides toward me, stopping right in front of me, so damn close I feel his whiskey breath dancing upon my skin.

He holds my stare as my legs involuntarily clench, the thought of this powerful man between my thighs unnerving me. I shouldn't want that, but the way those words so effortlessly rolled off his tongue has ignited something inside of me that I can't refuse.

This is wrong. So damn wrong. He's my captor, my owner, a man who could end my life with nothing more than a flick of his wrist. I should be searching for the exits, not wondering how good it would feel to have his mouth closing over my cunt, his tongue flicking past my clit, and those long, thick fingers plunging deep inside of me.

Fuck. FUCK. This man will have no issue taking me against my will. I cannot allow myself to see him this way.

Shake it from your thoughts, Chiara. Don't be a whore for this man.

As if seeing my inner turmoil, he takes pity on me and frees my stare, turning around as though he doesn't have me already messed up. "Come now," he says. "I will show you my home."

I follow in silence as he takes me around the estate, showing me the spaces he thinks I'll probably enjoy or find useful, and honestly, he's not wrong. As we make our way through a home library that overlooks the mountain range, he tells me how he will have my closet stocked and suggests I speak to his head chef about my dietary needs.

With each new sentence out of his mouth, I find myself even more baffled by this strange man. I'm his property, the woman he claimed at an auction, and yet he's welcoming me into his home like a long-lost guest he wishes to pamper. Where's the cell? The dirty sheets and food scraps? This isn't what I was expecting, not even remotely.

We walk back to one of the many living rooms where he refills his whiskey, and I realize just how serious he was. Since asking my name back at the warehouse, he hasn't once used it. It's not exactly high on my list of priorities, but it's almost ironic. He knows my name and won't use it, probably some kind of fucked-up way to misplace the guilt he feels from taking me away from the life I once knew. Either that or some kind of power play. Yet here I am, without even a clue who he is. At this point, I'd pay to learn his name and then inquire with my good friend, Google.

Lifting his glass to his lips, he takes a quick sip and focuses that intense stare back to mine, his gaze slightly narrowed with suspicion. It's as if he's patiently waiting for me to ask whatever is on my mind. Understanding just how serious he was about his desire to punish me, the thought of questioning him unnerves me, but I have to know what the hell I've gotten myself into. "I don't know your name," I tell him.

"There is no need for you to know my name, who I am, or what I do. Your one requirement is to cater to me."

"How can I best cater to you when I don't know anything about you?"

"I will teach you what you need to know and what is required of you," he states. I hesitate, biting my bottom lip, and his gaze narrows. "What is it?"

"Can I be honest with you?" I question, feeling as though I'm about to shit myself with fear.

"I welcome your honesty," he says with a slight nod, encouraging me to go on.

I swallow hard, keeping my stare locked on him to make sure he's not about to flip the switch and send this whole strange vacation vibe crumbling down around me. After all, the alternative terrifies me. "I feel that I need to warn you that I am not someone who naturally follows rules. The idea that you claim to own me makes me sick. I've never answered to anyone in my life, and I don't like the idea of starting now. I didn't answer to the assholes who took me off the street, and I don't answer to you. I answer to me."

Darkness clouds his eyes, and he steps toward me, placing his glass down on a table as he passes by. "Understand me, girl," he says, his voice taking on a tone that chills me to the bone. "I don't care what you once did in a former life, who you fucked, or what you valued. You belong to me now. You answer to me and me alone. I own you."

I shake my head, hating that my need to argue every case rears its ugly head right now. "But you don't," I tell him. "You might have claimed me at that bullshit auction, but you didn't purchase me because I was never for sale. I was stolen off the street and offered to the highest bidder. Besides, I don't know how many auctions you've been to, but when you purchase something, an exchange must occur. But you didn't dig into those deep pockets of yours and pay what you owed. You simply walked in and told the world that I was yours. There was no payment made. Therefore, you don't own me."

Those dark eyes are like two raging pits leading straight to hell, and as I try to back up, I find myself unable to move. "I paid by allowing those scum to keep breathing," he states, that low tone like poison in my veins. "A price unmatched by any other. Now, I understand this is your first night here. You're scared, uncertain, and nervous. You don't know what's coming your way and probably haven't had a decent meal in a while, so I will put your outburst aside. I am not a forgiving man, but considering the circumstances, I will excuse your actions. *This time.* But know, if you speak out of line one more time, you will see a side of me that you will never be able to come back from. Do we have an understanding?"

Fear consumes me, and I hold his stare for a while, absolutely hating this, but the one thing I feel deep in my gut is that this unnamed man keeps his word, whether those words are threatening my life or not. He will follow through if he feels challenged, no matter the cost. "I fear that this is going to be a bigger adjustment than you had anticipated," I tell him, keeping it honest. "However, I know you don't know me, and my word probably doesn't mean shit to you, but it means something to me. So, I will give you my word that I will try and do things your way. You said you hoped our time together would be pleasant, and I am honest in telling you that I hope it can be too. I'm not interested in experiencing this other side of you."

He nods, and his stormy eyes seem to relax. "Then we have an understanding," he says. "Now, I know it is late, and I am sure you are wanting to retire to your room. However, there is one thing I need from you before you are excused."

My brows furrow, and I meet his dark gaze. "What's that?"

He steps into me, closer than ever before, that sweet whiskey breath brushing over my neck and sending a shiver sailing across my body. He leans in, his voice low and thick with desire. "You're going to show me how you come."

CHAPTER 5

Chiara

Nerves pound through my body as my captor leads me through his home. I feel my hands shaking, but I'm far too focused on his words still ringing in my ear.

You're going to show me how you come.

Is he for real? Shit. What a stupid question. Of course he's for real.

He refuses to give me his name, and yet somehow, I already know he's one of the most powerful men on the planet. If he asks a woman to spread her legs and fuck herself in front of him, then that's exactly what she will do. This isn't a man who enjoys being told no. Hell, when he is told no, he fixes it by taking lives. At least, that's what I assume he does. He all but confirmed it when he suggested that he paid for me by allowing my original captor to live.

So why the hell am I so giddy with excitement?

This is wrong. So fucking wrong.

This man is terrifying, and if I deny him, I don't doubt that he will force me to see it through. And yet, I still want to please him. Surely that must mean there's something wrong with me. He hasn't once claimed to be the hero. He's not a good guy and doesn't deny that. So why am I not repulsed?

He heads in a direction we hadn't taken on his initial tour, which piques my curiosity. When he walks into a small, darkened room, my eyes widen, that same unease coming back to haunt me. I follow him right into the center of the room and stand awkwardly as I look around. The walls are either painted or covered with material. It's too dark to tell which.

There's a small stage behind me, and directly in front of it, there's an armchair he lowers himself into. He relaxes back, propping his foot onto his knee, just as he did in the car. He lowers his elbow against the armrest, his whiskey refilled and hanging from his fingers.

It's private in here, and as he fixes that alluring gaze on me, the tension builds in the room. I'm not the nervous type when it comes to performing for a man. I'm comfortable with my sexuality. Hell, I'm more than just comfortable, I'm a firm believer in getting down and dirty. And yet right now, I'm scared to death.

What happens if he doesn't like what I have to offer? Will I be prosecuted to the highest degree? Sent to a dirty basement to live as his prisoner?

The darkness of the room helps, and I anxiously make my way

toward the small stage. "How do you want me?" I ask, my tone coming out a shitload more confident than how I feel.

"On the stage," he instructs, nodding to the space right in front of the armchair. He watches me as I move across the room and take a seat on the stage, my stomach clenched with nervous energy. My tongue rolls over my lips, the adrenaline of this moment spurring me on. His dark gaze is barely visible in this dimly lit room, but just the knowledge of having his eyes on me like this is tantalizing.

"Now what?"

"Move back," he rumbles, watching as I scoot further onto the stage—so far that I have to put my feet up. "Lean back and open your legs. Slowly. I want to be able to smell you."

Oh, God.

Electricity shoots through me, right down to my core at the way he instructs me. Is he going to do this the whole way through? Or is he going to allow me to take the reins at some point? Either way, I lock my gaze onto his and watch him as I slowly spread my thighs, my heels making my legs look a million miles long.

Need slams through me, and I find myself already wet and desperate for his touch, but tonight is all me. I don't doubt that I'll experience his hands on me soon enough, I just hope it's under my terms.

He sips his whiskey before giving a slight nod, indicating for me to get started, and good God, I don't hesitate to get the show on the road. With my legs as wide as they will go and my knees up, it gives him perfect view of my pussy. I bring my hand up, trailing my fingers over my body and pushing the strap of my harness off my shoulder. The hard leather of the harness slips down enough for my nipple to peek out and join the party.

I continue moving, brushing my fingertips over my sensitive skin as my pussy begs for attention. I skim over my nipple, pushing the leather down further and watching how the gathered leather pushes my tit higher. But while it sure is a stunning sight, we both know that's not what he brought me here to see.

Trailing my fingers down lower, I suck in a breath as my fingers brush my waist, my sensitive skin not immune to the sweet tickle of a feather-soft touch. A breathy groan slips from my lips, and I push my hand down further as I watch my captive audience, my hand dropping lower over my hips until finally hitting the sweet spot.

I cup my pussy, giving a gentle squeeze to try and relieve the building ache between my legs, but it's not nearly enough. Moving slowly, I pull at the flimsy material of my lace thong and push it aside before trailing my fingers through my folds.

My head tips back, just enough that I don't lose sight of my Romanian jailer, and I roll my thumb over my clit, my needy moan breaking the silence.

The tension builds as he adjusts himself and takes another sip of whiskey. "Remove them," he says in that seductive accent, his tone thick with hunger and driving me wild with need. "Let me see your tight cunt."

Oh God. He's a dirty talker.

Not one to disappoint, I adjust myself slightly and make a show of peeling my lace thong down my legs and kicking it off at the end of the stage. I widen my legs once again, this time completely open, vulnerable, and available to him.

Unable to help myself, I bring my hand back down between my legs and show him exactly how I like it. I rub circles over my clit with my thumb as my fingers drop lower to my entrance. I push them inside of me without pause, watching the way his eyes darken with desire.

I'm soaking wet, and the tension in the room is so damn thick, it's almost impossible to breathe. I'm right on the edge, my fingers massaging my walls from within as my thumb continues rubbing tight circles over my clit. My hips start to rock, my thighs trying to push themselves wider, to open myself up even more. My fingers aren't enough. I need him to take me deep. Need him to fuck me until I scream.

"Why don't you come and join me?" I say with a breathy groan, our eyes locked together in a fiery war, fighting for dominance when we both know I don't stand a chance in hell.

He doesn't move, and I almost drown in devastation. "Remove your fingers," he instructs.

Disappointment fires through me as I free my fingers from within, wondering if this is all part of his game—getting me all hot and bothered, waiting until I'm just about to come, and depriving me of my release. I watch him expectantly, waiting to hear what he wants from me next. "Now, tell me how you taste."

Well, shit. I wasn't expecting that one, but if he insists . . .

A sly smile settles onto my face. If this is just day one and he's already hitting me with this, he must be one hell of a kinky bastard. Just the way I like them.

My eyes sparkle with a twisted satisfaction, and I see the curiosity deep in his stare, watching as I press my fingers to my mouth. I trail my wetness over my bottom lip before my tongue shoots out, rolling over my lip and tasting just how sweet I am. His eyes darken as I open wide, sucking both my fingers clean before returning them to my pussy. I trail them through my wetness and release a low groan. "I taste like I need to be fucked hard, deep, and fast."

"Good girl," he tells me. "Now let me see you come."

Goddamn.

I plunge my fingers deep, my whole body jolting with electricity as I picture his cock slamming into me, his fingers rolling over my clit instead of my own. I work my body right to the edge, the intensity of his eyes on me making me come alive like never before.

I give it my all, crying out as I finally come hard on the stage.

My orgasm tears through me, my pussy spasming around my fingers as I reach an unbelievable high. I throw my head back, wishing I knew his name just so I could scream it as I came.

My high shoots through my body like the sweetest victory, my toes curl in my heels, and I start to shake from the intensity of my orgasm. I keep my fingers moving, keep working my clit as my pussy continues to convulse, not wanting to come back to reality.

Taking a breath, my body starts to relax, and I catch myself against the stage, utterly exhausted. But I keep my gaze on my Romanian captor, assuming he's only getting started for the night. I try to calm myself, preparing for whatever he might have in store when he places his empty glass down at his feet.

Anxious energy flutters through me as he stands, and my gaze becomes hooded as I watch his tall frame rise before me. Whatever he wants, whatever he asks for, I'll give it to him. Exactly how he wants it.

He takes a step, his hungry stare still locked on mine, and just as I think he's about to make his move and throw me around like a goddamn ragdoll, he simply strides out of the private room, not a single word spoken between us. He leaves me wanting so much more, and I realize that I was just used for nothing more than a show.

As the ugliness of it all fills my veins, I simply collect my discarded thong off the ground and make my way up to my room, wondering what the fuck just went down.

CHAPTER 6

Killian

Hot water cascades around me as I brace my hand against the shower wall. My other hand grips my cock in a fucking chokehold, furiously jerking off.

I expected a lot of things from my new prize, but what she just did on that fucking stage . . . I wasn't ready.

She truly is a sweet angel.

I've been with plenty of women, each of them rare in their own way, but never have I come across a woman so confident in herself or so sure about what she wants and how to get there. The way she wanted me despite her declaration of independence. The way she begged me to touch her, to fuck her, and the soft pleasure-filled moans that slipped from her lips. God, I wanted her, and if I had crept just an inch closer, I would have bent her over that fucking stage and fucked her until she screamed, but there will be time for that, and believe me, I will have my way with her.

I won't stop until I've felt the warmth of her cunt squeezing around me and the way she comes undone and shatters as I thrust inside of her. I know it's going to be worth the wait.

When I fuck her, when I take her on her knees and bend her over, I need her to be ready for me, and while she was desperate to feel my touch tonight, she wasn't ready. I need her well-rested and fed. She needs to wash away the filth from Ezekiel's warehouse and restore the energy she lost during her confinement, otherwise, she won't possibly keep up. When I fuck her, it will be all night. She won't just scream for more, she will ache for it, she will beg until her throat is raw, and I will oblige her every need. But most of all, I need to know how she tastes, or just how far I can push her before she breaks—and she will. I will break her every fucking night, over and over until she can't take another fucking second.

The scent of her arousal in the air almost brought me to my knees. It's ingrained in my memory, and as I furiously pump my thick cock up and down, I need to smell it again. My jaw clenches, already knowing that no amount of pleasure I give to myself is ever going to compare to how it would feel being inside her. The way her petite fingers pushed inside her tight little cunt and massaged her walls made my hands ball into fists at my sides. I've never felt such an overwhelming or desperate need to take what's mine and claim every inch of her. I need to see the way her creamy skin reddens beneath my fierce touch, see the way her cheeks hollow out as she takes my cock deep in her throat. But nothing compares to the moment she lifted her fingers to her lips and told me just how hard she needed to be fucked. It was my undoing.

She's going to be such a good girl. She'll be the perfect whore for me, on her knees at my command.

A loud groan tears from the back of my throat as my fist tightens around my cock, and as I replay the memory of my sweet angel pushing her fingers deep inside her cunt, my balls tighten, and I shatter, shooting hot spurts of cum across my opulent shower.

I lean against my hand that's braced on the tiles, hanging my head as the high rocks through me. The water cascades over my face, but all I can do is stand here, gripping my dick as I try to calm myself.

The last thing I expected from this girl was to get me wound up like this. Don't get me wrong, she's fucking beautiful. I knew it the moment I laid my eyes on her. But when her fear begins to fade and she can look at me with confidence, she'll be fucking radiant. I knew I would enjoy her body, but it's the small snippets of her personality that have begun to shine through that are surprising me. She's not compliant, and while I thought I wanted a woman to submit, perhaps her resistance is what I've needed. Her need to argue and hold on to her independence intrigues me, and for the first time in my life, I find a woman's defiance sexy as hell. Though nothing will ever beat the confidence I saw from her when she was on that stage. If I allow her, she'll be the one trying to force my submission, but that will never happen. She just needs to learn her place here, needs to find where she fits into this fucked-up world and understand what it means to be the woman I come home to fuck each night. Once she's figured it out, something tells me she'll be unstoppable.

Getting out of the shower, I dry off and dress for another long day. It's almost seven in the morning, and I'm sure my employees are wondering what the fuck is going on with the half-naked woman I stormed through the door with only a few short hours ago. They need to know what's going on and what I expect of them where my new prize is concerned, and by the time I've finished filling them in, Sergiu should be in my office with an update on the raid downtown and a folder filled with every detail of Chiara Matthews' life.

As I finish buttoning my suit shirt and roll up my sleeves, I take my phone and call down to the kitchen. Putting the call on speakerphone, I wait all of three seconds before my head chef, Krista, accepts the call. "Mr. DeLorenzo, what can I help you with?"

"Call for a full staff meeting in the dining room. I'll be down in ten minutes."

"Of course, Sir. And for breakfast?"

"No breakfast this morning. Just a coffee will be fine."

"Coming right up."

I end the call and finish getting myself ready for the day, dreading the long hours ahead before I finally get to crash, but unfortunately, a lack of sleep is simply a hazard of the job.

Making my way out of my bedroom, I pass the closed door that my latest mystery soundlessly sleeps behind, and considering the sedatives that were slipped into the glass of water on her bedside table, she should sleep for most of the day, assuming she was brave enough to drink it, of course.

Either way, I've offered her the privacy of a closed door in a luxurious bedroom with a private bathroom, and that's far more than she would have received in Ezekiel's warehouse. She should be quite happy here, and if she's not . . . then that's not my problem. She will have to figure out a way to find happiness here, otherwise, she will lead a very dull and lonely life.

Ignoring the lure of her creamy thighs, I head down the stairs and detour past the kitchen before scooping up my steaming coffee off the edge of the counter.

Krista has worked as my personal chef for a little over twelve years now—after I found her in a similar situation to Chiara. She was too young, and there was never an attraction there for me, so instead of offering her my bed, I gave her my kitchen and she flourished there, and now, I can't imagine having anyone else working my kitchen. She's got it down to a fine art, and I fear the day she decides to move on. Don't get me wrong, she is free. I don't hold her to the same bounds as I do my new prize. Krista is an employee and can walk away at any point, just like the rest of my staff, and despite knowing exactly who I am and what I'm capable of, she sticks around, not out of fear, but out of loyalty.

Lifting my coffee to my lips, I take a quick sip before letting out a heavy breath and striding through my home. I make my way into the formal dining room and find my staff waiting for me, all but a few of my main security team who would have stayed at their posts, patrolling my property for potential threats. I take my security very seriously and have the best of the best. My security detail is made up of ex-military special ops members, former champion MMA fighters, and the kind of men you wouldn't want to run into in a back alley. They make a deadly team, and yet not one of them is more deadly than me.

Moving around the dining table, I survey my staff, watching how they all straighten and offer me every bit of their attention as I snake my way to the head of the table.

Everyone is here. My housekeeper. Rohan, my doorman. My personal butler. The maids and the groundskeepers. They all remain standing, knowing they all have duties to attend to and that I don't usually waste any time.

"Some of you may have noticed that we currently have a woman occupying the private suite on the second floor," I start as I settle at the top of the table, not bothering to take a seat. "She is my guest and is to be treated with the utmost respect, just as you would anyone else who steps foot inside my home. Not a single hand is to be laid on her, or any wandering eyes feasting upon her beauty. She has already been through enough, and I wish for her to find comfort within my home."

My gaze subtly meets Krista's across the formal dining table, and when her lips press into a hard line and her gaze fills with pity, I know she understands exactly what kind of life I have stolen this woman from. And let's be clear when I say *stolen*, Krista knows exactly what that means. After all, I stole her just as I did Chiara, and hopefully as she begins to find solace in my home, she will be able to connect with Krista and the two of them can heal together, or in the least, offer the other some kind of friendship.

55

Focusing back on the many faces around my table, I continue with my expectations. "I have granted her full access to my estate, including the outdoor facilities. However, it is imperative that I be made aware of her daily movements. Until I know she can be trusted, she is to be watched like a hawk. I need to know her whereabouts at all times of the day, and it is to be noted that she is not permitted to step even a foot outside my estate without my approval. Is that understood?"

Everybody nods their head, and I turn my attention back to my personal chef. "Krista, I trust you will find some time in your day to meet with our new guest and discuss her dietary requirements."

"Of course, Sir," she responds with a subtle drop of her chin. "Anything else she requires for her stay? Clothes? Prescriptions? Electronics? Toiletries?"

"No electronics," I state firmly. "As for clothes and toiletries, yes. Please see to it that her closet is fully stocked. She will be staying indefinitely, so be sure to provide clothing for all seasons and occasions. Stock her bathroom with basic necessities to get her started, and when she wakes and is feeling up to it, you can ask her about her preferred brands."

"Yes, Sir," Krista says with another nod.

Digging my hand into my pocket, I pull out my wallet and fish for my credit card when Rohan's tone sails through the dining room. "Her name, Sir? What shall we refer to her as?"

I blindly hand my credit card to Krista, and she takes it without question, being one of the only members of my staff I trust with it. "Her name is not important," I say, choosing to keep them in the dark. After all, the less they know, the better. However, considering the strict level of professionalism and how it directly stands against my requirements to show respect to my guests, I relent and offer an alternative. "You may refer to her as ma'am, and nothing more until further notice."

Rohan nods in acknowledgment, and to be honest, out of all of my staff, Krista and Rohan are probably the only ones my new prize will have to deal with. The rest are to be seen and not heard. However, if she wishes to make friends with them down the line, then I suppose that will be okay.

"Are there any questions?"

"Sir," one of my security team pipes. "What are your expectations security-wise? Does she require a shadow, someone stationed outside her door? Or will the security footage surveillance be satisfactory?"

I consider his question, trying to figure out exactly what I want. On one hand, I want her comfortable here, and having some ex-con stationed outside her bedroom door isn't going to help with that. On the other hand, I don't know anything about this girl. I don't know her capabilities or her intentions, and until I can look her in the eye and read exactly what she's thinking, I have to play it safe.

Unsure how to answer it just yet, I meet his waiting stare. "Let me get back to you on that. I need to look further into her history before making an informed decision on how to move forward. Expect a response before lunch."

He nods. "I'll let my head of security know to expect your instructions."

"Good," I say before looking back at everyone else. "Unless there are any further questions, this meeting is adjourned. Please get back to your posts in a timely manner."

With that, the dining room quickly empties until I'm left with just Krista's heavy stare on me. I arch a brow, waiting to hear what she needs. She lets out a heavy breath, and her lips flinch in the corners as if she's trying to be brave. "Trafficking?" she asks in a small tone.

I hold her stare a moment longer. She's usually not so bold when it comes to the details of my house guests. She tends to turn a blind eye, knowing exactly what kind of company I keep, but she can tell that this one is different. It hits harder and because of the respect I hold for her and the challenges she's had to overcome, I won't disrespect her by lying about it now. "Yes."

Krista nods, and as she slips my credit card into the back pocket of her jeans, she forces a smile across her face. "You're a good man, Killian. You did the right thing," she tells me, reaching out and squeezing my arm. "I'll do everything I can to help her feel at home."

I nod, and without another word, Krista is gone.

Letting out a heavy breath, I brace my fists against the table and lean into them. Heavy is the head that wears the crown. That's what my grandfather always told me, and I never truly understood it until he was murdered in cold blood. Before his body was even cold, I took over as head of the DeLorenzo Mafia family. Now, I understand it as clearly as if the words had been engraved on my skin. It's a lonely life here at the top, and with the lives of so many in the palm of my hands, I can't afford to put even one foot out of line. One wrong move, and this whole family could burn to ashes. That much was proven last night during the raid at my warehouse. While it wasn't my family members who were slain, they were my workers. They were my responsibility, and last night, I failed them. The blood of those twenty-three workers is on my hands, and I will make this right.

Having too much to get through, I scoop my coffee off the dining table and cringe at the circle it left on the hardwood. I've always been a fan of a good coaster, only whenever I need one, there's never any in sight. I suppose it doesn't matter. The second I walk out of here, my housekeeper will sweep through and leave the room looking untouched.

Moving through my home, I find myself passing the main staircase that leads up to the private suites, right where Chiara sleeps, and I feel a pull, urging me to go check on her. I pause, my gaze sweeping up the long staircase, and I immediately berate myself. I shouldn't feel this way. She's just some random woman who I happened to find locked in a cage at Ezekiel's auction. She isn't anyone special, certainly not someone who is worthy enough for me to take time away from work.

Anger at my lack of self-control surges through my body, and I push myself to keep walking toward my office, but a movement out of the corner of my eye catches my attention. I pause again, watching Rohan reach for the front door and pull it open just in time for Sergiu to stride through, not bothering to spare a single second to thank Rohan for opening the door.

"Cousin," Sergiu booms as he stalks through my foyer and meets me in the middle with two manila folders tucked under his arm.

He claps me on the back, making a move to greet me, but I hold back, not having the patience for it today and needing answers about last night's bullshit raid. "Have you got a name for me?"

Sergiu nods. "I'm waiting for the call to come through any minute now," he says before handing me the manila folders. "In the meantime, I come bearing gifts. Everything you requested on your new . . . pet. And the names and contact details of the workers killed in the raid last night."

I nod and flip through the list of names, not recognizing any of them, and yet each one seems to sting harder than the last.

There are a million more questions I need to ask to follow up on the conversation we had last night, but I move on to the next folder instead, and right on top, I find a photograph of Chiara. She must be only a few years younger here, maybe nineteen or twenty. Her cheeks are full, and her green eyes are so bright, a stark contrast to the girl I met last night. One thing is for sure, when she's not plagued by fear, starved, or covered in grime, she's fucking gorgeous.

My attention is piqued, and I flip through the pages inside, quickly scanning over her birth certificate and the copy of the missing person's report that was filed two days ago when she failed to show up for her shift at the bar she worked at. "I trust you've taken care of this?" I ask Sergiu.

"Just about," he says. "The report mysteriously went missing from police records, but this was filed a few days ago, so I can't guarantee that there aren't physical copies on a desk somewhere, but with her name scrubbed from existence and her birth certificate suddenly gone, we should be okay. I've got men keeping a close eye on that though."

"Good, and—"

Sergiu's ringing phone cuts me off, and as he reaches for it and glances at the caller ID, a familiar excitement flashes in his eyes. He holds up a finger, telling me to hold that thought while he takes his call. "Speak to me," he says into the phone.

I listen to his call, keeping a keen eye on my cousin as he takes in the information that's being shared, and the second his lip quirks up into a wicked grin, I know we've got exactly what we need.

Sergiu ends the call with his gaze locked on mine. "We got 'em."

"Call a meeting," I tell him, excitement drumming through my veins. "We're going hunting tonight."

CHAPTER 7

Chiara

I t's well into the afternoon when I wake from yesterday's exhaustion, and while I'm still a little groggy, I feel well-rested and ready for my day. I've never woken up feeling so refreshed in my life. Could it be the expensive bed and the fancy Egyptian linen? Or . . . My gaze shifts to the glass of water that was left out for me last night.

No, it couldn't be. There's no way he slipped me something again. First in the car and then again in my drink. This is bullshit. How stupid could I be to have fallen for that? I should have known better, but I was so exhausted and confused when I came to bed last night that it didn't even occur to me not to trust the glass of water that had been left on my bedside table. God, I'm an idiot.

Throwing the blankets back, I trudge out of bed and across the room to my private bathroom before closing and locking the door behind me. Turning to the vanity, I face my disheveled reflection and barely recognize myself. My hair is a mess, there are deep circles under my eyes, and despite only being gone from my home for three or four days, I look as though I've lost weight.

The body harness still decorating my skin makes me feel dirty. Wanting to put this bullshit behind me, I grip the thick leather and yank it off my body, loosening it to speed up the process. It's not easy, and the complicated straps quickly send me into a blind panic. I need to get it off and burn the fucker. I need to be free of what it represents, but I don't think I'll ever be free again.

This Romanian jailer is never going to let me go. I'm never going to be blessed with a life of my own. I will be at his beck and call until he decides I have nothing left to offer. When that day comes, all I can hope for is a bullet between my eyes to end this life of misery.

Forcing myself to take slow, calming breaths, I focus on one strap at a time until the leather harness and thong are discarded in a messy heap on the bathroom floor. Finally able to breathe just a little easier, I walk into the oversized shower. I step to the side as I turn on the taps, then hold my hand out under the stream of water, waiting for it to warm.

After scrubbing my hair and washing the filth from my body, I tip my head back under the cascading water and let the soothing warmth wash over me. I have to get used to this. I have to somehow find the beauty in this world. Otherwise, I'm going to live my life in misery, and that's simply unacceptable. I have to learn to embrace these changes, but it's going to take time and a shitload of patience—patience I simply don't have.

Stepping out of the shower, I quickly dry off before wrapping my towel firmly around my body and running a brush through my hair. Glancing down at the filthy harness, I let out a heavy sigh. What the hell am I supposed to wear? There's no way I'm putting that thing back on. I'd die before sinking that low again. Hell, the second I can, I'll be burning it to a crisp.

Wandering back out to my room, I step up to my closet and open the door with a gasp. It's fully stocked with clothes, but how?

Walking deeper into the closet, I scan over the variety of items. Sun dresses, formal dresses, night dresses. There are leggings, jeggings, and jeans. Workout clothes, bras, and underwear. Full briefs right down to tiny G-strings. Every single item of clothing a girl could need for every possible occasion has been catered, and all the tags say they're in my size. But the biggest question is, when the hell was all this done?

He really did put something in my water. I would have known if someone was delivering a truckload of clothes into my room. It's not a quick job. They're all organized and hung on expensive-looking hangers. This took someone hours.

I wonder if Mr. Romanian Jailer will shrug it off or be honest if I ask. Is he the type to be ashamed of his twisted actions, or will he own it?

Shit. I suppose it doesn't really matter now. I'm his to do with as he pleases. The only light in this darkness is the knowledge he wouldn't have personally hand-delivered these clothes to my room and spent time sorting and folding them into my drawers. No, he would have had one of his hired helpers take care of that, and all I can hope is that it was the little old lady who I'd thought was his housekeeper.

In the big scheme of things, having clothes to wear is minuscule in cIn the grand scheme of things, having clothes to wear is minuscule in comparison to the fact I've been trafficked and sold, so I try not to dwell on it. I suppose my owner likes his prisoners well-fed, well-dressed, and squeaky clean. Maybe the dirty, starving sex doll in the basement isn't his thing after all.

Going for comfort, I find a pair of high-waisted workout shorts and a matching crop before scanning through the array of shoes. Grabbing a pair of white sneakers, I hastily put them on and pull my hair into a messy bun.

Survival 101 kicks in, and after my Romanian jailer promised I'd have free rein of this property, I leave my room, determined to explore every inch of this place to find out where I can hide, and where I can run if need be. My hand hovers on my door handle and nerves spike deep in my gut. The second I step out of my room, I'm opening myself up to his world. Allowing myself to be ridiculed and used at his will. But if I don't leave this room or take this opportunity to learn and memorize my surroundings, I'm setting myself up to fail.

Shaking off the nerves, I forge ahead, opening the door into the silence of the hallway. Creeping out, I peer left and right and come up empty, not even a whisper of the staff who are no doubt roaming the pristine property.

I'm on the second floor. During my tour last night, all I saw up here were more bedroom suites, open sitting areas, and bathrooms. Nothing special apart from the master bedroom, which naturally, I wasn't offered a peek into, which is honestly a shame. I was curious to see if that massive balcony overlooking the front of the property really was attached to the main bedroom.

Anything worth exploring is going to be on the ground floor, so I grip the banister and make my way down the grand staircase. The subtle padding of my sneakers against the marble tiles somehow sounds like an airhorn in this silence.

Reaching the bottom, I find myself hovering in the foyer, coming face-to-face with the doorman. He looks at me before reaching for the door handle. "Out for a run, Ma'am?" he asks in a thick accent I didn't notice last night.

"I . . . uhhmmmm," I say a little too awkwardly while glancing around the foyer, waiting for my world to crash down around me. "Am I allowed to go out for a run?"

"Why would you not?" he questions, his brows furrowed as he watches me with suspicion.

Not knowing how to respond or what fresh hell I'd be in if I were to step outside that door, I shuffle to the side. "I think I'll grab something to eat first," I say. "Can you tell me where I can find the kitchen?"

"Of course, Ma'am," he says with a polite nod before raising his arm toward the right. "Follow the hall past the formal dining area. You'll find a sitting area to your left. Turn there and you'll find the kitchen. It is a lovely day, perhaps you would enjoy a sandwich out by the pool."

"Yes," I say with a smile, wondering just how much this guy knows. "That does sound nice. Thank you."

With that, I turn on my heel, following his instructions toward the kitchen, taking my time while trying to take in as much as possible. I pass living spaces, the formal dining area, and what I can only guess is an office dedicated solely to security. Peeking in, I see many screens across the wall showing a live security feed that captures every inch of the property.

Shit. I suppose that takes a daring escape out of the equation. Besides, where the hell would I go where he wouldn't find me? He knows my name, and a man like him would do his research. I'm sure by now he knows everything there is to know about me. My full name, address, and social security number. The school I went to. What I passed and failed. What dance school I attended as a kid. Which asshole I gave up my virginity to, and which piece of shit Mustang it happened in the back of.

Finding the kitchen, I stop and gape at it. It's huge. Unnecessarily huge. But damn, it's gorgeous.

A woman is busy in the butler's pantry, and I shuffle toward her, unsure if I'm supposed to help myself or if she's supposed to organize something for me. Either way, I'm a do-it-myself kind of girl. "Hi," I say in a small voice.

Her gaze whips toward me, startled by my appearance in her kitchen. "Oh, goodness," she says, her hand flying to her chest. "You scared me."

"Sorry," I say, a soft smile playing on my lips. "I didn't mean to scare you. I was just getting a bit hungry and thought—"

"Oh yes," she says, stepping back and welcoming me in. "You must be our new house guest. I was told to keep an eye out for you. I'm Krista."

"Chiara," I say with a small smile.

"Lovely to meet you, Chiara," she says, something lighting up in her pale green eyes. "Is there anything I can get you?"

"It's okay, you don't need to go through any hassle," I tell her. "I'm used to scavenging for myself."

"It'll be my pleasure," Krista says. "In fact, I insist. It'll save me from organizing this pantry for the hundredth time."

"Okay, sure," I say, not wanting to ruffle any feathers on day one. "The doorman suggested a sandwich out by the pool, and honestly, ever since the idea entered my head, it's all I've been able to think about."

Krista laughs. "One sandwich coming right up."

She motions for me to take a seat at the kitchen island bench as she goes about fetching everything for one hell of a good sandwich, and I watch in awe as she works. I was thinking a few slices of cheese, maybe tomato and cucumber slapped between two pieces of bread would be sufficient, but she's giving me the royal treatment. "So, what brings you to live here?" she questions absently, her attention focused solely on the sandwich, as if trying really hard not to meet my eye.

Not sure of what I can and can't say, I offer her a tight smile. "I, uhhh . . . don't think I got a choice in the matter," I tell her in a light tone, trying not to suggest any wrongdoing on her boss's part. Not that he deserves the kindness.

"Oh, I can imagine," she laughs as though extremely fond of the man, making me wonder where he is. "That man is a force to be reckoned with."

My brows bounce involuntarily, and I mutter under my breath. "Ain't that the truth."

As she works, Krista asks me about my dietary requirements, and when she offers me the plate, I take it eagerly. My sandwich looks back at me, presented like a work of art in small triangles, complete with a garnish and a glass of ice water. "Here you go, dear. Enjoy."

"Thank you," I say, collecting the plate off the island and getting up. I give her a smile before taking the glass of water and trudging out to find the back door. I don't have to go far to find an adjoining room complete with floor-to-ceiling bi-fold doors opening up to the jaw-dropping outdoor entertainment area.

I make my way out to the poolside patio and put my plate down as I gaze out at the sparkling water, which is just as breathtaking as I'd imagined. I'd kill to be able to spend my day lounging around a pool like this. It'd be an endless vacation. Just last night I was hell-bent on finding my escape, but being in the presence of such luxury makes my feelings about leaving one thousand percent more complicated. It's not as though I really have anything great to go back to. Hell, I doubt I even still have a job at this point.

As I soak up the sun, my gaze sails around the back of the property, taking in the tennis courts and gardens when something makes my back stiffen with unease. "I trust you slept well," that deep, thick Romanian tone rings out.

I swallow my bite of sandwich and glance back to find my captor staring down at me wearing another black suit, and yet somehow this one seems a little more casual. Those dark eyes still hold me hostage. I place my sandwich down and hold his gaze, my chin raised high, remembering the vulnerable position he had me in last night. "Did you have someone put something in my water last night?"

"Yes," he says, without skipping a beat. "You needed to rest, and I don't believe you would have slept soundly without intervention."

"That simple, huh? You could have asked."

"Would you have taken it had I asked?"

"No."

"Exactly."

I gape at him. "Not even an apology for drugging me?"

He arches a brow as though bored of the conversation. "Are you well-rested?"

"Yes."

"Then you will receive no apology."

Picking up my sandwich, I take a slow bite, chew, and swallow, glaring at him the entire time. "Has anyone ever told you that you're possibly the most infuriating human being on the planet?"

He shrugs his shoulders as if that's not news to him, and I'm surprised to find he doesn't call me out on having an attitude. Perhaps it's only in the middle of the night when he's tired and pissed off that he won't tolerate my bullshit.

He steps around the small table and pulls out a chair, casually taking a seat and leaning back. He doesn't say a word, just continues watching me, and as the seconds tick by, the silence becomes too loud. "Your doorman asked if I wanted to go out for a run."

He gives me a blank stare. "And?" he questions, his gaze dropping down my body. "You're dressed for a run. Why wouldn't he ask if you wanted to go for a run?"

"I just . . . I wasn't sure if I was allowed to go out for a run."

"Then why get dressed for a run at all?"

"I didn't get dressed for a run," I say, frustration gnawing at me. "I just like to wear comfortable clothes, and as it happened, I just look like I want to go for a run."

"So, what's your problem?" he questions. "You want me to put a bullet between his eyes for suggesting you wanted to go for a run?"

"What the hell is wrong with you?" I gape. "Absolutely not. I just wanted to know how much trouble I was going to get in if I did happen to walk out the door and go for a run?"

"Why would you get in trouble?" he pushes, staring at me as though I'm the one losing my mind here. "I told you last night, you have free rein of my home. That includes the outdoor areas. However, I suggest you do not venture into the woods. I cannot guarantee that there won't be creatures lurking after dark."

A shiver sails down my spine, and I nod, my gaze dropping to the table. "I don't like to run."

He watches me a moment longer, and I feel that intense, dark gaze lingering on my face. As I look back up to meet his stare, I find a strange fondness in his eyes. "I find your awkward ramblings quite . . . amusing."

I nervously worry at my bottom lip. "Is that why you haven't threatened me with some kind of horrendous punishment yet?"

He nods and there's a rich honesty in his eyes. "I believe so."

I swallow hard, continuing to watch him, and the longer I hold his stare, the harder it becomes to breathe. "Why did you save me from that place?"

My Romanian captor leans forward, reaching across the table until his fingertips brush against my chin before curling them around my jaw and holding my stare. The tension booms between us, and I can barely breathe as a flurry of nerves shoots through me. He holds me there, refusing to let me look away. "Do not mistake me for your hero. I am not," he says, that thick accent wrapping around me, his fingers so soft against my skin. "You are my property to do with as I please. And given time, you will learn to embrace it. Whatever life you had before this, forget about it. You belong to me now."

I nod, the need to please him flourishing through my veins.

Why does he make me feel this way? I should be running or figuring out how to get out. Yet, every time he's around me, I fall into his trap. He's already warned me he's not the hero in my story, and yet I crave to be near him.

In that warehouse, when he stood in the shadows with his stare locked on mine, I felt something. There's a strange pull every time our eyes meet, and if he hadn't felt the connection, surely he wouldn't have claimed me as his own. The other men in that warehouse looked surprised to see him, shocked that he would take a girl as his own, so why now? There must be something more. Something he sees in me that intrigues him, draws him in. All I know is that if he didn't care, he would have allowed Broken Nose to take me home, and my night would have been very different.

I shake my head, and his hand falls away. Maybe I'm reading too much into this. Maybe he just felt it was time he took someone home to fuck, and I just happened to be the easiest to claim. "Why me?" I ask him. "There were four other girls in that room. You could have easily taken any one of them."

He leans back in his chair with a stiff stare, and I don't bother waiting for a response that obviously isn't coming. I get to my feet as a wave of disappointment crashes through me, scooping my glass of water off the table and lifting it to my lips before taking a quick sip.

Taking a breath, I fix him with a stare. "Are you ever going to tell me who you are?"

He doesn't move, not even the slightest flinch of his lips, yet the way he stares back at me is filled with such cockiness that I'm ready to break all his rules and put this motherfucker right in his place. Knowing what's good for me, I rein it in and let out a disappointed sigh before finally averting my gaze.

I stride past him, my appetite gone, when his strong fingers curl around my elbow, pulling me up short. "I must attend business this evening," he tells me as my gaze drops to meet his, that thick accent doing wicked things to me. But it's got nothing on his touch. "However, after I return, you will meet me in my chambers."

I swallow hard, searching deep into those dark pits of hell. "Why?"

My Romanian captor stands, towering over me as my gaze rises, locked within his vicious stare. He leans in, his body pressed against mine as his fingers trail down to my wrist, his scent overwhelming me and making my knees weak. "Because I'm going to fuck you just hard enough to make you believe you want this."

And with that, he releases his grip and strides past me, disappearing back inside his home. I'm left gaping after him with my heart racing, equal parts terrified and giddy for what's about to come.

CHAPTER 8

Killian

My fleet of blackout SUVs rolls to a stop outside the home of Deago Donatelli, the scum who ordered the raid on my warehouse. He's the head of a small mafia family trying to climb the ranks—and burning bridges in the process—but after tonight, the Donatelli family will be nothing but ruins.

Under the cover of darkness, my men are barely visible as they pour from the SUVs and surround the Donatelli estate. I've brought overwhelming numbers, and while I certainly don't need it to be successful tonight, it also acts as a warning to anybody else who wishes to stand against the DeLorenzo family.

I've spent the day calling the wives and families of those who were slain in the raid last night to help organize funeral arrangements, with every grieving wife I spoke to, I vowed that come nightfall, I would get the justice they deserve.

It was a rough day, and while dealing with death is just another part of the job, I won't lie and say it doesn't affect me. The horror of what I do and who I've become has always lingered on my soul, and one day, I will fail to recognize the man who stares back at me in the mirror, but until then, I will continue to be the man this family needs me to be.

The only respite I've received today was the stolen moment with the beautiful woman I now call mine out by the pool. It was brief, and while my intent was to simply check in on her from afar, I found myself lingering, even taking a seat at the table.

I'm curious about her, and while I spent an hour this morning sitting by her bedside as I looked into the file Sergiu gave me, I'm finding that curiosity getting stronger. I wish to get to know her better. I want to know why she hasn't attempted to run, why her eyes flash with intrigue instead of fear every time she looks my way, but more so, I need to know why my pulse quickens every time I'm in her presence.

I want to touch her, want to know how it would feel to sink inside of her. Taste her and claim her in every way possible.

She is mine, every piece of her belongs to me. When her gaze locks onto mine, I feel that she belongs right here in my world. I feel a connection, an electricity that pulses between us, and I'm intrigued. I want to know her on a deeper level, and the fact that I don't has been grating on my nerves all day.

I felt it at the auction, the moment her innocent gaze locked onto mine and she silently screamed for help, that some kind of bond was forged between us, and while I stand by my statement that I am not her hero, I can't help but wish to be. However, villains cannot afford to be heroes, not in my world. Men like me are not bred for the limelight. We are not made to be celebrated. We live within the darkness, away from the watchful eyes of the general population, where corruption, money, and bloodshed are seen as power.

While she is a sultry fox and certainly not innocent by normal standards, compared to the world I live in, she's nothing but a helpless rabbit, and the right thing to do would be to let her go. But I'm not known for doing what's right. I do what I want, and right now, I want nothing more than to fuck that innocence out of her.

And that's exactly what I plan to do the moment I get home.

Wanting to get this shit over and done with so I can get back home and sink into my new prize, I glance around at my men as they surround the Donatelli estate. Everybody is exactly where they're supposed to be, guns at the ready.

Sergiu stands at my side, his finger at his ear as he listens to the intel he's receiving from my security team as they run my infrared software, telling us exactly what to expect once we penetrate the property.

"We good?" I ask him.

Sergiu gives a firm nod and a fierce hunger tears through me.

It's game time.

My gaze turns back to the estate. It's large, but nothing compared to the scale of my home. Our intel tells us that most of the home's occupants are on the lower level. At least fifteen men lingering within the main dining room, and a few others strolling the ground floor, possibly part of Deago's security team—all of whom need to be fired considering their lack of movement. We've been here for almost a full two minutes and haven't heard a peep from inside. If this had been an attack on my home, every single one of them would already be dead on the ground before they'd even stepped foot onto my property.

There are guns inside—probably my guns—but considering the casual stance of the assholes within, they still have not yet been alerted to our presence. There seems to be no children inside, but I'm not surprised. Deago wouldn't be foolish enough to have his family here tonight, not so soon after waging war with the most powerful mafia family in the country. And the fact that he fails to have a security team on standby only goes to show just how naive he is. He thinks he's untouchable, that my team would not be able to sniff him out, yet here we are, more than ready to take back what belongs to us.

Giving the signal to my men, we all move in as one. Like a well-oiled machine, we all know our part, and within seconds, we've breached every entrance on the ground level. The gunfire commences around me, and the deafening sound is cathartic. The world comes into hyper-focus, and everything around me slows. I can all but see the bullets whizzing through the air as Donatelli's men realize too slowly what's going on.

Before they can even get to their feet and reach for the guns that lay haphazardly around the living room, my men have every single one of them surrounded, and like the greatest symphony, gunfire booms through my ears, and Donatelli's men begin dropping like flies, not a hint of remorse coming from my men.

They're soldiers, just as I've trained them to be. They're relentless, callous, and cruel. My will is their way, and if they were to fail me, they'd be nothing but a forgotten body next to the men they've slain tonight.

Deago stands in a panic in the center of his living room, watching in horror as his men fall around him like toy soldiers. Screams ricochet from every corner of the mansion as my men spread out, searching for anyone who might have gotten away. The staccato beat of gunshots begins to slow as my men search the upper levels.

I don't need to say a word, I don't need to even whisper an order, my men just know what's expected of them, and without fail, they execute my every desire. There has always been unrest within my family, always a power struggle—especially with men like Sergiu who will never be satisfied with second best—but when it comes to defending our family, we have never been so in sync.

BANG! BANG!

Two more bodies fall with a heavy thump against the floor as the echo of the gunshots bursts through my chest, and a sick satisfaction fills my veins.

Blood splatters the walls and lines the marble tiles in a deep crimson that would look absolutely delicious on Chiara's lips, and the moment Deago finally pulls himself together enough to try and command control of the few men left on their feet, it's already too late. He knows this is a losing game, but that doesn't stop him from trying.

"KILL THEM," he orders what's left of his men in a last-ditch effort to save himself.

With blood coating his face and shaking hands, he scrambles for a gun dropped by one of his fallen men, but I don't dare allow him the chance—not with the twenty-three lives that were lost last night still fresh in my head. Just as his fingers curl around the handle, I lift my hand and shoot a perfect, clean shot straight through the center of his wrist.

Deago screams and drops to his knees as he clutches his hand, his attention now firmly on me. I stride toward him with Sergiu at my side, and I watch with amusement as Deago tries to inch away.

He knows what's coming for him.

"Even think about touching me, and my men will end you," Deago spits.

I hold my hands out, making a show of searching the room. "What men?" I ask. "Take a look around. You have no men left."

As if not having realized, Deago spares a quick glance around the blood-soaked living room, taking note of the bodies sprawled across the marble floor, not a single body belonging to one of my men. The room falls quiet, the screams fading to nothing but a haunted silence, and the *drip, drip, drip* of spilled blood spurs me on.

"No," Deago breathes, shaking his head as he scrambles back to his feet and backs up toward the wall—a blatant mistake my grandfather would have beaten me for. You never back yourself into a corner. Always leave an escape. "No. You can't kill me. I have a family."

"As did the men you slaughtered last night," I growl as his self-importance grates on my nerves.

He shakes his head. "I swear, it was an accident. We never meant to kill anybody. We were only going for the drugs. Nobody was meant to get hurt. We were only attempting to make a name for ourselves. We wanted everyone to know we meant business."

"And you thought making a stand against the DeLorenzo family was the right way to do that?" I scoff, barely holding back a laugh. "Let me break the bad news. When word of this spreads, you will not be known as a brave man for stealing from me, you will be known as a foolish one who sent your men to be slaughtered. Let me be clear, you will perish here tonight, and you will be remembered as nothing more than a joke. Men will forever hear your name and laugh at your cowardice."

"Please," he begs. "I'll give it all back. Just let me go. Surely you are a forgiving man. It was a moment of weakness, a bad judgment call, but I swear, I'll never make a stand against you again. I have a wife and three young girls. They need me."

I shake my head. "Oh, you believe this to be a negotiation? That I was coming here tonight to give you a chance to grovel for forgiveness?" I scoff. "Come on now, Deago. Surely you must know better than that."

His face drains of all color as my men file out of the property, leaving only my most trusted within the room with me.

"Now," I start. "You are going to tell me exactly where my product and weapons are and once I have confirmation of their whereabouts, I will then brutally slaughter you like the animal that you are."

Horror flashes in his dark eyes as he looks around the room for a way out, but he realizes all too late that he's trapped in a fucking corner.

"Kill me then," he spits, realizing that he's not making it out of here alive. "But I'm not telling you shit."

I shrug my shoulders, more than happy to play his little game. "Have it your way, Donatelli," I murmur, stepping closer with my gun in my hand. "But just know that if I don't have my product returned, you will die with a debt, and it will be that lovely family you speak of who will inherit that debt. Your wife is probably dried up and overused, but those little girls. I bet I could fetch a fair price for them."

The suggestion makes me feel sick. I would never lower myself to making a move like that, not even on my worst day. Family is off-limits, no matter if it's mine or my greatest enemy. There are some lines I simply won't cross, but Deago certainly doesn't know that. Hell, once I'm through with Deago, I'll ensure his family is looked after. Have a home to live in, food on the table, and a good education for his children. The crimes of a father should never burden his children.

Deago's eyes widen, and he begins to weep, falling back to his knees in surrender as blood pours from the gaping bullet hole in his wrist. It wasn't a lethal shot, and the artery hasn't been compromised, but I've done this long enough to know that anything could go wrong at a moment's notice. "Please," he sobs. "I'll tell you, just . . . leave my family out of this. They didn't do anything. They don't deserve that."

"Then tell me where my product is, and you will have my word, your family will be left in peace."

Donatelli sobs, hanging his head low. "My uncle's home in the Valley. There's a hidden room behind the tool bench in his garage. You will find all your product there."

"And my weapons?"

"Look around," he says, ushering to the weapons that lay strewn across the room. "They're all here."

Just as I thought.

I nod toward Sergiu, and without skipping a beat, he lifts his phone to his ear and makes a call. Within seconds, half of my men are taking off down the street toward his uncle's home in the Valley. It will be a little while until I get the word that my product has been secured, and as we wait, a few of my men collect every weapon in the home. They'll all need to be cleaned and checked before I will even consider boxing them up for a shipment for the DeAngelis brothers, but at least we're back on track. The last thing I'd ever want to do is let those brothers down. My army is far greater than theirs, but those brothers are fucked in the head, and they're not the kind of men one wishes to make an enemy out of.

"Wh . . . What are you going to do to me?" Deago asks as we wait to hear word on my product.

"It's simple," I tell him as I survey the massacre around me. "Tonight I will be your judge, jury, and executioner. You slaughtered twenty-three of my people, and I promised every single one of their families that I would get vengeance, so tonight, you will experience the agony of twenty-three deaths, and only then will I put you out of your misery."

He nods, the weight of his actions falling heavily on his shoulders. "Will you allow me to say goodbye to my family?"

"Did you allow my men the chance to farewell theirs before you slaughtered them?"

Deago visibly swallows, and I press my lips into a tight line, pitying the pathetic excuse of a man before me. "Well, it seems you have your answer," I tell him.

The call comes in a moment later, confirming that all my product is right where Deago said it would be, along with everything else the Donatelli family has stolen, and after ensuring that it is all back in my possession and on its way to one of my more protected warehouses, I turn my attention back to Deago. "This is going to be slow and agonizing," I warn him. "However, if you scream, I will make it worse. I don't care for a man who cannot contain his pain. Is that understood?"

I hold my hand out to Sergiu and without question, he places a dagger right in the center of my palm as Deago watches on with fear.

"Understood," he mutters.

And with that, three of my men step forward and grab Deago, tying him down on the coffee table as he foolishly attempts to fight them off, wasting what little energy he has.

"Shall we get started?" Sergiu asks.

I nod, and he produces the same manila folder he gave me first thing this morning and begins reading out the details I've already memorized. "Paolo DeCosta," Sergiu says. "First to perish in last night's raid. Single father of two boys. Died from a bullet wound to the chest. Possible collapsed lung."

I nod, and with that, I sink the blade deep into Deago's chest, making sure I angle the blade so it punctures his lung just enough to keep him breathing, but not so much that he doesn't experience the absolute agony that comes along with it.

Deago screams out, and one of my men grabs a cloth and shoves it into his mouth, none of us willing to put up with his screams quite this late at night. "One down. Twenty-two to go," I tell him before lifting my gaze to Sergiu. "Who's next?"

"Phillip Lancaster. Father of four adult children and—"

"Grandfather to six," I continue. "Died from a blown artery. Bullet wound straight through the neck."

Sergiu nods, and I glance down at Deago. "Get ready, this one is going to hurt."

An hour later, I stride out of the Donatelli mansion, leaving behind the type of massacre that I know will be splashed across the news first thing in the morning. However, not a single scrap of evidence will point in my direction. My men are too careful.

Sergiu hands me a cloth, and I wipe the smeared blood off my face as we make our way back to my SUV. "Security has confirmed our product has been returned to our warehouse," Sergiu informs me. "I have a team checking over it to make sure it hasn't been contaminated."

"Good. I want an update first thing in the morning," I tell him as we pile into the back of the SUV, my driver already waiting and ready to go.

The second the door closes behind Sergiu, he turns to face me. "You know, Monica is quite excited for the DeLorenzo annual gathering next week. She always feels it's her moment to shine."

I roll my eyes. Monica is Sergiu's wife and a pain in my ass, but if it weren't for her, our family events would be nothing more than a lunch put on in my home. Monica likes perfection, and event planning gives her purpose so she always goes above and beyond, and as the most senior wife of the family, she tends to let the power go to her head.

One of these days, it would be my honor to put her in her place, but in doing that, I would be giving Sergiu a reason to act out, and we have enough drama coming from outside of the family to have to deal with it coming from within.

"I'm sure she will look dazzling."

"Yes, as expected," Sergiu mutters. "Tell me, do you plan on bringing a date?"

I shrug my shoulders. I never bring dates to these family events, but the idea of seeing Chiara all dolled up in a gown has been playing on my mind today. "Perhaps," I tell him. "I am undecided if I will bring someone."

"Chiara?" Sergiu splutters, saying the one name I've gone out of my way not to use. "The whore you picked up from the auctions? Be serious, cousin. Bringing her would be a slap in the face. I'm sure Monica will happily find you a more suitable date. You're the head of our family, you can't be seen with some whore on your arm. We can find you better options if you truly wish to bring someone. Whores like that should be locked away in secret, not flaunted in front of the other women. Have some respect."

My gaze sweeps to my cousin, and I don't need to say a word for him to feel the wrath of my displeasure. She is certainly no whore, and while I may enjoy calling her as such when I finally get to sink into her sweet cunt, no other man shall be rewarded the same honor.

Sergiu visibly swallows and inches back, pressing his lips into a hard line. "*Chiara* is not some cheap prostitute offering herself up on the street," I inform him. "And if you call her that again, I will see to it that you are made to understand the nature of that term. Perhaps Monica shall be offered up to every man of the family and you can gain a true understanding of what it means."

Sergiu shakes his head, anger flashing in his eyes. "That's not what I—"

"She was an innocent woman going about her day when she was stolen and caged," I continue. "She's spent the last few days terrified of what was to become of her, and now she's been thrust into a world where she has to adapt quickly. That doesn't make her a whore. It makes her a survivor, and if you are ever allowed the pleasure of meeting her, you will treat her as such. Do I make myself clear?"

Sergiu clenches his jaw, but knowing exactly who holds the power here, he quickly relents and nods. "Of course, cousin. It was an innocent slip of the tongue. I didn't realize she meant so much to you."

I narrow my gaze on my cousin, not trusting him for one moment, but he knows if he crosses a line with me, I won't hesitate to take him out. "She does not mean anything to me," I counter. "However, that does not mean that she is not entitled to some respect. She is a guest in my home, and she shall be treated with the same respect in which I offer your wife in her home."

Sergiu watches me far too closely. "Are you sure, cousin? She seems to have you in a bind. You've had many guests in the past, none of whom you've cared to defend before."

I simply shrug my shoulders and right myself in my seat, focusing my attention out the front windshield of the SUV, calling an end to the conversation because honestly, I don't like what he's implying. The blonde bombshell that's currently residing in my guest suite really has been taking up a lot of my attention today. Every moment I've wondered about her, wanting to know what she is doing, what she's feeling about being here in my world, and if she fears me the way she should.

Just as Sergiu said, I've never cared for those who've ventured into my home before, so why now? I'm all too aware that I require an heir, and the fact that I'm even considering her to be the woman who bears my children tells me more than enough—I care.

But why?

I have no fucking idea.

I've become infatuated with a woman I know nothing about.

Any child would be lucky to inherit her beauty and backbone. She's stronger than I think I've even realized, and for some reason, I fully believe that she will surprise me. In fact, I really hope she does, and it's that thought alone that has me excited to get home, more than ready to see her again.

CHAPTER 9

Chiara

My hands shake as I approach the master bedroom, my fingers curling around the handle. I hesitate, swallowing hard and trying to ease the anxiety pulsing through my veins. I shouldn't entertain this. I should be locking myself in my bedroom and figuring out how the hell to get out of here.

But I'm intrigued.

He wants to fuck, and goddamn, in the space of a day and a half, I've become a needy whore for this man. He's barely touched me, barely even spoken to me, yet the overwhelming need to please him has me in a violent chokehold. Is this some kind of intense Stockholm Syndrome, or am I just as fucked up as he is?

Either way, I have to see this through. I have to know exactly what he's going to do to me. How he's going to touch me, how he's going to use my body, and goddamn, I have to feel him slamming deep inside of me. I can take it. If anything, my Romanian jailer has finally met his match.

Ever since I spread my legs for him on his fucked-up little stage last night and felt the weight of his stare on my pussy, I've been craving his touch. The second the thought of him fucking me entered my brain, it was over for me. All sense of survival burned to ashes at my feet. If only he knew what kind of devil he'd unleashed.

Despite this roaring need burning inside of me, I'm still incredibly aware of his rules. Instead of pushing my way through the door and demanding he hurries up and fucks me, I find myself hesitating. Do I knock? Or does he expect me to welcome myself in and settle on the ground with my knees spread, hoping to play out a bit of kinky Christian Grey fuckery? Because if that's the case, he should know I can't braid my own hair, and I'll have more than enough trouble allowing myself to be dominated in that way. When it comes to getting down and dirty, I'm the furthest thing from submissive.

Letting out a shaky breath, I rap my knuckles against the door before hearing that smooth accent call out. "Come in."

Gently pressing the handle, I ease the door open and ready myself for a whole world full of new possibilities.

His room is dimly lit, and there's just enough light for me to make him out across the room. He's shirtless, and my mouth waters at the sight of his strong torso. Those perfectly wide shoulders and defined pecs lead down to chiseled abs and a deep V that points right to the promised land. His dark pants are riding low on his hips, and I greedily take him in, more than ready to discover what he has in store for me.

My hands shake, and while I feel ready, the fear of the unknown still grips me.

Hunger flashes in his eyes, dark and disturbed, and pride tears at my chest, knowing he likes what he sees. And damn it, I do too. I went all out for him tonight. Black lace lingerie, suspenders, and thigh-high stockings. I don't know what he likes when it comes to stuff like this, so I kept it simple. Safe. I dressed up in natural makeup, just enough to accentuate my features, and I left my long hair down so that he can wrap his hand around it if the desire strikes.

"Don't be nervous," he says, slowly moving across his room. I track each of his steps like a vulture, but in reality, he's the predator tonight. His eyes are like beacons, capturing me, drawing me in, and demanding obedience. "Go to my bed."

Swallowing hard, I divert my gaze toward the big bed. A huge king-size mattress sits atop four steps at the head of the room, like the main attraction. I hastily make my way toward it before stopping at the bottom step, waiting for his next instructions.

He moves toward me until he stands only a foot away, his gaze sailing over me, taking in the subtle curves of my body. "Strip for me, Sweet Angel."

Oh, dear God.

His words are like a shot of pure adrenaline sailing right down to my core. I obey him, needing his approval more than I need my next breath. Wanting to make this a show, I slowly turn and make my way up two steps before propping my foot up onto the next one. Glancing back over my shoulder, I slowly bend and watch as his gaze drops to my ass.

Brushing my fingers over my thigh to the top of my stocking, I push it down, exposing the skin beneath inch by inch. I mean sure, I would have liked to see him tear it from my body with his teeth, but the way his stare is so heavily focused on my body is getting me hotter by the second.

When I kick the stocking off, I place my foot back on the second step and switch to the other leg. Once both stockings are gone, I turn back to face him and detach the suspenders from around my waist, leaving me in nothing but my bra and thong.

His eyes flame as I reach behind me, not saying a damn word. This time, he's the one captivated. Unhooking my bra, I let the flimsy fabric fall slowly down my arms before hearing it softly hit the ground. I wait a moment, letting him take me in. He saw all the goodies last night, but not quite like this.

His gaze is intense, sailing over my body, and I feel as though every inch of skin he takes in leaves me physically branded. My thumbs slide into the sides of my thong, ready to push it down, but the slightest shake of his head gives me pause.

Lifting my chin, I meet his eyes as my thumbs fall away, and the way he stares back at me with pure, animalistic lust is the most thrilling and terrifying thing I've ever experienced. Adrenaline pulses through me like raging water as I fix my heated stare to his. "Tell me what you want," I purr, a little bolder than I feel, but I'm so wet and ready for this.

"Bed," he says with a slight lift of his chin, indicating for me to move the rest of the way up the stairs. "On your knees."

Yes, Sir.

I nod and slowly turn on my heel before walking up the last two steps and settling onto the edge of his bed, hovering on my knees as I watch him. I can see the straining outline of his cock through his pants, twitching with readiness.

His body stills as he watches me, and the need to touch myself is too strong. My fingers skim over my tits, feeling how they pebble under my fingers, and a soft moan slips from my lips. My head rolls as my hand trails further down my body, past my waist, and over my mound.

Cupping my pussy, I grind against my hand through the flimsy material of my thong before pushing the lace aside and sinking down onto my fingers. Gripping my tit with my other hand, I ride myself, groaning with the sweetest pleasure as I watch the way he watches me.

Releasing my fingers, I push them into my mouth and suck them dry, loving the way his dark gaze grows more intense. "Again," he orders.

Not one to disappoint, I lower my hand once again, this time pushing my fingers inside so damn slow, he groans in agony. Pumping my fingers in and out, I grind down against the heel of my palm, my clit finally getting some relief before pulling my fingers back out again with the sweetest torture.

His eyes flame, pooling with hunger, and I suck in a breath as he makes his way toward me. He reaches the platform and pushes his pants down over his hips. "I hope you like it rough, Angel," he rumbles, just as he frees his thick erection. My gaze sails down his body, and I suck in a gasp as I take him in.

He's huge, thick, and girthy, with angry veins leading right to his tip. There's no way I'll be able to close my fingers around him. This is a two-hand job.

Good God, just thinking about the way he will stretch me has me quivering.

Fuck.

"Take me in your mouth, Angel."

Say no more.

Adjusting myself on his bed, I lower on my knees, keeping them spread wide. A giddy thrill sails through my veins, desperate to please him, and I lick my lips, more than ready to see how he tastes.

He steps up to the edge, right in front of me, and that giddy excitement quickly morphs into nerves. What if I can't fuck him the way he likes? What if I'm not enough for him?

"Open wide," he orders, reaching around me and knotting his hand into my hair, gripping hard, and taking complete control of my movements.

My heart races erratically in my ears. His thick cock is right there in all its glory, fucking gorgeous and waiting for me to do as he's asked. All I have to do is open wide and he'll be pushing inside, fucking my mouth. But I hesitate, not knowing where he draws the line. "Can I touch you?" I ask, not wanting to fuck this up.

His gaze narrows, really considering my question before nodding. "Yes, you may touch me," he says. "Now don't make me wait."

Yes, Sir.

Reaching up, I curl my hand around his thick base, and just as expected, I can't close my fingers around him. My tongue peeks out, wetting my lips as my fist slowly pumps up and down. While everything screams at me to open wide and take him hard and fast, I want to enjoy him first, not knowing when I might get the chance to play again.

My thumb rolls over the bead of moisture on his tip, circling it before making a show of sucking my thumb into my mouth. He's salty and delicious, just as I knew he would be.

Needing so much more, I grip him again before leaning in and trailing my tongue up his thick cock, right to the tip. I circle his head with my tongue, tasting more of him before the hunger really hits me, and I finally close my mouth around him.

I take him right to the back of my throat, his low groan doing wicked things to me as I soak through my thong, desperate to feel him stretching me wide. He lets me do my thing, my fist tightening around the base of his cock as I take him even deeper. Needing to feel him, I lift my other hand and curl it around the back of his strong thigh. His body tightens at my touch, but I keep working his cock, letting my tongue roll over his tip before feeling him finally start to relax.

My hand trails up the back of his thigh to his defined ass as my pussy all but screams for attention. Not wanting to cross any lines, I keep moving, sailing up his strong back before bringing my hand around to his chest. My nails dig in and drag over the tight ridges of his abs and then lower, past his cock. I take his balls in my hand, firmly massaging them in my palm as I feel him right in the back of my throat.

My captor growls his approval, and the way I almost come on his bed is so fucked up. I love it.

His hand tightens in my hair, and having enough of my games, he holds me still before thrusting into my mouth. He slams into the back of my throat, and I nearly choke on his delicious cock. I moan for more, and he does it again, not shying away from his warning of liking it rough.

He fucks my mouth hard as my grip tightens around the base of his cock, working up and down with his movements. My hand clenches harder around his balls, feeling the way they tighten within my grasp. He's close, and fucking hell, I want to be a greedy whore for him. I need him to come. I need it all.

Without warning, he stills, and I feel his hot cum shooting into the back of my throat. "Fuck," he growls, clenching his jaw as his hand loosens in my hair, falling to grip the side of my face. He closes his eyes, and I continue moving, swallowing every last drop.

He pulls free of my mouth, breathing heavily as I look up at him, waiting to hear what else he needs from me. His thumb stretches out across my bottom lip, taking in his handiwork. "You liked that, didn't you?" he questions, that sexy-as-sin rasp in his voice reminding me just how dangerous he is.

I nod. "I did."

He watches me for a second, his gaze narrowing as if unsure of what to make of me. He takes a step back, his gaze sweeping down my body and then between my legs, noticing just how needy I am.

"Turn around," he growls.

My brows furrow, unsure of what he plans to do, but I don't hesitate to move around until I'm on my knees at the end of his bed. My heart races, and hearing something behind me, I glance over my shoulder to find him pulling something from the pocket of his discarded pants.

He steps right into my back before brushing his fingers over my shoulder and trailing them right down to my wrist. His fingers curl around it, pulling it behind my back before joining it with my other. He closes something around my wrists, and I gasp in realization before he pulls it tight, leaving me bound.

"Don't be nervous," he rasps.

I swallow hard, deciding to trust him just as he reaches around me, fixing a thick, black piece of material over my eyes and tying it at the back of my head, leaving me blind.

My heart races, not sure if I'm willing to trust him this much. He could do anything to me, and I'd be powerless to stop him. I feel his fingers brushing over my skin, and now that I'm relying on all of my other senses, every brush of his hand feels so much more intense.

"Come up on your knees," he instructs, his lips right by my ear.

I do as I'm asked, rising up until I feel his chest at my back and his hand at my hip. He suddenly pushes me down onto his bed, my tits firmly against the mattress. My knees are spread wide with my ass and cunt offered up like an all-you-can-eat buffet, my thong the only barrier holding us back.

His hand lowers to my ass, and I suck in a breath trying to push back against him, but with my hands tied at my back, I can't go far. His fingers trail across my ass until he reaches the flimsy fabric of my thong and follows it down, right through my center. I groan, pushing back against him as he passes over my cunt and down to my clit.

He cups my pussy, giving a firm squeeze, and I try to grind down against him, but then he's gone. Disappointment wells in my chest, and before my pained groan escapes my lips, his hands are suddenly there again, gripping my thong.

He gives one sharp tug and the material rips in two with ease, leaving me bare. I suck in a gasp, feeling the cool rush of air against my pussy before his fingers are there, pushing deep into my cunt.

I groan and push back against him, my eyes rolling as he curves his fingers and massages my walls. I can feel two of his fingers in there, and what I wouldn't give for a third. He does it again and again until I'm wound right up, but he pulls his fingers free, continuing the sweet torture. He glides his hand down to my clit and rolls it over the tight, sensitive bud, keeping me right on the edge as my hips jolt with fiery pleasure. Then just when I expect him to line up with my entrance and slam that thick cock deep inside me, he steps away, leaving me needy and unsure.

All I hear is the sound of my own heavy panting as the anticipation of what's to come threatens to end me. Barely a second passes when I hear a soft thud, and before I can try and work out what that was, his mouth closes over my pussy.

"Oh God," I cry out, my eyes immediately rolling to the back of my head as his warm tongue flicks over my clit before trailing up to my cunt. He plunges his tongue inside me, and I push back against him, so damn sensitive to his touch.

He sucks and nips, and just when I think it can't get any better, I feel his fingers at my ass, applying just enough pressure to make my eyes roll again. "Oh fuck," I hiss through a clenched jaw, releasing a groan as he takes my ass deeper.

He gives me everything, working my body until I detonate beneath his skilled tongue. I come hard and fast, and he laps up every ounce of my arousal as my pussy convulses and my high tears through my body. "YES," I cry out. "Oh God, yes."

His tongue keeps working me, not letting a single drop go to waste until I come down from my high, and then he's gone again.

I try to pull against my binds, assuming he's about to free me, but I hear him making his way down the stairs. The soft padding of his footsteps sounds from across the room, followed by the familiar sound of a drawer opening and closing. "You taste divine, Sweet Angel," he rumbles, that accent making me wet all over again. "But I'm a man of my word, and I am not nearly done with you yet."

I swallow hard, listening as he strides back toward me. As he slowly comes back up the steps, his fingers brush over my ass. "What did I tell you out by the pool?" he questions.

I shake my head, barely able to remember the words when his hand comes down in a sharp sting against my ass. "What did I tell you?"

"That you'd fuck me until I believe I want this."

"Exactly," he purrs, stepping right up behind me.

His fingers trail through my wetness, drawing it up to my ass and rubbing slow, teasing circles before they're replaced by something cold at my entrance—something heavy and made of metal. He pushes it inside of me, and I gasp at its sudden, delicious intrusion. My walls contract around it, welcoming it in, but not a moment later, it's gone again.

I'm just about to ask what he plans on doing to me when I feel something cold and wet. He rubs it around my ass, and with the faint, fruity scent in the air, I realize it's lube.

A soft moan slips through my lips, understanding that my ass is about to be railed. The cold, metal object is pressed to my ass, and I shiver with anticipation. He starts to push it inside of me, and I gasp with excitement, leaning back against the object to take it deeper, welcoming the full stretch of my ass, only he doesn't stop until it's too much.

A soft, pained cry slips from the back of my throat, and I let out a shaky breath, trying to relax around the metal, realizing it must be some kind of butt plug. His fingers trail around my ass and down to my clit, rubbing slow circles, and after a second, the burn of the plug becomes manageable. Hell, it even becomes intoxicating. "Okay," I tell him, knowing he's waiting for me to be comfortable. "I'm good."

Without hesitation, his fingers plunge into my cunt, and I groan, already feeling so full. He massages my walls, making sure I'm ready for him, and not a moment later, his hand is at my hip, holding me still as I feel that big, thick cock at my entrance.

He pushes inside me, stretching me wide, and I suck in a breath as he just keeps going, taking me inch by inch until he's fully seated inside me. I've never taken someone this big, and with my ass already so full, I'm taken by surprise.

He grips my ass cheek, giving a firm squeeze, and then finally begins to pull back again. "Oh God," I groan low, my fingers itching to touch him. He gets all the way back before pushing in again, this time picking up his pace. His fingers tighten on my hip, holding me still, and despite not being able to see his face, I somehow know his gaze is locked on my cunt, watching the way his glistening cock moves in and out of me, stretching me wide.

He really starts to fuck me, slamming into me as he applies more pressure to the plug, making me cry out, pushing back against him for more, and without a damn word between us, he gives me exactly what I want. My wrists are freed, and then that intoxicating accent tears through the room. "Touch yourself, Angel," he growls. "Rub that sweet clit."

I've never obliged so damn fast.

My hand shoots beneath me, pushing between my legs and grazing over my sensitive clit. Electricity pulses through my veins, making my whole body jolt as he fucks me, rotating his hips to take me deeper at every damn angle.

He gets faster, grunting as he thrusts into me, and my eyes roll, wishing desperately to see his face. My orgasm starts to build, pushing me closer and closer to the edge, but I hold on to it, not nearly ready for this to be over.

He fucks me like a goddamn pro, and just as he promised, I scream out, and why I'm here doesn't seem so important to me anymore. All that matters is reaching that climax.

I apply more pressure to my clit as his hand comes down over the plug, gently pulsing against it and sending me right over the edge. "OH FUCK," I cry out, coming so hard my pussy spasms continuously around his thick, dominating cock.

My eyes clench as my other hand fists his bed sheets. My orgasm is so powerful, I don't know how to take it. It's too much, too hard. My high tears through my body, and I feel as though I could explode. Then just when I thought it couldn't get better, my Romanian savior comes with me, shooting hot spurts of cum deep inside my cunt.

He makes me feel like a fucking goddess. Just the thought of having that delicious cum inside me is doing wicked things to my body.

My high starts to ease, and as he stills, the exhaustion weighs down on me. I close my eyes beneath the blindfold, trying to catch my breath as he gently removes the plug from my ass, all while his cock remains buried deep inside me.

The metal plug clatters against the ground and rolls one step at a time until it hits the bottom. As much as I loved the feel of the plug, I'm more than ready to take a break.

My Romanian Sex God pulls out of me, and my knees flatten out, dropping right onto his mattress with complete, utter exhaustion. I hear as he pulls his pants back on, and not a moment later, he's reaching across the bed and freeing the blindfold from around my eyes.

I peer back at him, watching as he reaches down and scoops me into his arms, his cum beginning to slowly leak out of me and spread between my thighs. He walks down the stairs, leaving my discarded lingerie scattered across his floor as he steps out of his room.

Walking down the hall, I look up at him, scanning over his chiseled jawline and gazing at the darkness of his eyes, still not used to their intensity. "You're staring," he mutters, not meeting my eye.

I cling to him, barely able to keep my head up as the exhaustion weighs me down. "What's your name?" I whisper into the silence.

His jaw tenses as we reach my room, and he adjusts me in his hold, freeing a hand to reach out and open the door. He walks into the dark room and takes me straight to my bed, laying me down without making eye contact. I quickly realize that my effort to discover this man's mysterious identity is going to be harder than I ever thought.

"You know," I say as he pulls my blankets up to my chin. "The next time you fuck me like that, I want to be able to scream your name."

"Oh, I'll make you scream," he tells me, walking back to the door. "But it is not my name that will be on your lips."

"Dare I ask what it will be?"

He watches me for a breath, his wicked gaze so intense and full of mystery. "I have not yet decided, Sweet Angel," he says. "Now get your rest. You'll be needing it."

And with that, he's gone, leaving me in the darkness as the memories of being spread out on his bed send me off to sleep with the sweetest lullaby I've ever heard.

CHAPTER 10

Chiara

The bed dips beside me, and just as my eyes spring open into the brightness of a new day, a heavy hand presses over my mouth. "Hush now, pretty girl," a thick Romanian accent murmurs into the room, only it's not the Romanian accent I'm familiar with. "If you even try to make a single peep, I'll snap your neck before a sound can even leave your mouth."

Fear pounds through my chest as I gaze up at a strange man, somewhat similar to the man who claimed me at the auctions, and yet completely different. A brother maybe? A cousin? His face is wider and his eyes somehow seem too close together to be deemed handsome.

He leans right into me, pressing down against my mouth to keep me quiet. His large hand almost covers my nose, making it almost impossible to breathe. There's an awful stench lingering on his skin that has bile rising in the back of my throat, but when he snatches my blanket with his other hand and tears it off me, the fear turns to a sickening horror.

His dark eyes begin scanning over my naked body, and I immediately curse myself for falling asleep so quickly last night. I should have forced myself to dress. I shouldn't have let my guard down, but when my Romanian captor was finished with me, the exhaustion quickly took over. Just as he promised, I'd forgotten how the hell I'd come to be here, but now in the wake of a new day, the sex fog has cleared, and I'm all too aware of the dangers around me.

I go to squirm out from under his hold, but he quickly captures my hands, holding me under his weight. "I don't get it," he says, his hungry stare rolling over my body and sending a cold chill over my skin. "There is nothing special here. What does Killian see in you?"

Killian? Is that his name?

I swallow hard, tears forming in my eyes, but I refuse to blink them away, terrified that they'll fall, and he'll somehow win in . . . whatever the hell this is.

All I know is that this isn't good. There's a wickedness in his eyes that I haven't witnessed from the other guy—Killian. There's a nastiness about him that warns me to run as far as I can. Hell, I can't even allow myself a moment to wonder where I've heard that name before.

He presses his body weight against me, moving over me and forcing my legs apart as he lifts both of my wrists to my face and gathers them in the hand that's braced over my mouth. I'm immobilized, unable to move an inch, and when he presses his knees painfully over the top of my thighs, I'm completely pinned and spread apart, my body now freely open for him to take as he pleases.

I can't hold it back a moment longer, and the tears finally begin to fall down my cheeks.

I'm incapable of screaming or doing a damn thing to save myself, and when he takes his free hand and moves it down between my thighs, I give one last fruitless attempt to fight him off.

He's too big. Too strong. I don't stand a chance.

I'm at his mercy.

I feel his fingers at my entrance just moments before he roughly slams them inside of me. I cry out, the sounds muffled by his hand over my mouth. "Ahhhh, it makes sense now," he murmurs, thrusting his fingers again and again. "You've got a tight little cunt to go along with that pretty little face."

The tears come in heavy streams, blurring my vision, but I keep my gaze locked on the window, refusing to meet this asshole's eyes as he violates my body, taking me as though he's entitled to. And while I don't truly know my captor or what he's capable of, I somehow feel he won't be okay with this. At least I hope he's not. The alternative is that he knows exactly what's going down in here and has given this asshole his full approval to violate me in any way he sees fit.

He tears his fingers from inside of me and reaches for the front of his pants, popping the button with ease. "I wonder just how tight you really are," he murmurs as he works the zipper down.

I try to buck him off as his knees begin to bruise my thighs, desperately trying to cry out beneath him, but not a sound comes from my mouth. I gasp around his hand, struggling to take a deep breath, and just as he reaches inside his pants and fists his cock, a knock sounds at the door.

He freezes, and the brief flash of fear in his eyes tells me that my suspicions were right. He's not supposed to be in here, and if he fears my captor, that must mean he's below him on the food chain.

"Chiara, honey. Are you awake?" a feminine voice comes from the other side of the door. I immediately recognize the sweet tone of the personal chef I'd met yesterday. Kiersten, maybe. Kristy? My head is in no place to try and remember her name right now.

My chest heaves as my attacker bares down on me, pressing harder against my mouth, a stern warning to keep quiet as his words from earlier circle my mind—*make a single peep, and I'll snap your fucking neck*. I don't doubt that he means every word, and all I can do is try to swallow the fear.

His glare is like two lasers penetrating right through my eyeballs as the knock sounds again. "Okay, you must still be sleeping. I've made you breakfast. I'll just leave it here at your door. I'll come back in a few minutes to make sure you're eating. You need your energy."

I hear the soft rattles as the chef places something down in front of my door, and not a moment later, she's gone.

My gaze snaps back to my attacker's just in time to see anger flashing in his putrid stare. He clenches his jaw before finally pulling away from me, clearly realizing that if he lingers in here just a moment too long, it'll be his head on the chopping block. "You got lucky today, girl," he spits, getting to his feet and fixing his pants. "But let me make one thing clear. If I find out that you've even whispered about this, I'll come back here every fucking night, and what happened in here today will seem like child's play in comparison. And if you even think about offering him a DeLorenzo heir, I will tear your baby right out of your womb."

I swallow hard, unable to make even a single noise as my chest heaves with unease.

Did he just say DeLorenzo? As in the DeLorenzo Mafia family?

Oh fuck. I'm in bigger trouble than I thought.

I watch as he finally walks away, taking big strides to the door. He reaches for the handle, turning it just an inch before looking back at me, and while he doesn't say a word, the venom in his glare is enough of a warning to get his message across.

One word from me, and my life will become a living hell.

He finally leaves, plunging my room into silence, and before the door has even closed behind him, heavy sobs tear from deep in my chest. I bail out of my bed, my stomach clenching with unease, and within seconds, I'm hanging my head over the toilet, throwing up what little resides in the pit of my stomach.

He's right. I got lucky today, but what about tomorrow or the day after that? A man like that doesn't simply accept defeat. He will be back, and when he does, I'll be ready for him.

CHAPTER 11

Chiara

S itting at the kitchen island, I watch as Krista busily prepares a late lunch for Killian's business meeting this afternoon. I've been here for a little over a week, and so far, it's not as bad as I thought. I think.

Those first few days after Sergiu—which I've now learned is his name—visited me in my bedroom, I turned into a recluse. I didn't know how to feel about it or how to navigate it. My thighs were bruised, and one look from Killian would have told him exactly what he needed to know—that someone had put their hands on me, and I wasn't ready for that conversation. I believe every word that Sergiu said, that he will return with a vengeance if I breathe even a single word of what happened in my bedroom that morning.

I've lived the last week in fear of his return, but as I've crept through the mansion, searching around every corner, I've seen no sight of him. Krista has mentioned in passing that he's here quite often, which turned my blood to ice.

In those days when my bruises healed, I told Killian I was unwell, and with his busy schedule, he didn't bother to question me on it. Instead, he simply ordered Krista to make me soup and check in on me every few hours. I think she knows something went down, and I'm grateful that she hasn't attempted to bring it up. Hell, I can't help but wonder if her bringing me breakfast that morning was a planned move on her part. I'd like to think it was, that she had a part in saving me from the ugliness of Sergiu's abuse, and because of that, I've allowed myself to become closer to her over the past week.

She truly is wonderful, and judging by the way she speaks of Killian and her loyalty toward him, I can't help but wonder if he truly is a good man beneath all of that darkness. I haven't dared to tell anyone that I know his name or what he does for a living. If I'm honest with myself, I think I'm too scared to even entertain that conversation. Plus, it's not information he has yet volunteered to me directly, and until then, I'll be keeping my mouth shut.

He's visited me a few times over the past week, and I hate how much I've enjoyed those visits. Some were physical, but other times he simply came and sat at the table with me and shared a meal. He watches me a lot. Every time he silently walks into a room, I feel him before I see him. My skin always prickles with goosebumps, and the weight of his delicious stare makes something flutter deep within me.

I think I like him, but it's so much more than just a physical need for him. I want to please him, want to be the only woman who holds his attention, and perhaps that's wrong of me, but I can't seem to turn it off. There's a raw electricity that pulses between us, and I'm quickly becoming addicted to it. Though I won't lie, one comment Sergiu made has me concerned.

A DeLorenzo heir.

Is that why I'm here? Does Killian expect me to give him a child? I really hope not. I'm way too young for that shit. I'm not ready to be someone's mom. When I was out there in the real world, I could barely keep myself alive, let alone someone else.

"Where'd you go?" Krista asks as she searches through her cupboards and pulls out a cheese grater. "You disappeared just now. Is there something on your mind?"

I scoff. "Understatement of the year," I tell her. "I was claimed at an auction and brought here into this crazy world with a man who equally intrigues and terrifies me, so yeah, I think it's safe to say that there's been a lot on my mind."

Krista offers me a small smile. "I know it's hard to see right now, but he truly is a generous man, and he certainly is worthy of that intrigue," she offers, giving me a knowing smile before taking a heavy breath and fixing her stare on me. Her eyes fill with a heaviness that puts me on edge, and I watch her a moment before she finally says what she needs to say. "I've been warring with myself whether I should open up about this or not. I don't know anything about the place you were kept before you came here, the conditions or the horrors you were subjected to, but I do know that you're going to be okay."

Krista offers me a small smile, and when my brows furrow, confused by why she's bringing this up, she goes on. "When I was sixteen, I was stolen right out of my family's home. Three men broke into my home, and after being forced to watch them murder my father and rape my mother, I was taken."

I suck in a gasp, my mind jumping right back to the night I was stolen off the sidewalk.

"I was held in a basement for three months before being sold into the sex trade," Krista continues. "I was young and perky, so the older men flocked toward me, and seeing that I was worth some kind of value, I was sold once again. There was an auction, which I can only assume was somewhat like yours, and by the end of the night, I was claimed by some rich man in Siberia. However, on my journey to what would have been my new home and quite possibly my death, we were intercepted by Killian and his men. He claimed me as his own, much like he did you."

Hearing her story brings tears to my eyes, and I hastily wipe them away as she hands me a tissue. "Do not feel sorry for me," she says. "I don't see myself as a victim, nor should you. While I have had a horrifying journey, all roads led me here, and this is where I've found my happiness and was able to rebuild my life."

I nod and swallow over the lump in my throat. "Whether you wish for me to feel sorry for you or not, I'm still sorry that you had to go through those things," I tell her. "My story, while terrible, isn't as gut-wrenching as yours. I didn't have a family growing up. I was in the foster system and jumped from home to home, but I always wished for a family. I couldn't imagine how terrible it would have been having to watch your parents being hurt in that way."

Krista nods and forces a tight smile, though there's no denying the pain in her eyes. "It was a long time ago."

My heart aches for her, and not wanting to linger on such a painful time in her life, I move on. "So, you and Killian," I ask, my mind lingering on the way she said he claimed her in a similar way he did me. "Were you . . . together?"

"Oh, gosh no," Krista laughs. "Don't get me wrong, being saved by Killian at such a young age, I thought I was in love with him. For years, all I wanted was to please him and be something to him, but he never once touched me. He only ever looked at me like a little sister, and looking back, I'm grateful that he never laid a hand on me. I was too young and still healing from everything I'd experienced. Instead, he gave me a kitchen, and I fell in love with cooking. I owe my life to him, and I truly hope that one of these days, you'll be able to see beneath the cruel exterior to the wonderful man that I see."

I nod, hoping she's right because the alternative—a life living in fear—simply won't do.

Once Krista finishes preparing lunch for Killian's meeting and his *associates* begin to arrive, I take myself deeper into his home where I can keep myself hidden away until they're gone. I have no doubt that Sergiu is here, wandering the hallways, and considering how boldly he walked into my bedroom, I have no desire to be in there if he chooses to do it again.

I find the library and try to immerse myself in a book in the furthest corner from the entrance, which also allows me the perfect view of the expansive driveway through the bay windows. I keep my gaze focused on the pages of the book, but after two hours of hiding out in here, I haven't taken in a single word.

Instead, my attention has been on the bay window, watching and waiting for everyone to leave.

The property is so big with dozens of cars lingering outside. It's impossible to tell which of those cars belongs to staff or guests, so until I can be sure that the meeting is over, I'll be staying right here.

Another hour passes when I realize the bay windows open up into a small balcony that overlooks the front of the property, and I put the unread book down before spending a few minutes trying to figure out how to actually open it.

After realizing I'm just an idiot who doesn't understand a basic locking mechanism, I finally get it open and step out into the sun, pleasantly surprised to find a well-tended garden taking up the majority of the small balcony. Vines creep along the handrail and up the side of the home with flowers blooming and begging for attention. It's like I've stepped out of reality and into a magical garden of beauty, and despite how much I love the rest of Killian's home, this is easily my favorite part of the estate. However, that incredible pool comes in a close second.

I've barely had a second to take in all the beauty of the balcony garden when I hear someone making their way through the library, and the moment I feel his intense gaze on my back, I don't even bother looking to see who it is.

A strange flutter builds in the pit of my stomach as he steps out onto the balcony and moves in behind me. When his breath hits my skin, my whole body trembles.

"You've been hiding up here," Killian murmurs in that rich Romanian accent that sends burning electricity pulsing through my veins like wildfire. He reaches around me, bracing both hands on the balcony railing and keeping me caged.

"Not hiding," I say, refusing to tell him the real reason I've been locked away in his library for the past three hours. "Krista mentioned that you had a meeting, so I figured I'd keep out of your way. I wouldn't want to be a disturbance while you were working."

Killian lifts his hand and brushes his fingers across my chin before turning my face to meet his stare. "You are anything but a disturbance," he rumbles, those deep eyes locking right onto mine.

I suck in a breath as he steps in closer, his chest right up against my back. His fingers drop from my chin to my shoulder before trailing lower to my waist and finally to the hem of my skirt. He grinds his thick cock against my ass, and I push back against him, wanting to take anything he can offer me.

Within moments, my skirt is at my waist and as he takes my hip, he pushes inside of me, stretching me wide. I grip the railing, tilting my hips just enough to take him deeper, and in this position, knowing he can't see my fading bruises from this angle, I welcome his every touch.

Killian takes me slowly, and with every thrust, I'm pushed closer and closer to the edge. "Oh God, Killian," I groan. "More."

His fingers bite into my hip. "You know my name."

Oh shit.

My body stiffens, and I start to panic. "I do," I breathe, unable to relax. "I'm sorry. I know you were intentionally keeping that from me. I didn't go seeking that information, it just kinda fell into my lap."

He's silent for a moment when his hand slides around to my front and finds my clit. He rolls his fingers over the sensitive bud, and I push back for more, my hips jolting with desperation.

"F—fuck," I stutter, my eyes rolling in the back of my head.

"It's okay, my sweet angel. Relax. I don't mind that you know my name. In fact, I like how it sounds on your lips," he tells me, thrusting deep into me and stretching me so damn wide. "The question is, do you truly know who I am? What I do?"

My knuckles whiten as I clutch the railing tighter, the intense pleasure quickly overwhelming my system. I nod as I begin to pant, feeling my orgasm already building deep within. "Yes," I breathe. "You're Killian DeLorenzo, the head of the DeLorenzo Mafia."

"And?" he says through a clenched jaw. "Are you scared of me?"

"Terrified," I admit, swallowing over the lump in my throat, and standing by my word that I would always be honest with him . . . mostly.

"And yet," he says with a forceful thrust that has me crying out with pleasure. "You still allow me inside of you."

I nod again. "What you do and what you're capable of is what terrifies me, but when it comes to you and me, you've shown nothing but kindness. I don't believe you would ever intentionally hurt me," I tell him. "I know I don't know you nearly well enough to make a judgment call, but I feel like I can trust you."

"Good," he says as his fingers move faster over my clit, sending me into a world of pure ecstasy. "Now, squeeze me. Come on my cock like the good little girl you are."

His words send me into overdrive, and as he thrusts into me again, my world detonates, and I come for him, just as he demanded. "Oh God, Killian," I cry out, gripping his other hand and squeezing it tight as my body trembles, my walls shattering around him like flimsy glass.

Killian grunts his approval, and not a moment later, he growls deep in my ear as he lets himself go, shooting hot spurts of cum deep inside of me.

"That's my good little whore," he grumbles as he tilts his head forward, dropping his forehead to my shoulder. "You're mine. All fucking mine. No other man will ever touch you again, do you understand me?"

"All yours," I agree as my pussy continues convulsing around his thick cock.

He holds on to me a moment longer, and as he comes down from his high, I can't help but recall the words his putrid cousin said to me— *And if you even think about offering him a DeLorenzo heir, I will tear your baby right out of your womb.*

Is this why I'm here? Is that what he wants with me?

I honestly can't tell at this point, but now isn't the right time to ask. Hell, I doubt there's ever a right time to question Killian DeLorenzo's intentions and motives.

When I've finally caught my breath, Killian pulls out of me and fixes my skirt back into place. "I have an event tomorrow evening, and I wish for you to accompany me," he says as I finally turn to face him, my gaze floating over the man's striking jawline that bears just the right amount of stubble, reminding me for the millionth time just how damn gorgeous he is.

My tongue peeks out and rolls over my dry lips as I trail my greedy gaze up to meet his intense stare. "What kind of event?" I ask, instantly on edge.

As if sensing my unease, Killian hesitates for a moment. "A business event where you will be on your best behavior. You will smile when spoken to, be polite, and engage with our company. I will provide you with a gown, and come seven in the evening, I expect you to be ready. It is a formal event in which most of my family will be in attendance. A ball, as you Americans like to call them."

My brows furrow, skipping right over the part where he said his family will be there, because that could only mean that Sergiu will be there, but what could really happen in the presence of Killian? "You're taking me to a ball?" I ask, wondering what kind of badass mafia boss hosts a fancy ball with gowns.

That intense stare hardens, reminding me that he doesn't appreciate being questioned. "That is what I said, is it not?"

"It is."

"Then I'm glad we're on the same page," he says. "I will be out in the morning attending to business. When I return, Sweet Angel, the night is yours."

CHAPTER 12

Chiara

The sun has barely risen when I wake to find a floor-length gown hanging over the door frame of my walk-in closet. I gape at it in awe, throwing the blankets back and trudging across the room while also irritated with myself for not noticing when someone entered my room.

My fingers brush over the gorgeous champagne silk, and butterflies take flight in my stomach.

I swallow hard, confusion claiming me.

That first time we were together, he told me he would fuck me until I forgot why I was here, until I believed I wanted this. And goddamn it, I think he might have succeeded. He's fucked with my head, calling me *Sweet Angel* and treating me like the queen I always be. What woman wouldn't want this? Living rent-free in a beautiful mansion, deep in the mountains, and far away from the harsh realities of real life. I have it all here, the perfect life, and he's offering it to me on a silver platter.

Everything except his cousin, of course.

All I have to do is accept it.

He warns me about his dark side if I should refuse him, that it would be something I could never recover from. I won't lie, I trust him when he says that he's a man of his word. He always seems to follow through.

He has me in knots, so damn confused about what I want. I should be trying to find a way out of here, but all I want is to see the approval in his eyes when I fuck him and hear those sweet words whispered in that captivating accent.

What the fuck is wrong with me? When did I stop seeing him as my captor and start seeing him as the man I want to please?

My gaze sails over the gown, taking in the plunging neckline and the hip-high split that will show off my legs perfectly. And all I can do is wonder why he claimed me as his own. Even on the balcony after his meeting, he said no other man would ever touch me again, but if I'm just a toy, why take me as a date to a family event? I can't claim that I know anything about the ins and outs of mafia life, but wouldn't bringing me as a date make a statement? I just wish I knew what.

All I know is that being here with him is a million times better than any other outcome that could have come from being auctioned off in that warehouse. I should thank him for saving me, but he insists he's no hero. If only he could see it the way I do. He offered me salvation, and while he might think of it as satisfying his wicked needs, I see it as a chance to live.

Striding across my room, I gaze out my big window that looks over the back of the property, admiring how the soft hues of gold shine across the mountaintops. It's dazzling, unbelievably gorgeous, and a sight I could happily wake up to every day of my life. It sure as hell beats waking up to the sound of my landlord banging on the door, demanding rent.

I slept like a baby last night, completely satisfied. Despite the fear of someone unwelcome sneaking into my room and the comments about bearing Killian an heir, I couldn't help the need to step into the shower and clean up. Now, barely twelve hours later, the need to have him inside me is stronger than ever before.

He said he was going out to attend to business this morning . . . whatever business that might be. But I wonder if he needs a wake-up call.

That first time we were together was his opportunity to exercise control over me. Hell, every moment since the warehouse he's had his chance. I've pushed the limits with him and tested the waters with just how far I can assert my will. But I'm not the type to simply allow a man to rule over my world. I'm far too independent for that. If this little arrangement is going to work out, I need a better understanding of my boundaries, and I need to have some control. Even if it's just a little.

He got to dictate how he was going to take my body, but now it's my turn.

If he gets to take me however and whenever he pleases, then he better be prepared for me to demand the same in return.

Before I've even had a chance to truly think this through, I'm marching out of my bedroom, uncaring about the fact that beneath my silk robe, I'm still as naked as the day I was born.

Finding his room, I grip the door handle and slowly push it open before peering in. The sun rises on the opposite side of the property, so it's still mostly covered in darkness, but there's just enough morning light for me to make out his sleeping body dead center on his bed.

His arm is propped behind his head, and while he's sound asleep, his usually tense jaw hangs slack, and his serious expression has melted into a soft, boyish innocence. During the day, there are deep lines in his forehead and his posture is cold and rigid, but there have been a few times when I've caught him watching me with his guard down. He doesn't look at me with the same disgusting disregard that I received from the other men at the auction. There is a connection between us, something that pulls him in, an odd infatuation, and as long as he'll have me, I'm willing to stay.

Swallowing over the growing lump of unease caught in my throat, I let out a shaky breath and make my move. My hands shake, but I forge ahead, determined to make my point.

Climbing the four steps up to his bed, I hit the platform before slipping out of my robe and slowly sliding in beside him. I'm certain that if he were to wake up right now, this wouldn't go down well. My Romanian mystery stirs as the bed dips under my weight, and I hold my breath, trying not to move as he settles back into a deep sleep.

Scooching closer to him, I inhale deeply, letting his magical scent wrap around me.

I don't know what it is about this man. Perhaps it's the knowledge that he could kill me without mercy, but he's so enraptured by me that he won't.

Fuck, I can't think like that. Or can I?

Testing the waters, my hand drops to his bare chest with a feather-soft touch, and I take in his handsome face to find him staring right back at me.

Oh shit.

I freeze, waiting for him to bitch me out, but he doesn't say a word as his eyes remain locked on me. If he didn't want my touch, he's the type of man to throw me out of here so damn fast, I'd never see it coming. The fact that he hasn't stopped me suggests he's down to see where this goes.

So, I do what any other insane girl would do and trail my hand down his body, holding my breath as I sail over the tight ridges of his abs until my hand closes around his thick cock.

I gently stroke him, my fingers roaming over his velvety skin, and not a moment later, he's rock-fucking-hard. I lick my lips, excitement drumming through my veins. Taking every ounce of determination I possess, I straddle his hips and lower myself onto his cock.

I suck in a breath through my teeth, hissing as he stretches me wider than ever. He feels so deep at this angle that it's almost painful, but I'm not about to bitch out. He keeps one hand propped behind his head, and his other comes up to rest on my hip.

His hand is so big and strong across my body that he could throw me off him without even trying. But he doesn't. He just watches me, keeping those dark eyes locked on mine. The tension and electricity grow between us until I finally start to move, and that tension morphs into undeniable pleasure.

I rock my hips, taking him deep, grinding and moving over him. I take every bit of pleasure from him, and when his other hand comes to my hip and tries to raise me up to take control, I smack his hand away. "No," I growl, letting him hear the authority in my tone. "You've had your chance to fuck me the way you please, and now it's my turn. Either lay back and take it, or I'll leave you high and dry. Take your pick, bossman."

He just stares at me, and as my heart races, I do what I can to mask my fear.

What the hell was I thinking? I'm done for.

He's going to curl his hand around my throat and suffocate me with his dick still inside of me. The uncontrollable jolting of my body giving up would probably be enough to get him off.

I'm a fucking idiot.

Not giving him another second to decide on a game plan, I start rocking my hips again. Only this time, I pick up my pace, fucking him just like he did me—with every ounce of control and demanding submission.

He relaxes, and I balance myself against his strong chest. He's seated so deeply, and I watch as he sucks in a breath, already on the edge. "You're not gonna come until I do," I warn him before leaning down, my lips right by his ear. "And when you do, I want to hear my name on your lips. Not Sweet Angel, *my name.*"

Something flashes in his eyes, and without warning, his hand closes around my throat and pushes me back up until I'm right where I was before. "I told you to forget your name," he spits through his teeth, so close to the edge. "She doesn't exist anymore."

I keep fucking him and his hand tightens around my throat, just as my walls tighten around his cock. My hips roll as I move up and down on his impressive length, driving him wild with need. "I can't do that," I rasp, groaning as I feel that familiar burn deep inside of me, desperate for release. "You can take my name, but you can't change who I am."

"And who the fuck are you?" he questions, clenching his jaw, determined to see this through. Just as I demanded.

But that accent, holy shit. It's just enough to throw me right over the edge, and I come hard and fast, my orgasm tearing through me. I cry out, catching myself against his strong chest, gasping for air as I come undone, my pussy convulsing around him. Then looking him dead in the eye, I give it to him straight. "I'm your goddamn equal."

And with that, he shoots his hot load deep inside my cunt, his gaze locked on mine in disbelief. He doesn't say a word as he comes, just stares at me unsure. It's as though for the first time in his life, he's lost for words.

Certain I've managed to prove some kind of point and regain just a fraction of control—or at least tried to—I climb off him. And with that electrifying, intense stare locked on my back, I stride out of his room with his warm cum spreading between my thighs, more determined than ever to see this through.

CHAPTER 13

Killian

She's fucking insane.

My equal? Surely she bumped her head last night because it would be a cold day in hell when anybody in this world could even attempt to stand as my equal. Though I have to give her credit where credit is due, she showed courage this morning. Walking into my room like that and demanding control has seen weaker women dead on the spot. But not her. She's different. Her boldness excites me, and when she reached beneath the blanket and took charge, I couldn't wait to see what she would do.

Making my way downstairs, I pass her door and hear the familiar sound of a hair dryer, and it pleases me that she's the type of woman to have a healthy respect for herself. Every morning she wakes up and takes a shower before spending twenty minutes blow-drying her hair and putting on just a touch of makeup, even if it's to spend her day snooping around my home. She always puts in an effort, and while she is absolutely gorgeous with her hair in a messy bun and without a shred of makeup, when she does put in that little bit of extra effort, it never fails to blow me away.

She truly is a sweet angel, so fucking beautiful, it's blinding.

Stopping by the kitchen, I find Krista busily working away, my coffee waiting for me on the corner of the island counter. "Morning, Sir," Krista says, wiping over the bench. "You're up early."

"Yes, I had a bit of an . . . unexpected wake-up call."

Krista laughs under her breath as though knowing exactly what kind of unexpected wake-up call I had. "I see," she says, her cheeks flushing. "Then I take it you'll be needing a protein-filled breakfast to replenish your energy."

I roll my eyes and drop down at the counter as I sip my coffee. "Comments like that will see your pay docked," I warn, knowing she's only teasing. Over these past twelve years with Krista, she's become one of my true friends. I care for her more than I care to admit, and she knows it, which is exactly how she knows I'd never dock her pay for making jokes at my expense. She's like the little sister I never had.

Krista laughs to herself as she goes about making me the protein-filled breakfast she joked about.

"She knows who I am," I murmur, filling the silence.

"And?" Krista prompts, knowing there's more here.

I press my lips into a tight line, wondering where the hell I'm going with this. "She doesn't seem to fear me."

"Have you given her a reason to?"

"My name alone should be enough to terrify her."

"And yet, she rises with the sun just for the chance to sneak into your room."

I let out a heavy breath and raise my gaze to meet Krista's. "I seem to be very intrigued by her."

"And so you should," Krista tells me. "Have you taken the chance to speak with her? While she is dazzling and breathtaking in her beauty, she also has a personality worth getting to know. She's stronger than I think you know."

"She talks back to me."

"Well," Krista laughs. "I said she had a personality worth getting to know, not that she was overwhelmingly clever. I believe she's just trying to understand where your boundaries are and just how far she can push them."

I scoff. "She's delusional."

"No, she's strong."

"This morning she insisted that she was my equal."

"Oh, okay. Perhaps she's a little delusional, but it's not as though that's a crime," she teases before a seriousness creeps into her tone. "I know you weren't asking for my opinion, but if I dare be so bold. As an outsider looking in, it's clear that she's just trying to understand her place here, and I think you should allow her the chance to do that."

My brows furrow as I stare at my chef, not understanding what she's getting at. "How do you mean?"

"She's a young, impressionable woman, Killian. Despite how you claim to not be her savior or her hero, that's exactly what you are, and I see it every day in the way you interact with her. You treat her like the queen you've always deserved to have. You claim that she belongs to you, and I think she's trying to determine if this is a two-way street where she will be the woman who stands proudly at your side and you will be her man and protector, or if she will simply exist as a dirty secret."

I shake my head. "I see."

Krista fixes me with a hard stare. "Do you?" I watch her a moment, waiting for her to continue. "Last night you asked me to steam her gown for the annual DeLorenzo Family Gala, an event that's been going on for longer than I've known you, and not once have you ever taken a date. But tonight, for some reason, you are."

"And? That doesn't mean anything."

"By turning up with her on your arm, you are making a statement. You are telling the members of your family that you have found someone worthy of standing at your side and giving you an heir. Is that your intention?"

I lift my coffee to my lips and take a quick sip, unsure how to respond to that, but there's no denying that she's right. Bringing a date tonight is making a statement to my family, and the second I walk in with her on my arm, I am making a formal demand that my family shows respect to this woman, that she is important to me, and yet, I still can't figure out why.

I think I've already come to the conclusion that she will bear my child. Seeing that boldness in her this morning only cemented the fact that she would make a great mother. That strength and courage I've seen in her are the traits I require of my offspring in order to be successful as the next ruler of this family. My sweet angel is not timid or shy, and she certainly isn't afraid of speaking her mind and going after what she wants. Any child would be lucky to obtain those traits, and along with my demanding nature and leadership, we could create the strongest ruler this family has ever encountered.

Excitement bursts through my chest, and I do what I can to mask the emotions brimming in my eyes as I fix Krista with a stare, unsure of what to say. "You might be right," I tell her. "However, she will never be my equal."

Krista rolls her eyes and slides my breakfast toward me. "No, she won't, but I think you can learn to love the idea of having her standing at your side and being the woman you come home to. Everybody can see it, Killian. There's a spark between you every time you're in the same room. It's electrifying, and I think you'd be foolish not to see where it goes. Who knows, you might even allow yourself to love her."

I clench my jaw and drop my gaze.

That's the problem with Krista. She has a way of forcing you to see what's right in front of your face, and she's not afraid to call you out on it either.

She's right.

The electricity that sparks between us is like nothing I've ever felt before, and because of it, I am constantly seeking her out. I want to be around her and see the way her face lights up with happiness when she smiles, but mostly, I want to claim more than just her body. It's a long road we must travel before we get there first. While she claims to understand who I am and what I do, it's not the same as accepting it, and I don't believe that will be easy for her.

Can I love her? Possibly.

But is she capable of loving me in return? That, I don't know.

She has been hesitant during the week. Nervous perhaps. It's hard to tell. She faked an illness earlier in the week to remain locked away in her room. I figured she required a few days to adjust to this new life, and I willingly gave it to her. Coming into my world isn't an easy adjustment, and that much was obvious when she hid in the library yesterday during my meeting. She insisted she wasn't hiding, but I felt the nervousness coming off her when I first walked in. She might trust me not to hurt her, but she does not trust the company I keep, and that is fair enough. She will soon learn, and after I introduce her tonight, they will all know that she is off-limits.

In the past few days, she's blossomed right out of her shell, and this morning when she so boldly came into my bedroom and took what she wanted, she proved to me that she could handle it. It will be hard, and there will be trials she must overcome, but once she climbs through the wreckage and takes her stand by my side, nothing will ever hurt her. Though she must be prepared to fight for what she wants because nothing in this world comes without a price.

CHAPTER 14

Chiara

After spending my day lounging around the pool and getting to know Krista a little better, I stand in my room, staring at my reflection in the full-length mirror. I've never worn a gown like this. On second thought, I don't think I've ever worn a gown at all. I was too cool when it came to participating in school events and skipped out on my senior prom, robbing myself of a moment just like this.

I barely recognize myself.

The plunging neckline and high slit add just enough sex appeal while somehow keeping the overall look elegant and sophisticated. The perfect puppet for my Romanian mystery to parade on his arm. My hair is pulled up with a few loose curls framing my face, while also

I'm just finishing the final touches of my makeup when a knock sounds at my door. There's still an hour or so before we need to leave, and assuming it's Krista with something to eat, I call out over my shoulder. "Come in."

The door opens just a sliver, and there's a slight hesitation before it finally pushes open all the way. I glance up in the mirror, but when my Romanian jailer appears in the doorway, my back stiffens.

I haven't seen him all day. Not since I demanded that he treat me as an equal while riding his cock.

As he goes to step into my room, he catches sight of me in my gown and pauses, that dark, lethal gaze sailing over my body. He looks back up at me, meeting my eyes through the mirror, and I watch as he visibly swallows as though the mere sight of me in this gown is tripping him up. "I, uhh . . . I came to remind you that we're due to leave in an hour and that it would be prudent to start getting ready. However, it seems my reminder is unnecessary."

I slowly turn to face him, taking in the five-piece designer suit covering his strong body, and goddamn, all I want to do is tear it off him with my teeth. Every time I've seen him, apart from in his bedroom, he's been wearing suits, so I have no idea if he's ready for tonight or not. All I know is he looks good enough to eat.

"It is," I agree, watching as he hesitantly takes a step deeper into my room.

Trailing my fingers over my collarbone and down through the plunging neckline, I watch his gaze follow my movements. "Thank you for the gown. I've never worn anything like this before."

He simply nods. "You look . . ." He hesitates for just a moment, seeming out of his comfort zone. "Nice."

"Nice?" I say with a breathy scoff. "A woman stands before you in a silk gown and you tell her she looks *nice?* What about breathtaking? Dazzling? Unbelievably stunning?"

His gaze hardens before he strides through my room, stopping right in front of me. He reaches out and brushes his fingers over the soft silk of the gown, trailing up my body until his hand is at the base of my throat. He slowly squeezes until I'm left gasping for air. "You're not ready to hear the way I feel about you in this dress, Angel," he growls in my ear before finally easing up on my throat. "The things that I would do. The way I would tear it to shreds. You might think you can take it because you're a whore for my cock, but you're not ready. Not yet. Soon, Sweet Angel. But not yet."

Hoooooly fuck.

He pulls back just an inch so that he can meet my stare, and my heart races.

How is he able to do this to me? One second, I'm terrified of his reaction to my demands this morning, and the next, I'm ready to bend myself into a pretzel and let him fuck me into oblivion.

A seriousness flashes in his eyes, and his hand falls away from my throat. He watches me for a moment, the silence so thick between us. "It seems you made your point this morning," he says in that rich accent that could almost drop me to my knees.

Oh shit. We're doing this now.

"And what point would that be?" I question for the sake of clarity.

Frustration flickers in that lethal stare, and I swallow back my fear. "Don't do that, Angel. Don't pretend you don't know what I'm referring to. It's beneath you."

I roll my tongue over my lips, my throat suddenly very dry. "I'm sorry. You're right. I do know," I whisper, my hands shaking at my sides. "You told me you encourage my honesty, and I hope that's true."

"How many times must I tell you that I am a man of my word?"

"I'm not the type of woman who can easily accept changes, nor do I easily trust," I tell him. "I'm sure you can understand that. Which is why I can't easily accept the terms of our . . . arrangement. I need more. I need you to meet me halfway."

"Dare I ask what that means? *More?*" he muses. "Surely you must know that I cannot offer you equal standing."

"I know," I say with a small sigh. "I knew you'd never agree to that before the words even came out of my mouth. But I'm not ashamed to admit I was mid-orgasm and sometimes words just have this way of coming out at the worst times."

"Angel," he prompts, getting me back on track.

Balling my hands into fists to hide how they shake, I try to come to him with confidence. "I have terms of my own, and if you're able to agree to them, then I think I can learn to be happy here . . . *with* you."

He watches me for a long moment, his gaze narrowed as if contemplating actually entertaining my bullshit. As the seconds tick by, I become certain that he's about to walk out of here, leaving me hanging, but then he raises his chin. "Go on," he instructs. "What is it you need from me?"

"Okay," I say, ripping it off like a Band-Aid, starting with the basics. "I consent to you using my body at will. However, it's a two-way street. If you get to fuck me whenever the feeling strikes, then I get to ride your cock at my say-so. If you're in some kind of business meeting and I need to fuck, then you'll excuse yourself to take care of me, just as I'm expected to spread my thighs and bend over for you."

He rubs a hand down his face, taking a step back to put space between us. "Business is business. I will not *excuse myself* to fuck you," he states. "However, I brought you here, and if you have needs, then they are my responsibility. If you need to fuck, we'll fuck."

I nod, feeling as though we're gaining traction. "Okay," I continue. "I'm on board with you referring to me as Angel or Sweet Angel. However, I would like it if you could call me by my name. It's the only piece of me that is truly mine, and I wish to hold on to it."

His gaze hardens. "I will not."

"You will," I push, fixing him with a hard stare, letting him know that this is a hill I'm one hundred percent ready to die on. "My name is Chiara and when you call for me, you will use it. I will not forfeit my identity for you or any man."

"In my line of business, I cannot have anything linking you back to your old life. You belong to me now."

"Are you willing to compromise?" I question, all too curious about what this particular line of business is that would require me to lose my name. Though considering he's kidnapped me from a trafficking ring, it couldn't be anything good. "I am not attached to my surname. I never knew my parents. I grew up in foster care, jumping from home to home. I believe my surname was given to me by the state after I was dumped at the doors of an orphanage with no way to identify myself. I can part with that if you wish."

He considers me a moment before finally nodding. "Okay," he says. "You have yourself a deal. I will call you by your name. Is there anything else?"

Nerves sink heavily into my stomach, and I figure now might be my only chance to get this out. "I know that you claimed me as your own in that underground warehouse, and for some reason, you saved me from that misery. I will never be able to thank you enough. But you will not address me as your property. I wish to be your equal, and I know that's not something you can offer me. However, I would like it if you could try, or if it could be something we work toward. I wish to come and go as I please and you need to trust that I will come home to you."

He shakes his head. "No. I cannot allow that."

Clenching my jaw, I push him a little harder, relying on his infatuation to carry this home. "You can and will. This is your home after all, is it not? You can allow anything you like, and while you have offered me free rein, you have also offered me limitations. I don't do well when someone puts limits on me. If you wish for me to have free rein, then offer it openly and freely. I won't lie to you. I am intrigued by you, and while you scare the shit out of me, you also draw me in. You have warned me of the dangers of betraying you, of refusing you, and I trust you to keep your word. So I am asking the same of you. Trust me. Trust me when I tell you that I will not betray you."

"That's not something I am willing to bend on, *Chiara*," he says, using my name for the first time. "However, given time, it is something I am willing to discuss again."

"Okay, good."

"I do wonder, if I am not to refer to you as my *property*, then what shall you be?"

I shake my head, hesitating as I step in a little closer and rest my hand against his chest, feeling the rapid beat of his heart through his suit.

I look up into those dark, stormy eyes, my chin lifting. "That's for you to decide."

His eyes flame as his hand comes down on top of mine, maybe just a little more than a slight infatuation. He takes my waist with his other hand, pulling me in against him as he leans in, letting me see the dangerous man who lives inside. "I am not the hero you think I am, Angel. I am not a good man."

I swallow hard, my voice a breathy whisper through my room. "I'm under no illusion that you are a hero. However, when I look into your eyes, I know that you won't hurt me."

He holds my stare, almost looking just as confused about this as I am. "No, I will not."

"I don't know what this is," I murmur, our hands still joined over his chest, "this connection between us, but I know you feel it too."

He nods. "I find it better not to ask questions. Don't try to confuse this."

I nod, realizing I'm starting to push him too far. I pull back out of his hold and fix him with another stare. "I just have one more condition," I whisper, my hands starting to shake again. He narrows his gaze, probably wondering what else I could possibly want, but considering he's been so generous in our negotiations, I figure now is the best time to ask. "I need to know if you only brought me here because you want me to give you a child."

His eyes widen with surprise. "How do you know about that?"

I shrug my shoulders. "You're the head of the DeLorenzo family and splashed all over every news channel that ever existed. You're the world's most wanted man, so would I be crazy in admitting that I've watched more than one true crime documentary about you?" I question. "Now, I don't know much about mafia politics or how things are supposed to work, but what I do know is that you require an heir to inherit your position after you pass. I guess I can't help but wonder if that's the reason why I'm here. Also," I admit, "I kinda heard whispers about it."

Killian arches a brow as he watches me. "I won't lie to you, Chiara," he says, and my name in that accent does wicked things to me. "The thought of impregnating you with my heir has occurred to me on more than one occasion, and in case you haven't noticed, we haven't exactly been practicing safe sex. If you were to fall pregnant, then so be it."

"And if I'm not ready to be someone's mother?"

"Nobody is asking you to be a mother," he offers. "Not unless you feel that you're ready to take that step. However, I see how strong and courageous you are and believe any child would be lucky to have you as his mother."

I let out a shaky breath. "Okay. Shit just got real," I tell him, trying not to let on just how shaken the idea has made me. Is he actively trying to knock me up? Fuck that. I'm not ready for this. I'm barely even an adult myself. "How is it that I'm cool living in the home of the world's most terrifying man, but the thought of having a baby at twenty-three makes me want to hurl?"

"Do you need a moment?"

I stumble back, breathing heavily as my ass finds the edge of my bed. I bury my face into my hands, leaning forward as I try not to fall into a panic attack, but truth be told, I think I'm already there.

"I forgot to feed my goldfish once," I tell him. "He died. I can't be trusted with a baby. You know they need constant supervision, right? Plus, they suck the life out of your tits."

"Okay," he says, moving to my side. "We'll shelve the heir idea for now, but just know that in time, I will require a child. Just as you require honesty and equality from me, I require an heir from you. It's non-negotiable."

Non-negotiable.

I glance up at him. "So, it doesn't have to be now?" I confirm, a sliver of hope beginning to burn through my chest. "It can happen in ten, maybe twenty years down the track?"

"I am not waiting twenty years," he growls in that thick, delicious accent. "You get two."

"TWO YEARS?" I panic, my eyes widening like saucers. "Holy fuck."

"Alright, I see that I've upset you," he tells me, beginning to back up from the hysterical woman, clearly way out of his comfort zone. "That was not my intention. I don't know how to fix this."

"Vodka," I say. "Lots and lots of vodka."

He laughs, and the sound lifts my gaze from my hands. I hadn't realized a man like this was even capable of laughter. "That," he says. "I can do."

CHAPTER 15

Chiara

I'm surrounded by the Romanian Mafia. Every damn member is dressed in five-piece suits while their wives sip red wine in their spectacular gowns, eyeing me with distaste. One thing is for sure, if Killian hadn't filled me with vodka before making our way here, I probably wouldn't have the balls to look a single person in the eye.

I knew my Romanian captor was the head of the DeLorenzo family, but hearing it and seeing it are two very different things. The people here—the very ones he calls family—fear him, and it's clear that Killian DeLorenzo is a wicked man.

He's callous and cruel, unforgiving and twisted. The things I've heard on the news about his family are enough to send me into a blind panic. And yet here I am, standing in the middle of their annual family ball.

I can't say I'm well educated on the Romanian Mafia, and I don't recognize a single face, but I imagine that Killian isn't the only wanted man in the room. There must be at least five hundred people here. It's probably an FBI agent's wet dream. I wouldn't want to be the sorry asshole who decided to bust this party wide open. He would be dead before he even stepped foot inside the building.

The very thought makes my palms sweat. Just the thought of what the men in this room are capable of makes my blood turn to ice.

My hand curls around Killian's strong arm as he leads me through the room, holding conversations in Romanian, and I can't even begin to understand what sick deals they are discussing right in front of me. But I do my best to be polite, and whenever he gestures toward me, I give subtle smiles to play my part.

Women stare at me from every corner of the room, and I hate it. I feel like a butterfly with pinned wings, forced under someone's microscope. They watch me as though having a woman on his arm is unheard of. Their callous stares burn up and down my body with disapproval, comparing me to themselves, and probably wondering what the hell is so special about me. If only they knew how I came to be here. Hell, in this type of company, perhaps my story isn't as unique as I think. Who knows how many of the women in this room started just like I did. Some poor girl snatched away from her world only to be dazzled by this crazy, glamorous life.

And glamorous it is.

The room is huge, decked out in what I can only assume is the most luxurious Italian marble. Subtle geometric patterns cover the floors, sailing right out to the wide dance floor where a string quartet plays the most hypnotic music.

It's a scene right out of a Jane Austen film, but absolutely none of it prepares me for the high ceilings and stunning crystal chandelier. The room is a masterpiece. I suck in a breath, needing to hold on to Killian tighter as he leads me through the crowd, far too distracted by the stunning architecture and design of the ballroom.

God, I'm a sucker for good architecture.

The deeper into the room we get, the more people step in to say hello, attempting to get into good favor with the most powerful man in the world. Yet somehow, out of all the women who could have fallen at his feet, he chose me.

The thought has a thrill sailing through my body, and I find myself stepping even closer to his side. I know he probably doesn't hold any real affection for me, but I feel there's a possibility here. A possibility for this to be real, for something more to develop.

I feel I could maybe even love him one day.

Shit. I really do have some fucked-up version of Stockholm Syndrome.

What the hell is wrong with me? I'm smitten with my captor, but how can I not be? The way he looks, the way he smells, and good God, the way he fucks! I'm not just smitten, I'm completely taken with him. He's captured me in more ways than he ever bargained for. But something tells me I might have done the same.

Killian was intent on keeping me at arm's length. I was to keep my mouth shut and bend to his will, but he's allowed me freedom within his home. He's allowed me to set my own boundaries and promised to revisit the ones he wasn't ready for. Hell, he woke up this morning to me sneaking into his bed with the intention to fuck him and allowed me to take what I needed.

He might say we're not equals, but in my eyes, we're just about there.

Killian accepts two glasses of champagne from a nearby waitress and gingerly hands one to me as a couple approaches us, and my heart instantly kicks into gear, racing with fear.

Sergiu.

He eyes me with suspicion, the dark secret of what he did to me flashing in his eyes as the woman on his arm throws me a haughty look.

"Ahh, Sergiu," Killian says with sharp eyes, watching the man closely as I clutch his arm with everything I have. "Salut, cousin."

They take each other's wrists before pulling in close and clapping one another on the back. "Salut," Sergiu responds, still watching me as Killian moves back and steps into the woman, giving her a curt kiss on each cheek, something I've seen a lot of tonight.

The woman wears a bored expression as her partner gestures toward me, unaware of the way my whole body shakes. "Do introduce me," Sergiu says with a hard stare at Killian before shifting his sick gaze back to me. The request sounds friendly, yet his icy stare sends a wave of fear snaking down my spine.

God, when will this end?

Killian's hand rests over mine on his arm, and I find myself almost folding into him, trying to escape the heaviness of his cousin's stare. "Sergiu, this is Chiara DeLorenzo, my new bride. You will do well to accept her into the family."

"Bride?" he sputters, gaping at Killian as my heart stops, my whole body freezing. I'm certain I must have heard him wrong. "Tell me you did not wed this common whore?"

Killian's hand snaps out so damn fast, I barely see it moving, but damn, there's no mistaking the sound of his palm smacking across his cousin's face. "Watch your mouth," Killian growls, the tone in his voice making me tremble. "The whore you refer to is my *wife*. My family, *our family*. You will show respect, or must I remind you what happens to men who disrespect what's mine?"

Sergiu dips his head, finally dropping his lingering stare away from me, allowing me a false sense of reprieve. But with Killian's words still circling my head, peace is not something I'm capable of finding. "Of course not, Killian," he says, taking the smallest step back, trying to be discreet as the woman sneers at me, her gaze now shifting from disgusted to calculated. Sergiu looks back up before fixing me with a kind smile that doesn't meet his eyes, but I have to give him credit for trying. "On behalf of myself, my wife, Monica, and the DeLorenzo family, we welcome you with open arms."

Fucking bullshit.

I nod my head, really not knowing what to say when he pats his wife's hand on his arm. "If you would excuse us. I promised my wife a dance before dinner is served."

Killian gives a curt nod and watches his cousin as they step away, and once the fear of his proximity has finally faded from my veins, I'm left with nothing to do but gape at the intoxicating man beside me.

Wife?

I know this man is psychotic, callous, and cruel, but is he also deranged? I know we discussed our requirements this afternoon, but I could have sworn the word wife or bride was never brought up in conversation. Surely I would remember that. Though to be fair, I don't think I remember a single thing after he said I'd be birthing a child within the next two years. I'm still sweating from that revelation.

Noticing my stare, Killian lets out an exasperated breath before fixing me with a heavy stare, though the way his eyes flash lets me know he has all the time in the world for me right now. "What is it now, *Chiara?*" he questions, leading me deeper into the room, and not allowing me a single moment to melt at the way my name sounds on his skilled tongue.

"Uhhhh . . . Are you kidding me?" I stutter, barely able to meet the intensity of his rich stare. "You just referred to me as your *wife*. What the hell, Killian? I know we have an . . . odd arrangement, but *wife?* I don't remember signing a marriage license. Hell, I don't remember walking down the aisle in a big-ass poofy dress and vowing to love you in sickness and health either. Though to be fair, you have a tendency to drug me, so who knows what could have happened while I was out cold."

Killian pulls me in closer and lowers his hand to the small of my back before leading me toward the dance floor and away from prying eyes. "Must everything be so dramatic with you?" he questions, stepping out onto the dance floor, taking my hand, and spinning me out, unaware of the way I tremble being this much closer to Sergiu.

Killian gives a gentle tug, and I come spinning right back, my body pressing up against his as my hand lands on his wide chest, his proximity leaving Sergiu nothing but a distant memory. "As discussed this afternoon, for your own protection and the protection of my family, I cannot allow you to keep your name. So I have decided that you will take mine."

I gape at him. "As your *wife?*"

He nods. "You expressed that you were not comfortable being referred to as my property. Is that still true?"

"Yes," I rush out. "Of course that's still true. I haven't changed my mind in the past hour."

"Then this is what I can offer you," he tells me, casually leading me around the dance floor as the whispering about our current marital status spreads around the room like wildfire. "As my wife, you will hold a name that will not put my family or business in jeopardy. The world will know you not as my *property*, but as my *spouse. My wife.* And while I know we are not there yet, in the eyes of the outside world, that's exactly what you will be."

Holy fuck. I take a shaky breath. "I don't know how marriages work where you're from, but here in the US, a marriage is a partnership. *Equals.*"

His movements slow as he focuses on my terrified stare, his arm locking around my waist and holding me to him. "No, Sweet Angel.

This marriage is only for the public and to keep your identity concealed. When we are in the confounds of my home, we will continue as originally discussed. Nothing changes. You belong to me, Chiara. I am a powerful man, and I cannot simply give up that power to another. I was not raised that way. Already succumbing to your many requests has been a challenge."

"I wouldn't exactly call that succumbing."

"No?" he questions with an arched brow, his fingers dipping inside the material of my dress and brushing across my lower back. "I do not think you realize just how much pull you have over me."

I suck in a breath, swallowing hard over the lump in my throat as my heart races erratically. A little over a week ago, my life looked like a sack of shit, and I could have sworn that it would only go downhill from there. But now, Killian DeLorenzo, the most wanted and powerful man in the world, is looking at me as though I hold his whole future in the palm of my hand.

Words escape me, and he spins me around, letting the silk gown flow out around me before pulling me back in, allowing me a small chance to collect myself and process his words. I gaze up at him, feeling the stare of every last person in the room. "I think . . . I would very much like to be your wife, not just in the public eye."

His face softens as he brushes his fingers down my spine. "You've been with me a week, Chiara. You do not understand what it is you are asking."

"Perhaps not," I agree. "But I know how I feel, and I know that this electricity between us isn't something you come by every day.

Don't tell me you can't feel it."

"Of course I feel it. From the moment our eyes connected in that warehouse, I could feel a connection to you. Your soul cried out for help, and I've been mesmerized since that very moment, but that is no reason to take you as my wife in a world you are not yet familiar with. I know you may not see it this way, but it would be cruel. When I truly make you mine, it will be with your eyes wide open."

He spins me again, our pace slowing as the words spoken between us start to hold so much weight. "I'm terrified of what this life with you could mean, but at the same time, I'm also terrified that you'll let me go."

"I know, Sweet Angel."

He pulls me back into his chest as my heart continues to race. Somehow, my life has turned into some kind of twisted fairy tale, and all my darkest fantasies have become reality. Only, I don't get to take home the hero. I get the villain, and it's ten times more thrilling than having a white knight could ever be. I mean, damn. I doubt a white knight would have the balls to plunge a butt plug so deep in his girl's ass the first time he touched her.

A sly grin pulls at the corner of my mouth, and I watch the way his eyes spark with excitement. "Just for the record, I'm no sweet angel."

"Oh, I know. You're the devil in disguise, and I'm going to enjoy fucking you into submission."

He dips me low before I get a chance to say a word, and the way he looks down at me so full of desire makes my whole body clench with need. He pulls me back up against him, this time knocking the breath right out of my lungs. "You will stand at my side at the head of my family as my queen, and you will learn to play the role. It will take time, and there will be trials and tribulations, but one day, once you're fully able to grasp the magnitude of who I am and what I do, you will embrace this new world."

I stare up at him, absolutely dazzled by this perfectly lethal man. Then before I even get a chance to figure out how to respond, his full lips are crashing down on mine. I sink into him, my eyes fluttering closed as something settles within me.

His tongue delves into my mouth, claiming me as his own, just as he did the very first time I saw him. I was his then, but I can't help to wonder if he is mine now.

I kiss him back, letting him feel the rush of emotions I've felt over the past nine days. The fear, the anxiety, the nerves, the unadulterated passion, and the raw need I feel for him.

The music shifts, and he reluctantly pulls back from me, those dark eyes holding me captive. I can barely breathe; the rush of emotion is almost too much for me to keep up with. My tongue rolls over my bottom lip as I lift my chin, keeping as close as possible. "Did you really mean it when you agreed that I could take you whenever I needed?"

Those dark eyes fill with hunger as his hand bunches into the fabric of my gown. "What did I tell you about being a man of my word?" he growls, his chest rising and falling just a little bit faster.

"Well then. It's time to put your word to the test," I purr, letting him see the desire pooling in my eyes. "I need you now, and when I tell you I need it hard and fast, you better come through for me."

Killian clenches his jaw, his gaze lifting to the crowd around us. "I told you, business is business," he says, discreetly shaking his head.

A wicked grin stretches across my face. He said I was a devil in disguise, and he's about to find out just how true that is. "Then I suppose you're lucky you're not attending to business. We're dancing, Killian, not working, and I need you to fuck me right now."

His eyes flash, realizing I've just used and abused one of the best loopholes I'll ever find. He dips me low, a gasp sailing from between my lips as a ferocious growl tears from his. He kisses me deeply, and being a man of his word, his hand sails straight up the high split of my gown and right between my legs.

He pulls back from our kiss, his eyes sparkling with a wicked excitement, then watching the pure elation on my face, he pushes two thick fingers deep inside my tight cunt, more than ready to rock my world right here in the middle of the dance floor.

CHAPTER 16

Killian

We barrel through the door of a supply closet, Chiara's gown already bunched in my hands before the door even closes behind us. I slam her against the wall, her desperate gasp like music to my ears as she reaches for the front of my pants.

The hunger in her eyes is intoxicating. She's surprised me at every turn we've taken. I expected hesitance from her, fearfulness, and nerves, and instead, I've been rewarded with a woman whose confidence shines brighter than the sun. She is not timid like I expected; she is bold and unafraid, and with each passing day, another piece of me becomes drunk on her. Addicted.

I need to be inside of her, dominate her, to feel the way my hands grip her hips. Fuck, I need that release.

Two minutes ago, as I danced with her in front of my gossiping family, I was calm and collected, but this woman has turned me into a crazed, desperate man in the space of seconds.

Chiara frees my straining erection and squeezes her hand around me, so fucking tight I can barely breathe. "Fuck me, Killian," she begs, pulling me impossibly closer. With her gown bunched up to her waist, I go to reach for her underwear, only to pause when I realize she's not wearing any.

My gaze lifts to hers, my brow arching, but all she can do is smirk back at me as her eyes sparkle with her wicked intentions. She's been waiting for this since before we left my estate, and there's nothing that gets me harder than a patient woman.

"You planned this," I rumble, my fingers digging into her creamy skin as she pumps her tight fist up and down my cock.

The sweetest seduction flashes in her eyes and without even trying, she's got me right where she wants me. "No," she whispers, her tongue rolling over her bottom lip. "I hoped for it."

I groan, that same desperation in her, now rocking through my chest. I drop my gaze down her body, taking in her bare mound, and as my hungry stare trails just a little bit further, I notice the fading bruises on her thighs. They're almost gone, as though this happened a while ago.

Have I been too rough with her?

Fuck. That wasn't my intention.

I warned her that I would be rough, that I would make her scream and forget why she should fear me, but to leave marks on her body?

No.

I drop to my knees before her, my lips grazing over the faded bruises. "Did I do this?" I ask, gripping her thighs as my lips move to her center and dive between her legs. My tongue works its way through her center, tasting how fucking sweet she is as my mouth closes around her clit.

Chiara's knees buckle as she grips the back of my head, her fingers knotting into my hair. She widens her stance, giving me more access to her sweet cunt. "No," she pants, her grip tightening in my hair as if trying to control my movements. "Not you."

"How?" I rumble against her.

"It's nothing," she says, her body tensing up and only relaxing when my tongue flicks against her needy clit, making her hips jolt. "It happened while I was locked in that cage. It's nothing you did."

Anger seeps into my veins, pulsing through my body until it overwhelms my system, and I get back to my feet, my hand closing around her narrow throat. Chiara gasps, her eyes wide as she holds my stare. "Don't lie to me, Angel," I growl, tightening my hold on her throat just enough to allow her a shallow breath. "When you first arrived, I took my time to memorize every inch of your body. Those bruises were not there before."

Her eyes dance with excitement, and I realize the tighter I squeeze, the more she likes it, even more so when she reaches down between us and curls her hand around my cock again, her thumb gently stroking over my tip. "Does it really matter?" she breathes. "It's just a little bruise, and it's almost gone. Now, I don't know about you, but I'd rather feel you slamming inside of me than having a conversation about old bruises."

As if to bring her point home, she tightens her grip on my cock, pumping up and down, but I know exactly what she's doing, and while that trick might work on weaker men, it won't work on me. "No woman of mine will lie to me, Chiara."

"Then punish me, Killian. Fuck me," she demands, tilting her chin up with defiance. "Put us both out of our misery."

I groan, the fire burning within me, and in a flash, my hands are on her ass, lifting her against the wall as she guides my tip to her entrance. Her legs snake around my waist, opening herself to me, and with one solid thrust, I bury my cock deep inside of her, more than ready to fuck the truth out of her.

Her warmth surrounds me, squeezing me tight as if to welcome me home, and my whole body jolts with pure satisfaction. There's nothing better than the feeling of being deep inside this woman. It's as though she were made just for me.

"YES!" Chiara cries out, locking her arms around my neck for stability as I ram into her again, taking her even deeper.

My fingers dig into the globes of her ass, and this time, I know for sure that I'll leave marks there, but these are the kind of marks that we're both happy to see lining her flawless skin.

I thrust and grind, both of us teetering on the edge of satisfaction. "Fuck, I'm gonna come," Chiara grunts, clutching on to me with everything she's got, panting heavily.

"Hold on to it, my little devil. You'll come when I tell you to."

"Oh God," she groans, closing her eyes and tipping her head back against the wall.

I fuck her furiously, taking her hard and deep and stretching that sweet little cunt to its limits.

"Please," she begs.

I clench my jaw, desperate for my release, but she hasn't suffered nearly enough, and until she falls apart, I'll continue to punish her with this devilish torture. "Are you going to lie to me, Chiara?"

"No. Never again."

I push her further, rolling my hips and taking her at every angle. "What do you say, my Sweet Angel?"

Her grip tightens in my hair, the desperation radiating out of her. "Please, Killian. Please. Let me come," she cries out. "I'm sorry. I'll never lie to you again. I just . . . It wasn't important enough to tell you. Please, let me come on your cock. I can't hold on to it any longer."

I thrust three more furious times, each one rubbing right up against her G-spot and stretching her wider as my cock strains for release, the prominent veins angry and desperate.

One.

Two.

Three.

"Have you learned your lesson, Angel? If you lie to me, I will punish you, and believe me when I tell you, this is only a taste of what I will do to you."

"Yes, Killian. Please. I've learned my lesson."

"Good. Then come for me, Chiara. Let me feel how hard you

squeeze my cock."

She doesn't hesitate, releasing the hold on her orgasm and allowing it to explode through her body, shattering her like glass. Her sweet little cunt violently convulses around me, so damn tight that I can't hold on a second longer. I come with her, shooting hot spurts of cum deep inside of her, filling her with my seed.

I keep moving as she rides out the high, her head thrown back against the wall in elation as her death grip finally eases in my hair. "Holy fuck," she pants, struggling to catch her breath, but I'm right there with her, needing to release one of my hands to brace against the wall.

"So fucking perfect, Angel," I murmur, dropping my lips to her shoulder.

Chiara goes limp in my arms, a satisfied sigh slipping from her lips. "If that's the punishment I get, maybe I should lie to you more often."

I lift my head, my fiery gaze locking onto hers, finding nothing but an intrigued challenge staring back at me. "Don't try me, Chiara," I warn, my cock still buried deep inside of her. "You won't enjoy the consequences."

"I don't know," she teases, a playful smirk stretching across her lips and making a rush of . . . *something* pound in my chest. "I certainly enjoyed those consequences."

I shake my head, unsure how to respond. Nobody challenges me like this. I don't let them close enough to even try, and yet here she is, giving it her all, and what's more? I fucking love it.

"Come now," I say, pulling out of her and stepping back before helping to settle her on her feet. "If I'm gone for too long, people will come looking, and when they see you with those flushed cheeks and hard peaks of your nipples straining through your dress, they're going to want a taste of what's mine, but let me make this clear—I don't intend on sharing you."

A nervousness flashes in her eyes. "And if someone were to put their hands on me?"

"I would cut their hands off and deliver them right to your door."

Chiara grins and inches toward me as she fixes her dress back into place, though I have no doubt she's currently feeling the way my warm cum leaks out of her and spreads between those juicy thighs. She'll be excusing herself to go to the bathroom in no time. She lifts her chin, her lips barely a breath away. "I don't know whether to panic because that was the most messed-up thing you've said yet, or to start blushing at your misguided attempt at romance."

Taking her chin, I capture her gaze, and she becomes still. "Understand me, Chiara, that was not a misguided attempt to sweep you off your feet. It was honest. If someone were to put their hands on you, I would end them. Nobody steals from me."

She visibly swallows, and I wave my hand toward the door, a subtle demand to get her ass moving. She does as she's asked, and I follow behind her before reaching around her to open the door, only as she goes to step out of the supply closet, the deep rumble of my tone stops her.

"For what it's worth, my sweet angel. When I do decide to romance you, it won't be a misguided attempt, and you'll do a shitload more than just blush."

She sucks in a gasp, her cheeks flushing under my heated stare. "Go now," I prompt to get her moving again.

Chiara walks out before me, and as the door closes and my hand falls to her lower back, I can't help but notice a shift in the atmosphere within the room. The dancing has stopped, replaced by the wives gossiping between themselves and glancing around the room as though searching for something . . . or someone. And there's no doubt this is the result of my new *marriage* becoming public knowledge.

As I lead Chiara through the room and toward our table, those gazes land on her. Full of judgment, jealousy, and spite. Every single one of these women has shamelessly thrown themselves at me over the years in hopes of standing by my side at the head of this family, their husbands be damned.

I see the questions in their eyes, wondering why her? What's so special about this girl who appeared out of thin air? What does she have that they don't? And the answer to it all—everything. She is everything that they aren't, and that's exactly why I'm so drawn to her.

"Everyone is looking at us," Chiara says under her breath, clearly not comfortable with the speculation.

"Let them look, Angel," I tell her. "They're curious and confused why after all these years I've finally decided to take a wife, and on top of that, they're questioning why the usual steps weren't taken. Any wedding of mine should have been a grand event, a show of money, and tradition, and the fact that there wasn't is causing a stir. I'm sure you can understand that. But mostly, they're looking at you, and to that? I say let them feast on your beauty. Their jealousy and hatred will be their undoing."

"Jealousy?" she questions, her gaze lifting to mine. "Why would they be jealous?"

"Look at you, Angel. Look at the life that's been thrust upon you. The luxurious lifestyle and highest level of protection. Nobody can touch you, and as long as you are standing at my side, you stand at the top with me. These women have clawed the eyes out of weaker women just to take their place. They've each had to fight their way to where they are, but not you. This life was handed to you without question. They have a right to be jealous, but what they do with that is up to them, and how you respond will determine the kind of strength you possess."

Chiara cringes and glances back over her shoulder, taking in the huddle of women surrounding the bar. There's a nervousness in her eyes, a look I've never seen from her before today, and I realize that she would prefer to face my wrath than a bunch of spiteful women.

"Tell me about yourself," I say, more than ready to move this along and take her mind off the inevitable.

Chiara glances back at me, fixing a smile across her face, but I've come to realize it's fake. Her true smile, now that's where her beauty really shines. "I, umm . . . There's not much to tell," she says, seemingly caught off guard by my question.

We finally reach our table, and I pull her chair out before helping her sit, and the soft groan that rumbles through her lips tells me that she's sore from the thorough fucking I just gave her in the supply closet. But she asked for it. She begged me to fuck her, and I don't do anything halfway.

"Tell me what you feel is worth sharing," I say as I take my seat beside her, positioning myself in the best seat in the room that gives me a vantage point of the whole ballroom and is closest to the entrance of the secret underground tunnels that lead to a safe house.

"Okay, well, I was a foster kid. I was abandoned by my mother as a baby and dumped at an orphanage without any form of identification. I grew up in the system, bouncing from house to house until I was about fifteen when I finally found a bit of stability. The family I was with wasn't that great, but they treated me okay and were happy to let me do my own thing, as long as I kept my space clean, maintained my grades, and didn't get myself in trouble."

I nod, having known all of this from the information Sergiu found for me. "After that?"

She shrugs her shoulders, looking slightly uncomfortable. "Like I said, there's really not much to tell. I graduated high school and was accepted into college, and after a few months of working my ass off, I was able to afford a little apartment of my own while also paying my tuition, and since then, that's what my life has looked like. I work to eat and keep a roof over my head while I go to school . . . at least, I used to."

"Used to?" I question.

"I've been gone from my home for at least two weeks, and I can guarantee that my landlord would have already given me an eviction notice. He's an ass like that. As for school, I was one year from graduating when I was snatched off the side of the road, and I don't mean this in a snarky way or anything, but I seriously doubt that you're going to allow me the chance to finish that."

"No, I won't," I agree. "You no longer require a college degree."

Chiara nods and forces a tight smile. Disappointment flashes in her eyes, but there's also an understanding there that gives me just a fraction of hope that we can make this work between us. "I was going to be an architect," she tells me. "I've always loved it, which is why I'm so taken with your home. Whoever designed it has an incredible eye."

"I believe so too," I agree. "What about your personal life? Have you left anyone behind that I need to be concerned about?"

"Not really," she says, squirming in her seat. "With how often I worked, there really wasn't a lot of time for friends. As for a boyfriend. There was this one guy who I was with on and off for a few years, but we officially broke up a few months ago, and I haven't heard from him since. In hindsight, I probably should have ended it much sooner. He wasn't always so . . . nice to me, but I was afraid of having no one, so I stuck it out. Now that I look back, I see how much of a loser he was. I deserved much better."

"I'm glad you see your worth—" I pause, noticing the way she continues to squirm. "Is something the matter?"

"I'm sorry," she murmurs, leaning closer. "I'm trying to not make a scene, but I can feel you leaking out of me, and soon enough, it's going to smear on the back of my dress. Then there will be a whole new reason why everybody is looking at me."

A smirk settles across my lips, and I lean into her, taking her chin and lifting it just enough to meet her eyes. Feeling the stares of multiple people in the room, I lean just a little closer and brush my lips across her temple. "Go get yourself cleaned up, Angel. I'll be right here waiting for you when you get back."

CHAPTER 17

Chiara

Cum spreads between my thighs, and I clench everything south of the border as I scurry across the room, the desperation weighing down on me. Any second now, I'll feel Killian's cum at my ankles, but what truly has me concerned is just how long I was sitting down. There's a good chance the back of my silk gown is already destroyed, and if anyone were to see me like that . . . shit. I'll never live it down. How am I supposed to look like the type of woman who deserves to stand at Killian's side while looking as though I've just pissed myself?

Fuck me.

This isn't going well.

I rush across the luxurious room, my eyes glued to the little sign on the door indicating the ladies' room. Only another few steps.

It trickles lower, now at the inside of my knee.

I try to walk cautiously, not allowing my dress to get caught between my legs while scolding myself for being reckless enough to forgo underwear tonight. What the hell was I thinking? What a rookie error.

Fuck. Fuck. Fuck. Fuck. I'm so close, but yet so far. Just a few more steps, and I'll be good.

I try to avoid the eyes of all the women tracking me across the room, but as I feel the slimy trickle spreading so much further, my desperation turns into a sheer panic, and I hopscotch my ass the rest of the way to the bathroom.

Barreling through the door, I bunch up my gown, doing everything I can to keep the expensive silk fabric away from Killian's jizz massacre between my thighs while thanking the Hemsworth Gods that I'm all alone in here.

Hurrying into one of the stalls, I do my best to clean myself up, tearing off squares of toilet paper and trying to scoop up the slimy mess, but at this point, nothing is truly going to help apart from a nice warm shower.

Doing the best I can, I get myself fixed up before finally freeing myself from the small stall. Finding myself still alone, I go the extra mile to dampen some paper towels and give myself one final wipe before deeming my situation officially under control.

Taking a moment to myself, I turn on the tap and hold my fingers under the water while taking in my reflection. My hair is a little out of place, but considering just how thoroughly Killian fucked me in that supply closet, I've come out pretty well.

Speaking of Killian. I know he's the head of the DeLorenzo family and all that, but I wonder just how far his pull is. Do these people bow at his feet and obey his every command? Because some underwear really wouldn't go astray if he so happened to feel like ordering one of his men to go fetch me a pair. I highly doubt Killian's going to allow me to walk out those beautiful doors all by myself to go buy a pair of granny panties. He's starting to trust me, but certainly not that much. To be completely honest, I don't think I could run anyway. Even if he opened the doors as wide as they could go and told me I was free from this world, I'd stay right there by his side.

This strange world is my life now, and navigating it is going to be the most terrifying thing I'll ever do. Though, it's not like I'm really leaving much behind. Opening up to Killian like that—assuming I can call a speed-date run-through of my life *opening up*—caught me off guard. I was always proud of the life I was able to build for myself, no matter how shitty it was. I came from nothing and was well on my way to reaching for the stars, but I hadn't realized just how little I had until this world was staring me in the eyes.

These people live insane lives. It truly is the polar opposite of the world I was able to build for myself. They have everything I always dreamed of having, even the loyalty of a solid family who will always have your back no matter what. And me? I was lucky if I managed to stay in a foster home for more than a year at a time.

My past isn't something I usually like to talk about. I'm a here-and-now kind of girl, but there's something about Killian that has me willing to share every shitty era of my life. Shit, I even told him about my good-for-nothing ex, Derek. I've gone out of my way not to think about him over the past few months, and there I was, sitting across from the most powerful man on the planet, telling him about the asshole who treated me like nothing more than a convenient hole to fuck.

God, I wonder what Killian must think of me after that?

Realizing I've been in here just a moment too long, I turn off the water and grab a fresh paper towel to dry my hands. The last thing I need is Killian sending a search party in the form of Sergiu. Fuck, I don't even want to imagine what that asshole would try to do to me if he got me alone again. Hell, the bruises are only just starting to truly fade, and to be honest, I thought I'd gotten away with it without Killian noticing, but apparently, I'm not as clever as I thought.

The bathroom door opens, and I plaster a smile across my face as a few women saunter into the small space, doing my best to appear graceful and deserving of being the woman who stands at Killian's side.

When they don't make their way toward the stalls and gather behind me instead, I lift my head as a wave of nerves settles deep in my stomach. There are four of them, each one just as beautiful as the last, but I don't dare underestimate them. I know women . . . mostly. And this is the furthest from a friendly introduction to welcome me to the family. These bitches are looking for blood.

The words Killian uttered to me just moments ago flash through my head—*How you respond will determine the kind of strength you possess.*

They'd sounded so graceful coming out of his mouth, but now, just moments away from having that strength put to the test, it doesn't seem so motivating.

Fuck. It sounds downright terrifying.

These aren't the kind of women I'm used to dealing with in the bars I've worked at or the mean bitches from school who look down on you for not having a life worthy of their upper-class tastes. These women are on a whole new level, and I don't know if I'm ready for it.

The woman who stands closest holds my stare through the mirror, and I immediately recognize her as Sergiu's wife, but her name doesn't appear inside my head. Letting out a heavy breath, I turn to face her while doing what I can to hide my shaking hands. "Let's just get this over and done with so we can get back to the party," I say, not ready to be some pushover despite the fear rocketing through my chest.

"You don't belong here," she says.

An unladylike scoff tears from the back of my throat, and I instantly regret the laugh that booms in her face. "Are you serious right now?" I ask dumbfounded. "That's what you came in here to intimidate me with? That I don't belong? Wow. Are you trying to point out the obvious? I could have told you that."

"Oh my God," one of the other women says, arching her brow in disbelief. "She thinks she's better than us."

Fucking hell. This really isn't going to go well.

"I never said that," I throw back at her, fixing her with a stare that would have made my ex wet his pants, though somehow I doubt it would even make Killian flinch. "However, I'm not the one ganging up with her little friends trying to corner some woman in a bathroom, so take what you want from that."

The woman sneers at me, but Sergiu's wife takes the lead once again. "My husband has told me all about you, all about the whorehouse Killian took you from. You're nothing but a whore made to cater on the mattress of greater men. You're no wife, and soon enough, Killian will see that, and you'll be handed around like the common whore that you are. Forgotten and discarded."

"If that's so, why are you so pressed about it?" I challenge. "If I'm just some whore who'll be tossed aside when the next best thing comes along, why bother putting on this little show at all? It doesn't make sense. Unless you're threatened, of course."

"Threatened?" she scoffs in disgust. "Of you? I hardly think so."

"Right," I say with a devilish smirk that clearly grates on her nerves if her sneer is anything to judge by. "Well, here's the thing. Just because I don't believe I belong here, doesn't mean Killian agrees, and as long as he's willing to hold on to me as the woman who shares his bed and his name, then I'm willing to stick around. I'm not going anywhere, but what does it even matter to you? You have your own husband to worry about. My marriage to Killian has nothing to do with you."

"It has everything to do with me," she spits in a rage. "I haven't put in all these years, putting up with the wild abuse from my husband and loitering in Killian's shadow just for some tramp like you to come along and snatch it out from beneath me. The moment you give him an heir, my husband is one step further from taking that damn crown and I won't allow it to happen, no matter what I have to do."

My heart races, realizing this is much deeper than I could have imagined. There's a hierarchy here, and me stepping right into the middle of it means others who have done their time are pushed down the line, but that's not my problem. If she wanted to be at the head of the family and spend her days wearing a crown she didn't deserve, she should have married Killian instead. "Look, this really sounds like a *you* problem," I tell her, not knowing how she thinks I can possibly do anything about this. What Killian wants, I don't doubt he'll get, and I really don't think he gives a shit what this bitch thinks. "If Killian chooses to knock me up, that's our business, but I'll be sure to send you an invite to the baby shower."

She glares at me, and all I can do is smile and step around her before she has the chance to respond. "Anyway, this has been lovely. We should do it again sometime, but right now, I need to go see if my husband wants me to ride him again. He's got a very healthy appetite if you know what I mean." I take another step, turning my back on her before glancing back and catching her eye. "Word of advice, it would do you well to stop spending your time worrying about what my husband is doing and focus on satisfying the one you've got."

"What the hell is that supposed to mean?"

"It means that I've been here less than two weeks, and I already know what kind of man your husband is. But just know that when my husband goes to bed, it's me he's burying himself inside of. As for you, tell me. When your husband kisses you goodnight, how often do you taste another woman's pussy on his lips?"

I give her a salty smile before finally looking back toward the door and aiming for my escape when a loud screech comes from behind me. Before I even have the chance to react, a fist is knotted into the back of my hair, pulling me back with a violent tug.

I falter, struggling to keep myself on my feet when my head is shoved forward and barrels down into the porcelain sink. "THE FUCK DID YOU JUST SAY TO ME, BITCH?" she screams as the women around her gasp in shock.

Pain ricochets through my face, and as I scream, I feel blood trickling down my face. Her hold on me doesn't falter, and sheer panic pounds through my chest as my head spins, unable to catch myself or find traction to stop this insanity.

"LET HER GO, MONICA! FUCK!" Someone rushes out, only the grip on my hair is tightened, and I'm yanked back before being slammed down again. "KILLIAN IS GOING TO END YOU."

My lip splits against the porcelain as pain blasts through the side of my mouth, my teeth aching as I taste the familiar rust of blood in my mouth. My eyes roll in my head, disorientation quickly claiming me. The hold in my hair suddenly releases, and I drop heavily to the ground, my head smacking against the hard tiles. Before I can even cry out in agony, the sharply pointed toe of her designer heel rams into the side of my ribs.

I'm kicked up against the wall of the ladies' bathroom. Nowhere to run. Nowhere to hide. Something cracks as tears stream down my face, and hearing the sound of her stiletto heels against the tiles, I risk a glance just in time to see as she kneels down right in front of me. "You don't want to try me, bitch," she says. "Consider this your warning. Even think about showing your face again, and I will destroy you. You're a whore, and you're going to disappear like one."

One of the other women grabs her arm and starts dragging her away. "Come on, we have to go," she rushes out, dragging the bitch along. I don't dare take my eyes off her, watching every step as the four of them make their way out of the bathroom. I hold my breath until the door finally closes behind them, and when it does and I'm all alone, I let the fear and pain consume me until the dizziness finally claims me and my world turns to ashes.

CHAPTER 18

Killian

My fingers drum impatiently against the table, looking out at the dance floor as my cousins dance with their wives. Chiara has been gone for far too long, and my patience is wearing thin. I am trying to be respectful, trying to give her the time she needs to clean herself up, and no doubt have a moment of solitude. These family events can be daunting to an outsider. We're an intimidating bunch, and for most people, standing in the same room can be terrifying, but Chiara was doing well holding herself together. She has nothing to fear as my wife. Nobody will touch her.

Another minute ticks by, and my limits have been met. She will be punished for this. Nobody makes me wait, even women as dazzling as her.

My gaze swings back toward the ladies' room. She's too smart to try to escape me, not that any attempt would have been successful, so what the hell is she doing in there?

Frustration burns through me, and as I get to my feet, I press one hand into a tight fist, cracking my knuckles—a sign to every motherfucker in the room to keep out of my way.

I start to move through the room when Sergiu steps into my side. "What's going on?" he asks, his gaze shifting around the massive ballroom as if searching for a threat.

"Go back to your wife," I tell him, not pausing to even look his way. "This is between me and mine."

Sergiu immediately falters, falling back as I continue toward the ladies' room, not bothered by the hundred sets of eyes locked on my back. My jaw clenches as I consider what the fuck I'm supposed to say to her or what I'm even about to find, but as I continue, the ladies' room door opens.

A young woman runs out, perhaps one of my distant cousins' daughters whom I certainly haven't taken the time to get to know. Her eyes are wide and filled with horror, and as she stumbles through the door, she pauses and searches the room.

Her wide-open stare locks onto mine, and there's enough fear there to really get me moving.

Something's happened.

I run, my feet pounding against the marble tiles as the girl scrambles toward me in a blind panic. "It's . . . She . . . Killian, she needs—"

I don't hang around to hear what she has to say, bolting past the girl to the ladies' bathroom. My heart booms erratically in my chest, and for the first time in my life, I feel fear. My forearm slams against the door, swinging it open, and as I barrel inside, I pull to a hasty stop, finding Chiara in a pool of blood on the dirty ground.

She's not moving, and a fierce rage blasts through my chest.

"Chiara?" I rush out, throwing myself toward her and dropping to my knees as my gaze trails up and down her body, trying to figure out where the blood is coming from. My knees instantly soak in her blood, but all that matters is making sure she's still breathing.

Please, God. If you fucking exist, don't take her from me. I'm not ready for her to leave yet.

I cradle her face in my hands while gently stroking my thumbs across her cheeks. "Chiara, Angel. Please," I beg, her split lip and cheekbone only fueling my anger.

Her chest slowly rises and falls, and the relief that fills me is like nothing I've ever experienced, but when those gorgeous green eyes peel open and stare back at me, my whole fucking world comes into focus.

"Killi—" she tries to say my name but cuts herself off with a deep cringe, and I can only assume it's from the pain.

"Thank fuck, Angel," I breathe as my men barrel into the bathroom behind me. "Are you okay? Who? Tell me who did this?"

Chiara groans as tears begin filling her eyes, and I quickly realize that an interrogation on what happened in this fucking bathroom is going to have to wait. I need to get her out of here. Besides, I already have a good idea of what happened here tonight. However, in the name of keeping peace within the family, I wouldn't dare make such an accusation without the proof to go along with it.

"Home," she croaks out. "Take me home."

"Chiara," I warn, my patience wearing thin. "Who hurt you?"

"Please. Not here," she cries, almost seeming disappointed with herself. "Just take me home."

My brows furrow as I scan over her beautiful face, and even marred by cuts and bruises, she's still the most radiant creature I've ever laid eyes on. But it doesn't make sense why she would be disappointed right now. She should be thirsty for blood and ready to take revenge.

"Talk to me, Chiara. What's wrong?"

She visibly swallows as she reaches up and clutches my hand. "You told me how I respond will define the strength I possess. I failed, Killian. I'm not strong enough."

Something shatters inside me, and I realize I'm the cause of her brokenness.

I did this.

In the face of an enemy, she responded by showing her strength because of the words I said. Instead of calling for help or backing out peacefully, she stayed and faced this without a shred of training or preparation.

I've failed her. I marched her into this building and labeled her as my wife. I painted a target on her back without preparing her for what that truly means, so the cuts and bruises that linger on her skin, they're my burden to bear, and while I don't know how I'm supposed to fix that right now, I sure as fuck can ensure I fix everything else. "*Îmi pare atât de rău, iubirea mea,*" I whisper. "*E vina mea.*"

"Killian?" Sergiu murmurs, creeping in behind me.

"EVERYBODY OUT!" I roar, not wanting a single one of the assholes behind me to witness my wife in such a vulnerable state.

Chiara flinches at my tone, and on cue, the bathroom empties out, leaving just the two of us again. "You faced an enemy today, Chiara. While they may have taken you down, your strength will shine in the way you rise and hold your chin up high. You bear the name DeLorenzo and the weight that comes with it. You're my wife, and we do not fail. You will get back up, Angel. I will train you and see to it that nobody ever touches you again. You hear me? I will find who has done this to you, and when I do, you will spill their blood."

She presses her hand against the tiles in an attempt to push herself up, but she's too weak, and as she collapses, I catch her in my arms and scoop her into my chest. "It's going to be okay, Angel," I murmur as her tears quickly begin soaking the front of my suit jacket.

After standing with her still cradled to my chest, I make my way out of the bathroom. Sergiu pushes the door open from the opposite side, helping me with my exit. "What do you need?" he asks, his gaze lingering on the blood trickling down the side of Chiara's face.

"Call the doctor. I want him at my place in no less than fifteen minutes. She'll need a full examination. I need to know if anything is broken," I tell him. "Then I want every senior member in my formal dining room within the hour. One of your wives is responsible for this, and I'm going to find out who."

His eyes widen. "The wives?" he questions, his gaze shooting toward Chiara. "Is that what she said? She's been here two minutes, and you're going to allow her to make accusations like that? Don't you see what she's doing to this family? She is going to be your downfall, cousin. Open your eyes."

I clench my jaw, and if my arms weren't full with my wife, I would have already had the bastard against the wall. I've already warned him about disrespecting Chiara, and sooner or later, I'm going to break. "She said no such thing. I am the one making the accusation, *cousin*," I spit the word back at him like the insult that it is. "Chiara is refusing to talk. However, in the time she was in this bathroom, only five women walked in and came out, and four of those women were the wives of my most senior members, all of whom have been glaring at my wife since the moment she walked in here on my arm. So, please, tell me what I am supposed to assume."

Sergiu doesn't respond, and I watch as the color drains from his face, coming to the conclusion that I've already made—someone will die for this, and when they do, unrest is bound to follow.

A civil war is on the horizon, and he has a choice to make. Will he value his loyalty, or will I be signing his death certificate?

I don't bother to wait for his response, knowing that he will see to it that everything gets done. Instead, I focus my attention on Chiara while ignoring the gasps that come from around the room. The main doors open for me as my security team automatically falls in around us, scanning our surroundings for a threat. Within two minutes, I have Chiara in the back of my SUV with her head resting in my lap and her hand clutched in mine.

Blood soaks into her gold hair, and I have to assume that's where the majority of the blood is coming from. As my driver flies through the streets, I do what I can to get control of the bleeding. Now in the safety of my car, Chiara's tears begin to dry as my head of security sits up front, scrambling through the center console before handing me a few painkillers and a bottle of water.

"I need you to take these, Angel," I tell her. "They won't knock you out, but it'll help with the pain."

She nods and reluctantly allows me to pull her up. She opens her mouth, and I place the pill on her tongue before lifting the water to help her drink. She takes a small sip and cringes with the pain of her split lip.

Satisfied that she'll be able to relax, I pull her back into me, holding her in my arms the whole way home. We pull up just as the doctor storms down the driveway, and by the time I'm carrying Chiara through the door, he's right there on my heels getting a rundown by my head of security.

I barrel through the door, ignoring Krista's horrified gasp as she takes in my bleeding wife in my arms. I take her straight up to her room with both the doctor and Krista following behind me. Krista races ahead to open the door, and the moment I have Chiara back on her feet, I start tearing off the fragile material of her gown, desperate to see the damage beneath.

Krista gets to work releasing all the pins from Chiara's hair, and the second her long blonde hair is freed, Krista hurries off into Chiara's closet, scrambling around for some underwear. I help her dress into a soft tank and a pair of sleep shorts before lifting her into bed.

The doctor immediately steps in and starts looking over her injuries when Krista steps up to the head of Chiara's bed to wipe the blood from her face.

All I can do is watch as the doctor stitches her up, and with every drop of blood that runs from her body, the blazing anger within me intensifies.

How could I let this happen?

I saw the way the wives watched her, saw the disdain and ugliness within their horrid stares, and yet I foolishly believed they wouldn't touch her, especially when I was so close. I will find out what happened in that bathroom if it's the last thing I do, and when I do, justice will be served.

It takes nearly forty minutes for the doctor to finish up with her, and by the time he's done, I step into Krista's side and take the damp washcloth from her. "Thank you," I tell her. "I'll take it from here."

"Of course," she says, bowing her head. "Is there anything you need? I'm assuming there will be a meeting about this?"

"There will be, but nothing is required of you. You may retire for the night. However, tomorrow I'd like you to watch over Chiara. Make sure she is comfortable and tended to."

"Sure thing," she says before offering me a sad smile.

Krista leaves, and I step around Chiara's bed, watching as she tracks my every movement. I take the seat beside her bed that the doctor just vacated and continue cleaning the blood stains off her body. We remain in silence for a heavy moment, unanswered questions lingering in the air between us, heavy emotions, confusion, and tension thickening with every passing second.

"The senior members of my family are due to arrive any moment," I tell her, breaking the silence and giving us a reprieve from the tension within the room. "I saw their wives enter the bathroom, Angel. I know one of them, or all of them, are responsible for this. Time for games is over. I need to know which one of them put their hands on you."

Fear flashes in her eyes, and she looks away from me, a heavy sob tearing from the back of her throat. "What are you going to do when you find out?"

"That has not yet been decided."

"But she will be hurt in some way, right?"

"Yes," I say, already knowing where she's going with this. "An eye for an eye, Chiara. That is how we handle betrayal in this world. I am the head of this family, and as my wife, your protection is my top priority. Having another member of my family put their hands on you is a despicable betrayal of loyalty, and I have no choice but to see them punished."

She nods, her face turning white. "You're going to kill her," she states in horror. "I don't want that. I won't be responsible for the death of another human being, no matter how shitty they are. I can't do it. I'm sorry, but I can't. I won't give you a name."

"Whether you give me her name or not, I will discover who did this. My family knows the price of their betrayal. So, when they walked into that bathroom, they knew what they were doing, and they knew the price they would have to pay if anything were to happen to you."

SHERIDAN ANNE

"I'm sorry, Killian," she murmurs. "Punish me if you must, but I can't give you a name."

I nod, not prepared to force her to betray her morals like that, especially if she feels she will bear the burden of how I serve justice if she were to give up a name. If she were anyone else, I would probably force it out of her, but not with Chiara. She's shown a great deal of respect and loyalty by standing at my side. She's trying to find her place here, and now that she's starting to trust me, I won't break that.

Disappointed, I press my lips into a firm line and lean into her before dropping a soft kiss to her cheek. "I won't punish you for doing what you feel is right," I tell her before meeting her green stare. "But just know that with or without your cooperation, I will find out the truth."

Chiara nods, sadness brimming in her eyes. "I know."

Getting up, I start making my way to the door when her soft tone cuts through the room. "Killian," she murmurs, pausing a second as I turn back to meet her gaze, only the weariness in her stare has my brows furrowing. "I know it's a lot to ask, but do you think there's any chance you could just . . . let it go? I just want to heal and forget this ever happened."

Trying to soften the blow, I offer a small smile. "No, Chiara. I cannot do that. However, if you wish to forget about it, I will keep my dealings private. You will not need to know what happens from here," I tell her, watching as she nods with gratitude. "Now get some rest. I will check on you in the morning."

She doesn't respond, just watches me as I turn around and walk out of her room. I pull the door closed behind me, hoping that can offer her some peace to sleep. From the hallway, I hear demanding voices downstairs, and I make my way to meet with the senior members of my family.

Striding into the formal dining room, I find Sergiu and three of my other cousins—Phillip, Adrian, and Cristian—seated around the table in heated conversation, the blame already flying between them. Not bothering with niceties, I simply stride to the head of the table and brace my fists against the hard wood. "One of your wives betrayed me, and they will pay the ultimate price."

"This is absurd," Phillip roars, throwing himself to his feet. "You take the word of some woman you just met over our family. These are the mothers of our children, the very women who bore the future generation of our family."

"I don't care if they gave birth to the next fucking Pope. One of them is guilty, and I will get to the bottom of this no matter what."

Sergiu slams his fist against the table. "What is that supposed to mean? You intend to interrogate my wife with your brutal tactics? She's not some criminal mastermind like the men you're used to dealing with. You know Monica would never lay a hand on your woman."

Cristian scoffs at Sergiu. "Your wife is a loose cannon. If anything, she's the one responsible for this. Everyone knows that woman is a snake in sheep's clothing."

Sergiu flies to his feet, his gun in his hand. "What did you say about my wife?"

I roll my eyes at Sergiu's ridiculous display. "You look like a fool pretending you don't know what type of woman you take to bed each night. Put the gun down, cousin."

Adrian lets out a heavy sigh, not affected in the least considering his wife has crippling social anxiety and can't even look someone new in the eyes. He's got nothing to worry about. She wouldn't hurt a fly, but having said that, if it comes down to questioning the wives, she'll be the one to break first. "Has anybody even bothered to ask them what happened? There was another girl in the bathroom, was there not? How do we know it wasn't her?"

"It wasn't," I say, remembering the exact moment the young woman barreled out of the ladies' room. "I saw the look in her eyes when she ran out of there. She was terrified. She has nothing to do with this."

"Well, it sure as hell wasn't Evie," Cristian says. "She knows better than to get involved in something like that. She'd never betray you."

"All four of them betrayed me," I roar. "The fact that not one of them came to me to let me know that my wife was passed out bleeding on the bathroom floor tells me more than I need to know. They're all guilty, and they will all be punished."

"Why does this matter?" Phillip demands. "So what if our women pushed your boundaries? If this was one of our daughters bringing home a man, challenging him would be expected. So why is it so terrible that our wives wished to test the woman you claim will stand at the head of our family with you? They have a right to know if she can hack it or if she will bend under the pressure. We all do, and clearly, she failed their test."

I clench my jaw, my hands balling into fists, feeling my patience begin to snap.

"Do you even know anything about this girl?" he continues. "Or is she in your head because she has a golden pussy? You just met her and are already willing to risk the peace within our family. For fuck's sake, Killian. You married her without consulting the rest of your family."

Without a second of warning, my hand snaps behind my back, curling around the cool handle of my gun, and like a boom of thunder during a fierce storm, the gunshot rings out through my formal dining room. The bullet pierces straight through Phillip's skull, and he falls behind the table as though he never existed.

The room falls into a heavy silence as I stare at the place where my cousin once stood. "Does anybody else dare question my marriage or disrespect my wife?" I ask, my ferocious stare slowly swiveling to meet Sergiu's. After all, he's disrespected Chiara on more than one occasion.

"No, Killian. You are right. We have not been welcoming enough to your new bride," Sergiu says, kissing my ass. "We will do better."

"See to it that you do," I tell him before addressing the remaining senior members of my family. "I will be speaking to your wives, so I suggest you each ensure that they are readily available when I come looking, and if even one of them suddenly goes missing, I will automatically assume their guilt and they'll be buried in a shallow grave beside Phillip. Am I understood?"

"Yes, Killian," Cristian and Adrian say in unison before getting to their feet. And with that, I walk out of the formal dining room, more determined than ever to find out which of my cousins' wives will be next to go.

CHAPTER 19

Chiara

"**Y**ou wanna get out of here, Lara?" my boss asks with a ridiculous smirk across his face, one that I've become all too accustomed to over the past few years working in his run-down bar.

He's called me Lara since the day I started, and after telling him a billion times that my name is Chiara, it eventually became a running joke. Since then, the name has stuck.

"I thought you needed me to close," I ask, positive I was on the late shift tonight.

"Nah, it's all good. Give yourself an early night," he says. "It's quiet. I'm gonna close up early."

"You sure?"

"Positive. Finish up what you're doing and get out of here," he says, reaching *for a discarded glass on the bar. "Hell, maybe even enjoy your weekend for a change. Fuck knows you need it."*

I roll my eyes, but I can't help feeling grateful. I'm behind on three assessments, and while an extra few hours isn't going to help that much, it means I can get to bed earlier, have a decent night's sleep, and spend all weekend trying to smash them out.

I'm so close. Only one more year of college and I'll be free. I can get a proper job with decent pay and maybe even save some cash for a better life, but I can't slip yet. Twelve more months until everything changes. I can practically feel the optimism burning inside of me.

After closing out my register and grabbing my bag from under the bar, I take off. It's a little after ten, and I can't help but smile to myself as I make my way down the street. I never get to leave this early. Don't get me wrong, I love my job and the tips it brings in, and not having the extra tips from a busy night tonight is going to suck, but getting to leave early for a change is too good of an opportunity to skip out on. I'm usually the first to raise my hand for a close shift. The other girls prefer getting out early so they can have a life, but unfortunately, I don't have one of those, so I don't mind the late shift. I usually get off work at one in the morning, but most of the customers are gone by eleven, so I spend two hours with my face shoved in textbooks while filling the occasional beer. It's perfect for me.

It's a short walk, and on a good night, I'm usually home in eight minutes. When the bar has been crazy busy, and I've been run off my feet, crawling home can then take up to thirteen minutes, but tonight, I'm flying.

My attention is locked on my phone, scrolling through anything I've missed on social media over the past few hours, and surprise, surprise, there's not a lot to hold my focus.

My gaze shifts to the busy road, and I take in one of the bars that's a little closer to the college campus. This bar is always packed, and while I feel for the girls working the bar, I can't help but feel a little jealous. Their tips must be insane.

A scowl stretches across my face, and as I turn the corner, I do what I can to put it out of my mind. I'm lucky to have my job. While the tips aren't incredible, they're still considered good, and that's more than I could ask for.

As I get closer to my shitty little apartment, I dig through my bag for my keys, passing under the one streetlight that's been out since before I even moved here. Everything darkens as shadows stretch out across the road, and I can't help but notice the random guy leaning up against the neighboring apartment complex.

I meet his eye for a moment, hoping like fuck this guy doesn't intend to try something, but when he looks away, seeming bored and disinterested, I let out a soft sigh of relief.

Continuing on my way, I keep searching for my keys, feeling around every crevice of my bag, when I hear a scuffle behind me. My brows furrow, and I whip around to find the man launching toward me. My eyes widen in horror, and I suck in a deep breath, preparing to scream, but before I can make a single sound, he clamps one hand over my mouth as his other arm locks around me, keeping my arms pinned to my side.

My heart races as fear pounds heavily through my veins, and I do what I can to fight back, scratching the asshole's arms as I desperately try to fight for my freedom. Fear-filled tears spring from my eyes when he starts dragging me backward.
"Scream and I'll fucking kill you right here, you little bitch."

What the fuck?
What the hell does he want with me?
My attempts to fight are useless as his arm tightens like a boa constrictor around me, threatening to squeeze the life out of me. I can barely move or breathe

when a blacked-out van screeches to a stop on the sidewalk. "Hurry up," the asshole seethes as the back sliding door tears open, revealing another three men inside.

No. No. No. This can't be happening.

I'm dragged toward the van as my panic begins to overwhelm me. He shoves me toward the door, and I kick my foot up against the side of the van, refusing with every last bit of strength I possess, but it's not nearly enough as he pulls me back just out of reach of the van and tries again, only this time he throws me around like a ragdoll.

The men inside hastily reach for me, their fingers digging into my skin as I cry out in agony. They work together with the man on the street to get me inside the van, and before I know it, I'm thrown down on the hard ground.

"Go. Go. Go," someone yells out as I scramble to sit up and find my bearings, only as I do, I come face-to-face with the man from the street. His eyes are impossibly dark, filled with pure evil, and as he grins at me, my stomach coils.

A hand clamps over my mouth, and my eyes spring open to find myself in the darkness of my bedroom in Killian's home. I'm covered in sweat, my heart racing as consciousness brings the agony of my body to the forefront of my mind.

Something weighs down on the bed beside me as I try to suck in a breath, but it's almost impossible with the hand clamped over my mouth. I try to make out the person sitting on my bed, but it's too dark to make out any features, though judging by the size of the hand and the heavy weight on the bed, it's a man, and considering the scent of his cologne, it's not Killian.

"Even try to scream, and I will make your life a fucking misery," the familiar chilling tone rumbles through my room. "Do you understand me?"

Sergiu.

Fuck.

Tears fill my eyes, and I can't work out if it's fear from having him in my room or the panic of having to relive the night that asshole snatched me off the side of the street—the same nightmare which haunts me every time I close my eyes.

Trying to make out Sergiu's stare through the darkness, I nod while trying to figure out what the hell he wants. I kept his dirty little secret. I didn't tell a soul about what he did, so why is he here? If he was planning on fucking me, he wouldn't have bothered to warn me about my silence.

No, this asshole is here to talk. But why?

The weight of his hand pressing down on my split lip aches, and I immediately taste the blood in my mouth, but I do what I can to ignore the pain, determined to save my strength in case I need it.

My eyes finally adjust to the darkness, and I can just make out the too-sharp features of his face when he hesitantly lifts his hand off my mouth. I suck in a deep breath. "I don't like you," he states as though it was a secret.

"The feeling is mutual."

Fury flashes in his deadly stare, and without warning, I'm torn from my bed, a tight hand locking around my throat as I'm thrown against the wall. Sergiu leans into me, and I smell the stench of his hot breath against my skin.

"Foolish girl," he spits, keeping his tone low as my whole body violently shakes. "If you think being Killian's little pet is enough to keep you protected, you are sorely mistaken."

His other hand jabs against my ribs, right where his wife kicked me with her ridiculous designer heels, and I whimper under the pain, but I won't dare succumb to this asshole. His wife has already stolen my dignity, and after his last visit to my bedroom, I won't allow him to get the best of me again. "I am not mistaken. I have no illusion of what you could do to me. However, it seems you're the only foolish one here tonight," I say while struggling to take a deep breath. "It is clear your loyalty is to yourself, and if you ask me, as Killian's second-in-command, that's the deepest betrayal one could possibly commit in this world. But ask yourself, where do his loyalties lie? If he were to discover what you did here in this room last week or if I accidentally slipped up and gave the name of the woman who put her hands on me tonight, what would he do? Would he have your back, or mine?"

"You don't know what you're talking about," he spits.

I arch a brow and hold his ferocious stare. "Don't I?"

"You even think about running that mouth of yours—"

"You'll what?" I challenge. "If I run my mouth and tell him everything you and your bitch of a wife have done to me, you'll both be dead before you could even think about laying another hand on me. Time to face the facts, Sergiu. You've put yourself in a position where your fate now lies in the palm of my hands, and the more you threaten me, the more inclined I am to . . . slip."

Sergiu clenches his jaw, and fury flashes in his eyes. Without warning, he rears back, and in a flash, his hand slaps hard across my face. I cry out in shock as my cheek burns from the hit. "This is not a war you want to start, girl," he spits.

"Careful now," I warn. "You're threatening Killian's *wife*."

His hand clenches harder around my throat, completely cutting off my airway, but I don't falter as I hold his putrid stare. My lungs begin to scream for oxygen, and just as I start to see dark spots dancing in my vision, he releases me. I drop heavily to the ground, gasping for air.

Tears fill my eyes, and I watch as Sergiu turns on his heel and stalks out of my room, my heart racing with every step he takes. In a flash, he's gone, and my body finally relaxes.

Holy fuck. That was stupid.

What was I thinking challenging him like that? If I allowed him to believe he could continue walking all over me, he would have never seen me as a threat. He would have believed that I was too afraid to ever open my mouth, but now . . .

I openly just threatened his and his wife's existence, and what's worse, I based it all on the hope that Killian would have my back—a man that I haven't even known for two weeks—over the man who stands as his second-in-command. He grew up with Sergiu. The man is his own flesh and blood.

What the fuck was I thinking?

Grabbing the edge of my bed, I haul myself back to my feet and drop my ass onto the mattress when a soft knock sounds at my door. My back stiffens, and I desperately search the bedside table for something I can use as a weapon when the door opens and Killian strides in. "Chiara?" he asks, hovering by the door. "Everything okay? I thought I heard something in here."

This is my chance. I can tell him everything that just went down and both Sergiu and Monica will be names I'll never have to think of again, and yet, I can't bring myself to open my mouth. If I talk, two people's lives are on the line, and I don't know if I can stomach that burden.

Feeling the weight of this decision resting on my shoulders, I force a small smile across my face, hating the concern in his dark eyes. "Yeah, I'm fine," I tell him. "Bad dream."

Killian nods and strides further into my room before plucking the glass of water off my bedside table. He hands it to me before dropping down in front of me, his warm hands resting on my thighs. "Have some water, Angel. It will help."

Not wanting to disappoint him, I take small sips until half the glass is gone before handing it back to him. He puts the glass back where it was, right on top of the small circle of condensation the glass had already begun to form. Only he doesn't leave, he remains right there in front of me, his deep eyes locked onto mine. "Was it about your time at the auction house?"

My brows furrow and he goes on to clarify. "Your dream."

"Oh, umm . . . no. Well, kind of. It was about the night I was snatched off the street. I tend to dream about that night a lot, but in hindsight, the time at the auction house was worse. If anything, you'd think those were the memories that would play on repeat every night."

"Not necessarily. The night you were taken was the night

everything changed. Your mind didn't know it needed to be on alert, so the adrenaline and fear would have been a shock to your system. By the time you made it to the auction house, you were already aware of your surroundings, so you may have felt that same fear and adrenaline, but you were already in survival mode. While you remember those things, your unconscious mind is working overtime to block it out."

I nod and lift my gaze to meet his. "You really think that's true?"

"I have no reason to doubt it," he tells me. "I have been through many unforgiving circumstances, and if the only scars you bear are those on your unconscious mind, then I consider you lucky."

I swallow hard and really look at him, seeing the depth within his eyes. "Here I am whining about a bad dream to a man who has no doubt suffered through so much worse."

Killian reaches up and cups the side of my face, and I instinctively lean into him. "Everybody's trauma is different," he murmurs. "It's what sets us apart from one another, and what happened at the gala tonight is the first of many stepping stones that will pave your way to greatness. When you survive the unthinkable, others begin to fear the strength you possess, and that strength is the greatest power you will ever know."

I shake my head. "I don't think I'm capable of that kind of strength."

"Don't doubt yourself, Angel. You are. I've seen it, and one day, you will see it too."

Killian stands and inches back to the door before turning back and meeting my stare. "Get some rest, Chiara. You will feel better in the morning."

I nod, and with that, Killian slips out of my room, leaving me to contemplate his words. *When you survive the unthinkable, others begin to fear the strength you possess, and that strength is the greatest power you will ever know.* I'm not sure about the power part, but I sure as hell have survived the unthinkable. I survived a human trafficking ring. I survived Sergiu, and now his wife, and despite all of that, I remain right here, ready to earn my position at Killian's side.

I'm not running, and I sure as hell don't want to hide. Perhaps this is the strength Killian was speaking of. Either way, I have shown that I'm not some problem that can be swept under the rug. I'm here to stay, and if Sergiu and Monica have a problem with it, then they better prepare themselves, because I'm not going down without a fight.

I intend to rise up and be the woman Killian believes I can be, and as for Monica, that's the last time she'll ever put her hands on me. Next time—and I don't doubt there will be a next time—I'll be ready.

CHAPTER 20

Chiara

A subtle knock sounds at my door, and I peel my eyes open to find my room flooded with daylight. Pain throbs behind my eyes, and I instantly scrunch my face.

"Goddamn," I groan.

It's way too early to be awake.

"Chiara, honey?" I hear Krista at the door as she peeks inside. "I was just coming to check on you. How are you feeling?"

"Like I've barely even closed my eyes," I murmur into my pillow. "What's the time?"

Krista laughs to herself. "Almost midday," she says. "You've slept almost twelve hours."

My brows furrow as I sit up straight in bed, my wide eyes locking onto Krista's. "No, that couldn't be right," I mutter, rubbing my tired eyes and instantly regretting it as I pull at my stitches. "Ow. Shit."

I gently press against the stitches, making sure I haven't popped any as Krista carries in a tray of bacon, eggs, and orange juice. My mouth is so dry that the glass of OJ is practically calling to me. I don't think I've ever been so thirsty in my life. "How could it almost be midday?" I ask her as I help make space on the small bedside table, moving the glass of water Killian offered me last night. Only I pause, staring at the water as though it could answer all of life's big questions. "Holy shit. He drugged me again."

Krista cringes as though knowing exactly what I'm talking about. "Only a little," she admits. "He asked me to put a mild sedative in your water, just something to help you get a good sleep but not enough to knock you out. He was being thoughtful."

"Thoughtful," I scoff. "More like insane."

"You were hurting," Krista continues. "Believe me, the sedative was a kindness. I don't know if you've ever been beaten black and blue before last night, but trying to sleep when your face is aching like that isn't fun. He's trying to take care of you in the best way he knows how."

I scrunch my face and try to see where she's coming from. I suppose she has a point. He could have completely knocked me out like he did on the drive here after the auction house, but he didn't. He's learning my boundaries, and if he's able to put in that kind of effort, then I suppose I can put aside my hang-ups and be grateful for his kind gesture. After all, he could have left me to suffer through the pain. Hell, he could have left me bleeding on the bathroom floor, but he didn't. He scooped me up as though I was the most important thing to him and raced me to get help, and honestly, I don't think a man like that just comes around every day.

Shit. I'm getting way too deep here.

"Here," Krista says, handing me some painkillers. "You're going to need these."

Grateful that she didn't feel the need to linger on Killian being a respectable man with great intentions, I put the glass of water aside and replace it with the orange juice. "This is safe to drink, right?" I ask her in a teasing tone.

Krista rolls her eyes but can't help the laugh that bubbles up her throat. "Yes, it's fine," she says. "Now hurry up and eat your breakfast before it gets cold. I bet you're starving. Those galas wouldn't know how to serve a decent-sized meal if it smacked them right in the face."

I snort a laugh, recalling the tiny meal I was served last night, and honestly, it looked too fancy for me. I couldn't even tell what it was.

As if on cue, my stomach growls, and I don't hesitate to dig into my breakfast. My first bite is a learning curve, and my split lip screams with agony. After cursing myself for being too eager with my meal, I take smaller bites.

Krista hangs out as I eat, making her way around my room, opening my curtains, and making sure I'm actually eating. As she moves from one end of the room to the next, she tells me all about her life.

She helps me out of bed, and the movement reminds me just how brutal Monica's kick to my ribs was. I'm grateful when Krista offers me her hand and leads me into the bathroom. She helps me pull my top over my head, and I do my best not to let the pain show. My ribs aren't broken, but damn, they might as well be with how bad they hurt. The doctor said something about deep bruising last night, but to be completely honest, I was fading in and out. The words that were tumbling out of his mouth sure as hell weren't registering in my head. Hell, I worked hard to zone out a lot of the shit that happened last night . . . until Sergiu decided my closed door was an open invitation for him.

What a fucking asshole.

I have no idea how I'm supposed to play that card, but what I do know is that I need to keep my eyes wide open. I might feel as though I have the upper hand here, but truth be told, I'm fighting a war I know nothing about, and right now, all I am to Sergiu is a barricade that stands directly in the path of what he wants.

Krista helps me into the shower, and after making sure I'm not about to slip and hurt myself further, she leaves me be, and I take my time to wash the dried blood out of my hair. Killian and Krista gave it a good try last night, but there's nothing quite like a proper shower to make you feel clean.

I take my time to scrub the scum off my body, and then just because I spent a good portion of my night laying on the bathroom floor, I scrub myself again. When I finally feel clean and my body has relaxed under the warm water, I turn off the taps and reach for my towel before noticing the clean underwear and silk robe that's been placed just inside the bathroom door.

A small smile stretches across my face. I barely know Krista, but she cares for me in a way I've never been cared for before, and while I know she's just doing her job and following orders, she always goes the extra mile.

After getting myself dressed, I dry my hair and spend a few moments rubbing moisturizer into my sore skin while doing everything I can to avoid my reflection in the mirror. It's not pretty. The bruises are dark and unforgiving, and the stitches just make everything look worse. The less I look at them, the more I'm able to pretend they don't exist—until I yawn or move in the wrong way, then it all comes crashing back.

Once the painkillers have started to do their thing, and my headache dulls, I venture downstairs to find Krista putting the finishing touches on what looks to be Killian's lunch. "Is that for Killian?" I ask, eyeing the meal and wondering just how much of it I can steal. Despite just having breakfast, I could still eat.

"Sure is," she says, eyeing me suspiciously. "He's due to be back any minute. I was going to leave it in his office for him."

I lift my gaze to Krista's as a sheepish smile pulls at my lips. "Would you mind if I took it in for him?"

She grins back at me as if some kind of secret just passed between us, but honestly, I have no idea what. "I wouldn't mind at all," she murmurs, trying to smother her smile.

Wanting to escape before she tries to find meaning in this, I grab a knife and fork and scoop up the plate, all while Krista watches my every move. Taking off, I make my way through the massive estate, weaving through hallways until I finally come to Killian's office. It's huge. I've walked past here before, stopping by the door to peer in, but I never had the nerve to go inside. Things seem different now. It's as though something has shifted between us, and I no longer fear him as I should.

Stepping inside, my gaze shifts around the luxurious office, taking in the big mahogany desk and the matching bookshelf. There's a private bar area with a few armchairs that give off gentlemen's club vibes and a private storage room that I can only assume holds secrets that someone like me should never be privy to.

Making my way to his desk, I put his lunch down, making sure it's perfectly centered, but I can't help but notice there's nothing personal in here. In fact, there's nothing personal in the whole estate. No photos, certificates, or little knickknacks on the shelves. It's as though Killian's home could belong to anyone. He could just walk out, and a new owner could move right in without having to change a single thing. It's impersonal, a stark contrast to the small apartment I've lived in for the past few years. I went out of my way to decorate each space with my personal taste—not that I could afford much, but I tried wherever I could.

Curiosity gets the best of me, and I search through his office for any sign that he's human or that he has a single sentimental bone in his body. I start with the desk drawers, but after seeing a manila folder with my name on it, I decide that perhaps the desk drawers of a mafia boss really aren't somewhere I should be peeking into.

Am I surprised? No. I expected it. But seeing it in the flesh has something clenching within me, and it's not exactly a comforting feeling.

Moving around his office, I make my way over to the massive shelf. He has meetings in here all the time. So surely what he has on display are things he won't mind curious eyes skimming over. Right?

Shit. Maybe I should just leave.

Killian has been so patient with me. He's kind and allows himself to be somewhat vulnerable with me, but I don't know how he would feel about me snooping through his personal space—not that there's anything personal in here. It's a breach of privacy, and I'm sure if the tables were turned, I wouldn't be so welcoming of it either.

Damn. Besides, it's not like he's going out of his way to mask his life from me. I'm sure he would answer any questions I might have with probably more details than my mind can handle. He keeps warning me that I should fear him, that he's not a good man, and while I'm perfectly happy in my little bubble of delusion, a part of me wants to know the extent of it. What have I really got myself involved in here?

Deciding it's probably best to scram, I turn on my heel and hightail it out of Killian's office, but something on the shelf brings me to a stop.

My brows furrow, and I inch closer, not really sure what I'm seeing. It looks like a little tube of lipstick, but it's so out of place in this terrifying space of Killian's home. Why the hell would he have lipstick in here?

My brows furrow, and I reach for it, finding it abnormally heavy. As I scan over the little black tube, I realize there's something more to this than meets the eye. I go to open it when I realize it's not lipstick at all. There are two little buttons and a circle at the top, and when my ridiculous need to touch everything pops up and rears its ugly head, I press down on the button.

A loud zapping sound cuts through the room, and my eyes widen in horror as I instinctively drop the little lipstick tube.

It clatters to the marble tiles, and I follow it the whole way down, my heart racing.

Holy shit. It's a Taser.

A moment passes where I simply stand and stare at it, not knowing what to do, but in a flash of pure insanity, I scramble for it, scooping it back into the palm of my hand and capping the lid back on. I can guarantee that Killian probably wouldn't be comfortable with me having any sort of weapon. At least, I don't think he would, but the idea of having something to fend off Monica or Sergiu if they came looking for me again is too good of an opportunity to pass up.

Taking the little lipstick Taser with me, I slip out of Killian's office and hastily make my way back up to my room. As the door swings shut, I promptly whip out my new weapon in a move that could rival anything you'd see in a James Bond movie, flipping the lid and hitting that little button like a fucking demoness intent on causing havoc.

A swell of confidence booms through my chest. I won't exactly be unstoppable with this thing, but I'll sure as hell be able to protect myself just long enough to make an escape.

Not knowing how long the battery will last, I make my way over to my bed and drop my ass to the edge. A wide grin stretches across my lips as I imagine the very moment I'll Taser Sergiu right in the balls. Opening my bedside drawer to drop the little Taser in, I pause in confusion.

"What the fuck?" I murmur, opening it wider and peering in.

It looks like a "Dildos R Us" superstore in here.

Every shape, size, and color stares back at me. Little guys for those casual late nights right up to the monster cocks that literally look as though they were designed straight from some alien life form.

Six inches. Eight. Ten.

Holy fuck! Is that twelve? There's no way that would physically fit inside a woman, not without it puncturing a lung.

Curiosity gets the best of me, and I can't help but pull them all out and line them up across my bedroom floor like some kind of dick shrine, but I can't decide if I should arrange them by size or color. I could turn this room into a whole dick rainbow.

God, just imagine all the fun I could have in here, though I don't know what I'm expected to do with all of these. I only have a handful of holes. Just one would have sufficed. Or two. Maybe three. A girl needs a little variety in her life.

BUT SEVENTEEN? This is just ridiculous. Though there's no denying that a few of them are sparking just a little curiosity. I can't say I've ever fucked an alien before, but looking at the massive cock with all the angles, curves, and a base thicker than my fist, it makes me wonder what kind of rollercoaster it could take me on.

Once all the dildos are spread out in my room, I notice the array of vibrators that also fill the drawer, and my mind goes into overdrive. Did Killian put all of these in here or did he have Krista do it for him?

Oh God, I hope not.

Did she personally pick out the massive alien cock?

I can imagine her scanning over it and thinking to herself, *Yes, this is the perfect fit for Chiara.*

Holy shit. I'll never be able to look her in the eye again. What kind of sexual deviant does she think I am? I mean, fuck. I know I allowed Killian to take me any way he wanted, but I assumed that was information that only the both of us were privy to. Unless the walls aren't quite as soundproof as I thought they were. Is the whole estate hearing me when he gets me off?

My cheeks burn with humiliation when a soft knock sounds at my door and it's pushed open. Horror rocks through me, realizing that whoever's about to walk through that door is about to get a shitload more than they bargained for, but it's far too late to try and save myself now.

Killian steps into my room, and I watch in fascination as his usually hard features morph into surprise. His sharp gaze sweeps the room, and he's silent for a moment before his eyes meet mine. "Did you arrange them by color?"

"Seventeen, Killian," I state, ignoring his question as I grab hold of the monster alien cock and hold it up like a trophy. "There are seventeen rubber cocks in my drawer."

"I think you'll find they're silicone," he tells me.

I give him a blank stare as he hovers by the door, his gaze sailing over the darkening bruises on my face. "I don't care if they're hand carved from stone, why are there so many of them?"

Killian arches a brow. "Oh? Forgive me if I have offended. That was not my intention. I had assumed you were not opposed to using toys. I had planned on using every one of them on you."

My brows shoot up, looking at the monster cock in horror. "Even this one?"

"Even that one," Killian nods, his dark eyes somehow holding me captive.

"I . . . I'm not opposed to it, and I'm definitely not offended. I have a wide selection of overused toys back home. It's just," I say as a stupid grin begins stretching across my lips. "Why so many?"

Killian lets out a small breath before stepping deeper into my room. He moves right in front of me and offers me his hand before pulling me to my feet. A shiver sails down my spine as his fingers brush against my waist, making me wonder just how long it will take for my heart to stop racing every time he's around me. "As I mentioned, my work is . . . demanding, and there will be times that I can't always be here to satisfy your cravings. You seem to have quite a healthy sexual appetite, and I don't wish for you to be left . . . wanting." He gestures to the cock rainbow lining the floor. "With a collection like this, there shouldn't be any reason that you are left without having your needs met."

Hunger rumbles through my chest, and I creep closer, taking my time as I lift my hand to his warm chest. "Thank you," I murmur. "You look after me in a way I could have never imagined when I first arrived here, and while I truly appreciate your gesture to cater to my needs in your absence, surely you must realize by now that no amount of alien dildos could possibly satisfy me the way you do."

"Is that so?" he challenges, that same hunger flashing in his eyes. "You don't believe I could get you off just as well with one of these silicone cocks?"

I shake my head. "I don't deny you could definitely get me off. In fact, I welcome it. It would be hot and wild, but nothing could possibly compare to the way it feels having you inside of me and feeling the way your thick cock stretches my walls. Just the thought of it being you is enough to make me crumble," I whisper. "You're so powerful in your thrusts, so determined and precise. It's captivating. And while I know you might enjoy fucking me with one of those silicone cocks, it couldn't possibly compare to being inside me. I see the way you clench your jaw when you first push inside. It's like it's a shock to your system, like even though you know how good it is, it surprises you every damn time, and when my pussy clenches around you, claiming you all for myself, your whole body turns to stone, jolting with that overwhelming need that I have for you every moment of every day. God, Killian. Nothing could ever feel so good."

"Fuck, Angel. You're giving me far more than I bargained for. I came in here to check on you and find out why the fuck you felt the need to steal a Taser from my office," he rumbles, pulling me closer and grinding his thick cock against me. "But that interrogation might have to wait."

I grin as my tongue rolls over my suddenly dry lips. "What's it going to be, Killian? Are you going to fuck me with one of those fake cocks, or are you going to give me what I actually want?"

He grins, and the hunger in his eyes morphs into devilish desire, and as if taking my challenge and one-upping me, he reaches for the discarded monster cock and casually looks over it. "I don't see why I can't give you both," he says, returning that devilish gaze back to mine. "Now, strip for me, Chiara. Show me that pretty cunt."

CHAPTER 21

Chiara

G uilt eats at me as I make my way through the manicured maze garden that takes up a good portion of the backyard. It's absolutely beautiful, but truth be told, I think I'm lost. It's clear this garden was put here to disorientate anyone who comes through it, and right now, I wish that was something I'd realized before I decided to wander through it.

It's been an hour. This is getting ridiculous.

While it's been almost four days since the DeLorenzo Family Gala and my disastrous meetings with both Sergiu and his bitch wife, my body has not yet healed nearly enough for this kind of walk. Don't get me wrong, Killian has certainly put me through my paces in the bedroom, but he's been careful not to exhaust me, and he always makes sure he's the one putting in the work. I'm never at risk when I'm with him, and when I wandered into this damn maze, I never imagined that I could have been walking headfirst into a disaster. Yet here I am.

I'm a good walker. I could walk for miles before my calves start screaming at me, but the moment that walk turns into even the slightest jog, count me out. I've spent years having to walk to and from work. Don't get me wrong, I have a car—at least, I think I have a car. I really don't know what happened to it—or any of my belongings for that matter.

It's officially been two weeks since I've been here with Killian and two and a half since I was first snatched off the street. I can guarantee my apartment has been trashed and all my things stolen, and soon enough, there will be a squatter sleeping in my bed and eating all the food I had to work my ass off to buy.

Yet, I can't imagine leaving or going back to that life.

I want to explore this thing with Killian. I want to be his, and while he's already claimed my body, I want him to claim my heart too, and damn it, I think it might already be his. Is it even possible to fall for someone so soon? I barely know anything about him, but I want to know it all. I want to be his peace, the woman he comes home to, but this world terrifies me.

When my unhealed ribs begin screaming at me, I painstakingly wander another few steps to a little garden bench and plonk my ass right down, cringing as I gently rub my side. What was I thinking walking through here? I figured I'd be in and out within ten minutes, but if I knew I would spend the rest of eternity here, perhaps I would have chosen a stroll around the estate instead.

The guilt of not telling Killian about Monica or Sergiu eats at me as I catch my breath. I feel as though I owe him that much. He saved me from the auctions and gave me this life of luxury—one I could never achieve on my own—but the moment I tell him, they're as good as dead. Although they deserve nothing less, I can't stomach the thought of having their blood on my hands. I'm not built that way.

Perhaps it's something I'm going to have to get used to. Does anybody in this world stay an innocent bystander, or do we all become guilty by association? I'm the broken girl falling for a man who could destroy me without even flinching. I shouldn't keep anything this big from him, but I'm a sucker for punishment, or maybe I'm just a fool.

What it comes down to is that no matter what, Killian will always be the one with the power in this relationship. I will always be made to bow to him, and despite my useless efforts to demand I be his equal, we both know that's never going to happen.

Twisting to the side, I lay back on the small garden bench and put my feet up, staring at the sky. It's starting to get late in the day, and the warmth is beginning to fade from the air. It's going to be a brutal winter this year, but I suppose being here, I won't have to worry about affording the heating bill.

As I gently rub my side, trying to convince myself to get back up and find a way out of here, a familiar deep accent sounds within the maze. "You're lost."

I whip up, not having expected anyone to come looking for me. Hell, I didn't even realize he was home. "I am not," I say defiantly. "I'm just taking in the sights."

"My estate has surveillance everywhere, Chiara," Killian says, striding right up to me and kneeling down before me. "I've been watching you wander around in circles for twenty-five minutes. My security team has placed bets on how long it'd take you to find your way out."

My jaw drops, and I don't know whether to be offended or not. "And you were going to let that slide?"

"Of course I was," he scoffs. "Who do you think started it? My money was on three hours."

I gape at him while realizing that he was more than happy to leave me wandering around this maze for three long, torturous hours. "You're an ass."

"That may be so," he says while having the audacity to look offended. "However, I am here, am I not?"

My gaze narrows as I study his dark eyes, seeing a fondness within them that chokes me up. "Why?" I ask as a lump forms in my throat, making it hard to get the words out. "I would have eventually found my way out."

Killian reaches out, his fingers brushing over my side, right where my bruised ribs hide beneath my tank. "You're hurting, Angel. I couldn't take it any longer."

Letting out a heavy breath, I capture his hand in mine as something swells inside my chest, filling me with the most dazzling warmth and leaving me desperate for more. "You told me the other day that you were getting so much more than you bargained for," I murmur. "But

I think you're wrong. I think *I'm* the one who's getting more than she bargained for. My fate was sealed when I was snatched off the side of the road, but you've given me so much more than a second chance. I want to be your world, Killian."

He holds my stare, the depth of his gaze penetrating right through my chest. "Does it scare you?"

I nod, my whole body shaking with the realization. "It terrifies me."

"I wish to care for you, Chiara. I know this probably isn't the life you envisioned for yourself. It is a life filled with horrors you can't even begin to imagine, where bloodshed is power, and power is sought by those undeserving of it. Yet despite my position and the life I lead, I find myself mesmerized by you. I'm incapable of leaving you alone."

Leaning forward, I gently brush my lips across his. "I don't want you to."

"I know, but these feelings you have are based on an idea of who you think I am, and I so desperately wish I could be the man you hope me to be, but you don't truly understand what a monster I can be."

"You wouldn't hurt me," I insist, knowing it with every fiber of my soul.

"While that may be true, that doesn't mean you are capable of stomaching my true nature. I am callous, Chiara. The weight of my men's lives rests on my shoulders, and the things that I am capable of when those lives are at risk are worse than any nightmare you may have. The men who put you in that cage to sell you to the highest bidder are children in comparison."

I swallow hard, understanding what he's saying. I knew it from the moment he stepped out of the shadows at the auctions. I knew the power he possessed and the way every other man in that room shied away from him was a clear indicator that he wasn't someone who should be messed with.

He's the devil in a three-piece suit, but even the devil needs love too.

"And if I'm already falling for you?"

"Then you better hope like hell you're strong enough to handle the demands of this life," he says, leaning in and scooping me into his strong arms. He rises to his full height as I curl into the safety of his arms, resting my head against his wide chest. "You might only be my wife to the outside world, but for me, the moment those words fell from my lips, it felt right. I brought you here hoping that you would have my child, but I am not opposed to having something more with you, something real, Chiara."

"I don't get the feeling your family is too thrilled about this."

"My family will quickly learn their places. I won't lie to you, Angel. There will be backlash coming my way. I killed a senior member of my family the night of the gala," he tells me, and I nod, having heard the gunshot from my room. "However, I will protect you, even if it means protecting you from myself."

"You're a good man, Killian," I tell him. "I don't know if you realize that. Your life is clouded by darkness, and I'm not foolish enough to assume the things you've witnessed and experienced haven't left scars, but I believe there's still a good heart in there."

He nods and the way he shifts his stare away from mine suggests he doesn't believe me, but if I have to prove it to him, I will, even if it's the last thing I do.

Killian continues walking until I'm finally offered my freedom from the maze, and the second we're out, a deep relief pounds through my veins. I know it's irrational, but a part of me had started to wonder if I was going to spend the rest of my life on that little garden bench.

He makes his way inside, not stopping to put me down until we're in the den. He lowers me down on the couch, and I sink right into it. A part of me flutters, realizing he knows which is my favorite couch in the whole estate despite never having mentioned it before, and when he drops down beside me, the flutter intensifies. "It's been four days, Chiara. Nobody has been named responsible for the attack on you in the ladies' room. It's time. I need to know who did this to you."

A heaviness seeps into my veins, pulsing through my body and weighing me down, and just as I consider coming clean and giving him what he needs, Sergiu's terrifying threat sounds through my head—*If I find out that you've even whispered about this, I'll come back here every fucking night, and what happened in here today will seem like child's play in comparison. And if you even think about offering him a DeLorenzo heir, I will tear your baby right out of your womb.*

Sergiu's threat is a million times worse than anything Monica could ever do to me, and yet, I feel they come hand in hand. If I cross her, Sergiu comes for me either way.

Coldness penetrates my chest, and I gently shake my head, desperately wishing there was some way I could give him what he needs. "I'm sorry," I whisper, sitting up and cupping the side of his sharp jaw. "I've been thinking about this a lot these past few days, and I wondered if perhaps you'd be comfortable with me dealing with it myself? If you intend to hold on to me, then I will be facing these women for the rest of my life, and I want to send a message that I can't be broken, that they can't come at me without consequences. I know this is a betrayal for you that needs to be handled, but it's also a direct attack against me, and if you come sweeping in as my hero, saving the day, they'll never respect me as the woman who stands at your side. They think I'm weak, Killian, and I need to prove that I'm more than just some broken woman. I need to make my stand."

"And how do you intend to do that?"

"That's the part I haven't exactly worked out."

"You need to work it out fast, Angel," he tells me. "My patience is wearing thin."

"Promise."

With that, he's gone, leaving me here wondering how the hell I'm supposed to retaliate in a way that both serves justice for what Monica did to me and her betrayal against Killian, while also being a punishment that I can bear the weight of. And without even needing to truly consider it, I know it's an impossible task because the only acceptable form of punishment Killian will deem acceptable is death.

CHAPTER 22

Chiara

Staring out the window of the grand library on the top floor, a stupid smile cuts across my face seeing Killian's SUV barreling down the long driveway. It's officially been six days since the gala, and while the memories of that night still haunt me, the bruises have finally begun to fade, and I can move around with ease. It also means he's been fucking me more freely, and that's always a bonus. He's not someone who enjoys giving up control, but the days he lets me take the reins are the days I could drown in his ecstasy.

The SUV has barely come to a stop when I make my way out of the library. It's a hike to get all the way down to the ground floor, and by the time I'm in the lobby, I've already missed him.

Glancing around, I try to search for a clue as to where he's gone, when I give up and look to Rohan, the doorman. We don't exactly have a lot in common, and he's a man of few words, making it hard to form any sort of friendship, but he's always kind, and that's all a girl can ask for. Though, he insisted on calling me ma'am for the first few weeks, and it's taken me up until now to break the habit. "Did you see which way he went?"

"He took off to the left. Perhaps he's in his office."

"Thanks," I say, whipping myself around to the left of the stairs.

I weave through the corridors, proud of myself for learning how to navigate this maze—unlike the maze outside that I will never attempt again. I've been stuck on the *how to punish Monica for her crimes* train for two straight days, and I'm almost ready to admit defeat. The best I could come up with was a public beating like some kind of gladiator performance.

Killian claimed this world is ruled on the basis of an eye for an eye, and so I figured if she beat me in front of the other wives, then the equivalent would be for me to beat her in front of . . . Well, I don't really know who, but I don't think I care. I just want this shit over. Though there's no point even suggesting the idea. Killian won't accept a mere beating as punishment for betraying his loyalty. I was humiliated in front of everyone, made to appear weak, and a beating in return is nothing in comparison. I need to discover what Monica takes most pride in and exploit it. I want to ruin her, and it needs to be done in a way that she will never recover from.

The pressure from Killian to give a name has been getting worse, and soon enough, he'll snap. I don't mean to take so long, and I wish there were some way we could both get what we want, but it's becoming crystal clear there's not. He warned me though. He told me he was a callous monster and doubted that I could stomach what this world requires of him, but I'm choosing to see the good in him, and that's on me. Besides, the moment I open my mouth, everything gets worse. Monica and Sergiu won't stand for it, and honestly, the threat Sergiu gave that first time he came into my room hasn't been forgotten. If I even think about telling Killian, he will return every night, and what he does to me will pale in comparison.

Not bothering to knock on Killian's door, I stride right through the door of his office as though I have every right to be there. "Hey Killi—" I pause, cutting myself off as I find the luxurious office empty. My gaze sweeps left to right as my brows begin to furrow.

"Huh," I mutter to myself. Where the hell could he have disappeared to so quickly?

My gaze sails to the small store room, and I quickly cut across the room, twisting the door handle as I shove my hip against the solid door. "You in here?" I ask, stepping deeper into the store room.

It's bigger than I expected, and unlike the rest of the overly organized house, this room is different. There are papers, files, weapons, and briefcases scattered everywhere. It's a stark contrast to everything else I've come to know. The back wall is covered with surveillance screens, and I can only assume this is some kind of private security office, different than the normal cameras scattered across the property.

A strange nagging pulls deep in my gut, and it forces me farther into the room. My gaze shifts over the shelving full of boxes. Some look worn down and tired as though they're centuries old, while other boxes look as though they were only sealed yesterday.

There's a big table in the center of the room with paper scattered across it and a half-empty coffee mug that looks as though it was only placed here this morning. My gaze shifts to the papers, and while I've never taken the time to look over a police report, I can tell when I'm looking at one.

"What the hell?" I murmur, skimming over the pages as my heart races.

It says something about a massacre at the home of Deago Donatelli, the leader of the Donatelli crime family, and while that name means nothing to me, I'd bet everything I have that it means something to Killian. My curiosity gets the best of me, and I start flicking through the pages, but when I find crime scene photos, that curiosity turns into dread.

Horror rocks through me, taking in the blood pooled on the ground and the dead bodies littered with bullets. There are hundreds of images, one after the other, taken from a million different angles, but when the attention focuses on a different man, everything stops.

This one is different.

He's not littered with bullets like everyone else, he's been tortured to death. Deep, precise stab wounds cover his body. This man bled out in agony. His death wasn't quick or forgiving. It was brutal and callous, just like Killian.

I feel the blood drain from my face, leaving me faint and unsure.

Had I only seen the other photographs, I could have convinced myself that Killian had nothing to do with this, that he only had these police reports out of morbid curiosity for an opposing mafia family, but seeing the stab wounds over the body of the man I assume to be Deago Donatelli, I know it was him.

Killian orchestrated this massacre.

He did this.

Every bullet. Every death. Every last stab wound to that man's body. Killian was responsible for all of it.

My stomach clenches as fear pounds through my veins.

This is the man I've been allowing myself to fall for. Despite his warnings and demands that I fear him, I foolishly chose to believe there was something good buried beneath the darkness. But how could that be true? A man who's capable of wiping out a whole family couldn't possibly be capable of love. How could there be anything good inside his heart?

Fat tears stream down my face, and as I take in all the boxes of files around me, I realize they're all filled with the same thing—horrors of the crimes he's committed in the name of family. Horrors of the leaders who've come before him.

And this man wants me to give him a child—a child who will eventually stand in his place and be responsible for the same demented acts. How could I allow that to happen?

Moving to the wall of screens, the dread begins to drown me, but I can't walk out of here without truly knowing. After all, isn't this what he wants? What he's been trying to warn me about. He wants me to know who he is and what he's capable of. He wants me to have an informed fear and to know the man I said I was beginning to fall for. This might not be how he intended for me to find out, but isn't it best I know now before I fall too deeply?

I have to respect his decision to warn me. It's about as noble as it gets in the mafia world, but now that I'm peeking through the window of his soul, I don't know how I'm ever supposed to belong to him.

How can I give myself to a man who's capable of slaying an entire family line? A man who so unforgivingly can put a bullet through someone's head simply for existing in the wrong room at the wrong time. A man who shamelessly walks into a human trafficking auction house and is the one they fear?

How stupid could I be?

My hands shake as I reach for the power button at the bottom of the screen, and as the screens come to life, something within me dies.

Each screen is just as horrifying as the next.

The first screen has a naked man hanging from chains, his body broken and beaten. His eyes are swollen, barely able to open them, but there's no mistaking the tears staining his face.

The next is a frail-looking man in a cell with hollowed cheeks and his whole rib cage visible, even through this shitty camera. He looks as though he's been there for years, and I bet if he had the option, he would end his misery without a second thought. Though it makes me wonder, someone so frail should have perished long ago. Is Killian giving him just enough nutrition to keep him alive and prolong his misery?

Moving to the next screen, I see a woman strapped to a chair. She's filthy. Her hands are strapped to the arm rest, and while it's hard to tell through the camera, it looks as though each one of her fingernails have been pulled out. I can't imagine the pain, but I also can't imagine what kind of crime she committed to deserve such a punishment.

The tears fill my eyes to the point I can't make out the figures on the rest of the screens, but I've seen more than I can possibly stomach.

Feeling around the bottom of the screen, I turn it off before stumbling out of the store room, and as my mind becomes trapped by the horrid images, my stomach clenches.

Nausea sweeps over me, and I hurry from Killian's office, slamming through the door of what I thought was a bathroom, only to come face-to-face with the man. He spins, not having expected anyone to come through the door. His eyes widen just a fraction, and I swallow the nausea as it quickly turns to fear.

He strides toward me, fury in his eyes, but despite his sheer size and his imposing nature, I see past him into the small room to a familiar woman sitting in a stiff-back chair with absolute terror in her eyes.

"What—what are you doing?" I demand, my heart racing as my gaze locks onto the woman's pleading expression, but the longer I look at her, the more familiar she becomes. She's one of the wives. I spent the majority of that interaction with my gaze locked on Monica's, but there were three others. One of them clearly had Monica's back, but the other two were silent and unsure. This woman was there, but she didn't have a hand in any of Monica's bullshit.

"OUT," Killian roars, the venom in his tone making my whole body shake.

"No," I panic, my horrified stare flicking between Killian and the helpless woman. "What are you doing? I thought you were going to let me handle this. She didn't do anything. It wasn't her."

"Out, Chiara," he spits. "I told you your time was running out. You failed to give me a name or come up with a suitable solution, so now I will take matters into my own hands, and believe me when I tell you that I will enjoy my chance to break her."

Tears fall from my eyes, the horrors from that store room still too fresh in my mind to deal with this too. Is he going to strap her to a chair and pull her fingernails out one by one or hang her from an industrial chain and beat her black and blue?

"Killian, please," I beg. "Don't hurt her. She didn't do anything. She didn't know what was going to happen. She's innocent."

"None of them are innocent," he roars. "Their silence is a betrayal of their loyalty. In protecting the woman who put her hands on my wife, they betray the DeLorenzo name and will be punished."

I reach for him, fisting my hands into the front of his shirt, and I stare up into those dark, hollow eyes. "Please. If I give you a name, will you just . . . please. Don't do this. She doesn't deserve this. Let her go, Killian. I know there's still good left inside you. You don't have to be this way. You can still have power without the pain. Please, just let her go. For me."

A softness shimmers in his heavy stare, and as he forces my hands to release his shirt, he reaches up and wipes the fresh tears from my cheek. "Go, Chiara. It's too late. I will get the name I need, but it won't be from you."

The woman behind him sucks in a horrified breath, and I stand my ground, my chest heaving, knowing that despite everything I just saw on those screens, I trust that he won't hurt me, and a part of me has to trust that means he won't hurt her in front of me.

That softness still lingers in his eyes, and I struggle to believe that the same man who's capable of looking at me like this is the same man who could brutally murder someone in cold blood. "Chiara," he says after a tension-filled silence. "You said you didn't want to give a name because the burden of their punishment would rest on your shoulders. You didn't want their blood on your hands. Is that still true?"

"Yes," I say with a heavy heart. "But I'll accept that burden if it means preventing someone else's unneeded suffering."

"No, Angel. I won't allow that," he tells me. "Remember what I told you when we came in from the maze two days ago? What did I say to you?"

I swallow hard, knowing where he's going with this. "That you would protect me, even if it meant protecting me from yourself."

"Right, but as your husband, it's also my duty to protect you from yourself. So, no, Chiara. I will not allow you to give me a name. The crimes of another woman will not rest on the shoulders of my wife. Now leave."

There's a finality in his tone, and without question, I turn on my heel and walk straight out the door, an irrevocable darkness latching on to my soul.

CHAPTER 23

Killian

It's almost midnight as I finish in my office. It's been a long night and an even longer day, but the terror in Chiara's eyes made everything worse. There's no one to blame but myself for the fearful way she looked at me. This is what I asked for. It's imperative that the woman by my side throughout this life learns to fear me before she loves me, otherwise, there is no hope for us.

I am not a man who can hide my life from the woman I share it with. She must know who I am, and in order to love me, she must also love the devil within me—a feat no woman has ever been capable of.

Change is out of the question. In order to change, I must become weak, and that's not a risk I can take within this world. For her sake and mine, it's imperative to our survival. Instead, she must rise to meet me and bring a fierce will to survive. No less will be tolerated at my side.

Chiara has thick skin. She was raised as a fighter, but it's not enough. She has to be capable of seeing the darkness in the world around us. The vile things I must do to maintain fear are all that keep the other monsters at bay, and when I come home to her covered in blood, she needs to understand that the alternative would have been me not coming home at all. I want her to love the man I have to be, not love me despite it. I'm a cold-blooded killer standing before her, but if she can look past that, she'd see I'm the man who would sacrifice the world just to save her.

Getting up from my desk, I make my way out of my office as my phone rings in my hand, and I glance down to see Sergiu's name across the screen. Irritation burns through me. I've known it was his wife who put her hands on Chiara since the moment I found her on the ground. All I needed was confirmation, and despite what Chiara thinks, I got that from Evie on the drive over here.

As for Monica, I need to play my cards right. A part of me was holding on to hope that it might have been Phillip's wife, Rachael. I would have put her in the ground next to her husband without hesitation. We could have held a double funeral for the two of them, and I wouldn't have had a second thought about it. But Monica . . . that makes things difficult.

I can't simply execute her without causing issues with Sergiu. He will retaliate without a conscious thought for what he's doing, and it will start a mess none of us can possibly come back from. I need to figure out a game plan, and I need to be sure, confident, and precise in my plan, but I can't wait too long. Monica will soon discover that Evie gave the confirmation I required, and when that happens, the war will rage.

Hitting accept on Sergiu's call, I hold the phone to my ear and step out of my office. "Cousin," I say in greeting.

"The DeAngelis shipment has been secured and is ready for delivery. I've been in contact with Roman, and they're ready to take delivery. I'll have our drivers out within the next hour."

"Good. Go with them. We can't afford for anything to go wrong. We need a smooth delivery to ensure a good working relationship with the brothers, and remember, don't piss them off. They won't hesitate to put a bullet right between your eyes."

"Comforting," he mutters.

"Wasn't meant to be," I state before ending the call, and while I might not trust him to always have my back, I do trust him to get the job done better than anyone else. He can be a charming motherfucker when he needs to be, and on more than one occasion, that charm has saved our asses. As for me, I don't suck up to other men by acting like a charming fool. The only time you'll see me laying on the charm is when I have a woman on her knees and my cock in her throat, and as for Chiara, I've never seen a woman look so beautiful when she's working my cock.

I'm not going to lie, I feel like a fucking prick for speaking to Chiara like that when she walked in on me and Evie. She has been asked by Rachael to take care of the funeral arrangements for Phillip, and we were only just getting started when Chiara came running in looking as though she were about to be sick, and the moment she noticed Evie behind me, I knew exactly what was going through her head. Maybe it was cruel to not tell her what was really going on, but I need her to stop seeing me as her savior and more as the villain of her story.

As much as I wish I could be that for her, I need her to fear me, to truly understand who I am. It just happened that Evie is so socially awkward that the moment Chiara came racing in, Evie's anxiety peaked, and in Chiara's haste, she couldn't tell the difference between Evie's fear and her anxiety.

The moment Chiara was gone and the door closed behind her, Evie wasted no time to chastise me, but she couldn't deny that I'd done her a kindness. Refusing to allow Chiara to break on her resolve and give me Monica's name saved her from a burden that Evie knows all too well. Chiara won't always have the luxury of taking the high ground. Given enough time in this world, she will eventually have her hands stained by another's blood, and when that time comes, I'll be right here to hold her up.

Making my way up the stairs, my gaze lingers on Chiara's closed door, and I turn away, heading for my room instead. I haven't seen her since she barged in on me and Evie, and the sorrow that flashed in her eyes when she turned her back and walked away nearly destroyed me. She clearly has a lot she needs to work through, but for now, I'll allow her to rest. We'll talk in the morning.

Walking up to my bedroom door, I find it open just a sliver and I push my way through to find Chiara sitting on my bed, her knees pulled up to her chest as she focuses too hard on the black sheets beneath her.

I don't say anything, sensing she's the one who wants to do the talking. Instead, I stride through my room as I work the buttons on my shirt. A moment of tension-filled silence passes, and just as my shirt hits the floor, I finally hear the soft brokenness of her voice filling the air.

"I suppose you got a name then?" Chiara asks, not able to meet my eye.

I lean back against my dresser, simply watching her on my bed. "Yes," I say, deciding not to give her the whole truth about why Evie was really here. If they become close at any point, then that's a truth I'll leave up to her to share. Though to be completely honest, if Chiara did feel the need to make friends outside of my home, Evie would be the best option. She's entirely too guarded for Chiara's likes, but she's the only one who wouldn't intentionally stab her in the back.

Disappointment flashes in her lifeless eyes, and I realize that despite needing to be cruel in order to protect her from the burden of Monica's punishment, I've instead burdened her with the guilt of Evie's interrogation. She believes I broke her to get that information, and for now, she needs time to process that.

Her gaze flashes up briefly, but that second is more than enough to show her heartbreak. I've broken her, and I fucking hate myself for it, but she should learn now that just because I didn't have to resort to brutality this time doesn't mean I wouldn't have.

Chiara lets out a heavy breath before getting to her feet and walking to my door. She opens it wider and leaves her hand on the door, pausing and glancing back at me, the heaviness between us almost crippling. "The reason I was down there is because I was coming to look for you. I'd figured out a solution that I thought could be suitable and wanted to discuss that with you, but I see now I was foolish to assume you would actually allow me to take the reins on that one."

Her stab stings, but sensing she's not done yet, I don't respond.

"I looked for you in your office, and when you weren't there," she continues, pausing to meet my stare, but the darkness in her gaze puts me on edge. "I went looking in your little room of horrors."

"And?" I prompt, arching a brow.

"And you make me sick," she says. "I saw the pictures and the police report from the Donatelli massacre, and though your name wasn't anywhere on it, that brutality . . . it was you."

I nod, not willing to sugarcoat it. "It was."

Her bottom lip trembles, but she lifts her chin and goes on. "And the people you have locked up on those security screens. The man hanging from chains and the woman with her nails pulled." Chiara pauses and again I don't respond, giving her a moment to figure out what she wants to say. "You're really not the man I thought you were."

Meeting her broken stare, I take a step toward her, grateful when she doesn't flinch or try to move away. "Do you fear me, Chiara?"

She nods, not hesitating for even a moment. "Yes."

Her honesty wounds me, but when she first arrived here, honesty is what I demanded, and I can't fault her for giving me exactly what I asked for. "And do you still wish to love me?" I ask, remembering her words in that maze as clearly as though they were tattooed across my chest.

She visibly swallows as tears roll down her cheeks, and I want nothing more than to close the gap between us and pull her into my arms, giving every last reason for why I've done all the terrible things she accuses me of. Her hand shakes against the door, and I see the exact moment the last of her resolve breaks and the pain radiates from her beautiful eyes. "How could I possibly love someone like you?"

And with that, Chiara slips out the door and walks away, leaving me a fucking mess.

CHAPTER 24

Chiara

I'm a fucking mess.

It's been two days since I saw what Killian kept in his little room of horrors, and since then, I've done everything within my power to avoid him like the plague, but when you live within the same home and your bedroom doors are only feet apart, avoiding someone is a lot harder than it sounds.

I miss him. That's insane, right?

I miss his touch. His warmth. His stupid delicious rich accent.

I want his arms around me, his lips on my body, and those deadly eyes locked on mine. But most of all, I just want him. I want things to be the way they were before I discovered his little room of horrors.

Don't get me wrong, I see him more than I care for at the moment. His presence within this home is impossible to ignore. He's everywhere. Every room I walk into, he's right there taking care of business. I feel his deadly gaze on me like lasers in the night, and while I hear his voice, it's never directed at me.

He's trying to give me space. At least that's what I assume. A man like Killian DeLorenzo isn't the kind of man who would usually care about giving a woman the space she needs to process, but for some reason, he's always given me exactly what I needed in his own demanding way.

There's no doubt he cares for me, and I'm sure the words I spoke to him in his bedroom the other night have penetrated his soul in the worst ways, but I had to be honest with him. How could I not? What I saw in those pictures, on those screens . . . I haven't been the same since.

How could I ever love someone who's capable of such brutality? I can only imagine how he tore the woman to pieces in that interrogation room while searching for Monica's name. I don't even know who the woman is or which of the DeLorenzo men she's married to, and yet I feel a responsibility to her. Whatever she went through in that room is on me because I refused to give Killian Monica's name when I had the chance.

Is this what my life is going to be like? Am I damned to become that cruel and unforgiving? Will there be a point where my soul is so damaged that shit like this will simply roll off my back like water off a duck's feathers? I don't want that life. I just want him without all the bullshit that comes along with it. Why does that have to be so hard to ask for?

I was doomed from the moment I met him.

He told me he wasn't my hero. I should have believed him.

Making my way through this ridiculously ginormous house, I turn into the kitchen to find Krista hidden behind a mountain of boxes with a pair of kitchen scissors in her hands. She happily tears the boxes open like a kid on Christmas morning, and I can't help the smirk that pulls at my lips.

"What the hell is all this?" I ask, walking deeper into the room and making myself comfortable at the counter as I gaze over the few opened boxes, trying to figure out what's inside.

"I need help," Krista says. "The power has gone to my head."

"What the hell are you talking about?" I laugh, my brows furrowing.

"When you first arrived, Killian gave me his credit card and told me to purchase anything you required, and I haven't been able to give it back," she explains. "I can't stop shopping. *Add to cart* has become my favorite phrase, and that little rush you get when you click the checkout button . . . Holy shit, girl. I have a sickness. You have to take this card away from me."

"I don't want that thing," I say, horrified by the idea of having access to that much money. Actually, I wonder just how much money it is we're talking about here. Millions or billions? Surely it's not billions, right? Because that would be insane. Is this *swipe your card and suddenly you're the owner of an NBA team*, or is it more like *swipe your card and suddenly you're the owner of the free world?*

I'm willing to bet it's the second option.

The thought of that much money makes me sweat.

"Are you just going to sit there and look horrified, or are you going to help me open all these boxes?" Krista says as she pulls out a bedazzled dog collar. While it's absolutely stunning, I'm almost ninety-nine percent sure we don't have a dog here.

"What the hell is that for?" I ask, getting up and reaching for a box as she hands me a pair of scissors.

"I told you, it's a sickness," she says. "Besides, how am I supposed to know if you might need this or not? I was tasked with supplying you with everything you might need. I'm just trying to be efficient at my job."

"Wait," I say, my hands pausing on the box before me. "All of this shit is for me?"

"Who else would it be for?" she throws back at me. "I don't need any of this crap."

I roll my eyes and gesture toward the bedazzled dog collar. "And I do?" I ask, just as I feel the familiar shift in the air, warning me that Killian has just walked into the room. It's always the same. I sense him before I see him, and I feel his presence before I smell him.

Those laser eyes lock onto me, and it's almost a searing pain, but one that belongs only in my imagination as I do everything in my power to focus solely on the box in my hand.

Killian moves around the kitchen, each step bringing him closer and closer and making it harder to breathe. God, I wish I could simply get over it and be okay with this. I need to throw myself into his arms and feel that protection he can offer because when I'm with him, when his strong arms are wrapped around me, I feel as though nothing could ever harm me. I'm safe with him, despite the terror I feel simply being within his presence.

He strides past me, and I can't help but shift my gaze as I look over him, dragging my hungry stare over his wide shoulders and down his tall frame. He's so unbelievable.

"What the fuck is all this shit?" he questions, looking over the mountain of boxes.

Krista's eyes widen in panic. "Uhhhh . . . Just a few things I picked out for Chiara."

Killian pauses, his gaze shifting over the boxes before reaching toward the table and picking up the bedazzled collar. "Really? This is something she required?"

"Don't look at me," Krista says, shrugging her shoulders and glancing toward me. "It's none of my business what she intends to do with it. Besides, how well do we really know her? She could have a BDSM kink and is just waiting for the day you put her in a collar, and when that day comes, I think it's important that you're prepared."

My jaw drops as I gape at Krista, but before I can get the words out, Killian responds. "I will not be putting my wife in a dog collar. If she so desires to wear such articles, I have a perfectly acceptable collection for her to choose from."

"Okay, I'm just putting it out there because it's something I need to make clear—nobody is strapping a collar around my neck."

Killian nods as though this is normal conversation. "Understood.

Collars are out of the question. However, at some point, we should discuss what sexual fantasies you want to explore."

My cheeks immediately begin to burn, and I avert my gaze back to the boxes on the table, furiously cutting through the tape to avoid the awkwardness of having this conversation with Krista standing right here—a conversation I know she's going to demand more details about the moment Killian has taken off.

I feel his intense gaze on me as I tear open the box, but something seems off and my hands freeze. This box isn't packed like a normal order you'd receive from any online store, and it's taken me until now to realize there isn't even an address label on the front.

My brows furrow, and I open the box with caution, waiting for something horrible to jump out at me, only as I peer inside, I find nothing more than a crumpled piece of paper that looks as though it's been torn from a notebook.

Reaching in, I pull out the paper and straighten it out before glancing over the words.

SMILE, BITCH!

"What the fuck?" I mutter, grabbing the box again and checking over it to make sure I didn't miss an address label. "Is this supposed to be for me?"

Killian plucks the paper from my hand before quickly scanning over it, his whole body stiffening in the process. Barely a moment has passed before he turns and begins scanning the property line, way in the distance. "What are you looking—"

Movement far in the bushes catches my attention and before I even get a chance to finish my sentence, Killian grabs me and throws me to the ground. "DOWN!" he roars just as a loud BANG echoes through the distance and something shatters the floor-to-ceiling glass window.

My heart leaps right out of my chest as a panicked squeal tears out of me. "What the fuck?" I screech as Killian moves like lightning to return fire, but it happened so damn fast I can't even recall the moment he reached for a gun.

"Get her out of here," he roars. "Safe room."

Killian's men pour into the room, each of them quickly falling into position as Krista scrambles around the kitchen counter, gripping my wrists and pulling me toward her. "What's happening?" I yell over the sound of the gunfire.

"Don't know," she yells back. "But my guess is some kind of hired hit."

The fuck?

"Come on, we have to get out of here."

She pulls me harder, and my gaze shoots up to search for Killian, desperation pounding through my veins, but he's nowhere to be seen. Bullets whiz past me, plunging into the wall behind my head, and I quickly realize that had Killian not thrown me down, it'd be my blood and brain matter splattered around the wall, not an array of missed bullets.

My heart pounds faster than it ever has before, and when I don't move fast enough, one of Killian's men physically yanks me to my feet and clutches my arm in a death grip, shoving me along. Krista scrambles to her feet, and before I know it, I'm inside Krista's pantry being shoved through a wall into some kind of safe room.

"What's happening?" I rush out, whipping around to face the guy, but before I can even fully make out his features, a heavy metal door slams closed between us, plunging the room into a heavy silence.

"Hey," Krista says, clutching my arm and turning me to face her. "It's okay, we'll be safe in here until the threat is neutralized. Killian won't let anything happen to us."

"Holy fucking shit," I breathe, immediately beginning to pace the room, before actually taking a second to glance around and realizing this room could double as a livable bomb shelter. There's a small bed, an attached bathroom, and a shelf filled with food, water, and weapons. "What the hell is this place?"

"It's my safe room," Krista says. "There are a handful of safe rooms scattered throughout the property. You'd be surprised just how often they're used."

My hands shake, and I continue pacing. "This is insanity. There's a literal gunman outside."

"Killian will have him taken care of in a matter of seconds," she tells me before striding across the small safe room to a screen. She pulls a remote off the little shelf the screen rests on and turns it on, and I watch as she flicks through different camera feeds.

The front gate. The front door. The pool area. The maze. The kitchen. Then finally, the back portion of the property behind the pool, right where I'd seen the shooter hidden within the bushes.

Killian's men are everywhere, guns at the ready as they race toward the threat, bullets trading back and forth. Killian leads his men like a warrior, and I'm completely mesmerized—and honestly, a little turned on.

He's incredible. He didn't even flinch before throwing himself into battle. His strength and courage are like nothing I've ever witnessed, and it occurs to me that perhaps he is the way he is for a reason. He's not going around killing people for sport, he's defending the very family he vowed to protect, even if it means putting his life on the line. If his enemies saw the DeLorenzo family as weak, they would be picked off one by one, and that's not something Killian would ever allow.

He kills out of necessity.

He does the unthinkable because the weight of his family's survival rests solely on his shoulders. And right now, he's reacting to a threat. He's protecting the people he cares about, and in this case, he's out there protecting me.

Without him here right now, I'd surely already be dead.

I watch the very moment Killian disappears into the thick bushes at the very edge of the property line, the very bushes he warned me not to go running in, and I suck in a gasp. Fear booms through my veins, paralyzing me with every ferocious beat of my racing heart.

How can Krista stand by so calmly while he puts his life at risk? He could die at any moment, and the last proper thing I said to him was that I could never love a man like him.

Tears fill my eyes as my hands begin to shake. None of this is okay.

"He's going to be alright," Krista soothes, moving in beside me and latching on to my hand. She squeezes it tightly as her gaze remains locked on the same damn screen. "Killian knows what he's doing. He was trained to be the best."

The mere seconds feel like hours when I finally see Killian emerge from the thick bushes, his men dragging a man behind them. They stand just outside the bushes when they shove him to his knees in front of Killian.

There's no sound on the screen, but it's clear they're having a heated conversation, and judging by Killian's stance, he's pissed. The gunman obviously isn't giving him the answers he's looking for, and when his gaze shifts upward and he says something to his head of security, the gunman panics and launches to his feet.

I suck in a gasp, horror booming through my chest, and before a scream can even tear from the back of my throat, the hitman snatches a gun from the holster of one of the younger guards, shoves the tip to the bottom of his chin, and pulls the trigger.

Horror consumes me, and I watch as the gunman falls lifelessly to the ground—a portion of his skull no longer intact—and if I thought Killian was pissed before, now he's filled with rage.

"What—what just happened?" I ask, my heart booming so fast, it hurts.

"He chose imminent death over the brutality of Killian's interrogation," Krista explains. "And believe me, it was the wisest move he's made all day. Nobody comes out of interrogation without deep scars."

A shiver sails down my spine and I watch as Killian reprimands his security for allowing the hitman close enough to take his gun. And with that, he turns and stalks back toward the house. It's not long before he walks right out of frame, and for a moment, I'm filled with overwhelming heaviness.

Is this really what he has to deal with on the daily? No wonder his heart is so full of darkness. Had that been anyone else who had to deal with that, they'd be in therapy for years, but not Killian. He shakes it off as though the trauma will somehow make him stronger.

There's a sound at the door of the safe room, and as the mechanical locks release, the door opens wide, revealing Killian framed by the sunlight streaming in through the broken kitchen window. His dark eyes immediately come to mine, locking onto me like a hunter seeking his prey, and before I know it, I'm sprinting across the safe room.

I fly into his arms, crushing my face against his chest and inhaling that deep woodsy scent. His strong arms close around me, holding me tight enough to leave bruises across my ribs, but I don't dare pull away or complain.

"I'm so sorry," I murmur against his wide chest as he scoops me up and walks us out of the safe room and back through to the kitchen.

He places me down on the counter, stepping into me as he takes my chin and tips it up to meet my stare. "You have nothing to be sorry for, Angel," he tells me as his gaze sails across my face. "Are you okay? Did you get hurt?"

I shake my head. "I'm fine. I just . . . I hated seeing you run out there. You risked your life to protect me."

"A man came onto my property to launch an attack on my wife. What did you expect me to do? Let him have you?"

"No, of course not," I say, reaching up and cupping both sides of his face in my hands, sensing the fire burning within him and watching it slowly fade. "Seeing you like that . . . I was wrong to tell you that I could never love you. I misjudged you without giving you the chance to explain, and I hate that something could have happened to you and the last thing you would have remembered of me was being a bitch to you for the past few days."

Killian pulls back, freeing his face from my hands. "You were well within your rights, Chiara."

"No, I wasn't."

"It's not important," he says. "I'm sure you have many questions about what you saw, and we can talk about that when you decide you're ready, but for now, I need to know what happened in that bathroom with Monica."

"Monica?" I question. "What's that got to do with anything?"

"That hitman wasn't here for me, Chiara."

My brows furrow. "You think Monica hired him for . . . what? For me?"

"Yes. Now tell me what happened in the bathroom. Did she say anything to you before she attacked you?"

I shrug my shoulders, trying to remember everything that went down, despite having spent the past week doing everything in my power to try and forget. "She ummm—" I pause, letting out a heavy breath filled with reluctance. "I really don't want to make matters worse."

"You had a hitman shoot at you. How much worse do you think it's going to get?"

There's no denying it, the asshole has a good point, and I finally give in, telling him what he needs to know. "Okay, I'm paraphrasing here, but basically, she was saying that I was one more obstacle in the way of her and Sergiu taking over if you were to . . . you know, end up six feet under."

His face scrunches as if not following where I'm going with this. "If you were to knock me up, your child would inherit your . . . throne, or whatever you call it. But if I was out of the way with no chance of having your child, they would be one step closer to the top."

Killian's brows furrow. "That's what this is really about?" he questions, letting out a heavy sigh. "She's going to all this effort to try and take you out for the hope of one day getting to call the shots."

"Yep."

"Fuck, that woman has always been such a petty bitch."

My brow arches, a little shocked at the words that just came tumbling out of his mouth. I've heard the filthiest things a man could ever say from him behind locked doors, and I've seen the brutal evidence of what he's capable of in the name of protecting his family, but I've never quite heard him like that.

When speaking of his family, Killian always does so with high regard and respect, but now that Monica has shown her cards and her loyalty has been questioned, there's not even a scrap of respect left for her.

I can't lie, now that Monica has taken this bullshit so much further than a scrappy fight in a too-small bathroom, the idea of justice is suddenly a little more thrilling.

CHAPTER 25

Chiara

Darkness surrounds me as I stare up at my bedroom ceiling, finding it impossible to sleep. Today was a mess, and as a result, there's still fire pulsing through my veins.

A hitman was hired to take me out.

Like what the actual fuck? I'm just me. A nobody. I shouldn't be important enough to anyone to warrant the need for a hitman. All I want from life right now is to live it up in my new husband's McMansion and let him fuck me every way his incredible mind can possibly come up with. And yet, I'm being assaulted in bathrooms and shot at through the kitchen window. Not to mention Sergiu's belief that he's welcome into my room any damn time he likes.

How has this become my life?

I toss and turn, not able to silence the havoc inside my mind, but along with the havoc comes the memories of Killian's determination to protect me, and honestly, I've never been so turned on in my life. I shouldn't want him the way that I do. I shouldn't crave his touch, but the mere idea that he ran out into those bushes and risked his life just to save mine is something I can't ignore.

For the twentieth time tonight, I consider throwing myself out of my bed and going in search of the man in question and demanding that he fuck me until I can't possibly scream any longer. Yet, despite knowing that he would give me exactly what I need, something is keeping me from getting out of my bed.

Physically, Killian and I are the best match this planet has ever seen. Our bodies work together so damn well it's intoxicating and has quickly become my fiercest addiction. But emotionally, we still have a long way to go. Today has proven that I can trust him with my life, that if I were in danger, he's the one person I can rely on, but what about everything else? Can I trust him not to destroy me? Not to break my heart? Not to lie to me? That, I don't know.

Frustration claims me, and I let out a long groan as I clench my thighs, desperately trying to relieve the ache, but it's impossible. There's only one person who could possibly give me what I need. On second thought, there is a fully stocked drawer of toys right here by my bed, and it's not as though he put them there as a space filler. They were intended to be used, and honestly, I wouldn't want to offend him by simply ignoring the marvelous gift he's offered.

A sly grin pulls at my lips, excitement already pounding through my veins at finally getting the release I've been needing, and while I know it couldn't possibly compare to how Killian does it, it will at least get the job done. I hope.

Rolling over, I dive into my bedside drawer and blindly feel around for one of my vibrators. As much as I'd love to take advantage of one of those silicone cocks, that calls for a lot of energy . . . and probably a bit of acrobatics, but tonight, all I want is to relax.

Digging past all the silicone, I finally find one of the smaller vibrators in the bottom. Pulling it out, I roll back and get comfortable on my bed before reaching beneath the blanket and shimmying out of my underwear.

A hunger pulses through me, but knowing just how close I am to finally relieving the ache, my body begins to calm. My feet drag up the mattress as I bring my knees a little higher before finally spreading my thighs.

My pussy pulses with anticipation, and as I close my eyes and tilt my head back, I clutch the small vibrator and feel around for the button. Placing it against my clit, my brows furrow. It doesn't exactly feel like the vibrators I'm used to. It's not very soft against my skin or accommodating to a woman's shape, but there were a lot of things in that drawer I'd never seen before, and who am I to decide it's not worthy before even giving it a try?

With images of Killian dancing through my mind, my finger presses down over the button and a loud zapping noise fills the air in the same instant as a blood-curdling scream tears from the back of my throat. Pain booms through my pussy as volts of electricity penetrate my skin.

The agony is like nothing I've ever known, and I tear my hand away as fast as humanly possible. "FUCK. FUCK. FUCK. FUCK. FUCK," I scream.

The door barges open and Killian comes racing in, the room quickly filling with light. "What?" he rushes out, his eyes wild as they bounce around the room, searching for a threat, but the only threat is the fucking Taser laying by my hip. "What happened? What's wrong?"

I cry out as the sudden rush of electricity leaves me gasping for air. "I . . . FUCK," I cry out. "I TASERED MY FUCKING PUSSY!"

His brows furrow as he stares at me, looking as though he doesn't comprehend a single word I've said. "You did what to your pussy?"

"I Tasered it, Killian! My pussy. I thought it was a vibrator. I shoved my hand into the drawer and pulled it out because I was trying to avoid riding you all night, and NOW MY FUCKING PUSSY IS BURNING!"

I cry as I scoot to the edge of the bed, but each movement is excruciating. "Holy shit. Make it stop."

Killian strides toward me, a smirk resting on his stupidly gorgeous face. "Your pride is that important to you that you'd prefer to fuck yourself with a Taser than to walk the ten feet to my door and take what you really need?"

"Really?" I demand, my eyes filling with tears of pain as I attempt to glare at him, though to be honest, I don't think the message is getting across. "You want to give me a lecture right now?"

Killian laughs, and if I weren't in so much agony, I might even take a moment to linger on how smooth it sounds and how it somehow manages to heal something within me. It suits him in the best way, and while I want to throttle him for laughing at me right now, I can't deny how his laugh makes him seem so carefree. I bet he's the kind of man who doesn't laugh often, and the idea of getting to be someone who can give him that . . . well damn. There were a lot of things I wasn't expecting to get out of this relationship, and that certainly wasn't one, but now that I know what it feels like, I don't ever want to let go.

He reaches the side of my bed and kneels down to meet my stare. "Are you okay, Angel?"

The tears flow over, and I see as a softness creeps into his dark eyes. "Is it possible to singe your clit off? Because I swear, it's gone."

Killian reaches for the blanket and pulls it back before taking a quick glance between my legs. "I can confirm that your clit is still intact," he tells me, discreetly taking the taser away before those captivating eyes lock onto mine, and without even a whisper of warning, he blows out a soft breath of cool air against my clit and a needy moan pulls from deep within my chest. "Does that help?"

"Oh God," I groan. "So much."

Killian grins, and it's the most devilish thing I've ever seen, but before I can even work out what's going through that captivating mind of his, he slips his strong arm beneath my knees and pulls me into his arms.

The movement is crippling but as he pulls me against his chest, I suddenly don't care so much. Killian makes his way out of my room and carries me down the stairs, not saying a damn word. "You do realize you're carrying me through your home without panties on?"

"I am painfully aware of that fact."

I grin against his chest as he reaches the bottom step and rounds the corner into the oversized kitchen. It's late, and with Krista gone for the night, it's just us down here. The lights are out with nothing but the subtle moonlight shining through the window, and there's something so majestic about it. Maybe it's this home or the situation or maybe it's just him. I don't know, but whatever it is, I'm addicted.

Killian sits me on the table, and I watch as he turns and collects a glass from the cupboard. He walks to the freezer and fills the glass with ice as my brows furrow, wondering what the hell he's doing. I figured he was getting an ice pack of some sort to soothe my burning cooch, but a glass of ice? I don't know. Is he planning on putting that directly against my skin? That's going to be a hard pass for me.

He comes back to me, placing the glass of ice down by my thigh. "Still hurting?"

I nod. "Have you ever been Tasered on the tip of your dick before?"

"No, I can't say that I have. I've been shot, stabbed, and tortured within an inch of my life, but Tasered on the tip of my dick? No."

"Ahhh, so clearly you must not understand my current level of pain."

"Clearly not," he murmurs as he dips his fingers into the glass and scoops out a piece. He presses it to my thigh and slowly works it up toward my hip. "I may not understand your pain, Chiara, but I sure know how to take it away."

My brow arches, and I'm left speechless as he lifts the half-melted piece of ice to his mouth. His lips part, and the ice disappears inside before he grips the back of my knees and pulls me right to the edge.

I suck in a gasp, and before I know it, Killian DeLorenzo, the most powerful man in the world, is on his knees for me.

He leans in and blows out a soft, icy breath right against my core. "Here, Angel? Is this where it hurts?"

His mouth closes over my clit, and I draw in a deep breath as his freezing lips instantly soothe the burn. "Oh God," I groan, my eyes instantly rolling in the back of my head. He works his tongue over me, gently flicking and turning my pain into the sweetest pleasure.

His touch is like magic, every swipe of his tongue taking me closer to the edge, but when he works his fingers into my cunt and starts massaging me from within, I swear I'm seeing stars.

Killian is a man of power. He lives off others' fear. So cruel, conniving, and unforgiving that it's almost impossible to believe that he's capable of being so gentle with me. It's everything, and when I knot my fingers into his hair and hold on for dear life, he looks up, his dark gaze colliding with mine like an explosion in the night.

He holds my stare as his icy lips work my clit, and within seconds, I shatter like glass.

My orgasm consumes me, exploding from within like a million little fireworks overwhelming my body. "Oh God, Killian," I groan as my toes begin to curl, and I come undone in his grasp. His fingers don't stop moving as my walls contract around them.

Killian's tongue continues flicking over my clit as the melted ice

SHERIDAN ANNE

drives me wild, and he doesn't relent until I finally come down from my high. Only then does he get back to his feet and close the gap between us. He kisses me deeply, his chilly mouth against my burning one, and just before he pulls away, he pushes what's left of the ice cube into my mouth.

My tongue pokes out, rolling over my bottom lip as Killian simply stares at me with that devilish dark gaze. "Still hurting, Angel?"

"You know, I think I am," I lie as I reach down between us and work the button on his pants to free his massive cock. My hand wraps around him, feeling his protruding veins as I work my way to his tip. "Plus, it would be such a shame to waste all this ice."

"Oh yeah?"

"Definitely."

Those dark eyes flash with excitement, and before I know it, I'm spun around on the counter and put on my knees. He spreads my thighs as far as they will go and pushes my chest down against the cool marble counter, leaving me wondrously exposed.

Killian dips his fingers into the glass of ice and leaves them there for only a moment, and when he pulls them out, he swipes them right across my clit. He slowly rubs his cold fingers against me, and my hips jolt, desperate for more, but he doesn't dare hold out on me as he collects a piece of ice in his other hand.

"Now just remember, Angel," he murmurs, placing the ice at the top of my ass, letting it melt there as droplets of water roll down through my center and make everything clench. "You asked for this." And with that, he drags what's left of the ice cube down to my cunt and slowly pushes it inside.

An hour later, Killian and I lay naked on the soaked kitchen floor. My head rests against his defined chest, and all I can do is breathe him in. I don't think I've ever been so happy in my life. Despite all the terror that comes along with being a mafia wife, I'm truly starting to believe that I want this. The time I spend with him is worth a million hitmen, and I'll face down every last one of them if it means getting to peer into those dark eyes every day of the rest of my life.

I think I'm in love with this man.

"Holy shit, Killian. Remind me why I've been so stupidly trying to avoid you these past few days when we could have been doing that instead?"

"I do not claim to understand the inner workings of a woman's mind. However, if I had to take a guess, I would say it's because you're stubborn as hell and don't know what's good for you."

"Are you suggesting that you're what's good for me?"

"Not even a little bit," he tells me. "A life with me is a life of ruins, but that doesn't mean I can't make you feel more alive than you've ever felt before, and it sure as hell doesn't mean that I can't give you everything you've ever wanted and more. You're a priceless jewel, Chiara, and I want to give you the world, even if it means burning it to ashes to fit it in the palm of your hand."

My heart swells, and I push up on his chest so I can turn enough to meet his heavy stare, and the moment our eyes connect, I feel something solidifying between us like an invisible string tying itself to both of our souls. "How is it possible that you're so terrifying and yet so sweet at the same time?"

"I am not sweet, Chiara."

"You are though. To me, at least. Especially when I haven't deserved it. I've been cruel to you these past few days and judged you based on something I know nothing about. Even during those first two weeks before we really had a chance to get to know each other, you were patient with me when it's not in your nature. You've shown kindness when you didn't need to, and I don't think I've ever told you how grateful I am for that. You're making an effort to ensure I am comfortable with you, and I should be putting in more of an effort to return that favor."

"You do not owe me anything, Chiara. I am not the gallant man you make me out to be," he says. "The night I took you from the auctions, I had every opportunity to drive back into the city and let you go. I could have given you freedom, but instead, I chose to keep you for myself. That is not the act of a noble man."

A stupid grin cuts across my face. "Perhaps not," I agree. "But despite how I came to be here and how terrifying it was, I'm still grateful."

Killian watches me for a moment before sitting up and leaning against the kitchen cupboards. He lifts me onto him so I'm straddled over his thighs with his hands low on my hips. "The things you saw in my office—"

"You don't need to explain yourself," I say, cutting him off. "It's none of my business, and after seeing the way you protected me today, I don't believe I have a right to know."

"You're my wife. Of course you have the right to know."

"I'm your wife in public, remember? We don't have a real marriage."

"Stop fooling yourself, Chiara. I know I told you that it was all for show, but the moment I declared you my wife, it felt right. And though I know for you it may be different and you may not feel as strongly as I do regarding this, but for me, this is no longer just for show. For me, you are my wife for all intents and purposes."

My hands fall to his chest, feeling the heavy beat of his heart beneath his skin. "You want me to be your wife?" I murmur, my voice dropping so low I can barely hear it.

"Yes, my sweet angel, I want you to be my wife. I knew it the moment I saw you helpless in that cage, I just didn't understand what it was," he tells me, bringing his hand up and swiping his thumb across my cheek.

I blow my cheeks out and hold his heavy stare. "I mean, couldn't we start by putting some of my clothes in one of your drawers like normal people?"

"Or we could move you permanently into my bedroom. I wish to have you in my bed every night."

I nod. "I can manage that."

"Good, now as for the things in my office—"

"I told you, I don't think I need to know."

"It's important to me that you do," he tells me. "As I told you, it's important that you learn to fear me. You need to truly understand who I am and what I am capable of. You need to learn where my boundaries are. What I will tolerate and what I will not. But despite that, I also need you to love me, and in order to do that, you must see past all of my flaws. It's a balancing act, Chiara."

Leaning into him, I drop my forehead against his, feeling the electricity burning between us, and as he lifts his hands around my back and pulls me closer to his chest, my world explodes with the sweetest satisfaction. "I want to love you so bad it hurts," I whisper. "A part of me thinks I might already be there, but the other part . . . I don't know if it's possible to love someone you fear. But that's just it, Killian, no matter how much you push me away or how many horror stories you tell me, I don't know if I'm capable of fearing you . . . not anymore."

He nods and is silent for a short moment before finally going on. "The police report you found on the desk," he starts, this time not allowing me a chance to cut him off. "You were right, I was responsible for that massacre. Your second night here when you joined me in my bedroom, I had just returned and there was still blood on my clothes."

"Why did you do it?"

"The Donatelli family was responsible for a raid at one of my warehouses. Their men brutally murdered twenty-three of my workers for the sake of getting their hands on Ecstasy and guns. These were innocent men and women who were only trying to make a few dollars for the families and children they left behind."

I suck in a gasp as my mind begins to process, but before I have a chance to say anything. He goes on. "The surveillance screens. Tell me what you need clarified."

"Umm . . . There was a man hanging from chains."

Killian nods. "He raped and murdered my cousin's daughter six months ago. She was barely eighteen and only starting her life."

I swallow hard over the lump forming in my throat as tears begin to fill my eyes. "I'm so sorry," I whisper, feeling the weight of my cruelty slam down over my shoulders. I berated him for the things I saw in that office. I told him I could never love a man like that, but I was so wrong. I judged him too fast.

"I don't need your sympathies, Angel," he says, wiping the tears off my face. "It has been handled, and I don't wish to linger on the hurtful events that are now in the past. Now, what else do you need clarification on?"

"The woman," I say, sensing his need to move on. "She was strapped to a chair and had her nails pulled."

"Elaina Brinetti," Killian says. "The estranged daughter of Georgio Brinetti, a known enemy of the DeLorenzo family. She took it upon herself to seduce my uncle in order to learn my whereabouts. She then used that information to orchestrate an attack in order to return to her father's good graces. However, her attempts were fruitless considering her current predicament."

My lips twist. "She sounds like a bitch."

"Indeed she is," he agrees.

"I know there were other screens, but apart from the frail old man, I didn't look at the rest."

Killian nods, and something darkens in his deep stare. "That man is solely responsible for the unprovoked murder of both of my parents. I was only a child visiting my grandfather the night they were slaughtered. Losing them broke me, and in return, I vowed to break him. He has remained in that cell for over thirty years, receiving just enough food and water to ensure he lives in misery."

"Thirty years is a long time."

"It is," he agrees. "And yet, it hardly feels like enough."

I nod, not knowing how it feels to lose your parents, but knowing all too well what it's like to grow up without them. "I should never have judged you, Killian. Seeing all of that . . . It was a lot to take in, and it chilled me to the bone knowing what you're capable of doing, but I don't believe you're the type of man to hurt another unprovoked."

"I am not."

I raise my chin just enough to capture his lips in mine. "Okay," I tell him. "Then I'm ready. I'm ready to love you despite the fear of the unknown, despite the world you live in, and despite the people who actively wish to work against us. I'm ready to truly make this work."

CHAPTER 26

Killian

Chiara sleeps soundly in my bed as I sit in the corner of my room, watching the way her chest rises and falls with each soft breath. She's undoubtedly the most stunning creature I've ever laid my eyes on, but on the inside, she's absolutely breathtaking.

Since the moment I brought her here, I've been focused on being prepared for her to love me, to hate me, to discover who I truly am. I didn't take a moment to consider how I would feel if I were to reciprocate those feelings.

Last night while we spoke on the kitchen floor, it occurred to me that I wasn't the only one fighting this alien feeling inside of me. Every touch with her is electrifying, every smile stops my heart, every fucking time she looks at me, I'm captivated.

I'm in trouble.

This is what I wanted, what I demanded from her. I brought her here to be mine, but I had no intention of it becoming anything more than a sexual relationship, and if it progressed well, possibly the woman who would give me a child.

Don't get me wrong, I don't wish to fight this. I've always craved to have someone by my side who could love me despite my flaws, someone who would gift me her loyalty in exchange for my own, someone to share a life with, and now that it's right there within reach, it's suddenly the most terrifying prospect I've ever been faced with.

My world is no place for Chiara. She's too good, too innocent, and if I'm not the one who destroys her, someone else will. Yesterday was proof of that.

I will go to extreme lengths to protect her, but already, Monica has been able to get to her twice. If I hadn't been there yesterday, I don't know what would have happened. Just being with her is putting her life at risk, and up until yesterday, I thought that was something I could deal with, just something that came with the territory.

Not anymore.

I can't do it. I can't be her shadow every moment of the day, and I can't be the reason for her getting hurt. If something were to happen to her . . . fuck. I can't handle it. I'm supposed to be stronger than this, but she's making me weak. How am I supposed to be the head of this family while my every thought is focused on Chiara? How am I supposed to protect my people when all I want is to protect her?

Fuck.

The people in this world are either born into it or knowingly marry into it, but Chiara didn't ask for this. She didn't sign up for a life of fear. She didn't want to be in a world where she would constantly have to watch her back. I forced this on her, and now I've put her in a position where just being the woman who stands at my side is detrimental to her survival.

I won't always be there to protect her. Despite how much I want to, it's not physically possible, and there's only so much training I can offer. Monica was able to strike in the blink of an eye in the ladies' bathroom, but what could she concoct given time? She almost killed her in a spur-of-the moment attack, and even though I plan to deal with Monica, and she will soon cease to be a problem, what about the next threat? What about the next enemy who chooses to use Chiara to get to me?

Yesterday the shooter missed her by mere millimeters, but what would have happened had I been in a meeting or just simply a moment too late? What if Krista had gotten hurt in the process? What if I'd lost both of them?

Despite my needs and desires, there's only one true way to protect her. I need to let her go.

I need to offer her freedom and give Chiara the chance at a real life away from the dangers of mine. Despite how right it feels to have her by my side, I have to break her heart. I have to make her leave and never look back.

This world is going to kill her.

I'll watch her from a distance, ensuring she has everything she will ever need. A nicer home in a safer neighborhood away from men like Ezekiel, a car, money, and a full pantry of groceries. I can ensure she's enrolled back in college and that there will be no repercussions from her time missed while she was here with me. But most of all, I can ensure her life isn't in constant danger just by being the woman I love.

Fuck, and I do love her. I'm so fucking in love with her it aches. I hadn't even realized I was capable, but here we are. I let her in, and instead of pushing me away like any sane woman would, she clutched on and sank her nails in, claiming me just as I'd done to her.

I've never feared anything. Never been emotionally involved to the point it leaves a scar. I was a fool to believe I could have this. Men in my position don't get to have happiness. They don't get to have families and love, not without risking their lives.

I sit and watch her until the sun begins to peek through the window, and when she finally wakes, a soft moan slips from her lips as she clutches the blankets to her naked chest with one hand and stretches her other out across the mattress, right to where I should be sleeping.

Her body stiffens, finding my side of the bed cold, and I watch as she peels her eyes open into the morning light.

"Mmmmmm," she grumbles, rubbing her hand over her bright green eyes before pushing herself up into a sitting position and blowing me the fuck away. She looks incredible like this. Her hair is a mess, and her creamy skin looks good enough to eat as she clutches the blanket to cover her full tits. "What are you doing all the way over there? Did you sleep?"

"I'm sorry, Chiara."

"Sorry?" she questions. "What for? Do you need to work this morning, or do you want to come back to bed? You tired me out last night, but now that I'm feeling refreshed, it's my turn to give you the royal treatment."

I hold her soft stare, knowing that the words that are about to come out of my mouth are going to break her, but I've never been one to beat around the bush. I'm direct in my intentions so that no one misunderstands me, and the same will apply here.

"You need to leave."

Her brows furrow, and she stares at me confused. "Leave?" she mutters, her lips twisting with unease. "What do you mean? Is this too much? Do you need me to go back to sleeping in my room? If you do, that's fine, but I thought you wanted this."

"I don't mean that you need to leave my room, Chiara. You need to leave my estate. It's time for you to go back home. I'm releasing you. You're free to go and live your life. You're no longer a possession of mine."

"I'm . . . I'm confused," she says, clutching the blanket tighter to her chest like a security blanket. "What are you talking about? When you brought me here, you said I was here indefinitely. I was your property. There's no *get out of jail free* card. This is my home now. Hell, you told your family I was your wife for fuck's sake, and now all of a sudden, you're just going to tell me to get out. What the fuck, Killian?"

"I'm sorry, Chiara. It was certainly not my intention to cause you any grievance. However, our . . . relationship has progressed in a way that is no longer beneficial to me, and so now you must go."

"Must go?" she repeats as though trying the words out for herself. "I must go?"

"Yes."

Chiara shakes her head as tears begin to fill her eyes, and I watch as she scrambles out of bed, taking the blanket with her. "You'll have to forgive me because I'm not understanding," she blurts, hysteria beginning to creep into her tone. "It was only last night you opened up to me and told me how important it was that I truly understand who you are and said that you needed me to love you. You said that you wanted me to be your wife, and now I have to leave, just like that? It doesn't make any sense."

"I'm sorry, Chiara. I—"

"No, don't give me that bullshit," she says, striding across the room toward me. "You're scared. You opened up to someone for the first time in your life and now you're scared."

"I am not a man who fears his own heart, Chiara."

"Then what the fuck?" she demands, stepping right in front of me as I stand to meet her. "I told you I was ready. I've allowed you to fuck with my whole life to the point that I don't have anything to go back to, nor do I want to go back. I want this life with you. I want to be here with you."

Taking her waist, I pull her in and drop a kiss to her temple. "It simply cannot happen," I tell her, feeling as my heart shatters within my chest. "I will have my driver take you home, and I'll arrange for Krista to pack up your things and have them delivered."

Chiara scoffs, gaping at me as though she doesn't even recognize me. "Just like that, huh?" she asks, her tone breaking as a tear rolls down her cheek and falls to her collarbone.

I nod, feeling an ache forming deep in my gut. "Just like that."

She stares at me a moment as the silence grows heavy between us, and I hate the betrayal that grows within her eyes. She's breaking right in front of me, and there's not a damn thing I can do about it. My hands curl into balls at my sides, resisting the urge to reach out and comfort her again, but I've kissed her once, and that's all I will allow.

The betrayal in her eyes quickly morphs into blatant agony, and just like that, Chiara turns and walks out of my bedroom, not sparing even a second to turn back. The moment the slamming door cuts through the silence, I let the ache consume me and fall to my knees, knowing that without a doubt, I just lost my whole fucking world.

CHAPTER 27

Chiara

Everything hurts.

I sit in the back of Killian's SUV—the only time I've ever been in it without him, and I've never felt so alone. His driver flies through the long, windy streets that lead back toward the city I once called home, and every inch of distance he puts between us shatters me just a little bit more.

I thought I'd found my forever. I thought we were going to build a life together, and after the conversation we had in the kitchen last night, I simply don't understand what went wrong.

Waking up in his bed, I had the perfect vision of how our morning was supposed to go. We were going to spend hours wrapped in each other's bodies while experiencing the sweetest pleasure this world could offer. We would have had breakfast in bed and ended up in the shower together, only to fuck up against the wall. I would have gotten on my knees for him and worshiped every inch of his rock-hard body, and once I was thoroughly done, I would have started all over again because we were meant to be. We'd found our happiness, and this was our chance to finally see a glimpse of what our lives could look like together.

Never in my wildest dreams did I think I'd wake to hear those words spill from his mouth. *You need to leave.* Since the moment I walked out of his room, those words have terrorized me in every way possible.

You need to leave.

You need to leave.

They won't go away, no matter what I do. They're on a constant loop inside my mind, destroying me from the inside out.

How could he just toss me aside as though I never mattered? I know this is all still so new, but the moment he saved me from the auctions and took me to his home, I came to terms with the fact that I was never going back. I'd said goodbye to my old life and started to learn what this new world had in store for me, and while it scared the shit out of me, I knew it was going to be okay because I had Killian right there to protect me.

Don't get me wrong, the idea of marriage and babies at twenty-three also terrified me, but Killian made it seem so easy, so natural. He made me believe that I could have anything I wanted, but I didn't want anything . . . only him. And now . . . Am I ever going to see him again? Or is he always going to be nothing more than a memory, a figment of my imagination, or a story that nobody will ever believe?

It's a long drive back into the city, and the last time I did it, Killian knocked me out with one hell of a strong sedative. I was so pissed about it, but now, I would give anything to be able to fall unconscious and wake up in another lifetime where the memories of him won't hurt quite so much.

I was falling in love. There's no doubt about it, and in an instant, he pulled the rug out from under my feet.

How the hell am I supposed to go back to my bland lifestyle after that?

The tears continue to flow, but I manage to gain control of my gasping breaths, and after an hour, the driver finally glances at me through his rearview mirror. I'm under no illusion that Killian would have demanded he watch over me. I also don't doubt that someone will be watching me over the coming weeks. At least until I fade from Killian's mind and become some girl he used to know.

It's a long three hours by the time the driver pulls to a stop outside my apartment block. The moment the door opens, the fresh air hits my face, and I'm reminded of the night I was snatched off this very sidewalk.

A shiver sails down my body, but I'm too exhausted from the emotional rollercoaster to pay it much attention. "You good?" the driver asks.

"I ummm . . . I'm not sure actually," I say, struggling to get my voice above a mere whisper. "When I was first taken, I lost my bag that had my keys and everything in it. I'm not sure I can get into my apartment. Actually, I'm not sure I even still have an apartment."

"Mr. DeLorenzo was sure to take care of that, Miss. Your home is just as it was before you left, and your rent is up to date."

"Oh—"

"You should be able to find the spare key above the door frame." The driver glances at me through the mirror, and I force a smile across my face, but it falters when he goes to open his door. "Let me help you with your bags."

Waving him off, I scramble out of the car and peer at him through his open door. "No need. I won't be keeping any of the things Killian gifted me. Please take them back to him. They'll only get stolen around here, and truth be told, if they're in my apartment, I'll probably end up burning them before they even get a chance to be stolen."

"You sure, Miss?"

"Positive," I say. "Thanks again. And please let Krista know not to bother packing up the rest of my belongings. It'll only be a waste of her time."

He offers me a friendly smile, but I see the pity in his eyes, and not being able to handle it, I turn and make my way into my apartment complex before he gets a chance to destroy me further. The old, rickety stairwell looks just as unloved as it's always been as I make my way up, clutching the railing to avoid plummeting to my death on the creaky steps.

My apartment is on the third floor, and by the time I reach my door, my whole body is ready to give out. I push up onto my tippy toes to feel the top of the door frame for the key, and finding it a moment later, I make quick work shoving it into the lock.

The door opens, and as I walk in, I feel as though I'm taking a step back in time. This place has been my home for so long, but now it feels foreign—like it no longer belongs to me. All my things are here, but my heart belongs somewhere else.

It's a small apartment, and before I've even closed the door behind me, I see the wad of cash and the phone that's been left on the kitchen counter. Everything constricts within me. The last thing I want are his handouts. After all, they're only here because of his ridiculous need to clear his guilty conscience.

Closing the door behind me, I make a point to flick the lock, put the chain on, and deadbolt the door before finally making my way over to the kitchen counter and looking over the cash with a cringe. There must be at least ten grand here—the type of money I would have killed for before my life was turned upside down.

Taking the phone, I power it on and wait the agonizing seconds for everything to load before opening the contacts list. There's only one number programmed into it with no name, but I have a good idea who it belongs to.

Then just because I'm a petty bitch when I'm hurting, I open a new text and start typing.

Chiara — I don't need your dirty, blood money or your stupid phone. I survived on my own before you, and I'll be fine without you. I'm burning the cash, and the phone is going out the window. Thanks for nothing, asshole. I don't need you.

Feeling pretty damn proud of myself, I turn the phone off and just to be on the safe side, I take the little sim card out and leave it on the kitchen counter right where I first found it. Truth be told, I doubt I'll actually burn the cash. Money like that doesn't come around often, and in these times, it's always smart to have something hidden away just in case, but that's all it'll be. I have every intention of returning to work and picking up right where I left off. Assuming work and college will take me back.

Exhaustion quickly claims me, and I take myself off to the bathroom and run a warm bath before stripping out of the clothes Killian bought for me. From now on, it's back to my normal shitty clothes, my normal shitty bed sheets, and my normal shitty life.

I'm not usually a bath lover, but I'm feeling today is going to be a day filled with exceptions, and without a second thought, I slip into the too-small tub and do my best to get comfortable.

Closing my eyes, I try to relax my mind, and as the emotional turmoil catches up to me, I finally let it all out and turn into a sobbing mess. I stay in the tub until the water is cold and my fingers have begun to prune, and when I finally find the energy to pull myself out of the water, I wrap my towel around me and collapse into my bed, not even bothering to dress.

With my head squished against my favorite pillow and my sore eyes growing heavier by the second, I allow myself to give in and fall into a fitful sleep.

I'm woken by a soft creak across my room, and my eyes spring open to find my room clouded by darkness, and I realize I've slept most of the day away.

"*You don't need me*," a deep Romanian accent fills my room, and I whip my gaze toward the armchair at the end corner of my bed.

Oh shit.

"You shouldn't be here," I tell Killian with a heavy sigh as I scooch to the end of my bed and get to my feet while trying to feign indifference, but I know he sees my puffy eyes. He sees everything.

I move to walk out of my bedroom when Killian stands and blocks my path, his massive frame almost intimidating if I didn't know any better. "*You don't need me?*" he repeats, his brow arching as those dark eyes consume me. Then in an instant, he grabs my hips and whips me around so that my back is flush against his wide chest.

His hand curls around my body, roughly cupping my pussy as he grinds his palm right against my clit, making my hips jolt with involuntary desperation. He leans into me, his breath brushing my bare shoulder. "Let me remind you just how much *you don't need me.*"

Oh, fuck, fuck, fuck, fuck.

Without warning, Killian bends me over the end of my bed as he kicks my feet apart, and I can't help the desperate yelp that slips from my lips. My pussy is drenched, already so worked up, and when his hand comes down in a painful spank against my ass, my knees begin to tremble.

There's no doubt about it. I will always need him. Always crave him.

His fingers trail through my center, every touch sending me into a fucking meltdown when he slams his fingers inside of me. "OH GOD," I cry out, my body already spasming as his fingers reach my G-spot. He does it again and again, rotating his fingers and curling them deep inside me.

"*If you don't need me, Angel. Then I suppose you don't need this,*" he says before tearing his fingers free and leaving me empty.

I whimper at the loss as I quickly figure out his game plan. He's going to work me up and deny me at every chance until I admit just how desperately I need him. But he pushed me away. He told me to leave. In his actions, he was the one who told me I wasn't needed, so I won't dare give him what he came for.

"I don't need you," I tell him, the coldness of my tone feeling foreign on my lips.

Killian wraps his hand around my hair and pulls me up off my bed until my back is against his chest again, and when he brings his soaking fingers to my lips, I tremble again. "Open," he demands.

I do exactly what he asks, opening my mouth as he slowly pushes his fingers inside. I suck them clean, tasting my desperation on his skin. I work my tongue over his fingers until he finally pulls them free from my mouth, but the soft groan whispered in my ears lets me know that he's just as wound up as I am.

"You don't get to come here and play your games with me, Killian," I growl, feeling his heavy erection against my back. "If you want to fuck me, then do it. Give me everything you've got. Otherwise, you can leave. But this will be the last chance you ever get. You were the one who told me to get out, remember? You were the one who didn't need me."

He pulls me harder against him, his hands so rough on my body. There's a shift in the atmosphere, a heaviness that consumes us both, and I feel the very second the fight leaves him, and he's left feeling just as broken as I do. "I will never not need you, Chiara," he says through a clenched jaw.

Every part of me succumbs to the destructive man behind me, and I melt back into the comfort of his strong arms, desperately wishing things could be different. "Take me," I beg him. "Let me feel you just one more time."

His lips come down on the side of my neck, working up to the sensitive spot just below my ear as my eyes roll. His arm winds around my body, slipping down between my thighs and finding my center. He rubs tight circles over my clit, and my whole world falls to pieces.

"Killian," I breathe.

"I know, Angel," he murmurs, and I can't help but feel as though this is the goodbye I didn't get this morning. In an instant, he turns and lifts me into the safety of his warm arms.

My legs lock around his waist as he steps around the edge of my bed, bringing his lips to mine and kissing me deeply before lowering me to my bed. He comes down with me and reaches between us as he frees his straining erection against my stomach.

I feel his fingers curling around himself, pumping up and down as he continues to kiss me. His lips move down to my throat, and I reach for his face, lifting just enough for his dark gaze to lock onto mine. "I was falling in love with you," I tell him.

Killian nods, and the tip of his cock pushes at my entrance, slowly stretching me wide. "I know."

He keeps going until he's fully seated inside of me, and as he finally starts to fuck me, he holds on to me as though the idea of ever letting me go is simply unheard of. It's everything, yet excruciatingly heartbreaking at the same time.

He moves in and out, every thrust of his thick cock working me to the edge, and when he reaches down between us and gently rubs his fingers over my clit, my whole body begins to shake. I throw my head back as my chest heaves for sweet oxygen.

His other hand grips my waist, his fingers digging into me as he holds on for dear life. "Chiara," he murmurs.

"Don't stop," I gasp, feeling the familiar tightening deep inside of me, building like a coil preparing to spring. "Don't ever stop."

He gives me everything I need, just as he always has, and as that coil gets tighter and tighter, the intensity builds. I can't hold on to it a moment longer, and as he thrusts inside of me again, stretching me so damn wide, I explode in a dazzling mess around him.

My pussy wildly convulses, squeezing him so damn tight that he comes with me, shooting his hot load deep inside of me. His hold tightens on my waist, but he doesn't stop moving as my high consumes me, fucking me like his one and only queen.

My chest rises and falls with rapid movement, desperately trying to catch my breath as I finally begin to come back down to earth. My world is shattered like glass as I come undone, knowing that this part of me will always belong to him.

It was barely a month spent together, but it was enough to leave a scar right in the center of my chest, and I know without a doubt that I will never be the same.

Killian's body stills, but he leaves his cock seated deep inside of me, caging his arms around my body and rolling us until he's sitting against the headboard with me straddled over his strong thighs.

"You must know that it was never my intention to hurt you."

"Whether it was your intention or not, that's exactly what you did."

"I know, Angel. And I will live my life with the weight of your pain on my shoulders."

I nod, more than okay for him to have to carry around the guilt for how this went down as I desperately try to hold back the tears that threaten to spill. "You don't get to do this, Killian," I tell him. "You don't get to waltz back into my life whenever you want. If you're letting me go, then let me go. Give me a chance to try and find some kind of normalcy. You've broken me, and if I don't get to have you, then you don't get to have any part of me."

"It's not that simple," he says. "Letting go . . . It's not something I know how to do. I know I was the one to push you away, and despite how I feel, I have no choice but to stand by that. For your sake and for mine. This cannot work between us, not without consequence, and I refuse to put your life at risk for my own selfish desires. But for you, I will try. I will let go and give you the chance to rebuild your life."

My brows furrow, really taking in his words. "You told me this morning that we couldn't work because our relationship had progressed to a point where it was no longer beneficial for you, but that's not true, is it?" I ask, sitting up a little straighter. "This is because of Monica. Because she hired some asshole to try and take me out."

He nods. "Partly."

Anger burns through me, and I pull myself back from him, scrambling off the bed and grabbing the blanket to wrap around my naked body. "That's bullshit. Be honest for a change. You told me you were a man of your word, so give it to me straight for once. Why did you send me away?"

"Because I can't protect you like this, Chiara," he growls, throwing himself to his feet and reaching for his pants. He quickly pulls them on, does up the fly, but leaves the button hanging free. "This world . . . You're not suitable for it. You're a fighter, and you're everything that I need, but it's not enough. This world will destroy you. Just standing at my side automatically paints a target on your back, and I thought I could handle it. I thought I was okay knowing that at any time you could be taken from me, but I'm not. I can't do it. The thought of losing you like that . . . I can't fucking do it, Chiara."

He's losing it, the panic quickly overwhelming him, and I make my way toward him, gripping his arms and forcing him to meet my eyes. "I'm right here, Killian. Nobody can get to me here. I'm okay."

He presses his lips into a tight line as he pulls me against his chest and holds me tight. "I can't protect you. I'm sorry, Sweet Angel. If there were a way I could guarantee your safety, I would, but I just can't do it to you. I need you to distance yourself. Take off and start a new life, far away from me and my enemies. You have the world at your feet. You can do anything you want."

"But all I want is you."

Killian lets out a heavy breath and sits on the edge of my bed as I stand between his legs, holding on to his strong shoulders. "You deserve a life that isn't like mine. A life of massacres and hitmen isn't what I want for you. You shouldn't have to learn to fear the man you love, and I should never have asked you for that."

Silence pulses between us as I feel that invisible string between us begin to burn, and as the heaviness weighs down on us, he pulls me onto his lap. "I will leave you alone, Angel. I will give you the freedom to start over, but just know that if you call me, I will come. If you feel unsafe, I will be here, but I cannot guarantee that I will be capable of walking away from you again. If you call, be sure."

I swallow over the lump in my throat and nod, the weight of his words resting on my soul. "You know, when you told me last night that you wanted me to truly be your wife, I've never wanted anything more. I thought we were really starting our lives together."

"You don't know how badly I wish it could have been so," he tells me. "There's just one thing I need from you." My brows furrow, and I meet his stare as I wait for him to continue. "Tell me, Chiara. Tell me what it is you've been so afraid of where Monica is concerned. I know you've been hesitant to share, but I don't understand why. There's more to this than you've disclosed."

A spark of fear catches light inside my chest, and I lean into him, brushing my lips over his, wishing I was able to tell him what he needs to know, but just because I no longer live in his home doesn't mean I'm free from Sergiu's threats, and that's not a risk I'm willing to take.

Especially now that I'm out here on my own.

"I'm sorry," I whisper, hating to let him down again, but if I could give him the tools to discover for himself, maybe everything might be okay. "I wish I could tell you, but it's too much of a risk. All I can say is that perhaps it's time for a review of your surveillance footage. That should give you the answers you're looking for."

His brows furrow and he reluctantly nods. "Okay, Angel," he says, standing and balancing me back on my feet. "Let's not drag this out. I need to leave."

I can't hold on a second longer as the tears finally win the battle and begin rolling down my cheeks, and all I can do is watch as he leans in and kisses me one last time. "Goodbye, my love," he murmurs as those dark eyes capture mine, and then just like that, he turns and walks away, closing the door behind him.

CHAPTER 28

Killian

It was one hell of a long drive back to my home, and the moment I walked through the door, I beelined straight for my office.

Leaving Chiara like that killed me. Having to walk away from her as she silently cried was the most horrendous torture I have ever endured, and that's saying a lot considering the hell I've suffered through at the hands of my enemies. But I'd endure it all again if it meant I could change things and hold on to her for the rest of time.

Dropping into my office chair, I power on my computer as I drum my fingers against the desk. Impatience tears at me, and while I feel helpless and broken, she's given me something to focus on, a task that could hopefully give me some kind of answers.

I don't know what she hopes I'm going to find here, but if she thinks it's important enough to mention it, then I owe it to her to dig as deeply as I can into my surveillance footage.

Once the computer is on and ready, I waste no time bringing up the footage, and after spending the whole trip home debating on where to start, I scroll all the way back to the night she first arrived. Issues didn't start until after the gala where Monica first met Chiara, and despite wanting to desperately skip ahead to that night, I resist.

The screen comes alive from that night, and I fast-forward through the footage until I see my SUV coming down the driveway. I watch as Chiara steps out onto my property for the very first time in that piece of shit bondage outfit Ezekiel has all his girls wear.

We make our way up the stairs to the door, and after walking inside, I start to fast-forward. Nothing else happened that night that could possibly set off alarm bells. She gave me one hell of a performance that crippled me, and after I walked away, she crashed for the night, not waking until late the next day.

I scroll through as much as I can, following her movements throughout the house and pausing whenever she interacts with anyone. She had lunch out by the pool when I first requested her presence in my bedroom, and that night, I held up my vow to fuck her until she believed she wanted this.

She was so worn out that I carried her back to her bed, the moment we finished talking and I closed the door behind me. I fast-forward through the night, skipping ahead to when she woke.

The sun is just starting to brighten the screen when movement inside her room has me slowing the video down, and I can't fucking believe what I'm seeing. "What the fuck?" I mutter to myself, watching as Sergiu, the one man I'm supposed to be able to trust with my life, welcomes himself into Chiara's bedroom.

How the fuck could I not know about this? I sure as hell didn't approve of it. Sergiu knows my boundaries better than anyone. He knew she was off-limits to him, even if it was an innocent conversation.

I watch closer as Chiara sleeps soundly, unaware that she's not alone, but a moment later, Sergiu drops down on the edge of her bed, his hand clamped over her mouth to keep her from screaming. Chiara wakes with alarm, her eyes springing open with undiluted terror.

Anger drums through my veins, and I have to force myself to remain in my seat and keep watching, but suddenly Chiara's fear begins to make sense.

Sergiu leans down toward her, keeping his voice low, and it's clear as fucking day that he did so to keep me from finding out. Then as he starts to talk, I turn the volume up on my computer, making sure I'm able to make out every last word.

"Hush now, pretty girl. If you even try to make a single peep, I'll snap your neck before a sound can even leave your mouth."

He surveys her like cattle, like he has every right to be there, all while she stares back at him in fear. There's a moment of silence before he continues. *"I don't get it. There is nothing special here,"* he tells her in a conniving tone that makes me sick. *"What does Killian see in you?"*

My hands ball into fists, and just when I thought it couldn't get any worse, Sergiu moves on top of her, crushing her thighs with his knees to keep her pinned, and just like that I realize this is where those bruises came from.

I'd seen them the night of the DeLorenzo Gala. Hell, I'd even fucking asked her about them. She refused to tell me, she straight-up lied about it, and even after calling her out on it, I still didn't get any answers, but I chose to let it go. I believed that if there was something truly wrong, she would come to me, but she didn't. Was she too afraid? Too ashamed?

Why the hell didn't she tell me about this? Have I failed her that much that she didn't trust me to speak up? Didn't she believe that I cared enough to do something about it? All I know is that I let her down. I was with her multiple times and never noticed the bruises until it was already too late. I should have paid closer attention. I should have pushed harder for answers after I finally saw them.

Chiara tries to cry out, but his clamped hand over her mouth makes it impossible. Tears roll down her beautiful cheeks, and not a moment later, he violently thrusts his fingers inside of her. He does it again and again, and just as bile rises in my throat, the asshole has the nerve to belittle what's mine. *"Ahhhh, it makes sense now,"* he spits as he fucks her with his fingers. *"You've got a tight little cunt to go along with that pretty little face."*

I pause the footage, throwing myself out of my chair as I pace behind my desk, unable to catch my breath. My hands ball into fists, and I clench my jaw so tight my teeth almost shatter under the pressure. I'm going to fucking kill him. There's no doubt about it. He touched what was mine. He took from her, violated her precious body, and now I will get justice, but not before I discover the extent of his crimes.

A few minutes pass before I've calmed enough to press play, and I watch the rest of her assault as she fruitlessly tries to fight him off, but it's no use. She's not nearly strong enough. She's completely left at his mercy. I watch as he reaches for the front of his pants while trying to keep her quiet, but a knock sounds at the door.

Relief rushes through me as he pauses and Krista's tone sounds through the footage, asking if she's awake. No response comes from Chiara, but Krista remains just long enough to deter Sergiu. She tells Chiara that she will return soon, and it's exactly what Chiara needs to gain freedom.

Sergiu finally pulls away from her, and I watch with unease as his tone comes through my speakers once again *"You got lucky today, girl. But let me make one thing clear. If I find out that you've even whispered about this, I'll come back here every fucking night, and what happened in here today will seem like child's play in comparison. And if you even think about offering him a DeLorenzo heir, I will tear your baby right out of your womb."*

And that right there answers every fucking question I've ever had. Why she kept quiet. Why she stiffened when I first introduced the two at the family gala. Why she hid in the upstairs library during my meeting. She was terrified of him, and she had every right to be. Had I known, had she found the courage to take the leap and tell me what was going on, I would have done something about it. I would have ended his miserable life without a second thought.

Any act against my wife is a betrayal against the DeLorenzo name, and because of that, I will ensure that Sergiu never claims what belongs to me. My position in this family will never be his. The only place he's going is to a shallow grave.

Sergiu finally leaves her room, and I watch as she promptly falls apart. Heavy sobs tear from her chest and despite how every cry of fear shreds my soul to pieces, I force myself to watch the whole thing because her pain is mine to bear. I brought her into this, and I'm responsible for everything that happened to her while under my roof.

I failed to protect her. I brought her into my home and foolishly believed that she would be safe.

A hollowness tears my chest wide open as I force myself to continue looking through the footage, desperate to know just how often Sergiu welcomed himself into her room. I see all the nights we were together. I see the times she would search for me in my home, only to be disappointed to learn I was working. I watch as she cautiously allows herself to begin to trust me, and I watch as that trust begins to shift into something more.

I get through to the night of the gala, and I've just started to convince myself that Sergiu's visit was a one-time thing, when he betrays me once again. Chiara lays in her bed, tossing and turning in a fitful sleep after spending a portion of her night beaten on the bathroom floor. I'd demanded Sergiu's presence in my home. I gave him access to her.

He walks into her room, and just like the time before, he sits on the edge of her bed, clamping her mouth. She wakes immediately, that same fear from the first time flashing in her green eyes. *"Even try to scream, and I will make your life a fucking misery,"* he tells her. *"Do you understand me?"*

She's fucking terrified, but after a short conversation, it's clear he's there simply to deliver a warning. He pulls her out of bed and slams her against the wall, a move she was in no condition to handle, and yet she still kept her mouth shut.

Sergiu threatens her with the usual bullshit and jabs her in her bruised ribs—the very ribs his wife had almost broken—and just when I expect Chiara to crumble, she fights back, surprising me like never before. And even though she was new to my life, she knew her place at my side and knew exactly what to say to make him fear for his own life.

Their conversation is short, and he soon leaves, but the look in his eyes . . . He's just as terrified of her as she is of him. And while she doesn't hold the kind of power that he does and isn't capable of causing physical harm to him, she holds a different kind of power, one that Sergiu could only ever dream of having now—my loyalty.

She's stronger than I could ever have known, and she handled herself remarkably against a man like Sergiu, but I stand by my decision to send her home. If all of this happened under my roof within the space of two weeks, what else did I miss? Hell, Monica was able to get a hitman access to my home for fuck's sake.

I spend the next few hours watching through the rest of the footage and am relieved to find no other incident had taken place, but at least I have a solid understanding of why Chiara felt she couldn't tell me what was going on. I won't lie, her inability to trust that I could take care of it has a searing pain taking residence inside my chest. She feared Sergiu would return, and she was right to believe that he'd try. As for Monica, I'm unsure if Chiara truly worried about carrying the burden of what it would mean to get justice, but Sergiu made it clear what would happen if she even tried.

I don't know how I'm supposed to handle all of this, but I can't jump the gun without causing havoc and unrest with the family. I need to play it smart, plan this out like a game of chess, and when the time is right, I will strike. When I do, he's going to beg for the relief of death, but it won't come, not until he's fully paid for the crimes he's committed against the woman I love and the betrayals against the DeLorenzo name.

It's well past midnight by the time I finally leave my office and make my way up to bed, and despite knowing that Chiara will be asleep, I can't resist sending her a text.

Killian — I reviewed the footage, Angel. You should have told me.

I put my phone down on my bedside table, not expecting a response until morning, if at all, and start unbuttoning my shirt. The material falls to the floor, and just as I go to reach for the button of my pants, my phone chimes.

My brows furrow, and I look at my phone for a second before springing into action and scooping it off the table.

Chiara — You once told me nothing happens inside your home without your say-so. How was I to know you didn't send him?

Killian — How could you ever believe that I would allow such atrocities?

Chiara — Of course I know that now, but the days after it happened, before I knew you, I didn't. You told me you were a monster who I needed to fear. I thought you were testing me.

The guilt eats at me as I read over her words. I created an atmosphere for her in that first week where she didn't believe I could be trusted, to the point she thought it could have been a possibility that I sent Sergiu to her. The only reason she could ever think so poorly of me is if I'd given her reason to, and that's on me.

Killian — I failed you, Angel. I promise I will make this right.

Putting my phone back down, I go to finish undressing when I hear a noise outside my door, and I move across the room and swing the door open to find Krista in the middle of raising her hand to knock, a tray of food balanced on her forearm.

"You're still here?" I ask.

"You haven't eaten all day, Killian. I know you're hurting, but it would really help settle my worries if you ate a proper meal."

I give her a small smile and reluctantly take the tray, knowing she's bound to stand right here until every bite is gone. Striding out of my room, I put the tray down on the small table in the sitting area that stands between my room and what was Chiara's.

I drop down into an armchair, and as I collect the knife and fork to start eating, Krista smiles and turns to leave. "Krista, wait," I say, watching as she pauses and turns to look back at me. "A few weeks ago, the second morning Chiara was here, you came up to deliver her breakfast. You knocked on the door to see if she was awake."

"Yes," she says, her gaze flashing with unease.

"You usually serve breakfast in the kitchen."

Krista visibly swallows and averts her gaze, her nervousness as loud as the empty room beside us. "That's correct, I do."

"Why?"

Her stare comes back to mine as the color drains from her face. "Please don't, Killian," she begs. "I do not have sufficient evidence to support my theory, and I do not wish to make such accusations of your second-in-command. If I am wrong, he will make an attempt on my life."

"Krista, please," I say, not above begging. "I have already reviewed the surveillance footage, and you are not wrong in your assumptions. However, I need to know why, at that time, you thought it was imperative to check on her."

"He's a bad man, Killian. I have been here for years and met the likes of all kinds of men. I know the difference between a man who has a good heart, a man who is cunning, a man who is manipulative, and a man who is simply evil. Sergiu is that evil. He encompasses it, and the moment Chiara arrived, he was too curious for his own good. He hated her for no reason, despised her simply for being here despite her doing nothing to deserve such animosity," she explains. "That morning he arrived too early. You weren't due to meet him for another hour, and when he made his way upstairs, I just knew. I had no proof or any real reason to make such vile assumptions, but I felt it in my chest. He was going to attempt to hurt her, and so I did what little I could and hoped for the best."

"Thank you, Krista," I tell her. "I wish you had told me sooner."

"I do not wish to offend you, Killian. You truly are a wonderful soul, and I love you. You have given me this wonderful life and asked for nothing in return. However, let's not pretend there isn't a hierarchy within this home. I am an employee, and it is not my place to comment on the senior members of your family, the people who share your blood. Plus, I've already been through a hell of my own. I don't wish to draw Sergiu's attention to me any more than it already has. I do apologize for not bringing this to your attention. However, when Chiara was up for the day, she did not offer any signs that foul play had occurred. I thought maybe all he had done was talk to her."

"I understand," I say with a nod. "Why don't you retire for the night? I have a lot to consider, but just know that your name will be left out of this. You have nothing to worry about."

"Thank you, Killian."

"There's no need to thank me," I tell her. "I've already let both you and Chiara down by not seeing what was right in front of my face all these years, and it's about time that I make things right."

CHAPTER 29

Chiara

This fucking sucks.

It's been three days of agony where I've done nothing but feel sorry for myself, apart from last night when I took a breather from the agony of losing Killian and found the joy at the bottom of a tequila bottle.

Waking up this morning, I immediately regretted that decision, but at least I've been able to feel sorry for myself for a whole new reason, which has been refreshing.

These past three days have been miserable. I made this whole declaration about getting my life back on track, getting back to work, and making sure my college enrollment is still intact, and yet all I've done is hole up in my shitty apartment and stare at a blank wall. I'm really doing wonders with my newfound freedom. Killian should be so proud.

Tonight though, things change.

I'm not just going to talk about getting myself on track, I'm actually going to do it. I hope.

After swallowing a few painkillers to help manage the epic hangover, I take one final look in the mirror to make sure I'm presentable for a night at work. My hair looks dull, and the rest of me looks boring as hell compared to the expensive clothing Killian has had me in over the past few weeks. Hell, I've been in silk gowns and fancy lingerie, but tonight, I'm in a pair of black jeans with bleach stains and a boring cotton tank.

Knowing this is about as good as it's going to get, I grab my key off the counter and make my way out the door before quickly locking up, then because I no longer own a handbag, I shove the key into my bra and get going.

It's barely dusk with the sun only just beginning to duck down beyond the horizon, leaving enough daylight to make the walk to the bar not so daunting, though who knows how I'm going to cope tonight.

With every step I take, it's almost impossible to ignore the black SUV that creeps along the road, and every time I pause and glance back, the driver eases onto the brake and waits for me to continue.

I roll my eyes. There's no doubt these are Killian's men tasked with watching over me and making sure I'm okay, and despite how much I want to scream at them to leave me alone, it's not their fault. They're simply following orders that they're not permitted to refuse. I suppose I should be looking at it as a sweet gesture and not an insult that suggests I'm incapable of looking after myself. Though to be fair, I did manage to get myself kidnapped off the side of the street and thrown headfirst into a human trafficking ring, so it's not as though I have a great track record.

Arriving at the bar, I pause on the sidewalk before looking back at the SUV and warring with myself on whether to be a decent human being or not. Letting out a sigh, I turn back and make my way toward the SUV. Seeing me coming, the driver puts the window down.

"Miss Chiara, how lovely to see you again," Killian's hired help says, feigning surprise. "I didn't realize you'd be here tonight."

"Quit the bullshit and stop acting like I haven't been throwing old meatballs at you from my bedroom window for the past three days," I tell him. "But I'm planning on being here for a while. I'm getting my job back, so you might as well park the car and come in for dinner. If everything goes well with my boss, then I'll probably be here until one, maybe two in the morning."

The driver looks to the other guard, his brows arched in question. "That's a really long fucking time to go without dinner. You know how cranky I get when I don't eat."

The other guard lets out a heavy sigh and rolls his eyes. "Fine. But you're paying."

"YES!"

Feeling as though I've done my civic duty, I go to turn away before thinking better of it and looking back at the passenger who seems to be the one in charge of the two. "Out of curiosity," I say. "How long is this whole stalking me thing supposed to last?"

He offers me a tight smile as pity flashes in his eyes. "Indefinitely, ma'am. Killian has no plans to cease your security, so as far as I am concerned, you can consider us your personal security team. Travis and I will be working the night shift, and then Calvin and Harry will be with you during the day."

"Great," I mutter under my breath. "Exactly what I need."

The SUV pulls away, presumably to find somewhere to park, and I don't waste a moment making my way into the bar, nearly running directly into my boss, and damn it, he looks pissed.

"Oh, hell no," he says. "You can turn your ass right around and get out of here. Do you have any idea what kind of mess you left me with? Not even a call to tell me you won't be coming in. What the fuck, Lara? It's like you vanished out of thin air."

"Well . . . I guess that's exactly what happened," I tell him. "I've had a really messed up few weeks that includes getting snatched off the side of the road while I was walking home from here, and I don't mean to tell you that as some kind of sob story, I just want to be honest with you. But I'm home now and I'm ready to try and get back to normal life . . . If you'll still have me, of course."

His brows furrow as he steps closer to me, and I watch as his gaze focuses on the dark pink scar left on my lip, courtesy of Monica. "You're serious?" he questions, deep concern flashing in his gaze as he continues searching my face, noticing my other new scars. "What the hell happened to you, Lara? Do you need me to contact someone for you? Family? The police?"

"No. No, no. Please don't do anything like that," I tell him. "I was put into a really shitty situation, and I met somebody who was able to help me out. He kept me safe, but as I said, I'm home now, and it's over, and I'd really love it if you'd be able to look past the last few weeks of radio silence and remember that you actually really loved having me work at your bar."

"Shit, Lara," he says, gripping the back of his neck. "Of course you can have your job back. I just . . . You know you can always talk to me, right? I know I'm your boss and we've never really had that kind of relationship, but I care about you, and if you're going through something or someone's hurting you, I just need you to know that you have options. I can offer you a safe place to crash or give you cash for a ticket out of here, just say the word."

A fond smile stretches across my face, and I scold myself for the rush of emotion that floods me. "Thank you," I murmur. "I appreciate that, but really, I'm all good now."

"Alright, have it your way, but that's an open offer. There's no expiry date on that," he tells me, reaching out and gently squeezing my shoulder. "Now get back there. The bar's been kicking my ass for weeks. I really don't know how you do it."

Thank fuck for that.

Getting straight to work, I head to the back to clock in, and before I know it, I'm back behind the bar and falling into routine. It's a busy night, and the customers keep coming, making it easier to keep Killian off my mind.

My new security team occupies the corner booth, getting curious glances from the customers, knowing without a doubt they don't fit in here in their imposing black suits and buff frames, and considering the way they watch me like stalkers in the night, it doesn't take long for the other staff to figure out why they're here, but thankfully they don't ask.

Despite ordering their own meals—a meal paid for with a black card with the name Killian DeLorenzo on the front—I continuously bring them more fries and soda, doing my best to keep them comfortable despite their continued objections. But if they're forced to be here just to watch out for me, then I'll do what I can to make this easier for us all. Hell, I might even consider putting a hold on throwing food at them from my bedroom window. Though there's no doubting the rush of joy that floods me when the sauciest meatball splatters right across their windshield, only for the idiots to put on the wipers and smear the mess everywhere.

It's a little after ten when I deliver another round of sodas to their table and notice the way they both stiffen in their booth, their gazes locked on the woman walking through the door.

Whipping around, I take in Monica in her ridiculous designer outfit looking like some over-done Beverly Hills side chick. "Ma'am," my new head security dude says, a stark warning in his tone. "Just say the word and we'll escort her out of here."

"No, it's fine," I say, swallowing the fear as it tries to rear its ugly head. She's already destroyed me in so many ways, stolen my dignity, and taken out a hit on my life. She doesn't get to have my fear too. "She's not going to try anything here."

"Ma'am," he repeats. "I highly suggest you step away and allow us to handle this."

"She's not running me out of here. She's already cost me the one thing that matters to me. I've got nothing to lose. Not anymore."

Before he gets a chance to warn me again, I walk back toward the bar while watching her like a hawk, but it doesn't go unnoticed the way my new security team creeps in—one of them casually with their hand on the gun at his side and the other is already on the phone, probably filling Killian in on this little situation.

Making my way behind the bar, I grab a glass and fill it with the nastiest beer on tap, making sure to give it the biggest head of froth possible while spilling it all down the side of the glass. She watches my every move, and as I put the nasty beer down in front of her, I hold her stare, not finding her nearly as intimidating as she hopes.

"You lost?" I question.

Monica scowls at the beer in disgust before raising her gaze back to me. "This is your life, huh? The one woman who could make the great Killian DeLorenzo feel something, and this is what you are. He was right to let you go. You're beneath him. You're scum."

"Did you come all the way out here just to insult me?"

"I had to see for myself that he'd truly taken you out with the trash. You know how the rumor mill works, you can never really trust it until you've confirmed it for yourself, and it looks as though the rumors were right. You're back where you belong."

"Wonderful news all around," I mutter, my sarcasm thicker than ever before. "I suppose that means you can take your freshly done manicure and get your ass out of here. Lord knows what filth was on that stool before you sat your fake ass on it."

"You truly are a disgrace, Chiara."

"Says the woman who ordered a hit on me," I say, reaching for her drink. "You done with this?"

Her face scrunches and she goes to push the sticky glass away, but I pull on the small coaster beneath and watch with fascinating delight as the glass tips over, sending a wave of beer cascading over the edge of the bar and right into her lap.

Monica screeches, throwing herself to her feet. "You fucking bitch."

"Oh no," I gasp, holding my hand to my mouth in fake shock. "Is that a Givenchy jacket? You better hurry and get that to the dry cleaner before it stains."

Her face turns beet red, and as cheap beer rushes off her, she steps closer to the bar, her horrid stare locked on mine. "You're dead. You better watch your back, bitch."

"Who, me?" I ask. "What are you going to do, Monica? I'm out. You can't touch me without causing a scene. It's too messy and you know it. The police will be crawling all over it, and now that you've made a public declaration in an establishment covered with surveillance footage, all arrows point to you. But sure, give it your best crack. I'll be right here waiting."

Monica clenches her jaw and whips around as she grabs her designer bag off the bar. She goes to storm away, probably angling for something dramatic, but I call after her instead. "Oh, Monica," I say in a sugary-sweet tone. "It really was lovely seeing you again, but keep in mind that while I might be out here working some lousy bar, one call to Killian is all it would take to end you. That's assuming he doesn't already know and is waiting for his moment to strike. Exciting, isn't it?"

Her face drains of all color, and for a moment, I fear I'm going to have to scrape her off the dirty ground, but she quickly recovers and whips around before hightailing it out of here.

One of my security guards—Travis, I think his name was—follows her out, hopefully making sure she actually gets in her car and leaves, while I remain behind the bar, cringing at my boss as he gestures toward the mop and bucket. But despite the mess I'm left with, nothing has ever been so satisfying.

My other guard hovers way too close for the rest of my shift, and by the time I'm closing up and stepping out onto the street, it's well past two in the morning, and yet I find myself frozen to the spot. My gaze lingers on the dark street, and all I can picture is the asshole who snatched me.

My body shakes as the trauma of that night bubbles up, leaving me rooted to the sidewalk in fear. Despite being the type of woman who doesn't like to ask for handouts, I can't help but glance toward the two men lingering in the familiar SUV.

They watch me through the open window, probably wondering why the hell I haven't made a move yet. "You guys are heading back to hover in front of my apartment building like fucking stalkers, right?"

"Nowhere else we'd rather be," Travis mutters as he rolls his eyes.

"Would it be completely inappropriate if I rode back with you?"

"Thank fuck! I thought you'd never ask," Travis says with a heavy sigh of relief. "Do you have any idea how frustrating it is having to roll behind you at a snail's pace? Don't get me wrong, the view from behind was great, but goddamn, you need to put a little more motivation into your walk."

"Fuck, man," the other guard says, slapping his colleague's chest. "Are you trying to get us fired? Why the hell are you commenting on the view from behind? The boss is going to fucking slaughter you."

I roll my eyes as I cross the street and help myself into the back of the SUV. "What the boss doesn't know won't hurt him . . . or you for that matter."

I laugh to myself at my lame attempt at being funny, but truth be told, no joke is ever funny if your heart isn't in it.

The driver takes off, and within moments we're pulling to a stop outside my apartment complex, and the guard whose name I haven't gotten, looks back at me. "You good to make it up to your apartment or do you need one of us to accompany you?"

I give him a tight smile, grateful for their presence tonight. "I'll be good. Just make sure nobody attempts to snatch me off the street and put me into a human trafficking ring."

"Fucking hell," Travis mutters, sounding shocked by how blasé I speak about it, though he doesn't know the way my chest sinks with hollowness every time the images of that place flash in my mind.

"Alright, well . . . thanks," I say, pushing out of the SUV and cutting across the sidewalk to the door of my complex while noticing the streetlight that always used to be out is suddenly shining brighter than it ever has before.

Taking my ass upstairs, an exaggerated yawn tears out of me, and just as I turn the corner to make my way to my door, a shadow steps out at me. My heart lurches in my chest, fear consuming me until I force myself to take him in.

His hands are out, a universal sign that he means no harm, and I have to take a moment to catch my breath. "What the fuck, Derek?" I demand, taking in the ex I'd spent years going back and forth with. "What are you doing here?"

"I've been trying to call you for weeks, and after ghosting me for so long, I figured something happened to you, but then my friend from college was at the bar tonight and said you were back, so I figured I'd come around. But I suppose you've changed your locks."

"You were trying to get into my apartment?" I ask as a chill sails down my spine.

"Where the fuck have you been?"

"That's none of your business," I say, striding past him to the door and digging the key out of my bra. "Look, it's late, and I want to get to bed. So can we do this another day, or perhaps not at all? You and I were over a long time ago, and I've moved on and realized that we were never good together. I deserve better, and now that I know what that's like, I'm never going back."

"The fuck did you just say?" Derek demands, and as he steps closer to me, I smell the alcohol on his breath and let out a frustrated sigh. He was always particularly nasty when he'd been drinking. "I was the best fucking thing that ever happened to you, bitch, and after everything I did for you, you repaid me by kicking me out on my ass. All you were good for was a fucking payday, but now that you're back, it looks like my luck's about to change."

"What the hell are you talking about? What payday?"

Derek laughs, creeping closer. "Oh, you still haven't figured it out," he mocks as his gaze begins to darken with something sinister. "It'll just make taking you again that much better."

Horror grips me like a vise, but before I can fully comprehend what he's telling me, a voice sounds from down the hall. "Time for you to leave, asshole," Travis says, standing there all imposing and intimidating, a stark contrast to the laidback man who was commenting on the great view my ass offered.

Derek takes one look at him, and without question, we all know who'll come out second best here. He backs up, putting space between us, and I take a deep breath, not having realized just how badly my hands were shaking.

Derek spares one more look toward me, his stare making me sick. "See you 'round, Chiara," he purrs, and with that, he slinks away like the piece of shit he is.

Did he really just tell me he was responsible for me ending up at that fucking auction house? Surely not. I know he was an asshole, but we were together for years. I knew him better than that, and sure, he was an ass a lot of the time, but he would never have done that. At least, I don't think he would have.

Travis waits at the end of the hall for Derek to completely disappear, and once he's finally gone, he meets my horrified stare. "Tomorrow, we're leaving your bullshit pride behind and walking you right to your door."

"Yeah," I agree. "I think that might be a good idea."

Travis nods and gestures to my door. "Take yourself to bed, Chiara. I'll wait here until I hear your deadbolt sliding into place."

"Thanks," I murmur before turning on my heel and shoving the key into the lock. The door opens, and I offer Travis one more friendly smile before finally diving into my apartment, and despite the long night I've just endured, there's no comfort here, not anymore.

After putting all the locks into place, I wander into my home, putting the key on the counter and pausing, staring down at the phone I haven't touched since last night.

There's only one voice that could make me feel okay, but as the heartbreak washes over me and the words he last said to me sound in my head—*just know that if you call me, I will come. If you feel unsafe, I will be here, but I cannot guarantee that I will be capable of walking away from you again. If you call, be sure*—I walk away, leaving the phone behind, more determined than ever to try and put Killian DeLorenzo behind me.

CHAPTER 30

Chiara

Blowing out a heavy breath, I look around my bland apartment as I prepare for another night at work. I used to be so proud of my home, so pleased with everything I'd managed to accomplish on my own, but having Killian standing in my apartment, even for just a moment, made everything seem so small and insignificant.

He's larger than life, and seeing him in my home made me feel like everything I've accomplished in this life means absolutely nothing compared to his empire. I no longer feel excited by my life. It all feels so dull compared to the life I could have had with Killian, and I don't mean materialistic things.

Being by his side was thrilling. Getting to be in his arms was a rush. Being the woman who occupied his bed was explosive, but digging my nails into his heart and claiming him as my own was the whole fucking world.

God, I miss him.

Everything hurts without him, and I know the concept of being his within the world he rules meant constantly living with a target on my back, but despite all of that, I think he was wrong to push me away because people don't just feel like this. I've had boyfriends, and there were times in my life when I thought I was in love, but never like this.

It consumes me, and every moment trying not to think about him is crippling. I just need one more chance to be in his arms, one more night indulging in his insane orbit.

I need to be his. I belong to him. Every piece of my shattered soul is his, and without him, I've never felt so empty. But more than that, I don't just want to be his, I want him to belong to me too. I want every piece of who he is to be mine. I want to love him and be loved by him. I want it all. Hell, even if it means popping out a few kids and spending every day of the rest of my life calling myself his wife.

I've never wanted anything so bad, and I don't even care if that makes me sound like a lovestruck teenager, crazy about some stupid boy. I'll be that stupid teenager if it means getting to have him. I get it though, and I understand why he pushed me away. He's absolutely right, his world would have destroyed me. I wouldn't survive it, but I believed he'd be able to protect me. I still do, and his doubts about his ability to do so destroy me.

A stupid sigh tears from deep in my chest, and I whip around and cross my apartment to the lonely phone that sits on my kitchen counter. I scoop it up, open the text chain with Killian, and simply stare.

It's my closest connection to him right now. The words he wrote me, they're all I have left, but I need more.

Without a proper conscious thought, my fingers sweep across the screen.

Chiara — Take me home to you.

Delete.

Chiara — I miss you.

Delete.

Chiara — Stop being such an arrogant asshole and see what's right in front of your face. I belong right there with you. I love you, and I know you love me, too. Nothing else should matter.

Letting out a heavy sigh, I go to delete that too when a loud noise echoes out in the hallway, and as my brows furrow, I drop the phone to the table and hurry to my door to peer through the little peephole. Wherever the noise came from is too far down the hall, and all I'm able to see is my neighbor's dirty doorway. I let out a huff, wishing for just a little bit of excitement in my day.

I go to turn away when a loud, piercing scream sounds from out in the hall, this time much closer, but in an instant, the scream cuts off like someone physically silenced it.

My heart races as I shove my face against the door again, desperately trying to figure out what's going on, when a shadow cuts in front of my door. I suck in a gasp, pulling away and hoping like fuck whoever it is keeps on going, only the shadow hovers, soon turning into two and then three.

I shake my head as I back up a few steps, my stomach knotting with a deep dread knowing that somehow this is retaliation by Monica. I provoked her the other night. I foolishly believed I was untouchable, that she couldn't hurt me while I was outside her world . . . but now? Fuck.

How stupid could I have been?

I back up another step as fear clutches me with both hands, refusing to release me, and just when I think I could be wrong, that it's all in my head, a loud BANG sounds on the other side of my door, rattling the whole fucking wall.

"Oh fuck, no," I panic, frozen to the spot.

Another BANG sounds through the door, and when the flimsy wood begins to splinter, I'm thrown into action. I lunge for the phone on the kitchen counter, my hands scrambling to scoop it up as the door finally gives in.

Pieces of my front door go flying through my apartment as three masked men storm in. A piercing scream tears from the back of my throat as I make a break for it, gripping the phone as I race through my too-small apartment.

They storm after me, their shouts of 'get her' turning my blood to ice as my fingers desperately try to move across the screen, knowing there's only one man who could possibly help me now.

I somehow manage to get the call to connect, and just as it rings once, the phone is viciously stolen out of my hand as a vise-like grip circles around my arm, yanking me to a stop so hard, my shoulder joint almost dislocates.

Fuck. Fuck. Fuck. Fuck.

"Over my dead body, bitch," a sickening tone spits as the call disconnects, and they throw my phone across the room, shattering the screen against the hardwood floor.

There's something familiar about his voice, but as the other two men close in on me, my fight-or-flight instincts kick in. I bring my knee up with every ounce of power I have, slamming it right into the asshole's junk.

He roars in agony, immediately dropping to the ground and releasing the death grip on my arm, giving me mere seconds to spring back into action.

With the other two blocking my only two ways of getting to the door, all I can do is aim for my bedroom, and I sprint toward it as fast as humanly possible, my bare feet pounding against the old rickety floorboards.

Racing through my bedroom, I sprint toward my window in a last-ditch effort to save myself, hoping like fuck my new security team is downstairs and somehow able to save me, but hell, if I have to throw myself from the third-story window just to escape, I will because I've been here before.

I used to see the best in people, but not anymore. I know what the kind of men who break into women's apartments want, and I have a good fucking idea where they plan to take me, and I refuse to go back there or be treated like some whore who can be sold to the highest bidder.

I'd sooner die than have to face that bullshit again.

"FUCKING GET HER," the asshole nursing his balls roars just as I reach the window. My hands shake on the locking mechanism, and as I tear it open, I peer out into the street, preparing to scream for help when I see Travis lying lifelessly on the sidewalk, a pool of deep crimson blood beneath him.

His partner is motionless in the driver's seat of the SUV, but if the shattered windshield is anything to judge by, it's safe to say he's gone, and I'm out here on my own.

The dread is like nothing I've ever known, and as my heart beats right out of my chest, I realize I only have one option left—I have to jump.

Tears fill my eyes as I frantically haul myself through the window, but a bruising grip closes around my arm and tears me back. "Too fucking slow, bitch," a gravelly tone spits into my ear as I'm pinned against a big body. "You're gonna wish you fucking jumped now."

"No. No. No. No. No."

I frantically try to fight for my freedom. Kicking. Scratching. Clawing. Punching. Screaming. I try it all, but despite my every effort, I'm not strong enough. The third guy reaches me, and between the two of them, they tackle me face down onto my bed and painfully bind my wrists behind my back.

The tight rope bites into my skin, and as they grab hold of it to pull me up off the bed, both my wrists and shoulders scream for relief. I cry out in pain as I'm whipped around and shoved against the same big body. He grips my shoulders, and just as he goes to shove me to get moving, my bedroom door becomes crowded with familiar faces.

Sergiu.

Monica.

And fucking Derek.

"What?" I breathe, my chest heaving with heavy breaths as I try to understand the crooked smirk across Derek's face. Why is he here . . . with them?

It doesn't make sense.

Sergiu steps forward as Monica watches the show with a twisted look of obsession, but knowing the biggest threat in the room, I keep my stare on Sergiu. "He's going to fucking kill you," I spit through a clenched jaw, the anger and fear creating the worst kind of emotional storm within me. "And when he does, it'll be brutal. You'll fucking beg for him to end you, but he won't. You'll suffer the agony of a million deaths before he even thinks about finally ending your pathetic life."

Sergiu laughs, and that thick Romanian accent makes me want to be sick. "Sure, if he ever finds out, which he won't. I'm his second-in-command, his flesh and blood who has stood by him since childhood. You are some whore he picked out at an auction. He will soon forget about you," he says, producing a needle that induces the rawest terror within me. "It's time for you to go, Chiara. There's no room for you here."

And with that, he slams the needle into the side of my neck and empties the syringe straight into my bloodstream.

My body slams against the hard ground as consciousness comes back to me. My head pounds, but I'm all too aware of the familiar cell I'm sprawled across to take a moment to focus on the pain.

It's small and dirty, but that's the least of my problems. My pained wrists are bound to the wall to keep me down as an eager audience watches over me.

Sergiu and Monica stand outside my cell, watching me like a caged animal with another guy I don't know the name of, but I remember him from last time. He's the owner, the asshole who was responsible for all of this bullshit.

Pulling myself up off the ground, I sit against the blood-smeared wall as I keep my gaze locked on them, all too aware of the fact the cell door remains open. Sergiu watches me too closely, and the vile way he looks at me makes my skin crawl.

He steps around the metal bars and creeps into the opening of my small cell. "Not so pretty anymore, stupid girl," Sergiu muses as he crouches down. "I wonder if he will still care for you once you've been thoroughly destroyed by another man."

I swallow over the lump in my throat as I try to cling to the thought of what Killian will do to him once he finds out.

I don't bother responding, too fearful for what's supposed to come next. Will I be abused in here? Stripped of my clothing and dressed up as the perfect little whore like last time? Put on display and sold to the highest bidder, or is that the best outcome I could possibly hope for? I got lucky last time, but luck like that doesn't come around often. Will it be worse for me now?

Sergiu looks over me, that vile stare making me sick. "Such a waste," he mutters. "You're a foolish girl, Chiara. You should have taken my warnings a little more seriously. I told you what would become of you if you opened your mouth about my wife."

I scoff and spit at him before kicking up dirt all over his expensive suit. "Joke's on you, asshole," I say with a twisted smirk of my own. "Do what you want to me, it makes no difference because that's not all I told him. I might die here or be sold to some piece of shit who'll rape me over and over, but it's nothing compared to what Killian will do to you."

Sergiu watches me for a moment, his gaze narrowed as if trying to catch me in a bluff, but there's no bluff here. "He doesn't know shit."

My lips twist, the sweetest satisfaction coming from the fear in his eyes. "Is that really a risk you're willing to take? After all, I was more than happy to tell him all about your wife's betrayal. So why the hell wouldn't I tell him about yours? Only difference is, the shit you did to me comes with surveillance footage that Killian spent hours combing through last night. So the real question is, why the fuck haven't you started running yet? Are you that confident that he'll let your crimes slide?" I pause, meeting his horrid stare. "Ask yourself, Sergiu. Whose back will he truly have? Yours . . . or mine?"

Sergiu clenches his jaw and raises back to full height. He backs out of my cell, keeping his gaze locked on mine before finally turning to his wife. "Come on. We must leave."

"What?" Monica screeches. "No way. We're not leaving until that bitch gets what she deserves."

Sergiu lunges for his wife, closing his big hand around her throat before slamming her back against the metal bars of the cell. "You'll do as I fucking tell you to," he growls before holding her there until the fight leaves her.

"Yes, Sergiu," she says.

He releases her before glancing toward the asshole who runs this shitshow. "Make sure you get rid of her this time," he snaps. "If the bitch won't sell, put a bullet through her brain."

With that, Sergiu stalks off, not stopping to check if his wife is following, and if she knows what's good for her, she'll get moving. But instead, she turns back and meets my stare. "You're gonna wish I killed you when I had the chance."

"Don't worry," I taunt before winking at her. "I'll be seeing you really soon."

Monica scowls at me, not knowing what to say before quickly scurrying after her piece-of-shit husband, leaving me with the other guy. He stands behind the bars, his muscled arms crossed over his chest, just simply staring at me.

He doesn't say a word, but there's clear disdain in his eyes as though he's trying to figure out exactly what he intends to do with me. "You caused me a lot of trouble and cost me a good payday."

"Take it up with Killian," I say. "The way you run your business has got nothing to do with me."

His gaze narrows. "Is that so?" he growls.

"You know he's coming for you too," I tell him. "Once he figures out what happened to me—and he will—you'll be served the same fate that Sergiu has coming to him."

He scoffs. "You think you're that important, huh? You're a whore, a dirty piece of ass for him to throw around. He doesn't care about you, and he sure as fuck isn't coming to save you. There'll be a new whore warming his bed by the end of the night."

A grin pulls at my lips, and even though there's a good chance I might end up dead, I'll be so damn happy to watch Killian come for revenge. "You don't know, do you?"

"Know what?"

I laugh, all too amused by the fate that's waiting for him. "You haven't abducted some cheap whore. You abducted Killian DeLorenzo's *wife*—the woman who owns his heart. He is the most powerful man on this earth, and nothing will stop him from finding me. When he does, I can guarantee you are going to wish you never laid eyes on me."

"Wife, huh?"

"That's right."

He reaches for the front of his pants, working his belt. "In that case, if he's gonna kill me anyway," he drawls, striding into my cell, his limp cock in his hand. "I might as well get something out of it then."

No. Fuck no.

Horror consumes me, and I pull against my bound wrists, the too-tight rope digging into my flesh as I throw my legs out. "Don't fucking touch me," I spit, kicking the fucker in the shin.

He roars in agony, but the determination in his putrid stare only strengthens, and I watch in horror as he whistles loudly, calling for help. Then as if on cue, two big men storm into my cell. They come for me, all three of them smirking like this is the best game they've ever played.

They hold me down as one of them pulls a knife and starts cutting my clothes off my body, the sharp tip digging into my flesh. I cry out in agony, and when my thighs are forced apart, the tears roll heavily down my cheeks.

The owner moves into me, and when he violently slams his pathetic excuse of a cock deep inside of me, all I can do is turn my head and clench my eyes, hoping and begging for the brutal torture to end.

One after the other, they take their turns, until finally it's over.

My body is bruised and broken, covered in blood and gashes from the sharp tip of the blade. When I hear the loud clang of the metal door closing behind them, I curl into a ball, not even able to reach for the discarded remains of my clothes, and like that, I cry.

I cry for my dignity. The pain that consumes me. The violent thrusts on repeat inside my mind. Their sickening laughter. The shame. The fear. The blood that coats my skin. Their cum between my thighs that I'm unable to wipe away. The desperation for it to end.

I cry. And cry.

And I don't stop until exhaustion claims me, and I fall into a dark pit of nothingness.

CHAPTER 31

Killian

My driver pulls up outside Chiara's apartment complex, coming to a stop right in front of the SUV I assigned to Chiara's security team, though they shouldn't still be here. She should have left for work hours ago.

When she called me this afternoon, something didn't feel right. The call only rang once, not long enough for me to answer and figure out what she needed, and when I tried to call back, the call was disconnected. It could have been put down to her emotions running wild and missing me just as desperately as I've missed her these past few days, but when I checked in with her security detail, no one answered. My team always answers. Something is wrong.

I've barely stepped out of my car before I notice the dried blood staining the sidewalk, and as sheer panic captures me in a chokehold, I look back toward the SUV parked behind mine.

It's empty, but I'm more focused on the bullet hole that goes right through the windshield, directly through the center of where the driver would have been sitting.

Fuck.

Travis and Jake were my best men, which is exactly why I assigned them to Chiara. With them, I knew she was safe. They were focused, brutal, and paid sharp attention to detail, all while still being capable of blending in. They wouldn't have intimidated her, and given time, I'm sure they all would have become quite friendly.

Dread sinks heavily into my veins.

Chiara.

If something has happened to her . . . fuck.

As I cut across the sidewalk, I lift my gaze to Chiara's bedroom window and find it wide open. She doesn't strike me as the type to be careless about her safety, whether her apartment is on the third story or not. She's supposed to be at work, and I doubt she would leave for the night without locking up properly.

At the complex door, I use the spare key I had copied and make my way into the building, my pace quickening by the second.

Something doesn't feel right. I've been in enough situations like this to know when things aren't adding up. Hell, I've been the reason for this kind of dread more times than I could ever try to count.

What are the chances that the two men I assigned to Chiara just happened to lose their lives in a bad street mugging that turned deadly?

Because the only other explanation is that someone came for my girl, and if I open her door to find her lying in a pool of blood on the ground, the storm I will wield will bring this whole fucking world down.

Reaching the third floor, I storm toward Chiara's door, only to find it in shattered pieces on the floor.

I pause, quickly taking in the apartment.

It's dead quiet apart from the outside noise flowing in through the open bedroom window, but all that matters to me is the smashed phone I'd given Chiara left on the floor.

I stride deeper into the apartment and crouch down in front of the phone before scooping it up. The screen is smashed, but upon pressing the home button, it lights up and I brush my thumb across the shattered glass to find it open to our text chain with an unsent text.

The screen is too shattered to try and make out the words clearly, so I hit send and wait just a moment for the text to arrive on my phone.

Chiara — Stop being such an arrogant asshole and see what's right in front of your face. I belong right there with you. I love you, and I know you love me, too. Nothing else should matter.

Fuck me. She couldn't be so right.

I screwed up letting her go. I should have held on tighter, and instead of letting the fear of losing her keep me from loving her, I should have figured out the source of that fear and burned it to the ground.

After making a quick round of Chiara's apartment, it becomes all too clear that she's not here. Apart from the open window, shattered phone, and broken door, there doesn't appear to be any sign of foul play against her. If she was hurt here, it wasn't enough to draw blood.

Pulling up my driver's number on my phone, I give him a quick call. "Boss?"

"Head down to Chiara's bar, make sure she's not working and report back."

"On it."

I hear as he pulls away, and just as I start circling the apartment again, I hear someone in the hallway outside the apartment. "What the fuck was that? You were supposed to take her and leave. Now there's fucking dead bodies and witnesses. The cops are going to be crawling all over this."

There's silence for a moment, telling me he's on the phone as opposed to having someone with him. It's not a voice I recognize, but there could only be a small handful of people it could belong to. "I don't give a fuck. I did what you asked, and you got the fucking bitch. Why does it matter how it happened? Just pay me what you owe me."

Fuck. That could mean a million different things, but it confirms what I already know to be true. Chiara's been taken.

The storm begins brewing inside of me, and I can't wait to bring it down on the fucker who thought they could touch what's mine. I fucking meant it when I said she was my wife. I know there's no signature on a dotted line, but the moment I claimed her as my own, it felt right.

Fuck. If I'm too late . . .

Hearing the person out in the hallway come closer, I move around the kitchen, keeping out of sight from the door. He strides right in, completely unaware of the hurricane he's about to face.

I recognize him from the file Sergiu gave me on Chiara at the beginning. It's her ex, Derek Monroe, and from what I've been able to learn of him, he's nothing much. Just a misguided loser who uses the people around him for a step up. And clearly, that's exactly what he's done to Chiara. He gave her up for a payday, and that's not something I can possibly look past.

Moving out through the other end of the kitchen, I place myself between Derek and his only escape before clearing my throat.

He yelps before whipping around with wide eyes, his hands up in a fighter's stance that only makes him look weak. I don't fight with my fists, not when I can avoid it. I prefer bullets.

"Where is Chiara?" I ask, not willing to waste time dancing around the topic.

"Who the fuck are you?"

"The one man you don't want to cross. Now, tell me where she is."

Derek scoffs and goes to step around me. "Yeah, get fucked, bro. I'm not telling you shit."

As he steps past me, I grab the front of his shirt and throw him halfway across the apartment, watching as he tumbles back against the wall and falls to his ass. I stride toward him, not missing a beat as I draw my gun and point it directly between his eyes, my fingers twitching to pull the trigger. "Let's try that again, shall we?"

His eyes widen in fear, and I watch as the patch of denim over his dick begins to darken. I let out a heavy sigh. Why is it so hard for men to control their bladder in the face of fear? It truly isn't that hard. When I was younger and immature, I used to find it entertaining, now I only find it humiliating.

"Woah. Woah," he rushes out, putting his hands up in surrender. "I'll tell you anything you need to know. Just put the gun away."

"No. Talk."

He visibly swallows as his eyes remain locked on the gun, acting as though he's never seen one in his life. "I . . . I don't know what to tell you, man. This asshole called me up and said he knew what I did, and if I helped him do it again, he'd pay me a hundred grand."

I tilt my head just a fraction, looking like the psychopath many claim me to be. "And what exactly is it that you did?"

"I . . . fuck man. Please."

I shoot and the bullet penetrates straight through the center of his knee. Derek screams in agony, but I don't have time for his bullshit. I need answers, and I need them now. "Speak," I order like he's a fucking animal.

"I sold her to Ezekiel Lopez after the bitch dumped me. He's—"

"I know who he is," I roar as my patience wears thin.

"The deal was supposed to be that she'd be gone. Some asshole would purchase her, and she'd never come back here, but then she did. She acted like nothing even happened, and the bitch still didn't give me the time of day."

Crouching down, I press the gun right to the center of his

forehead. "What did you do?"

"I wasn't gonna do nothing, but then . . . How was I supposed to say no to a hundred grand?"

"WHAT DID YOU DO?" I roar. "WHERE IS CHIARA?"

He jumps at my tone but finally gives me the answers I need. "I . . . I don't know. That guy and his fucking bitch of a wife said they were taking her back to Ezekiel, but once they left here, I was done. How the fuck am I supposed to know if that's where they actually took her? But with any luck, she'll be gone by the end of the night."

My frustration gets the best of me, and as I stand from my crouch, Derek lets out a heavy sigh as though he just escaped death, but I am not a merciful man, and despite only playing a small role in this, it was enough to ensure the end of his life.

I pull the trigger without hesitation, turning away before his brain splatters against the wall, and with that, I walk away, preparing for a fucking battle.

I have to assume the asshole and his bitch of a wife is Sergiu and Monica, and assuming they stuck to the plan and Chiara is with Ezekiel, then my time is running out. The auctions will be starting soon, and this time, I'm not just going to find myself a prize; I'm taking what's mine and burning the rest to ashes.

CHAPTER 32

Chiara

It's déjà vu as they come for me again. It's been maybe an hour since their callous attack. The tears on my face haven't even had time to dry as they force me into black bondage lingerie.

They pull against the ropes binding my wrists, and each painful tug bites deeper into my burning flesh.

The last time they dragged me through here, I fought like a hero. I refused to give up, even after I saw Killian standing in the back and felt that magical connection. I gave it my all and valiantly tried to save myself until the very last moment, but this time is different.

I can barely stand, and my body feels broken beyond repair.

As they lead me to the main floor and shove me into a cage to be displayed for their eager bidders, I don't even bother looking around.

I've never felt so flat or alone in my life.

Soon I will be surrounded by the pitiful men who will bid for the chance to violate me in every way imaginable. Only unlike last time, I don't have any fight left in me. My only hope is that when Killian comes for me, which he will, I'll still be worth saving.

Though right now, I'm not so sure that I am.

How could he want me now?

I crumble in my cage, falling to the ground and curling into a ball, much like I've spent the past hour, only now my bound wrists are freed and offered just a bit of relief for the first time since being taken from my apartment.

The people around me busily prepare for the auction, and for the most part, I'm left alone, and I do what I can to recoup just a fraction of energy, but it's no use. I'm so thoroughly depleted that what little energy I'll be able to find won't do me much good. Not in the face of these assholes.

He's going to come for me. He has to.

Once he realizes the lack of communication from the security team he stationed outside my apartment, he'll make his move. He'll figure this out. I just hope that when he finally gets to me, it's to take me home and not to put me out of my misery.

How am I ever supposed to come back from this?

All I want is to be in the safety of his arms, pressed against his warm chest where I know nothing would ever happen to me. I want to be his sweet angel again. I want to be the woman he needs, and if I can't have that, and this here is my only option, then I hope whichever miserable bastard purchases me is merciful enough to put a bullet right between my eyes. But the likelihood of that happening doesn't seem great.

Why did I have to provoke Monica? I could have kept quiet when she came to gloat at the bar. I should have left her to Killian's capable hands and maybe they would have left me alone. Maybe this is all my fault.

From the moment Monica put her hands on me, Killian insisted that he deal with it, and instead of letting him do what he does best, I held back, and in doing so, I've failed myself. Same goes with Sergiu. The second I had the chance, I should have gone to Killian. I should have told him what his cousin did to me, and it would have been dealt with, but I chose to fear Sergiu instead of trusting that Killian had no part in his cousin's little visits.

He would have protected me. He would have made it right and ensured that Sergiu or Monica couldn't even hear my name without fearing it—assuming he would have allowed them to live, of course, but I doubt it. He isn't known for being a forgiving man. Only with me.

Fuck, I miss him. I'd give anything to see him stride through those doors and take me away from here.

Minutes turn into hours when the massive warehouse begins filling with men. Drinks are served as the other women in cages frantically look around for a way out. I envy their fight for freedom. They still hold on to the hope that they can get out of here, but they'll soon discover they were foolish to hold on to that hope. All it's doing is eating into what little energy they have.

Men circle my cage, but I don't dare look up. I don't perform for them or show off my body at their demand. I simply sit curled in a ball, waiting for some lowlife to decide my fate.

A laugh sounds before me, and the chilling tone of it has something sinking deep in my gut. The raw familiarity of it sends a chill down my spine, and I can't help but lift my gaze. His face is one that's been burned into my mind since the night I stood in this very cage and broke his fucking nose, only now, his nose is healed and there's one hell of a chip on his shoulder.

Broken-nose guy.

He was an ass that night, and I don't doubt he'll be an ass now. The only difference is that I don't have the fight in me to tell him to fuck off or to even attempt to break his nose again. It's definitely healed, but it sure as fuck wasn't set right, and something tells me he's not exactly thrilled about it. I wonder what bullshit excuse he gave his wife.

"Well, well. I didn't expect to see you back here," he chides as his wicked stare lights with excitement. "I'm going to have fun with you."

My gaze drops back to the floor of the dirty cage, not caring for anything he has to say, but my lack of fight only seems to get him off. "Wow. DeLorenzo really fucked you up, huh? Look at you, you haven't got even a scrap of dignity left. But don't worry, I've got the perfect place for used-up little whores like you."

I roll my eyes.

His intimidation tactics didn't work on me before, and they sure as hell aren't working on me now. Does he really think a woman who's spent time with Killian DeLorenzo is going to crumble at his lackluster threats? He's fucking kidding himself.

Clearly not receiving the show he's hoping for, Broken Nose eventually slinks away, and I go back to ignoring the world around me, desperately trying to get the images of the past few hours out of my head, but it's impossible. They're etched into my brain for eternity, and nothing will make it go away. Nothing will ever make this okay.

The auction gets underway, and I'm not surprised when I'm up first. They want the boring bitch out of the way so they can get to the exciting girls of the night—the girls who are putting on a show, the ones who are drumming up the wrong kind of interest in their desperation to survive.

The bidding is low, and when I hear Broken Nose join the party, sounding more chuffed than ever, all I can do is let out a resigned sigh. He's only put up three hundred grand so far, whereas last time, he was pushing his limits at over a million dollars. The asshole probably thinks he's getting a good deal.

Someone else bids, and I don't even bother to look up. "Four hundred."

"Five," Broken Nose says.

The other guy doesn't respond, and when the auctioneer calls it, declaring me sold, Broken Nose cheers, fist pumping the air as though he just won a prize, but what the hell does he think he won? A woman so broken she can't even find the energy to get up? A woman torn to shreds and marred by the actions of other men?

I guess congratulations are in order. He's just got himself a wreck. Good job, asshole. Even the other vile men walking around were capable of taking one look at me and seeing that I wasn't worth a single cent and knew to look past me.

But not this asshole—my brand-new owner.

Fun times.

His only goal was to break me, but how the hell does he think he's going to break someone who's already shattered beyond repair? What a fucking joke.

Needing to put my whirlwind depression on pause to know what the hell is about to happen to me, I watch Broken Nose march across the auction house to the piece of shit who just violated me in the tunnel cell to turn over his payment.

The two of them look at me, and the owner smirks, making my blood turn to poison in my veins. Bile rises in my throat at having his sickening stare on me, and though Killian isn't here, I still believe he'll come eventually. I won't be here when he does. It's too late for that, but when he finds this smug asshole, he'll end his miserable life and make him suffer the most brutal death, and that's the only thing that keeps me breathing.

Killian will learn who purchased me, and in a matter of hours, he'll be right there to take me home. He always told me not to think of him as my hero or a knight in shining armor, but how could I not? I know he'll come for me, and when he finally saves me from this wretched hell, everything can be just as it was.

The owner nods to one of the guards—the third man to force himself inside of me—and not a moment later, he makes his way across the auction floor to my cage. Taking the lock in his hand, he begins to release me as Broken Nose comes over to claim his prize, not even waiting for the end of the auction to take me back to his hell hole.

The cage door opens, and the guard reaches in and grips my arm, his dirty nails digging into my skin as he yanks me up off the ground. "Shame you're not going to be sticking around," he murmurs, a sickening grin lingering on his vile lips. "I wasn't nearly done having my fun with you."

I spit in his face as I hold his stare. "I'm really going to regret not being here to watch as my husband slaughters you like cattle."

Broken-nose guy laughs, booming with excitement as though he just made some risky bet in a casino, only to learn it's paying off. "Ooohhhh. I knew she had a little more fight in her," he grins before reaching for me and tugging me toward him. "Hope you're fucking ready, bitch."

I clench my jaw. It's one thing being destroyed by three grown-ass men holding me down, but this piece of shit? No. He's old, and while he's certainly not frail, there's a part of me that believes I might just be able to fend him off, if only for a little while. Maybe just long enough for Killian to find me. If he's coming for me—and I know that he is—then I'm going to give it my all. And when I'm through with him, the last thing he's going to be worried about is his fucked-up nose.

I'm going to destroy this bastard just as thoroughly as he thinks he's going to destroy me.

Not stupid enough to make a move within the confines of the auction house, I stand by as my wrists are bound and pulled tight, the rope biting into my already torn flesh. Agony rips through my body, but Broken Nose tugs me away like a dog on a leash, and I don't attempt to fight him on it.

Unlike when Killian took me from here, Broken Nose doesn't appear to have any guards to keep me in line, and my mind immediately starts to put together a plan. Surely he has a car around here somewhere, and with everyone still inside, who's going to stop me?

As I'm dragged through the crowd, men grope me, grabbing my ass and tits as Broken Nose pulls me along with his chest puffed out like a fucking peacock, showing off his new toy. But he's shown his hand now. A man with an ego is a man easily brought down. He's shown his weakness, and if and when I get the chance, I will exploit it.

My tits are grabbed and roughly squeezed as someone else shoves his hand between my thighs, but joke's on him, all he's going to find down there is the remnants of other men's dick juices.

My body is still weak, and I trip over my feet while cursing myself for not having been able to gain enough energy. But even if I had, I'd be holding on to it. The real battle for my life hasn't even begun yet, and when it does, I'm going to be ready.

Broken Nose leads me to the small metal staircase I first walked with Killian, and as he drags me up, the ropes around my wrists dig deeper into my flesh. My whimper catches in my throat, and I swallow it down.

I will not cry for this man. I will not show him weakness.

The guard lets us out into the cold night, and as the chill seeps into my bones, all I can do is follow Broken Nose as he makes his way around the side of the massive building. I suddenly don't feel quite so threatened. It's just me and him, but I'm not about to make any stupid moves. This could be my only shot at freedom.

There are parked cars farther down the road, and I try to figure out how I'm going to play this vile game. I need to somehow get my wrists free, knock the bastard out, and steal his car. I have no chance of figuring out how to find my way back to Killian's estate, but if I can get back to my shithole apartment, I can find my phone to call him, and he'll be there within seconds. I don't know how, but I trust that he will.

My feet stumble against the uneven ground, and when he pulls me again, my knees give out, twisting my ankle in these ridiculous heels and dropping heavily to the ground. My knees become embedded with gravel, and I cry out in pain as he finally stops, the sudden drop tearing the rope out of his hands.

I barely have a moment to catch myself on my sore palms before he kicks me in the ribs. "Get the fuck up, bitch."

I clench my jaw and hold my ground, but as he reaches for me, I flinch away from his putrid touch, and the rope loosens at my wrists. A flash of hope burns through me, sparking like a flame and capturing my full attention.

I don't dare look down at my wrists, terrified of giving it away. He grabs a handful of my hair and throws me across the uneven ground. "Ugh," I grunt as I drop heavily to the ground, but again, I don't dare try to get up.

"That's the way you want to play this?" he demands, kicking me again. "Alright, have it your way, bitch. But if you're so fucking determined to be on your knees, then I'll give you something to do."

He reaches for the front of his pants, quickly unbuckling his belt and pulling his flaccid cock out. He quickly pumps up and down, readying himself for what I assume he thinks is going to be something amazing, and as his grip tightens in my hair and the eye of his cock stares at me, bile rises in my throat.

"Open up, bitch."

"If you think I'm about to suck your pathetic excuse of a cock, you've got another thing coming."

"You don't want to cross me, girl. Now open your fucking mouth and be the good little whore that you are and take it. Otherwise, you'll find your brains splattered across this road, and whether you're alive or dead, I'll still be fucking that pretty little mouth, so take your pick."

My wrists loosen a little more, and as I clench my jaw and lift my gaze, lights appear behind him, much further in the distance, but only a massive fleet of SUVs moving at a million miles an hour could create a halo of light like that.

Killian.

It has to be.

He's coming for me just as I knew he would.

The wave of emotion that crashes through me is almost crippling, but with Broken Nose's attention focused solely on me, I mask every emotion within me while doing what I can to keep his stare on me. If he catches wind of someone coming, my chance of getting out of here will get smaller and smaller, and if he somehow worked out that it was Killian coming to get me back, that chance will become non-existent. And while I know I've made some foolish decisions in the past, I won't be making any tonight.

The SUVs are still too far to risk doing anything stupid, but I also can't risk moving from this spot. If this asshole scoops me up and somehow gets me into the trunk of his car, I'm fucked.

It's all or nothing.

Putting my pride and dignity aside and doing what I can to disassociate from everything around me, I open my mouth, and as tears fill my eyes, he slams his cock right to the back of my throat. "That's what I fucking thought," he says, his hold in my hair tighter than ever as he forces my head back and forth. "Now suck."

I gag on his cock, choking as it slams against the back of my throat over and over all while keeping my gaze locked on the blinding headlights that grow closer and closer, and the moment they're close enough for me to take the upper hand, I don't fucking hesitate.

I wait, just a microsecond for his cock to penetrate the back of my throat, and then with every ounce of strength I possess, I bite down as hard as fucking possible. Broken Nose roars in agony as a wave of blood fills my mouth, but I don't dare let go, I just keep grinding my teeth.

He viciously pulls on my hair, yanking out chunks, and as my wrists finally come free, I shove my hand between his shaking thighs and grab his balls in a death grip, squeezing until I feel something pop.

Broken Nose falls to the ground, and the heavy drop of his body is enough to tear the rest of his skin, completely castrating him, and the moment I can, I pull back, spitting what's left of his cock out onto the dirty ground.

Blood smears across my face, and as I shakily get back to my feet, I stare down at the pathetic man before me, watching as he succumbs to the agony. Blood pulses out of him in waves, and while I know nothing about the human body, I know people don't often survive that kind of blood loss.

"How's that for a little fight left in me?"

I rise like the fucking red queen, wearing my crown of blood. "YOU BITCH," Broken Nose roars, clutching on to his non-existent cock, but all I can do is laugh.

Maybe the events that unfolded tonight have ruined me. Maybe I'll never be the girl Killian fell in love with, but right now, it doesn't matter, because these assholes have blackened my soul, and I won't rest until justice has been served.

I hear the convoy of SUVs skidding to a halt, and as I glance back over my shoulder, I realize it's time to go. Killian is going to storm the auction house, and when he does, I want him to know exactly what he's getting justice for.

I turn to race toward the other half of my heart, but the gurgling of Broken Nose gives me pause, and as I look down at him, my dark heart creeps closer. "I hope I was worth it," I tell him as a twisted smirk stretches across my lips. "Now, if you don't mind. I've been away from my husband for far too long."

"I'm going to kill you," he spits through a clenched jaw. "Mark my fucking words, girl. I'm going to find you, and when I do, the pain I inflict on you would be like living in the darkest hell."

I laugh. "Cute," I say, as my gaze shifts down to the castrated penis and the rush of blood flowing from the wound. "With that kind of blood loss, you won't live past the next few minutes, let alone have the chance to get your hands on me again, but just in case some bullshit miracle occurs and you somehow survive, you'll never find me."

"What—"

With every bit of my weight, I slam my stiletto heel down right into his eye socket, feeling the exact moment the heel penetrates through his brain. It's lights out in an instant, and with a newfound hope burning brighter than ever, I yank my heel out of his brain, turn to face the angelic halo of light, and without a single glance back, I make a break for it and race toward the other half of my black soul.

CHAPTER 33

Killian

The fleet of SUVs screech to a halt outside the auction house, and I watch as fifty of my men pour out onto the gravel road, every last one of them ready to storm this fucking hell hole and find my girl.

The uneasiness of the past few hours has destroyed me. Since the moment I discovered she'd been taken, to having to spend precious minutes organizing our attack, it all felt like time I didn't have, but to go in unprepared means unnecessary loss of life, and I won't risk my men because I wasn't thoroughly prepared.

I just hope it's not too late.

These auctions usually happen late in the night, but it truly depends on the patience of the crowd. The men who frequent these auctions aren't exactly known for being respectable or capable of waiting.

They're demanding, and when they don't get what they want, it often turns dangerous. There's a good chance my girl might already be gone, but if she is, there's not a damn thing stopping me from going in there and finding out everything I need to know.

But if she is still there, just like she was that first night, then I'll bring this whole fucking ring down around her.

My men immediately disperse around the property to infiltrate from every exit, making sure not a soul inside is able to escape. I've reached my limit with Ezekiel, and if I'm bringing this fucker down, then I'm taking him down with the ship. There will be no escape for him tonight, no sneaking out through underground tunnels, or taking off through the roof emergency exit. I have them all covered, and tonight, Ezekiel Lopez is mine.

"We good?" Cristian—my new second-in-command—asks. He's the only senior member left I can trust, and honestly, I'm not sad about it. He and his wife, Evie, are exactly what Chiara needs to transition into this world. I should have thought of it first. Evie can help her, teach her everything she needs to know, because I'll be damned if I ever let her go again. As for Cristian, he's the only senior member who's never wanted the limelight, the only one I've never had to worry will stab me in the back. He is the perfect yes man, however, in the face of terror, he will always rise. If the worst happens and he's forced to take my place, he will take the role just as seriously as I have.

He's exactly what I need.

I go to nod when a broken cry sounds in the distance—a tone I would recognize anywhere—and I whip around, seeking it out, only to watch Chiara stumble around the corner of the building and step directly into the light from the SUVs.

My heart freezes for a moment before crippling me as it launches into a full attack, pounding faster than it ever has before. I start running, my eyes wide as she hurries toward me, but after one look, I know she's been through hell. Her knees are shaky and there's dried tears on her blood-soaked face, but all that matters is getting her into my arms.

The moment she realizes she's safe, she crumbles, dropping to the hard ground, and the moment I reach her, I fall with her. My knees crash against the gravel, and I pull her into me. "You're safe now, Angel," I murmur as she buries her head against my chest, letting me hold her. "I'm so sorry. I'll never let you go. You'll never have to be afraid again."

She begins to cry, but I sit there with her, giving her a moment to get it out, despite losing the element of surprise on our attack. Nothing matters more than having this moment with Chiara. She needs this more than I need to breathe her in.

"You're safe now," I repeat, brushing my hand gently over her hair and taking note of her injuries. Her knees are scraped, and there's bruising across her ribs, but it's nothing compared to the random slices in her skin. It's as though someone took a blade and cut her, but there's no pattern to it. It's all random, as though she were cut out of her clothing. "You're safe."

Her tears quickly dry, and I doubt her need to process and cry has barely even begun, but she puts it aside, knowing we're here for a reason. She's putting her needs aside to be strong for me, and a woman like that is a woman I should have never let go.

"Why are you out here, Angel? Did you escape?"

Chiara nods. "I . . . I was sold," she begins. "Maybe ten, fifteen minutes ago. He was dragging me out to his car, and I fell and . . ."

The tears return to her eyes, and seeing the pain within them, I don't try to push for information. At the end of the day, all that matters is that she was able to get away. Instead, I simply hold up my hand and point in the direction she came, knowing my men will deal with whatever she left behind.

"No," she says, reaching for my hand and pulling it back down. "You don't need to do that."

I catch her eye, my brows furrowed in confusion.

"I've already dealt with it," Chiara explains. "After I fell, I saw the headlights coming, and I knew it was you, so I refused to get up. I didn't want to risk him getting me in the trunk of his car, and he said that if I was on my knees, that I—"

My jaw clenches as she cuts herself off, and I can only imagine what kind of bullshit this asshole has put her through.

"I killed him," she says, trembling. "He forced his . . . into my mouth, but I wasn't about to let him walk away from it unscathed, so I bit down and didn't let go, even when it felt like all the blood was going to choke me. I just . . . I had no choice."

I nod and hold her to my chest, hating every moment of the torture she's had to endure, all because I pushed her away. If I had never let her go, none of this would have happened. "It's okay, Angel. You did what you had to do."

"I put my heel through his eye socket and punctured his brain."

I simply stare at her. I was expecting a lot of things to come out of her mouth, but that wasn't one of them. As she stares back at me, her lips quirk into a wicked grin, and for a moment, I don't recognize the woman within. She's harder. Colder. She's changed.

"When a man touches something that belongs to my husband, he must be punished."

I groan low. Those words out of her mouth are my undoing, and I pull her tighter against my chest, my lips pressing against her temple. "That's my girl," I soothe before taking her shoulders and gently pushing her back to meet her eyes. "Listen, my sweet angel. Let me take you to my car. You can sit in there with two of my men while I handle this. I need to put an end to this bullshit, and the moment I'm done, I'll take you home, and you won't ever have to leave."

She shakes her head, anger flashing in her eyes. "No. I'm going with you."

"Chiara—"

"Don't," she says, grabbing my shoulders as she shakily gets to her feet. "If you knew what those vile monsters did to me. What they . . . I'm going with you, Killian. They put their hands on me, so when you slaughter them like animals, I'm going to be right there to watch it happen."

I rise with her, holding on to her arms, terrified she'll crumble again. "What are you talking about, Chiara? What did they do to you?"

She glances away, refusing to meet my eyes as though she can't possibly divulge this information to my face. "They raped me, Killian," she whispers. "Three of them. The guy who runs it and two of the guards. They came into my cell, held me down, and took turns—" she pauses, closing her eyes as though the images running through her head are too much for her to handle. "They cut me. One of them had a knife, and they cut these deep gashes on my skin while they were trying to get my clothes off. But they'll scar. I'll forever have these reminders of what they did to me."

"Yes, every time you look in the mirror, you will remember. Some days you will fall apart and other days you will feel rage, shame, fear, and maybe even disgust. But those scars are also a reminder that you survived. Each one of them, while just as painful as the last, tells the story of what you have endured and overcome. You are stronger than them, and no scar is going to keep you from getting the justice you deserve. I know it may be impossible for you to see now, but one day, you will wear those scars as a trophy."

When she stares at me blankly, I know she doubts every word I say. She's not there yet. She has been through the kind of hell no woman should have to endure, and while the scars I bear are different, I'm a testament that strength can come from the worst of times.

Pressing my hand to her lower back, I begin leading her back toward my men when Cristian breaks off from the crowd and meets me in the middle. "Do you have the headshots of Ezekiel's men?"

Cristian nods and pulls out his phone. He brings up the files we need and hands me the phone. I scroll through the images as Chiara looks on. "Tell me when you see them," I instruct.

She nods, and as I continue flipping, she watches like a hawk.

"Stop," she finally says. "Go back one."

I do as asked and a hollowness appears in her eyes as she simply stares at him. "That's one of them," she murmurs before reaching out and flipping through the images herself. Another moment passes before she pauses again. "That's the other."

I nod and pull the phone away, not wanting her to have to look at them a second longer than necessary. Handing the phone back to Cristian, I give him my instructions. "Everyone apart from Ezekiel and these two men will be slaughtered. Those three will be returning with me."

"Yes, boss. Anything else?" he asks as I slip my suit jacket off and help Chiara into it to offer her just a little bit of dignity.

"No, we're good to get started."

"Wait," Chiara rushes out in a panic. "What about the other girls in there? There's a few of them. They don't deserve this. They're just innocent girls like me who were snatched off the street. We need to save them. Please, Killian. Let me save them. We can offer them a new life where they won't have to fear for their safety and face men like this ever again."

"Okay," I tell her, nodding at Cristian who immediately starts giving orders. "We'll make the girls a priority."

Chiara nods and sucks in a deep breath, giving herself a moment to mentally prepare to go back in there. "Alright, then let's do it."

"You sure, Angel? You don't need to witness this. It won't be pretty," I warn her. "The things you see will pale in comparison to what you've already been through, and I guarantee, I will bring these motherfuckers home for you. You will get your justice at your own leisure."

"I'm going in," she tells me with defiance in her tone. "I need to see this."

She holds my stare for a moment longer, and as I see the true hunger in her exhausted gaze, I finally nod. "Okay, Chiara. You stand at my side the whole time. When I tell you to move, you move. If I tell you to run, you run. Do you understand me?"

"Yes."

"Okay," I finally agree. "Then let's do it."

Moving over to the trunk of my SUV, I find a small handgun, and after checking it's properly loaded, I press it into Chiara's hand. "Do you know how to use this?"

"Point and shoot?" she asks.

Jesus Christ. I consider taking it off her, but as she looks over it, the confidence builds in her stare, and I won't dare take that from her, especially not tonight, even if it means I risk catching one of her bullets. It'll be worth it.

"Good enough, just keep your finger off the trigger until someone needs to die."

Cristian gives out the order for my men to prepare to infiltrate the warehouse, and though I'm sure we've lost our advantage of surprise, I don't hear any commotion coming from inside. Nobody is trying to escape, and there's sure as fuck no one going on the defense.

Perhaps we still hold on to that element of surprise.

Cristian nods, getting a message through his earpiece before he turns to me. "We're ready," he tells me.

"Good. Then call the order."

With that, Cristian gives the order for my men to go, and in a show of pure beauty, every door surrounding the building is blown to pieces. Multiple explosions boom through the night, and as the smoke billows high into the sky, my team races forward, guns at the ready.

Chiara stays right on my ass as we fly through the narrow opening, her hands wrapped around the gun as though she's trying to choke it. I pause by the door, taking a moment to survey the chaos below.

My men are pouring in like perfect soldiers, taking out every obstacle in their way, and I watch as men begin dropping like flies.

Girls scream, but the sound doesn't come from the few girls visible on the floor, and it leaves me wondering just how many girls Ezekiel was attempting to auction tonight.

"There," Chiara says, pointing out something in the chaos.

I follow her eyeline, and as if on cue, Ezekiel turns and meets my stare.

I've never seen a man look so terrified in my life, and that says a lot coming from me. Taking in his fear is like a drug to me, and within seconds I'm intoxicated by the simple need to make him suffer. This man put his hands on my wife, violated her body, and sold her to be someone's whore. He won't escape my wrath, no matter how hard he tries, and I will enjoy every second of it.

"Let's go," I tell Chiara.

She doesn't skip a beat as I storm through the chaos, my men having my back and taking out every threat before it even becomes a problem, all while I watch as Ezekiel desperately tries to get through the crowd.

He knows what's coming for him.

Purchasers are slaughtered left, right, and center, and I watch as women who were being carted away are suddenly freed and falling into the arms of my men. They run, desperate to get out of here, and I can't help but notice the way Chiara's spirits seem to rise.

It's as though she doesn't even see the blood pooling on the ground, doesn't feel the weight of the death within the room. She's here with a purpose, and despite the exhaustion that claims her, nothing else matters. It's fucking beautiful.

Ezekiel breaks out through a side exit that leads deeper into the maze of tunnels, and without hesitation, we follow him in. His feet pound against the concrete floor, leaving an audible trail for us to follow, and I shake my head at his pathetic attempt at escape.

"Is he for real?" Chiara asks, still clutching the gun.

"Unfortunately, for people like Ezekiel, stupidity comes naturally. It's why their businesses are so easy to obtain and corrupt."

Ezekiel runs into an office, and as we step into the open doorway, we watch him scramble through his desk drawer. "Ezekiel, how nice to see you again."

He holds up a gun, his hands shaking in fear. "Don't fucking touch me," he spits. "I'll kill the bitch before you even take a step."

I laugh. "Oh, I believe you've met my wife," I say, indicating to the blood-soaked warrior beside me. "Isn't she gorgeous?"

His putrid gaze flicks toward Chiara for barely a second, but it's a second too long. He looks back at me but doesn't respond. It's the first smart move he's made all day.

"Ezekiel, do you know what happens to men who put their hands on my wife?" I ask, so calmly anybody would assume I'm here for a lunch date.

His eyes fill with panic, clearly not knowing how to play this, but there's no hand he could possibly play to win. Every move he makes, he'll lose. And as if knowing that, he raises his gun just a little higher, aimed right between my eyes.

BANG!

Chiara shoots, and her bullet goes wide, penetrating the wall behind his head, but it's enough to startle him. He drops his gun in his panic, and all I can do is let out a heavy sigh as I stride deeper into the small office. "I asked a question," I say impatiently. "What do you believe happens to men who touch my wife?"

Ezekiel flashes his gaze between me and the door and seeing no way out, he backs up against the wall. "Just kill me now, you piece of shit," he spits over the horrendous noise coming from the main floor, dropping to his knees in surrender. "DO IT! FUCKING DO IT."

I laugh. "You think I will do you the honor of putting you out of your misery? Of giving you a simple bullet between your eyes and calling it even?" I ask, leaning toward him and holding his stare as he wets his pants. "You put your hands on my wife, you had your men hold her down while you took turns fucking what is mine. You scarred her body, left her broken and bruised, and then sold her for profit. You dared to touch the woman I love. So no, a simple bullet will not suffice.

You are about to experience the full wrath of the DeLorenzo Mafia."

I inch away from him, and on cue, three of my men pour into the small office to collect Ezekiel, cuffing his hands behind his back and pulling a black bag over his head. "Sir," one of my men says, pausing beside me. "We have the other two guards in custody."

"Good. Take the three of them back to my private cells. I'll be there shortly."

He nods and with that, he leaves with the others.

Alone with Chiara, I move back into her, taking her waist and forcing her stare to mine. "You good? We have what we came for. We can leave out the back door or return to the main floor and finish what we started."

"The girls?" she questions, fear in her eyes. "Have they got them all?"

"No. I don't believe so."

A profound determination comes over her and I realize in an instant that she is about to dedicate her life to helping girls just like her, girls who have suffered at the hands of unlawful men, girls who have been tossed aside and disregarded as nothing more than a toy for someone to use and abuse. And however she decides to do that, I'll be right there, helping her along.

"Then we stay," she says.

Without skipping a beat, Chiara pulls out of my hold and turns on her heel, heading back to the main floor, and the moment we pass through the tunnel and back into the chaos, she takes off at a sprint.

"CHIARA," I call after her, but she's already gone.

Most of the purchasers have been taken out by my men, but there are still a few left. Both sides exchange gunfire, but my girl races straight through the center like a fucking angel dancing across landmines.

She's fearsome and wild, and I've never been so fucking proud of her.

Reaching one of the cages, she drops to her knees in front of a girl on the ground of the dirty cage, her hands protectively covering her head as she sobs with fear. "I'm going to get you out," Chiara calls over the noise as a bullet whizzes straight past her face.

For fuck's sake. She's going to get herself killed.

Moving in behind Chiara, I shield her body with mine before taking the gun from her hand and shooting out the lock. The cage door swings open, and without wasting a single moment, Chiara dives into the cage and pulls the terrified girl out.

The two of them stumble through the dead bodies and indicate for one of my men to come collect the girls, only as the woman is taken from Chiara, she doubles back, refusing to call it quits just yet. "There's still more," she says, not fearing the world around her for even a second.

"Okay," I tell her. "Lead the way."

Twenty minutes later, every purchaser within the room is dead, along with every guard or person who had any hand in making these auctions happen. All while Chiara stands out by the convoy of SUVs, offering water and blankets she found in the warehouse to every last woman rescued.

"What's going to happen to them?" she asks, joining me a moment later.

"Whatever they want," I tell her. "I can offer them a new life far away from here, but I would assume that many of them already have lives they won't wish to leave behind. Friends, family, a support network. I can only help as much as they're willing to accept, but they're safe now, Chiara. Just as you are. Ezekiel and his men can't hurt them anymore."

She nods and steps right into my arms. "Thank you," she murmurs. "I know it's not common practice for you to run rescue missions for women you don't know, but I appreciate that you did."

"Anything for you, my sweet angel."

She nods and buries her face against my chest, simply breathing me in. "I think I'd like to help them. I don't know how, but I just feel . . . I have to."

"I know," I tell her. "We'll figure something out. A foundation perhaps, somewhere women who've been hurt in the way you have can find safety and start to rebuild their lives."

She nods and meets my stare. "You'd help me do that?"

"Of course, Angel. I'm sure both Krista and Evie would also commit to the cause."

"You know, I'm still annoyed that you interrogated Evie. She didn't deserve that."

My face scrunches, and though this isn't the time to get into it, I can't help but come clean. "About that. There was no interrogation. A pure heart like Evie, she wouldn't be able to handle it. She told me everything I needed to know on the car ride over and once in my office, we made funeral arrangements while she sipped on tea."

Her jaw drops and she stares at me in shock. "You're a real asshole, you know that, right?"

I nod. "I do."

Shaking it off, she lets out a heavy breath. "Okay. So, this foundation. We're going to do it. We'll make it happen."

I nod and a moment of heavy silence falls between us, and it's clear she's deep in thought. "Chiara," I say, drawing her attention. "I was wrong to send you away. I thought you were safer on the outside, that once you were separated from me, Monica would no longer see you as a threat. I am sorry. I was wrong. I should never have hurt you like that."

"I provoked her," she admits. "The night she came into the bar, I provoked her and led her to believe that I'd told you everything she'd done. I thought it would scare her into leaving me alone, but all of this happened because of her. They were there when I was taken, both Monica and Sergiu. They were the ones pulling the strings. They made this happen."

I nod as my gut tightens with unease. "I know," I tell her. "But they won't hurt you anymore. I'll make sure of it. Now, please, my sweet angel, let me take you home."

Chiara nods and lifts her gaze to mine. "I want them to pay, Killian. For everything they've done to me. I want them punished."

Clenching my jaw, my mind immediately takes me back to the surveillance footage I saw from Chiara's room, of Sergiu making himself welcome and violating her. While I know that pales in comparison to what happened to her here, he was the root of this. Monica doesn't have the brains or connections to pull this off, but she will still die for her part in it. Sergiu, however, he's going to wish he never crossed me, never put his hands on my girl or orchestrated her abduction.

He's going to wish he were already dead.

"I promise you, Chiara. Sergiu and Monica will pay for what they've put you through," I tell her. "I already have a team working on their location."

"Good," she finally says, allowing the exhaustion to claim her. "Then take me home. I need a bath, and after that, I intend to spend the rest of my life in your arms," she tells me. "I belong with you, Killian. Right here at your side, and I don't care how many times you try to push me away for my own wellbeing, I'm not going anywhere. You can't make me. I love you, and though I know we didn't make vows or have some elaborate wedding, it changes nothing. I'm your wife, and I fully intend to keep being your wife."

"I'm not pushing you away, Chiara. I'm taking you home to my bed, and that's where you're going to stay."

"About time," she says, and with that, she slips into the back of my SUV and curls up on the seat, more than ready to live the rest of her life as the only woman I've ever seen.

CHAPTER 34

Chiara

The sweet sound of Ezekiel's screams is like music to my ears as I watch my husband take his fingers one by one. "You should have heeded Chiara's warning," Killian chides, snapping the garden clippers closed and watching as his pinky finger falls to the ground. "When a woman tells you she is married to the most powerful man in the country, only a fool would assume that is an invitation to fuck her."

Ezekiel cries out, sobbing so much that snot falls into his mouth, and I cringe, wondering why I was so afraid of him. Next to Killian, I've never seen such a pathetic little man, and yet, this misery of a man held power over me. But never again.

"Please," Ezekiel begs as blood pours from his hand, pooling on the ground beneath. "I swear I didn't know. I never would have touched her."

Using the garden clippers, Killian backhands him, and I watch as teeth fly from Ezekiel's mouth, shattering against the wall of the cell. "Are you calling my wife a liar?"

"No. NO!" he panics, his eyes desperately flicking between me and Killian. "I knew. She told me, and I—"

"You what, Ezekiel?" Killian prompts in a tone that makes my skin crawl, but fuck, I love it so much. "And I suggest you be honest with me, otherwise, I'll keep you here for years, replaying the same torture over and over again."

Ezekiel frets, his whole body shaking as blood dribbles from the corner of his mouth. "She told me she was yours and that you'd kill me when you found out she was being sold again, and I said—" he pauses, and knowing exactly what he said, I can't blame him for his hesitation. Once those words are out of his mouth, he's a fucking goner. "I said that if you were gonna kill me anyway, I might as well get something out of it."

Killian moves like lightning. One minute the clippers are in his hand, angling toward the next finger, and the next, the handles are protruding from Ezekiel's stomach, the tip buried so deep I can't even tell what type of tool it is.

Ezekiel roars in agony, the sound of his pain mirroring the cries of his guards coming from the adjoining cells, and I'm not going to lie, most of the brutality I've seen today has had me nodding along in excitement, but even this one has me cringing.

"Damnnnnnn," I groan.

Killian turns and meets my stare, his brow raising as a stupid grin stretches across his face, and for the first time since meeting him in that terrifying auction house, he's giving me golden retriever vibes. "You like that one, Angel?"

I can't help but grin back at him. "That was messed up, even for you," I tell him. "Just one more inch and he would have swallowed it whole."

"That's what I was going for, but my hand was in the way," he says as Ezekiel groans behind him. "You're welcome to give it a go if you think you can do better."

My gaze shifts to Ezekiel, taking a moment to consider what kind of revenge I would find the sweetest, but when it comes down to it, I've always been an eye-for-an-eye kind of girl. Don't get me wrong, it's not as though I'm going to violently ram a dildo up his ass for an hour straight. The more brutal punishments I'm happy to leave for Killian, but everything else . . . I don't see why I shouldn't enjoy taking part.

Pushing off the edge of the metal bars, I stride toward Killian and watch as the curiosity flickers in his dark eyes. "Do you have a knife?"

He silently nods and pulls a switchblade from his pocket before handing it to me and backing out of the way, leaving me to take the reins. Nerves begin creeping into my veins, slowly at first until they've completely consumed me, and before I even start, I glance back at Killian. His simple nod of encouragement is all I need to remember who has the power here.

"As much or as little as you need, Chiara," Killian's soothing tone fills the cell, sending waves of confidence crashing through me.

I take a breath, and as I slowly let it out, I take one final step, settling in front of the man who abducted me twice. He sold me as a piece of meat, chained me, cuffed me, held me down and raped me. Suddenly, my morals no longer exist.

Ezekiel stares at me, his gaze narrowed to slits as I contemplate how I want to play this. "You treated me like an animal," I say as calmly as ever. "A toy put here for your sick entertainment. You held me down. You sliced my clothes from my body and forced yourself inside of me while I sobbed in agony."

My voice wavers, and I pause, needing a moment to find my composure before continuing. "Do you recall how many times I begged you to stop?"

Ezekiel doesn't respond, but I didn't expect him to.

"Thirty-six," I say. "Thirty-fucking-six times. I counted every single one of them because it gave me something else to focus on apart from your brutal attack, but now I'm the one with the power, and it's your turn to beg. It's your turn to crumble at the hands of someone else, to feel every ounce of your dignity be stolen from you, even if I have to come back here every damn day to make it so. You haven't scarred me, Ezekiel. All you've done is prove to me exactly what I'm capable of surviving."

He still refuses to respond, and it's clear that he doesn't fear me in the way he fears Killian, but he will learn to soon enough. However, to be fair, he kinda has a pair of garden clippers hanging out of his guts, so that could be putting a damper on things.

Wanting to start out slowly, I raise the hem of my shirt and show him the slice his men made in my torso when they began cutting me out of my clothes. My cuts are stitched up now after spending the majority of the night being tended to by Killian's doctor, but they're still just as painful as they were when they first happened.

"You see this?" I demand. "You left a scar on my body. Twenty-three of them, in fact. And now, you will bear the same scars so when you decend into hell, even the devil will know what a pitiful, little man you are."

And with that, I step even closer, and press the tip of the blade right to his torso before digging it deep. Ezekiel clenches his jaw and groans in agony as I simply stand back and look at my handiwork. It's certainly much deeper than the cut that was left on my skin, but nobody said it had to be fair.

Moving on, I lift my gaze to his chest, and as I plunge the knife into his skin, the burden of his abuse begins to lift off my shoulders. Each cut takes away just a bit of the shame, and I go on and on until every last scar is mirrored on his body.

I let out a heavy breath, turning to face Killian. His deep gaze locks on me, and the pride behind those dark eyes fills me with the deepest joy. Without a second thought, I know that I will do everything within my power to see this look in his eyes every damn day for the rest of my life.

His phone is wedged between his ear and shoulder as someone speaks to him, and to be honest, I didn't even notice his phone ring. He walks into me, his hand falling to my waist as he finishes his phone call, and the moment the phone slips away into his pocket, he lifts his other hand to my chin and leans in. Killian brushes the softest kiss upon my lips, and I savor every second of it, erasing the horrible memories and replacing them with ones like this.

"You know," I say, barely even aware of the dying man behind me. "It's almost comical how just a few days ago, the thought of these cells terrified me, but now . . . they seem to offer some kind of twisted justice."

"It does," he agrees before nodding toward Ezekiel behind me. "Are you finished with him? Or would you prefer I keep him alive?"

I shrug my shoulders. "It's your call. I'm done with him. I don't plan on ever coming into this cell again, as long as he occupies it, of course. As for you, if you feel what's been done here today isn't sufficient, then by all means, have at it. I don't care if you wish to keep him down here for an hour or a lifetime. It's up to you."

His eyes sparkle with excitement. "It seems I'm the one who needs to fear you, not the other way around."

I scoff. "Flattery will get you nowhere, Killian DeLorenzo."

He laughs before a wave of seriousness washes over him, and I feel a heavy weight drop into the pit of my stomach. "That was Cristian on the phone. We found them, Angel. Sergiu and Monica. They're in South France in an underground bunker," he tells me. "Now, I know you've already had a very long day, so the choice is yours. You can stay here and heal, or you can come with me. Either way, my jet is ready to take off."

My brows arch. "You have a jet."

"Of course I have a jet," he says. "I have three."

"Three?" I scoff. "Why the hell do you need three?"

"Why wouldn't I need three?"

I gape at him, realizing he's absolutely serious. He simply doesn't comprehend how three jets would be excessive, and all I can do is smile at him as I look up into those dark, deadly eyes. "You know, I've never been to France."

"You'd like to come?"

"Do I get to dress for the occasion?"

"Absolutely."

"And will you take me to see the Eiffel Tower afterward?"

"If you wish."

"And the Colosseum?"

His brows furrow. "That is in Rome, Angel."

"Oh, I know."

He lets out a breath, clearly working out my game plan. "Of course, Chiara. Any other stops you'd like to make along the way?"

My grin is bigger than ever before, instantly sending an ache deep into the apples of my cheeks. "Why don't I make you a list?"

Killian laughs and lowers his hand to my back before leading me out of the cell, neither one of us bothering to stop and glance back at the mess we've left behind. We make our way out of the cells and back to the main house, when we pass the doctor who spent the early hours of the morning stitching me back together and offering me the little pill that could prevent any unwanted pregnancies from my night of hell.

Killian stops and meets his curious gaze, clearly knowing there's more work for him to do. "Cell three. Find a way to keep the bastard alive without removing the sheers and that big property you've been looking at for your wife and kids is all yours."

His eyes bulge out of his head. "Certainly, Sir," he says before pausing and thinking better of it. "How long will he be required to live?"

"I'll return in . . . a month. I have business to attend to tonight and then I'll be taking Chiara on a European vacation. See what you can manage in the meantime."

The doctor is wise enough to nod and do everything he can to please Killian, but there's no denying the dread in his eyes. I'm certainly no doctor, but it doesn't take a genius to realize that those garden cutters will cause some pretty insane infections, and considering the likelihood that they punctured the stomach or intestines, the chances are high. But hell, if there's a possibility of getting the new home his wife and children have been wanting, then why not give it a try? I know I would.

The doctor scurries off, realizing the quicker he can start dealing with his new assignment, the better his chances are, and I'm left to go pack a bag. "A month? Really?" I ask as Killian helps me up the stairs.

"Does that seem too soon? I can make it two, but I can't guarantee Ezekiel will still be breathing when we return, and I really haven't finished with him yet."

"You're insane," I tell him. "A month is huge."

He grins, and as we reach the top of the stairs, I take off into my room. When I walk into my closet, I turn my ass back around. "Killian," I question, striding back out into the big seating area between our rooms. "Where are all of my clothes?"

"My room," he says, watching me from an armchair. "It didn't feel right having you so far away. You'll sleep in my bed from now on, Angel. In my arms. Nowhere else."

A flutter blooms through my stomach, quickly spreading throughout my body and leaving me a trembling mess. "I'd like that," I tell him, and then before I get carried away, I stride into Killian's bedroom and prepare to put this war to rest for good.

CHAPTER 35

Chiara

Stepping off Killian's private jet onto the tarmac in France is surreal. How the hell is this my life? Last night I was in the center of a human trafficking ring, being gang raped and sold, and tonight, I'm in France.

What are the chances?

Killian meets me at the bottom of the stairs, and as he places his hand on my lower back, the soft breeze sends my blood-red silk gown blowing behind me. Can't deny it, the moment he told me I could dress for the occasion, I took full advantage.

My gown is everything and makes me feel like the woman Killian deserves. The gown I wore to the dreaded family gala was dazzling in all the right ways, but this one is sexy and makes me feel alive. It plunges deep between my breasts as the slit in the side trails right up to my hip. Every scar those men left on me is visible, but I don't feel the need to cover them up, not around Killian.

The deep red of the gown seems fitting considering what we're here to do, and after bunching my thick hair into a high ponytail, I paired the dress with combat boots and a knife strapped to my thigh. Because what kind of mafia wife burns the world to ashes any other way?

Killian helps me into the car and explains that it's almost a two-hour drive into the countryside to the bunker, and as the driver hits the gas, Killian takes my hand. His thumb is soothing against my skin, gently roaming back and forth across my knuckles.

He's had no issues touching me since bringing me home, but he always allows me to determine how much I'm comfortable with. Though he should know where he's concerned, I don't ever want to hold back. I don't know how that relates to sex yet, but the idea of not being able to be physical with Killian kills me more than the memories of what those men did to me.

I gaze out at the picturesque view, taking in everything around me. It's still so surreal.

This is France! But not only that, I came here in a silk gown on a private jet with a man who looks at me as though I'm his entire world, as though everything could be burning to ashes around him and all he would see is me. This just doesn't happen for girls like me.

The drive to the bunker goes by faster than I could imagine, and as the driver rolls to a stop, I stare out the window and scrunch my face.

We must be lost.

All I see are rolling hills covered by the late afternoon sun. Don't get me wrong, it's one of the most stunning landscapes I've ever seen, but there's no bunker here. Not that I've ever been in a bunker or know what to even look for, but surely there'd be some sign, right?

Killian opens the door and gets out before striding around to my side and offering me his hand like a perfect gentleman. I get out, combat boots and all, and before I know it, we're marching out into the long grass.

There are lots of ways I pictured this going, but a trek through the countryside wasn't exactly on the bingo list.

For forty-five minutes, we walk over the rolling hills while Killian holds on to me, making sure I'm doing okay on the rough terrain, but as long as he's by my side, I'll always be okay. "Whose brilliant idea was it to build this thing so far away?"

"Mine," he states. "It's a safe house. The idea is that it is safe. If anybody were able to locate it, it wouldn't be so safe, now would it?"

"Don't you try and use logic with me mid-trek, bossman," I mutter. "Besides, I thought it was an underground bunker, not a safe house."

"Same thing."

"Same thing?" I scoff. "They are so not the same thing. To me, an underground bunker is an oversized shipping container dropped into the earth. Add a shitty cardboard bed, a scratchy blanket, and non-perishable food. But a safe house . . . I uhmmmm . . . I actually don't know what to expect out of a safe house, but I can assure you, it's not the same thing."

Killian rolls his eyes. "If you're done droning on about safe houses and bunkers, we're here."

"We're where?" I ask, looking around.

He lets out a heavy sigh, and as he cuts through the long grass, I begin to see the concealed opening cut into a hill. "What the fuck?" I breathe as we walk straight into the dugout and come to a huge metal door that looks capable of protecting the people inside from a missile strike.

Killian steps right up to it and leans in, and I watch in surprise as his eyeballs are scanned like some kind of entry code. "Okay, James Bond. Are we about to walk into your secret headquarters?"

Killian grins as the massive door begins to open. "One can never be too careful."

"One can definitely be a little too extravagant though," I mutter as we stride through the entrance into what I can only assume is the massive lobby area of what seems to be more of a safe mansion as opposed to a safe house. "I thought we were walking into some fancy bunker, not an underground estate."

"Wait until you see the pool."

I roll my eyes. Why am I not surprised? Though, I can't help but note how fucking moronic Sergiu must be to use one of the DeLorenzo safe houses in order to hide from the head of the DeLorenzo family. Bad move on his part.

A seriousness comes over him, and it occurs to me that both Sergiu and Monica are here somewhere, and at any moment, they could jump out at us. "Do they know we're here?"

"No, the surveillance cameras were looped before we arrived, and the alarm will only sound if the retina scanner is activated by anyone other than me. We're good."

The underground safe mansion certainly isn't anywhere near as luxurious or big as his home that I've become accustomed to, but it's certainly nothing to turn your nose up at. The finishings are exquisite, and it's clear that whoever was in charge of building this masterpiece did so with every bit of their heart. I could only dream of affording a home like this.

The polished marble and gold hand railing on the staircase are stunning, and the seating area that's centered around an open fireplace is jaw-dropping. Homes like this simply don't exist, and yet Killian has it basically unused, sitting here under a hill.

Killian goes quiet, and instead of giving me verbal directions around the mansion, he points to where he wants me to go, and I can only assume we're getting close.

I'm not sure what the plan is, and to be honest, I doubt Killian knows either. We're just making it up as we go, but what I do know is that one of the occupants of this mansion poses a significantly larger threat than the other. And while they both deserve a horrific ending for what they've done to me, I think it's safe to assume that one of them will receive a much quicker death than the other.

As if on cue, we turn into the open living room, and sitting right there, completely immersed by The Real Housewives of Beverly Hills is the woman who beat me in a bathroom and hired a hitman to take me out, only I suppose she didn't anticipate everything becoming this messed up.

There's no telling if she was the one behind the idea of sending me back to Ezekiel to be sold, but it's clear that Sergiu was the one who had the connections to make it happen.

Killian pulls out a gun, and I arch a brow, not having realized he was carrying it, but I suppose it makes sense. A man like Killian DeLorenzo doesn't go anywhere unarmed. Even when he's in bed, there's always a weapon close by.

He pulls something from his pocket, and I watch as he twists it onto the top of his gun, and I realize it must be a silencer, which makes me realize that if I'm going to be a part of Killian's life, I need to learn this shit . . . and fast.

Killian motions for me to follow him deeper into the living room, and as I do, he hands me the gun. My eyes widen as I take it from him in shock. I didn't realize that he wanted me to play any kind of role in this. I thought I was just along for the ride. Though, maybe I am. There's no telling what plans are pulsing through that wicked brain of his.

We stop a few feet away from Monica as she continues watching her show, completely unaware that she only has moments to live. Killian moves in behind me and adjusts my stance, widening my legs and lifting my arms until the gun is pointed directly at the back of her head. "If she tries to run," he murmurs into my ear. "Shoot."

I swallow hard and nod as the nerves creep in, but all I can do is watch as he strides around me and brazenly approaches her. He sits right on the back of the couch as though he were invited for lunch, and only after he clears his throat does she realize she's not alone.

Monica whips around, her eyes wide as she takes in Killian sitting a foot away from her, and when she turns her gaze to take me in, the horror on her face makes everything worth it. "No," she breathes, making it clear she didn't expect me to last the night with Ezekiel.

Killian lifts a single finger and holds it to his lips, warning her to remain silent and as she visibly swallows and her eyes fill with terror, she does as she's asked. That finger moves, indicating for Monica to stand, and like a trained robot, she lifts herself off the couch, not capable of moving her stare from his.

She's his captivated audience, and it only goes to show the kind of power he wields. It's both fascinating and terrifying, but I wouldn't want it any other way. A man in his position needs to be. He needs to terrify the very people he rules over so things like this don't happen. But Monica and Sergiu got too comfortable, and they foolishly believed they were above Killian's law.

Killian stands and slowly walks around the couch until he's standing right behind her, and now that he's stepped out of her line of vision, her gaze settles on me, and for the first time, I know what it's like to look directly into the eyes of death.

"You see my beautiful wife?" Killian murmurs, his voice barely sounding over the TV. "Do you know what happens to people who harm those I love?"

Monica's body visibly shakes, but she doesn't dare try to run. She knows her fate, and while she might be terrified, she's also accepting of it.

Then, being the kind man I know him to be, he raises his hands—one curled around her chin and the other at the back of her head—and with a violent twist, he puts her out of her misery, refusing to drag it out any longer than necessary.

A horrendous crack sails through the room, and just like that, Monica's lifeless body falls to the ground.

Killian's gaze comes directly to mine, making sure I'm okay. This death wasn't like the others I've witnessed so far. This was different. It wasn't bloody and reckless. There was nothing wild or brutal about it, just . . . simple. It was a woman, and while she did terrible things to me and deserved a million deaths, it sits uncomfortably inside my chest.

My gaze falls to her lifeless body as Killian comes to stand at my side. "It's over, Angel," he murmurs, pressing a gentle kiss to my temple. "She can never hurt you again."

I swallow over the lump in my throat and nod, and just like that, we turn and walk out of the living room. Because while Monica might be dead and gone, her husband certainly isn't, and until he takes his final breath, we won't stop searching for him.

CHAPTER 36

Chiara

K illian leads me through the massive underground safe mansion, and after circling the top level twice, we begin creeping down to the next. He reaches out and takes the gun from my hand, and I realize shit is about to get serious.

He's here. But where?

We move slowly through the home, and Killian is more cautious than I've ever seen him before, checking areas most wouldn't even think to look, but Sergiu isn't some random drug dealer off the street who needs to be punished. He's the man who stood at Killian's side all these years. He's just as brutal as Killian. The two of them were brought up together, trained side by side. They know each other's weaknesses, where to strike, and how to make it count.

It's the first time I'm at risk of losing him. This could go either way, so if Killian tells me to move, I'll move. If he tells me to run, I'll sprint faster than I ever have in my life. Whatever he needs from me, I'll do it without question, because the idea of leaving here without him isn't acceptable to me.

If Killian dies here today, then I will too. There's no doubt about it.

We move through the main bedrooms, past a sitting area, and to the other half of the downstairs area. There are a lot of closed doors, and each of them makes me nervous, not knowing what lies beyond.

We approach what I assume is a private office when the slightest movement in my peripheral vision catches my attention, and without hesitation, I drop to the ground. "Left!" I tell Killian, but he's already seen it. A bullet whizzes straight past where my head was only a moment ago, and Killian shoots back, a bullet plunging straight through Sergiu's knee.

"Ahhh fuck," Sergiu roars before diving behind a couch.

Killian glances toward me, his eyes wide as they scan over my body, making sure I wasn't hit. "I'm good," I tell him. "Now, go and get the fucker so we can really end this."

Killian nods and stalks toward the couch that Sergiu is hiding behind as I remain down on the ground, my gaze bouncing through the room to make sure nothing goes wrong. Killian walks with the kind of confidence that gets me hot, and as he approaches the couch, he holds his gun at the ready, but I'm not foolish enough to assume Sergiu isn't just as prepared.

"It's over," Killian taunts. "You and I both know how this is going to end, so you might as well come out so we can get this over and done with."

Killian remains on the opposite side of the couch, and without warning, he shoots through the cushions. I expect to hear a pained groan, or a gasp at the very least, but when we hear nothing, my heart starts to race just a little faster. "What the—"

A hand grips my ankle, and I'm dragged across the marble tiles as a sharp yelp tears from the back of my throat. I barely have a moment to register that Sergiu has crawled around the back of the couch and through the sitting area without detection.

Killian whirls around as I'm painfully yanked to my feet by my hair. Horror rushes through me, knowing he could kill me in an instant, just as quickly as Killian killed Monica. There's no time to think. No time to plan. I have to act now, and I have to do it fast.

Then before Killian can even attempt to make a move, my hand strikes like lightning, grabbing the knife strapped to my thigh and blindly whipping it up in a quick arc over my shoulder. I feel the bite of something in my waist at the same moment my blade plunges straight through Sergiu's eye.

Sergiu roars in agony as Killian lunges toward me, violently yanking me away from his cousin, and as my head whips back to take in Sergiu, all I see is the blade protruding from his eye socket as he crumbles to the ground.

"Holy fucking shit," I screech before I've even hit the ground.

Everything happens so quickly.

One minute Killian is flying toward me, and the next, I'm sprawled on the floor of his mega-underground mansion as he subdues his cousin. "You good?" Killian throws over his shoulder with a bite in his tone.

"I . . . I don't know," I say, scrambling to my feet and looking over myself to see a patch of blood beginning to seep into the soft silk at my waist. "I think he cut me. Maybe. I can't be sure."

Not wanting to risk turning away from Sergiu, he knocks him unconscious before finally moving toward me, his gaze roaming over my face. "You sure have a thing with eyeballs," he murmurs as his fingers dance across the high split of my dress and drag the material higher to my waist.

He looks over my body, taking in the fresh wound. "He got you, alright. But you moved just in time. It could have been worse."

"So I'll live?"

"You'll live," he tells me, that bite still in his tone. "Now, let's really finish this."

"Hey," I say, grabbing his chin and bringing his gaze back to mine. "What's wrong?"

His gaze darkens, and every bit of it eats at my already blackened soul. "I should have been able to play that out before it happened. He should never have gotten that close to you."

"You're not a mind reader."

"No, I am not," he agrees. "However, I was the one who taught him how to move like a ghost. I should have seen the signs."

"It's okay, Killian. We've got him now," I tell him as I reach up onto my tippy toes and brush a kiss to his lips, still so addicted to the way everything pulses within me just being this close to him. "And if you need, you can spend the rest of your life making it up to me. For now, though, we need to end this because I'm hungry, and dinner at the top of the Eiffel Tower is sounding pretty damn good to me right now."

Killian laughs and rolls his eyes, but he gets back into action, and twenty minutes later, all I can do is gape at the sight before me.

"What in the ever-loving fuck?" I murmur to myself.

We're standing in some kind of tiled chamber. It doesn't look like the cells back at his home, but there's definitely something eerie about it. Plus, any room that comes equipped with a hose and drainage system seems somewhat sketchy to me.

If I thought the room was bad, it's got nothing on what Killian actually plans to do in it.

All four of Sergiu's limbs are chained, and I watch with my jaw hanging open as Killian presses a button and the chains retract to each corner of the room. They pull him up off the ground and stretch him wide like a fucking chunky star, and it's got to be the most horrifying thing I've ever seen. Not to mention, the knife I jammed through his eye is still there, flopping around with every little movement.

I thought mafia wars were all about taking out family lines, the occasional standard torture, and a bit of unfriendly gunfire. But this goes to show just how deranged some of these men are. And the fact that this was already installed into the property says a lot. There's nothing spur-of-the-moment about this.

"Not going to lie," I tell Killian as he stands back to survey his handiwork. "This is messed up."

"I'm aware," he says, moving back toward my side. "However, this is about more than what he did to you. He was my second-in-command, the one I was supposed to trust to have my back. His vow of loyalty was broken, a betrayal of the highest treason. His actions against you were horrendous, and I will ensure he pays for that. However, his death sentence must also encompass the rage I feel when I look in his eyes."

I nod, not quite understanding. This isn't a world I know enough about to be able to compare the magnitude of his crimes, nor have I ever had a stable family situation to truly understand how it feels to be betrayed by someone who's supposed to love you unconditionally, but I'm sure I'll get there. One day, I'll understand and be able to share in his pain. Until then, all I can do is support him in whatever he needs to do to make this sit right in his soul.

I don't respond, but Killian doesn't need me to. He's not the type of man who needs to justify his actions. He does what's required of him, and if you have a problem with it, that's on you.

After offering me a sad smile, he moves across the room and reaches for the hose. "What are you doing?"

"I don't intend to start until he regains consciousness, and at this rate, we'll be here all night," he says.

"You're going to hit him with freezing water?"

"I am."

"Would ummm . . . Would it be entirely inappropriate if I did it?"

He turns to face me, and his brow arches in pleasant surprise. It's as though the idea of me taking an interest in his work couldn't make him happier. "Be my guest," he says, offering me the hose.

I smile wide as I gingerly take it from him, and after he turns on the tap, I twist the nozzle and watch the water shoot out of the hose. It drenches him, and then just for good measure, I raise the harsh spray of water to his face and watch as it ricochets off the blade in his eye. "Is this what waterboarding is?" I throw over my shoulder, not taking my eye off Sergiu.

"Not exactly," Killian says. "I can teach you all about it though. It's quite an effective interrogation tactic when performed correctly. However, I wouldn't wear anything of value. It can be quite messy."

A smirk settles across my face, but as the water hits the blade at the wrong angle, it dislodges and flings across the small room. "Damn," I say with a heavy sigh, but not a moment later, Sergiu re-enters the world with a loud gasp.

His one good eye widens in horror, realizing the unfortunate position he's in, but unlike his wife, there's no acceptance of his fate. He's filled with terror and pulls against the chains, desperately trying to find a way out, but there isn't one. He should know better.

Turning the hose off, I move out of the way as Killian steps forward to take control, slowly unbuttoning his shirt in the process. He tosses it aside, and something warns me that this is about to get messy.

There's an animalistic look in his eyes, and it speaks to me on a deep, primal level. This isn't just a man seeking justice, this is *my man* protecting both of us in the only way he knows how. And goddamn, the way he so confidently steps up to take care of business is like nothing I've ever experienced.

God, I love him so much. How could I have ever questioned that? How could I have ever allowed him to make me fear him? It's not possible. To love him isn't to fear him. He was wrong. He would never hurt me because he's not capable of it. His heart won't allow him to.

Killian DeLorenzo would sooner lay down his own life than allow harm to come to me, and because of that, I will always belong wholeheartedly to him. Everything that I am is his.

Trying to focus on what's about to happen, I watch Killian move right in front of Sergiu. "Release me," Sergiu demands. "Haven't you done enough? You're going to destroy the DeLorenzo legacy. You've already slaughtered my wife, and now me? What's next, Killian? You'll burn the empire I built to the ground."

"You built?" Killian questions, before striding across to the small table at the side of the room and scanning over the endless options of tools before picking up a power drill. "You didn't build anything, cousin. You thrived in the world I provided for you. Without me, you would be nothing. I gave you your position at the top of this family, and in return, all I asked for was your undying loyalty. You've betrayed me, Sergiu. You broke the solemn vow you made me. You put your hands on my wife, UNDER MY OWN FUCKING ROOF," he roars. "You stood by knowing Monica was the one who beat her black and blue and you kept quiet. You put your own priorities above mine, and for that, I will see to it that you are punished. You will never come back from this."

"SHE'S A FILTHY WHORE, KILLIAN," Sergiu throws back at

him. "You're destroying everything for a whore."

"You will not speak of my wife," Killian spits, stepping closer to him and looking him dead in the eye. "The thirty-odd years you've stood at my side pales in comparison to the past few weeks I've had with Chiara. She will always come before you. She encompasses everything that is good, and she is stronger than you could ever dream of being. You're nothing in comparison, and when I look at her, I will always know that what I did here was right. You're pitiful, Sergiu. A sorry excuse of a man. No one will miss you. No one will even remember you. There will only be gratitude for your absence."

Killian raises the power drill, giving it a test as he pulls the lever. The sound reverberates off the walls, sending a chill down my spine, and yet I find myself eagerly watching, anticipating how this will go down.

"Cousin," Sergiu warns. "Don't do this. I can be better."

Killian tunes out his desperate pleas, and not a moment later, he presses the drill against Sergiu's ribs and pulls the lever. Sergiu roars in agony as the drill effortlessly cuts through his flesh and down to the bone. I cringe, unable to imagine the pain as the sound of crunching bone fills the air.

I hear the exact moment Killian punctures his lung, and only then does he pull back on the drill. I expect him to put the drill down and pick another tool, but he doesn't. He just picks a new spot and goes again.

And again.

And again.

Thirty-six times.

One for every time I screamed for Ezekiel and his men to stop. One for each agonizing plea torn from the throat of a helpless woman. And now, he gets to feel just a fraction of the hell I endured.

This drill is for me, and once Killian is through with it, he places it back on the table, right where he found it. He switches it out for a machete, and as the blade catches in the light, I know that what comes next . . . This is for him.

CHAPTER 37

Chiara

Two hours we spend in the small torture chamber at the very bottom of the underground mansion, and when Sergiu dangles lifelessly from the suspended chains, Killian finally turns to face me. He's covered head to toe in Sergiu's blood, but all I see is him.

His chest rises and falls with rapid breaths, and it's clear he's on the edge. Yet despite everything he just did to a man he called family for so long, despite the rush of guilt and unease no doubt pulsing through his body, he's looking at me, silently asking if I'm okay.

He's selfless.

Incredible.

Absolutely everything I've ever needed.

And without question, I cross to him, throwing myself into his blood-soaked arms as the machete clatters to the ground behind me. My lips fuse to his with a deep desperation as he cradles the back of my head. Sergiu's blood smears across my body, but all that matters is Killian. All that matters is holding him tighter than I ever have before.

His tongue plunges into my mouth, warring with mine for dominance, but where Killian is concerned, he will always have the upper hand. The hunger intensifies within me and before I know it, I'm held within his strong arms as my legs lock around his waist.

"God, I have to have you," I groan against his lips.

"Are you sure, Angel?" he grunts, the hesitation in his tone coming in thick and hard. He doesn't want to stop, but if I'm not ready for this, if it's too soon, he'll stop.

"I'm sure," I pant. "I need you to remind me how much I love sex. Make me feel, Killian, but fuck, I need to know I'm in control. Don't take my control."

"You've always been in control," he tells me, dropping to his knees in the pool of blood marring the pristine marble tiles. "Since the very first time. Always you."

Killian pulls me to my knees, whipping me around so that his chest is flush against my back and when he grabs handfuls of my silk gown and tears it off my body, I shudder, unable to wait a moment longer to feel him inside of me.

I'm fucking drenched, and while a part of me is nervous about how this is going to go, that he's going to touch me and I'm going to shut down, he's always known exactly what I need. He's always read my body and the signals I give off better than I know my own mind, and

I trust him to do that now.

His hands roam over my blood-soaked body, setting my skin alight, and when his lips fall to my neck, working over my sensitive skin, I can't help the desperate groan that rumbles from deep in my chest.

My hand closes over his, and our fingers entwine as he roams over my body. It's like he's committing every last curve to memory. His cock grinds against my ass, and there's no doubting how big he is. He's starved of my touch, his desperation just as powerful as mine, and I can't resist reaching behind me and quickly working his belt.

Killian helps me to free his cock, and the moment his heavy shaft lands in the palm of my hand, I curl my fingers around him and start working up and down. My thumb circles his tip, feeling the small bead of moisture there, and every part of me wants to lap it up, but I won't dare take my hand off him.

He shudders behind me, his body becoming weak beneath my touch, and it's the most powerful thing I've ever done. Bringing a man like Killian DeLorenzo to his knees will always be my greatest achievement.

Killian groans, and the sound spurs me on, feeding my hunger in a way only he ever could, and when his hand trails down my waist and into the front of my thong, I crumble beneath him.

His skilled fingers push between my folds and instantly circle my clit, making my hips jolt. He doesn't dare stop as his lips continue working my neck, and I close my eyes, tip my head back against his wide chest, and let the intense pleasure rock through me.

It's too much, and he's barely started touching me.

"Please," I beg, the breathy word slipping through my lips. "God. Please, Killian. I need to feel the way you stretch me. I need you inside me."

His hand slips further beneath me, and I can't help but feel as though he's testing the waters, needing to see just how much I can take.

"How much do you need me, Angel?" he growls in my ear as he slowly pushes two thick fingers deep inside of me, taking all the time in the world. "How fucking ready are you?"

There's no denying how ready I am, and I know he feels it just as much as I do. I'm fucking drenched for him. "Again," I demand, and as if on cue, his fingers slowly pull out before thrusting them back in, only this time, he curls them and massages my walls from within.

My eyes roll, the satisfaction so intense it takes me by surprise, and before I know it, I start grinding down on his fingers, desperate to take everything he's got. "Don't keep me waiting, Killian DeLorenzo," I demand, tightening my grip on his heavy erection. "If you don't bend me over and fuck me right now, I'll do it myself."

"Mmmm, that's my girl," he rumbles, and the way I feel the vibration through his chest makes my whole body shudder. "Spread those pretty thighs, baby. As far as they'll go."

A sultry grin spreads across my face as I quickly do as I'm asked, spreading my thighs almost to the point of pain, and when I feel his hand at my back, I release my hold on his cock and voluntarily lower my chest to the ground.

The blood instantly stains my long golden hair, but right now, only his hands on my ass matter. He tears my thong from my body, and the vulnerability does wicked things to me. I feel his heavy gaze locked on my drenched cunt, and I've never felt so beautiful in my life, and when everything clenches, he lets out a low, desperate groan.

"Angel," he breathes as his fingers dig into my hips.

He takes his other hand and swipes his fingers through my center, and I push back against him, hungry for more. "Again."

This time, he pushes those same two fingers deep inside of me, twisting and curling his fingers with every movement, and at this angle, he might as well kill me now because there's no way I'm going to survive his wicked pleasure.

He works my body right to the edge, and I clench around his fingers as my whole body begins to shake. "Fuck," I groan.

"You ready for me, Angel?"

"God, yes. Now."

Killian wastes no time freeing his fingers from my cunt, and not a moment later, I feel that heavy tip at my entrance. "Touch yourself, Chiara. Show me how you like it."

I don't hesitate to slip my arm beneath me, and as I roll my fingers over my starved clit, Killian slowly pushes inside of me. He takes his time, taking me inch by inch, and I let out a breath of relief, not having realized just how much I was fearing this moment, but with him . . . it's only him.

He keeps pushing and stretching until he's fully seated inside of me, and I clench around him, my eyes rolling with the sweetest satisfaction. Everything pulses, and I'm so close to coming undone, but I won't dare let go, not until he's right there with me.

My fingers work manically over my clit, and as Killian begins to pull back, his fingers collect my wetness and dance across my ass. Without skipping a beat, I groan and push back, and he gently presses his thumb to my hole.

"Fuck. Fuck. Fuck," I breathe, and when he pushes back inside of me, I feel it all. Every inch of him, every angle he touches me, every pulse of my walls around him.

It's too much.

Too good.

"More," I tell him, determined to take it all, but damn it, he needs this release just as much as I do. "Faster."

Killian picks up his pace, thrusting harder and faster, and my body quickly comes undone. It's more than I can take, and it's absolutely everything. I've never felt so alive, so on fire. "KILLIAN!" I cry as the intensity builds to new heights within me. "I'm going to come."

"Give it to me, Angel. Let me feel how that pretty cunt squeezes me."

"Fuck."

His words are my undoing, and I fall to pieces, coming harder than ever before. My walls violently convulse around him as I cry out, every piece of me shuddering with the richest pleasure. It pulses through me, filling me with the sweetest intensity, and I clench my eyes as my hand curls into a tight fist.

The high blasts through me like an explosion, and as Killian groans behind me, my whole world seems to settle. He comes right along with me, each of his precise movements increasing the intensity until I physically can't take it anymore and begin to pull away.

He relaxes behind me, panting heavily, and with his cock still buried deep inside of me, he pulls me up so my back is against his chest once again. "Angel," he breathes, the sound so desperate it's as though I'm the only thing in the world holding him together right now.

"I love you," I whisper into the blood-soaked room. He remains silent, but as his arms tighten around me, I know he's soaking in every syllable that just came out of my mouth, so I look back over my shoulder and cup my hand to the side of his face as he meets my stare. "I love you, Killian. So fucking much."

"I know, my sweet angel. I feel it just as you do. Every beat of my heart belongs to you. Everything that I am is yours."

I melt into him, and not a moment later, he picks me up off the ground and lifts me into his strong arms. He walks us out of the torture chamber, blood dripping off us and staining the floors, and as he makes his way into the massive bathroom, I can't help but dance my fingers up and down his sculptured arms.

He's absolutely perfect.

Every ridge of his strong body, so perfectly carved out of stone, is a testament to years spent in excruciating training, and I get to call it all mine. Yet despite how entirely incredible he is to take in, nothing beats the soul inside. The man that I've come to know. He's so beautifully broken, but so am I, and the pieces of our shattered remains fit together like a complex puzzle.

"You know, I was nervous about that," I admit as he clutches me tighter and leans into the shower, turning on the taps.

"Which part? Sergiu or letting me fuck you?"

"Both," I say. "But in particular, the part where you bent me over and pushed inside of me."

His gaze softens and as he pushes my blood-soaked hair off my face, he steps into the warm water, only just when I think he's about to say something monumental, a cheesy smirk settles onto his full lips. "To be fair, you bent yourself over."

I roll my eyes, and as the water rushes over us, I can't help but notice the way it turns red, washing away the sins of what just went down. "I was worried that the second I felt you, their faces were going to torment my mind and suddenly it wouldn't be your hands on my body, it'd be theirs. But it didn't. It was only you I saw. Only you I felt."

Killian nods and settles me onto my feet. "You won't ever have to worry about them again. I've got you, Chiara. And I'm not letting you go. I was foolish to think I could do life without you." He pauses as I hold his stare, and as the water finally runs clear, he circles his arm around my waist and pulls me against his strong chest. "Grapes are *crushed* to form wine, and seeds only grow when in *darkness.*"

My brows furrow as I try to make sense of what he's saying, but he ignores my confusion and goes on. "Olives, they must be *pressed* to release their fine oils, but diamonds, my sweet angel. Diamonds are formed under *immense pressure*, and while they are undoubtedly beautiful and dazzling, their strength is unmatched. You, Chiara, you are my diamond."

Everything within me melts, and he lifts my chin to hold my stare. "You've overcome the impossible, Chiara. You balance me, and despite knowing what kind of man I am and what I am capable of, you continue to love me anyway. You see through the darkness, and I will never take that for granted. I wish to be your world, Chiara. I wish to give you everything you could ever desire."

"Don't you see?" I murmur, pushing up onto my toes and kissing him. "You've already given me everything. Just getting to be in your presence is more than I could have ever asked for, but you give me yourself, and within you, I've found where I truly belong. You once told me that when you declared me as your wife, it felt real, and while I know we were only starting to get to know each other, I couldn't have agreed more. I feel like I am your wife, and I want to keep being your wife. I want to give you joy and a family to be proud of. I want to give you everything you never thought you deserved because you do deserve them. You deserve it all."

Killian scoops me back into his arms and presses me against the wall as I feel him harden between us. He doesn't waste a moment, slipping back inside me, and as if on cue, we both let out a satisfied sigh. "I'm going to marry you, Chiara DeLorenzo."

A stupid grin pulls across my lips as he slowly starts to rock in and out of me. "You already did," I tease.

"For real, Angel. I want your signature on the little dotted line. I want to see you in a ridiculous white dress, walking down the aisle right into my arms. And once I officially make you mine, I'm going to spend the rest of my life between these pretty thighs and listening to the way you scream my name."

"Oh really?" I ask, seeing the rest of our lives playing out so clearly in my mind. "And just how soon do you plan on making this happen?"

Killian grins, and the way his gaze softens makes my heart race with undeniable happiness. "Who knows?" he murmurs, his dark eyes twinkling with excitement. "Got any plans tomorrow?"

Well, shit.

I grin right back at him, that same excitement brimming in my chest. "I do now," I tell him, and with that, the most dangerous and powerful man in the country pulls me off the shower wall and walks straight out to the bed, throwing me down and showing me exactly how he intends to spend every day of the rest of our lives.

THANKS FOR READING

If you enjoyed reading this book as much as I enjoyed writing it, please consider leaving an Amazon review to let me know.

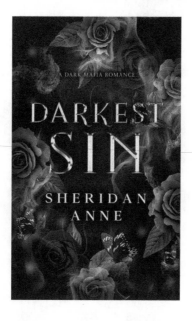

For more information on Haunted Love

find me on Facebook –

www.facebook.com/sheridansbookishbabes

SHERIDAN ANNE

STALK ME

Join me online with the rest of the stalkers!!
I swear, I don't bite. Not unless you say please!

Facebook Reader Group
www.facebook.com/SheridansBookishBabes

Facebook Page
www.facebook.com/sheridan.anne.author1

Instagram
www.instagram.com/Sheridan.Anne.Author

TikTok
www.tiktok.com/@Sheridan.Anne.Author

Subscribe to my Newsletter
https://landing.mailerlite.com/webforms/landing/a8q0y0

MORE BY SHERIDAN ANNE

www.amazon.com/Sheridan-Anne/e/B079TLXN6K

DARK ROMANCE STANDALONES
Pretty Monster (Stalker Romance) | Haunted Love (Brother's Best Friend) | Darkest Sin (Mafia)

DARK CONTEMPORARY ROMANCE SERIES - M/F
Broken Hill High | Haven Falls | Broken Hill Boys
Aston Creek High | Rejects Paradise | Bradford Bastard

DARK CONTEMPORARY ROMANCE - RH
Boys of Winter | Depraved Sinners | Empire

NEW ADULT SPORTS ROMANCE
Kings of Denver | Denver Royalty | Rebels Advocate

CONTEMPORARY ROMANCE
Play With Fire | Until Autumn (Happily Eva Alpha World)
The Naughty List (Christmas Standalone)

PARANORMAL ROMANCE
Slayer Academy [Pen name - Cassidy Summers]

SHERIDAN ANNE